SCORPIO

ALEX McDONOUGH

ibooks
new york
www.ibooks.net

DISTRIBUTED BY SIMON & SCHUSTER, INC.

A Publication of ibooks, inc.

Copyright © 1990, 2004 by
Byron Preiss Visual Publications, Inc.
All rights reserved.

An ibooks, inc. Book

Distributed by Simon & Schuster, Inc.
1230 Avenue of the Americas, New York, NY 10020

ibooks, inc.
24 West 25th Street
New York, NY 10010

The ibooks World Wide Web Site Address is:
www.ibooks.net

ISBN 0-7434-9776-7
First ibooks, inc. printing January 2005
10 9 8 7 6 5 4 3 2 1

Cover painting by John Jude Palencar
Cover design by Brandon Diaz
Maps by John Pierard

Printed in the U.S.A.

SCORPIO

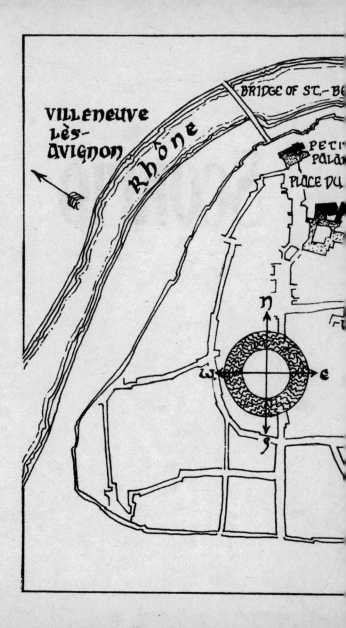

VILLENEUVE
LÈS-
AVIGNON

Rhône

BRIDGE OF ST.-BE

PETI
PALA

PLACE DU

n

w   e

s

et

as

ais

es

e carnot

EWISH
QUARTER
SEXTIER

⫷⫷ SYNAGOGUE

AVIGNON

1351

Prologue
Scorpio Landing

Maybe they've killed me. I think I'm not on Terrapin anymore.

The palace is gone, the ramparts and corridors of the Hunter stronghold, the steely cities and liquid globes of the vegetable gardens. I am seated in a strange field. The earth is unfamiliarly scented, cold and muddy, not spongy, not mossy. There is no dome. A single, pale moon. Grasses I've never seen, primitively sown in soil rather than water.

This is not Terrapin. So I have escaped.

Deity help me, perhaps I have died.

I remember the laserfire, I know I was hit. I felt the pain, it pierced my thigh. Where is the wound? *The orb*. Gracious Deity, I am healed! I can feel my body, it is whole. This earth, it is solid. It has a smell. I do not think that I am dead. No. But *I* have the orb—and I am triumphant!

I am triumphant, but where am I? I remember the noise before the swirling stopped, a loud, low-pitched whir; and the bubbling heat that threatened to burst my every molecule. And the pressure! as though blood and bone were straining to spring from the tips of my fingers, toes, scalp, pushing yet holding me still. Such a dizzying, frantic calm. Then the swirling and the watery greenness. Surely I was close to home?

I was certain I was safe, at home, when I let go of the orb. *The orb*.

1

It must have been the orb. I grasped the orb, wrenched it from its pedestal with both hands, my mind squirting instructions: *Run! Flee!*

What a surprise—I did not run or flee. I triumph! Even the terror now seems sweet. Oho, I led those Hunter assassins a merry chase! A greased, wet skin will slip like a snake through a steel corridor! They were going to murder me anyway, so what did it matter? The threat of extinction made me rash! My people are never rash. We are a placid, thoughtful folk, the Aquay.

But the Hunters were always, and only, Hunters. Perhaps it's the truth, Leandro's little joke, that our Deity and theirs have never met. A bitter joke, to be sure. Still, we lived cooperatively enough until the balance shifted. How foolish we were, how blind. No one understood what had happened. But one by one, group by group, it seemed we were evaporating. The older ones just vanished, herded to the harvester camps, it was said. The younger ones, and the Speakers, we would find their leaking bodies flayed or sliced open, a hole from a Hunter laser burnt between their eyes. I remember.

We remained a thoughtful, placid folk. At first we sent emissaries to the Hunter stronghold, but they were never seen again. Our lives soon blurred into an endless night spent breathing through hidden tubes in underwater lairs, murky holes the Hunters would not penetrate with their instantly waterlogged skins. Mute, sightless havens. But we had to surface sometimes. . . .

How has this happened, what have I done?

It seems an eon ago that we began to hear rumors about the orbs. There was news of a new power source, discovered by Hunter miners on one of their forays to some fledgling planet. The power source, the orb, generated much excitement. Then it was said the Hunters had ventured farther afield, sought more, gathered another and another. The rumors stopped at three— three orbs.

Later, the few elders who escaped from the harvester camps said it was the orbs that changed everything. The orbs stimulated growth in the thin soil of Terrapin, so the Hunters no longer needed our hydrogardens. And the orbs had other powers as well. The rumors began again, of mysterious conferences held among Hunter elders, of strange bursts of light from within the stronghold at Chanamek, of the eyes of the Hunter leaders, glazed and far away.

I remember, it all began innocently enough. Our elders were asked to tend two experimental gardens, soil farms. These became the harvester camps where our old ones were forced to water the orb fields. After the first wave of protests, the disappearances increased. The murders began, public, personal, each calculated to foster terror and despair among those of us who remained. Witnessed. Our Speakers were exterminated methodically, ruthlessly, and then those who rose like a new tide to replace them. Leandro. And the young ones, why so many of us? We could not stop grieving, we were numb from grief. . . .

It was Leandro who told us of the Hunter system of assigning to each of their targets a personal assassin from their warrior ranks. They borrowed the custom from their own mythology, he said. Leandro was a student of Hunter lore. The executions were judged by their variety and finesse. Success was a matter of honor. "Scorpio," he told me, "speak to no one and swim alone. Take care not to imagine a future, or they will hunt you too."

Leandro was an organizer, not placid or numb. He planned to bore water tunnels into the two orb fields and free those who labored there. But he knew there was a Hunter assassin already charged with his particular death—a talented ore-finder, a fanatic diviner. Leandro had seen him. Or been allowed to see him. The Hunter had shown himself, another of their customs, a Hunter notion of fair play.

I didn't see him afterward. They told me how they found Leandro, whispered the unspeakable. Oh, they told me, but the horror lifted, and something inside me snapped. And then they were after me too, so I had no more time to think.

The solution seemed so simple. The Hunters had three orbs, we had none. I would bring my people an orb of power and try to restore the balance. I could not tunnel into the orb fields alone. But I could try to steal into the stronghold at Chanamek and capture the third orb. What could be simpler? They were going to murder me anyway.

My heart quickens, I see it. Could it have been just hours ago, just a day? I have peeled off my garments and coated my skin with the thickest of grease. My eyes are wide—with fear, I know, but I pretend I am one with my exophthalmos, reptilian ancestors and I slither on my belly from water hole to rivulet, slip through dried and dying aquagardens, swim into the sewer system of Chanamek.

I am in a pipeline, swimming against the current toward the city. Water spews past me, the overflow on its way to feed the now unused and shriveling hydrogardens. It gushes through my first obstacle, a sewer valve that opens and closes like a sucking mollusk, a dilating pupil, the mouth of a sea-worm in the great city wall. But I am enthusiastic, not yet dread-filled, and I push through as the valve closes. Something has happened to make me rash, and I dive into the gut of the raptorial Chanamek.

The sewer pipes are used to cool a maze of buildings and draw the moisture from the atmosphere so the Hunters don't drown. Hunters can tolerate very little moisture; their skins tighten on their bodies and they turn a fiery red. They rub themselves with sand to keep clean, and they take their liquids in their foods. The sewers are filled with chemicals and acrid Hunter piss. It has not yet been filtered and the stink of Hunter water sets off signals in my agitated brain: *Alert! Freeze! Dive!* My skin burns slightly, but the grease serves me well. I try to circumvent the messages of panic. I hum hymns of praise. I amuse myself with ironies. For once I am grateful that solid Hunter waste is deposited in clay pits, dried and pressed into bricks to fuel their filthy smelting furnaces. At regular intervals, I add my own piss to circulate beneath Chanamek. Ha!

The hours pass, the waters quicken. Like a stubborn sperm, I wriggle onward. Sometimes I am carried forth in a rush of water and am able to float for a time. Finally, in the distance, I hear the hollow roar of the cooling pumps, punctuated by metallic *plinks* from dripping chemical feeders. I have reached the underbelly of the Chanamek stronghold.

I prowl along the smooth steel wall until I find a wide metal spout attached to a porthole. It is sealed with gum to keep all traces of moisture inside the pipes. Braced on the spout, I push until the porthole springs open with a sucking *pop*! And then, *zip*! I'm through the hole, tumbling onto a pyramid of packets, chemical coolant stacked neatly below the spout. It, and I, spilling onto a cold metal floor.

The noise brings no one running. But I feel my first wave of dread. I am in a basement chamber. The air is so dry the salve begins to soak into my skin and I turn as gray as the steel walls. I must hurry.

The rest is a blur of corridors, pillars and fear. Like a greased shadow, I whisk through the stronghold. I am on the third level when the alarm goes off and I shimmy up a pillar and cling to the top like one of the grotesques on its capital. Hunter warriors thunder below me, helmeted, booted, dedicated, intense. No one looks up.

The word is passed along through the ranks. "It's a moisture seal break in Cellar 10." The squadron clomps around a corner and I continue my eellike progress.

The next alarm is a bad one. The Hunters have discovered they have an intruder. I curl around the top of the tallest column, one of a pair opposite a set of monumental burnished doors. I begin to sweat. Have they found my oily trail? But my luck is strong. The doors burst open and a Hunter baronet sweeps into the corridor, barking orders at a quartet of guards. "You two! Come with me to the cellar. I'll track this audacious Aquay myself! He's sure to set off a trail of alarms, even his stinking breath is wet! You others—join the honor guard in the orbarium!"

I try to breathe in short, shallow puffs to spread my humid exhalations thin. But I stare, horrified, as a tiny droplet of sweat beads at the top of the pillar and slowly, tortuously, dribbles downward. The baronet marches off toward the cellar and the two guards trot dutifully toward the orb.

I am following my Hunter guides, stealthily gliding, silently running like a crazed pool of quicksilver, when the alarms are triggered. One after another, closer and closer. The result is good—the guards increase their pace toward the orb. We approach a solid wall of icy steel, a seamless, mirrored barrier. I skate along the shiny floor, staying boldly behind the two guards so the only reflections they see are their own. My mind is gushing instructions: *Freeze! Play dead!* I override them all.

There is stomping behind me, and an enraged Hunter shriek.

"There! He is almost to the orbarium! Shoot before the doors open! *Now!*"

I begin to fishtail wildly, skidding toward a slowly parting wall of steel. Laser blasts like crossed swords, blinding lines of whitest light, are ricocheting from walls to ceiling to floor, weaving a web of deadly rays. I know I am moving like an unstoppable wave; but I feel like a river that is frozen in winter. I am the eye of a cyclone!

Around me there is chaos. Ahead of me, the surprised guards duck through the parting doors and take cover on either side. Behind me is a cat's cradle of deadly laserfire, blocking the baronet's party from the orbarium. The baronet is baying orders in a fit of fury. "Stop! Hold your fire! Don't shoot near the orb!"

The two guards flanking the entrance to the orbarium hold their fire as I whisk between them and streak along a polished floor. I am wounded, and my blood sets off alarms. I hear nothing but my own voice, and I am screaming. I see only a glowing shape on a single pedestal, it is miles away. I zoom toward it, I wrench the orb from its pedestal, is that another voice I hear? Is it mine? Leandro's? Saying *Scorpio! Don't let go. . . .*

The orb! I open my eyes. It is as I feared, I am still here. I find the orb. It is right next to me, as comfortable as a melon. Its amber glow has dimmed and it seems to want to burrow into the earth. Already it is nestling up to its center. The growth around it seems soft and lush, greener than the rest. Perhaps, like me, it wishes to hide, to delay the trek across this foreign field. But the next step must be taken. My breathing isn't labored, my skin is pale, there is enough moisture, it seems. The future must be faced.

I am in a fallow field, among dark brown mounds of earth. The mounds are covered with long, silvery grasses that are flattened by wind. There are two or three stone huts in the distance; they look like insect hives. There are trees, rooted in earth, not in water. A crag rises beyond the field. There is a stone building there too, very large, a stronghold perhaps, with towers, and slits in its walls in the shape of a cross. No Hunters in sight.

But I know I'm not on Terrapin anymore. Oh, my beloved Aquay. How do I help you now?

I remember my triumph! I've got the orb! It *must* have been the orb. And if the orb brought me here, it can bring me home as well.

Alert! Run! Flee!
Hush, my mind, there is someone coming. *Hide!*

It comes closer. It is speaking a language in a heated, scratchy voice. So a cognizant species, it would seem. Limbs like an Aquay, but with long darkish fur that springs from its head. Not armed, I don't think. Clothed in flapping garments. Female, by the look of her. But is she young or old? I cannot tell. Gathering greenery—a good sign. Perhaps we will have something in common. But that raucous voice! Oh, my ears!

Still, I have become no stranger to risks. I will stand and show myself! Perhaps she can help me.

Chapter 1

Two hours after first light, Leah de Bernay had long since paid her five sous to pass through one of the three gates in the thick wall that separated the Jewish quarter from the rest of the citizenry of Avignon. A minute's walk from the gate, she had paused at the foot of the newly completed Papal Palace to gaze at the towers and ramparts, buttresses and arches soaring upward from their foundation of solid rock. The unyielding facades, twelve feet thick, were built of blocks of a gelid yellow limestone that had taken on an uncharacteristic, almost friendly hue in the pink light of dawn. But the glow soon faded to a cold morning gray, and Leah hurried on, down narrow and foul-smelling alleys to the turreted bridge of St.-Bénézet; across the quirky Rhône, the same shiny gray as the sky; past the aging tower of Philippe le Bel and the hills of Villeneuve-lès-Avignon, where the wealthy cardinals had their mansions; through outlying olive groves, heavy with autumn fruit; to a quiet forest that spread beyond the medieval city of Avignon.

It was a clear November morning in the year of Our Lord 1351. Leah loosened her cloak as the day began to warm, a small reprieve. Today the breeze was light and pleasant, but any time now the mistrals would begin to blow, freezing north winds that swept through the Rhône valley on their way to the sea. The mistrals were a mixed blessing, Leah thought. The unremitting, icy blasts would slice through the thickest clothing; but they also carried off with them some of the city's notorious stench.

For all its odors, Avignon in 1351 was one of the liveliest capitals of Europe, an international center of the arts that revolved around the learned and worldly Pope Clement VI. A generous patron, Clement attracted poets, architects and painters, scientists and scholars, as well as ecclesiastics seeking the lucrative benefices only the Pope could confer. The city was noisy, filthy, and overcrowded with fortune-seekers from all parts of the world: cardinals and bankers, emissaries and messengers, merchants and artisans, servants and soldiers, pickpockets and prostitutes, all ambitious satellites of the papal court.

The popes had been established, more or less comfortably, at Avignon since 1305. Clement had been Pontiff for almost a decade. And while Jean le Bon was newly King of France, Avignon belonged to the Holy See, recently purchased by Clement himself from the lovely teenage Queen, Joanna of Naples, Countess of Provence. The populace still vividly recalled Joanna's formal entry into the city three years earlier. She had come to face trial, accused of strangling her young husband, Prince Andrew of Hungary, and of having his body dragged by the genitals for some distance before having him hanged for good measure. The purchase of the city was arranged shortly before Joanna's absolution. Naturally, there was speculation that Clement had exchanged a regicide for real estate. But in 1348, the citizens of Avignon showed little concern for the affairs of state, there being a power far graver than king's or pope's to contend with; for in 1348 the Black Death reigned supreme. Its sovereignty endured for seven horrific months until, its hunger still raging, it departed for more northern haunts, having claimed fully half the city's inhabitants. By 1351, the half who remained were emphatically alive. They believed they had survived the end of the world.

The day was going to be glorious. Pausing at the edge of the forest, Leah sighed and stared at the sky, barely able to admire its luminous blue. She'd been feeling so restless and short-tempered lately. Normally, a day of freedom from the cramped Jewish quarter would have been a delight. But so far her outing had been spoiled by her own angry and confusing thoughts. Irritably she put a name to them: Aimeric de la Val d'Ouvèze.

Even his name had the easy grace of a young gallant. What a fool she felt now. How could she have known that he considered his nobility a given, and the code of chivalry just a game? Her budding knight had turned out to be a lout, and there was nothing to be done about it.

Leah banished Aimeric from her mind and concentrated on her herb-gathering expedition. Scouting the forest floor, she spotted an ivy-covered tree stump and yanked at a clump of ivy root. Good for treating her grandmother's failing eyesight, she thought. Maybe this will appease her. Grandmère Zarah wouldn't be pleased to learn that Leah had come so far alone. "Unmarried girls shouldn't venture forth unaccompanied," she would say. "I didn't go very far," Leah would answer. "You can drown just as easily close to the shore," Grandmère would counter. Or some such saying.

"Proverbs! Stories!" thought Leah, vigorously shaking the excess soil from the ivy root. She shoved the ivy into her apron and tucked the fabric into her belt. "I'm not a child!" she muttered, stamping her foot to repack the earth she had dislodged near the tree stump. Wasn't she her father's assistant? And wasn't he Nathan de Brenay, one of the most respected physicians in Avignon? Why, already she knew more than most boys her age; even her father said so. How could she be expected to learn if they kept her hidden behind the walls?

Today she'd been lucky. She and her father had planned to collect plants together. But just before sunup the doctor had been called to the home of M. Ferussol, the lute-master. His stomach was aching again. Leah had jumped at the chance to slip away by herself. Perhaps a good dose of solitude was all she needed, some room to breathe away from Grandmère's admonishments and Father's orders. He'd noticed her moodiness of late. If she wasn't careful, he'd have her drinking bitter draughts of wormwood to alleviate her melancholia.

Leah filled her apron with mosses and morels, ferns and barks, then headed for an open field adjoining the lands of the Benedictine Abbey of Montmajour. Father had said they needed more valerian for Mme. Roussillon's nerves—she *was* high-strung, Leah thought, but so charming! Did that mean they would be calling on her soon? It was at Mme. Roussillon's that she had first met Aimeric. How handsome and sophisticated he had looked, in his short tunic and elegantly pointed shoes! And how he had gazed at her! None of the boys in the quarter had ever looked at her so boldly. Much less dared to speak to her alone. It simply was not permitted.

So many rules! she thought wistfully. Often she had watched the carefree flirtations of the courtiers as they flocked to a banquet at the Papal Palace. Sometimes at night she could hear the music from the courtyard and banquet halls, wafting over the walls of the Jewish quarter. The ladies looked so gay in their finery. Perhaps some of them were immodest, as her father said. But how wonderful to laugh so freely! And to be able to talk with whomever one chose!

As her father's assistant, Leah knew she had had much broader experience of the world than the other girls her age. Not one of them had ever been outside the quarter after the gates were locked at night. That privilege was limited to doctors and midwives. Leah often accompanied her father when he was called to treat one of his many Christian patients, night or day. She'd been welcomed in Christian households.

Why did the Christians think they were so superior to Jews? Leah wondered. Their aches and pains were certainly the same—though the Christians bathed less, she had observed. But weren't they all respectful of her father's knowledge, and grateful for his treatment? They sought him eagerly enough when they were ill. So why were the Jews locked up at night?

"The gates are for our own protection," her father had once tried to convince her. Leah remembered only too well her nightmarish twelfth year: how her mother had gone to tend to a sick friend and died before she could return home; how the hideous piles of naked bodies had risen in the streets; and how the terrors of the Black Death were compounded by the attacks of an angry mob shouting that the Jews had poisoned the public wells. Pope Clement had issued a Bull protecting the Jews, and the violence in Avignon had stopped, though there had been massacres elsewhere. "They need a scapegoat," Grandmère Zarah had said. And every day she had told the story of the goat sent into the wilderness bearing the sins of the people, as though every day was a Day of Atonement.

But wasn't that all over now? Why didn't they take down

the walls? How ridiculous it all was, Leah thought bitterly. Just because we have our own well water. Hadn't the Jews died just as horribly as the Christians? Hadn't the pestilence taken her own stepmother, and her newborn stepbrother as well?

Her father had been devastated. Physicians were as helpless against the Black Death as were the astrologers, rabbis and priests. Nathan had tried to console the living and see that the dead were buried. But he had lost his only son. Leah knew that her father had despaired of ever having another.

At the time of the pestilence, no young man wanted to be apprenticed to a physician. But families tended to band together, and no one disapproved when Leah began to help her father. For the past three years, she had worked by his side daily, studying, trying to offer what comfort she could. She had learned quickly, and she knew her father was pleased. "She has a thirst for knowledge, just like a boy," Nathan would insist. But she wasn't a boy. And lately it was beginning to be obvious.

Grandmère was constantly bringing up marriage. Leah had even spied her just outside the synagogue, talking to a go-between from the nearby city of Carpentras. The sight made her stomach twist with anxiety. What if they chose someone she found repulsive? What if she had to leave Avignon?

Leah had been surprised by her own reaction. Ever since she was a little girl she had looked forward to her wedding day, had giggled with the other girls and daydreamed about her bridegroom, the ceremony, a home of her own. But now that she was old enough, she didn't want to be married! "Not to any of the boys in the quarter, anyway," she thought. "They are so serious and dull." *Not like Aimeric*. She squelched the image. "Besides, I want to continue my studies. And I'm too busy caring for Father, and for Grandmère as her sight dims."

Leah knew her value to the family was enormous, and Nathan had seemed in no hurry to marry her off. Since her stepmother died, she and Grandmère had shared most of the household responsibilities. But of late, Leah had taken on more than her share, as well as attending patients with her father and studying when she could. Only last week, Nathan had suggested he find a permanent apprentice so Leah could devote herself to her "proper duties." At Leah's vehement protest, he had let the matter drop. She decided he was just testing her commitment to her studies. But recently her father had been talking of marriage too.

It began after their last visit to Mme. Roussillon. Madame had introduced them to her visiting nephew, not yet twenty, but already welcome at court. Aimeric de la Val d'Ouvèze. Why, just last week, he had been falconing with his uncle—her brother, you know—Bishop So-and-So. . . . Mme. Roussillon had gone on and on.

Her father must have noticed how Aimeric stared at her, running his eyes from her face to her feet and then back again. His gaze was unnerving, persistent. She had blushed a deep crimson. Everywhere her eyes fell, there Aimeric would appear, boldly questioning.

"The arrogance!" Nathan had exploded after they left. Seeing Leah's confusion, his anger soon cooled. "You behaved very well," he told her. "You must cast your eyes downward when men look at you that way." He had gone on to make fun of the long, curling toes on Aimeric's shoes, twice the length of his feet. "How can he walk? And how can he breathe? His clothes are so tight he looks like a sausage!" Leah had nodded in agreement. But secretly she was thrilled. Aimeric was dressed in the height of fashion, and his taste was faultless.

Twice that week Aimeric had waited to catch a glimpse of her as she passed through the gate in the rue Jacob. Then it seemed she couldn't go to market without seeing him. Sometimes he would pass by her, very close, and whisper in her ear: "I yearn for you!" "I am dying!" "My dark angel!" "Your beauty is as a dream!" And soon she had been able to think of nothing but Aimeric de la Val d'Ouvèze.

Leah had heard all of the stories about Christian men seducing young Jewish women. But she didn't believe such a thing could be true of Aimeric. He waited for her every day. They had long discussions, or brief exchanges as time would permit. Once he had slipped her a book of the most current verse—not one of the dull moral tales that Mme. Roussillon was always reading. "This is what all of the ladies are reading at court," he told her. "It is the bible of courtly love." He quoted from it often: the *Roman de la Rose*. How impressed he had been at how well she could read! She had cherished the verses, and learned them by heart. Some days he would regale her with gossip from the palace—who had worn what to dinner, who had danced with whom, what music had been played. Always he told her what a bore it was to pretend to be gay when all he could think of was his "little Leah."

Their romance was impossible, and therefore pure, as only a courtly love could be. It was also a secret. On the days she was walking with her father, Aimeric wouldn't even meet her eyes. But she could feel his presence. He was so intense! So devoted! Hadn't he declared his love for her? Told her she was beautiful?

Hadn't he said that she could be a queen in a court of love? Their love had been ideal, just like in the *Roman de la Rose*.

Then, two days ago, he had asked her to sneak out of the quarter alone to meet him. Leah was alarmed. He must want to ask for her hand. She had spent a tormented day and a sleepless night worrying about how difficult it would all be. It would be lovely to live outside the quarter, to be able to come and go as she pleased. But her father would never allow her to marry outside the faith. She would have to convert. She could never do that; it would break her father's heart, and her grandmother's as well. Aimeric could lose his inheritance. It was all out of the question. Their love was doomed. She would have to meet him, and gently tell him that, for the sake of love, they must give one another up. Already she was pining for him. . . .

Then yesterday she had been out with her father and returned to the quarter through the gate in the rue des Marchands. Her father had stopped a short distance before the gate to speak to an associate when Leah spotted Aimeric with two of his friends, trailing lustfully after Rebekah de Milhaud and her mother on their way back from the market.

Her cheeks burned as she watched him stare pleadingly at Rebekah. She had seen the look before. Her heartsickness increased as she overheard Aimeric brag to his friends.

"Just think of them in there," he announced jovially. "Ripe fruits to be plucked!"

"Their beauty is exotic," agreed one of his friends. "But how can you even think of marrying a Jewess?"

"Who said anything about marriage?" said Aimeric. "I simply have a taste for something rare!"

The three had strutted away, laughing and jostling one another, without noticing the doctor and his daughter. Leah felt as though all of the air had been punched from her lungs. Somehow she had followed her father back into the quarter, stonily watched him pay their five sous and numbly gotten through the night.

Today, as she entered the fallow field of the Benedictine brothers, she resolved never to speak to Aimeric again. But what if he was just posturing in front of his friends? No, she had heard what she had heard. He'd been telling her lies. There was no sense hoping.

Leah headed for a bright patch of greenery in the meadow. "I must look for herbs," she told herself. Suddenly, all of her pain and humiliation came flooding back.

"Damn you, Aimeric de la Val d'Ouvèze!" she cried as her tears began to flow. "I wish a demon would sweep you off this earth!"

Cautiously, a naked demon rose from the field and spoke to her, hesitantly, in a warbly, watery voice.

"Can you help me, please?"

Chapter
2

At the sight of the demon, Leah felt as though all of the liquid had suddenly been sucked from her body. Her tears evaporated at once, leaving tight, crusty tracks that crackled along her cheeks, and her sobs dried into a knotted rag at the back of her throat. Her body grew stiff and drained of color, while her mind called up an image of Lot's wife turning to a pillar of salt. For although she was trying to run, her legs felt as heavy as sand, and they would not move.

This must be a delirium, Leah told herself. I was distressed, and now I am having a vision. She shut her eyes. She opened them. Then the terror began to rise.

"Don't be frightened," said the demon. The words echoed in Leah's mind like distant drips in an underground chasm. She registered little of their sense. But the liquid voice was strangely soothing. "I mean you no harm," it said. "I see we are both fond of plants. I gather vegetation in my own land, though it is all under water there."

Leah took in deep, calming breaths of air and willed her heart to slow down. She tried to think. There was a demon in the field. It did not disappear when she closed her eyes. It had stepped forth from a globe of glowing light and there it stood. It appeared to be real.

It had spoken to her. What had it said? What had *she* said? She remembered now, she had wished a demon on Aimeric, spoken aloud! She must have called it forth!

She gave a soft whimper of remorse and fear. Would it take

Aimeric away? Did she really have the power to make that happen? Despite her fear, Leah experienced a certain awed self-regard. Now that she had invoked this demon, was she also empowered to control it?

The demon blinked and stood quietly, expectantly, waiting for her to recover her senses.

She would have to try to remember everything Grandmère had told her of *shedim*. Leah had heard many tales about demons, *shedim*, both evil and benevolent. It was said they could assume human form. But she didn't know anyone who had actually seen one. That this one appeared to be real was fearful in itself, but although his face was misshappen, he didn't look malicious. A single bone swept sharply across his face, forming cheeks and nose in one unbroken line. Beneath this flesh-covered beak small nostrils showed, tiny punctures above a wide, lipless mouth. At the sides of his head were openings in awkward clumps of flesh, small and smooth as though the ears had been lopped off at birth and had long since healed. The effect, strikingly birdlike, was accentuated by large round, protruding eyes of a deep, soft green. These vanished completely when the demon blinked, leaving a seamless countenance with no lines visible from lashes or brows, which were absent. In fact, his body was entirely hairless—but quite human otherwise, with all of the requisite limbs in the usual positions and proportions. No wings that she could see; and a navel. But that would be only natural if the demon had assumed human form to come to her.

As a veteran of the plague years and a student of anatomy, Leah was little bothered by the demon's nakedness. But his coloration was another matter. He was as tall as she, and rather scrawny, Leah thought, with skin of the same pale, bilious green as some of her father's more miserable patients. This observation caused her panic to arise anew. What if the demon had come to afflict her with spleen?

"Oh, Lord, Creator of all things, grant me health and strength that I might resist all evil," she prayed aloud, fixing the demon with a defiant stare.

"Let it be so," Scorpio responded politely. "Sacred Deity, embrace your humble servants that we may receive your blessings."

● ● ●

Scorpio was pleased. The female being had welcomed him with a formal greeting or prayer. He sensed he had startled her, and observed that her eyes, which were outlined with hairs and separated by an angular bone, had widened in shock. Probably she was not familiar with his species. He stood passively still to allow her close scrutiny, and was glad of a chance to examine her in return.

Her form was female, there was no doubt. But she wore long garments that concealed most of her body: a close-fitting green gown or tunic, sleeveless, with contrasting red sleeves that showed beneath; a light-colored apron; a brown cloak.

Although she was eyeing him with unblinking intensity, she still seemed quite alarmed. Perhaps a response in kind would reassure her.

Scorpio fixed Leah with a reciprocal stare.

At the demon's unflinching gaze, Leah instinctively stepped backward, drawing her arms protectively across her chest. Then she recovered her nerve and glared back. She'd show this demon who was in charge.

Her expression turned to one of amazement as the demon studiously crossed his arms over his chest and took one step backward. Then he quietly returned her look. It certainly seemed he was taking his cues from her! Was he in her power? Perhaps he was awaiting her command.

"Begone, demon!" she tried, pointing skyward. At least her voice was firm, if not entirely authoritative. The demon dropped his arms and continued to look at her, sadly, Leah thought, or maybe with disappointment, it was difficult to tell.

"I'm afraid I can't do that," he said finally. "I apologize if I've frightened you."

There was that voice again, she thought, watery, pure, like the rippling echoes of the *mikvah*, the torchlit women's bath beneath the synagogue.

Leah's confusion mounted. The demon did not seem wicked. The sound of his voice made her feel safe. And the globe behind him gave off such a sunny light. He had said that he meant no harm. He had even condoned her prayer, and called for a blessing in return. Was he trying to trick her, to seduce her into passivity? Leah remembered stories that Grandmère had told of kindly demons who would come to the aid of those in special need. Maybe the demon intended to help her.

The silence was becoming unbearable, and Leah's curiosity was rapidly overcoming her fear, though her heart still pounded in her chest. She hoped it was not dangerous to speak directly to a demon.

"What are you, and why have you come?" she asked.

Scorpio relaxed a bit and answered truthfully:

"I am a being from another world, and I am not certain why I am here. My name is Scorpio."

Leah nodded, it was as she hoped. The demon had answered her call and would have to be informed as to her wishes.

"I am Leah de Bernay," she told him. "You, Scorpio, are here to do my bidding. I summoned you."

"You summoned me?" The demon's voice rose in a flutey trill. "And how was this done?"

"I cursed someone aloud in anger," Leah admitted, "but I may have been rash. I wouldn't want you to hurt anyone. You had best go back to wherever it is you come from."

"Rash, was it? I too know what it is to be rash—the results can be surprising, can they not?" The demon uttered a light warbling sound, not unlike a laugh. "But I have no wish to harm any of your kind, have no fear. I will gladly return to my world if you'll direct me."

"So you are a kindly demon!" said Leah, relieved. "But how shall I direct you? Can't you just appear and disappear at will?"

"I don't think so," answered Scorpio. "My people rarely travel, and I've never done this before."

"Well, try. All demons can appear and disappear at will."

"Perhaps I'm not a demon. I think not."

Leah felt her irritability returning. "What else could you be?" she demanded. "Did you not fly here from a world beyond?"

"I must have flown, in a way," answered Scorpio, looking skyward.

"Are you mortal? If you dry out, will you die?"

"Yes, I need moisture, that's certainly true," said Scorpio.

"You see? The only way a demon can die is to dry out. And can you foretell the future?"

"No," said Scorpio sadly. "That I cannot do. And I can die in many ways. Very many ways."

"What a poor kind of demon you are!" said Leah critically. Was it her imagination, or did the demon look crestfallen? His mouth, though lipless, had still turned downward, his lidless eyes had managed to droop. Immediately she felt remorse for her hasty words. Perhaps it was her own fault he was weak. It was her first time at invoking a demon, after all. "You must have some powers," she said charitably. "What is that ball of light at your feet?"

Scorpio was battling a wave of hopelessness. There were to be no easy solutions, it seemed. He was still stranded on an unknown planet. It was becoming clear to him that Leah hadn't summoned him, nor could she send him home. Obviously, she had mistaken him for some sort of supernatural being. What order of being was she, for that matter? Was she reliable? For all he could tell, he might be talking to a child. Nevertheless, he needed information. He must find the elders or leaders on this planet who could guide him homeward. He would risk revealing the orb to Leah.

With reverence and apprehension, Scorpio parted some of the verdant grasses that only partially screened the orb from the light of day. It had nestled into the dark earth, a marbled melon of a softly glowing bronze. Both Sorpio and Leah wondered at it for some moments. To Leah, it looked like the inflated bladder of some magical animal—metallic, but with the fine-lined texture of a skin. Scorpio, too, was studying the orb at leisure for the first time. Its peculiar rind or husk was unbroken, but from time to time he thought he could see something rolling or pulsing inside the small sphere. The effect was hypnotic.

At last he turned back to Leah. She was staring at the orb, her odd, fruity mouth wide open. "This orb has great but hidden powers," he told her. "I seek to unlock its secrets. Have you ever seen its like in your world?"

Leah wrenched her eyes from the golden light and regarded Scorpio with new respect. Perhaps she had underestimated his importance in the hierarchy of demons.

"I have never seen such a wondrous thing," she answered, "nor have I met with any demon before!" But even as she spoke, an image flitted through her mind. "Once, though," she added, "I did see a globe of gold, in a picture that hung at the home of one of my father's patients, a Christian gentleman attached to the court.''

Leah paused, but the demon seemed unimpressed with her father's connections. In fact, he was regarding her rather blankly.

"In the painting," she continued, "the Pope held a golden orb with a cross on its top, cupped in the palm of his hand. It was meant to signify divine power on this earth. But even an orb of pure gold would seem dull when placed next to your ball of light."

"Where could I find the owner of this golden orb?" asked Scorpio.

"Only a great ruler, an emperor or the Pope, would own such regalia," Leah answered patiently. Didn't this demon know anything? "If there is one here in Avignon, it would be locked away in the Treasury at the Palace of the Popes."

"I shall go to see this Pope," said Scorpio excitedly. "He is your king?"

Leah eyed Scorpio skeptically. "Surely even a Jewish demon has heard of Pope Clement VI! He is the ruler of kings, of all Christendom. He may not be sovereign to the Jews, but we live in Avignon at his mercy." Leah gestured in the direction of the papal city. "His power is far-reaching and unassailable. Have you come to challenge the Pope?"

Leah's eyes sparkled with amusement at the thought. How could a demon visit the Pope? And a Jewish demon at that!

"I wish only to ask his counsel regarding the orb," Scorpio answered. "This device will help me to return to my own kind."

"Why don't you use your wings?" asked Leah practically.

"I have none."

"Well, of course not, while you are in a human body. You'll have to resume your true form!"

Suddenly Leah blanched. She remembered what Grandmère had told her about demons, that they only regain their true forms after mating with a human being. What if . . . and what of that name, Scorpio? Didn't the sign of Scorpio rule the reproductive organs? What was she doing anyway, standing in a field, alone, talking to a naked demon who was trying to seduce her with a glowing ball of light?

Leah's volition suddenly returned to her in force. With no

further word, she bolted from the field as fast as her legs could carry her.

"Wait!" Scorpio called. "I have no other body! Please don't go! I have so many questions, Leah! Won't you tell me where I am?"

Leah did not slow down.

Scorpio felt a surge of desperation and homesickness as he watched the panicked being flee. What could he have said to have frightened her so? He followed her, calling reassurances, as far as the edge of the field. But she only ran faster, and Scorpio was soon overcome by the exhaustion born of futility. He stumbled toward the little stone huts at the field's edge. They were simple cone-shaped structures, doorless, with earthen floors. All three appeared to be deserted. Inside the first were a wooden bench and some metal tools with handles. Gardener's tools, thought Scorpio. These are gardener's huts.

Collapsing gratefully onto the bench, Scorpio looked from the dim interior of the hut to the brightness of the field. The greenery around the orb was a vivid patch among the grayness of the sleeping field. He would have to move the orb to safety before someone spotted the new growth from the bleak stone stronghold on the hill. And he would have to find water soon. His skin was beginning to flake, exposed to the atmosphere as it was. But first he would rest for a moment, and collect his thoughts.

Leah dashed into the cool silence of the forest beyond the edge of the Benedictine field. The demon no longer called her name, and she no longer felt his presence dogging her. Hugging a tree for dear life, panting to catch her breath, Leah risked a peek, past the stiff solid bark of the Aleppo pine, through the sun-speckled shadows of the wood, to the field where her nightmare had begun. Was there a figure standing near the three stone gardener's huts? She squeezed her eyes tightly shut, then peeked again.

The field was empty. The craggy hill and blue sky, the monastery, the gardener's huts and golden grasses, all stood serenely in picturesque innocence, as if to say, "Who, me? House a demon? Never!"

Leah regarded the scene for some moments. Her eyes stung,

and she wiped away the tears of relief that had sprung forth unbidden. There was no demon. But as her vision cleared, she could not help but notice a brilliant patch of green that seemed to have been dropped, like a silk kerchief, in the middle of the field. There must be an underground spring, she thought. How fortunate for the monks.

Scorpio's eyes wearily adjusted to the cool darkness of the gardener's hut. He had to blink repeatedly now, using the last of his precious moisture to keep them lubricated, and the flickering effect was irritating. But he was pleased to find, thrown over a primitive wooden wheelbarrow, a garment of rough woven cloth, once a light color, now a dirty white. It was a loose gown, patched at the knees, with long sleeves, a full hood and a belt of knotted cord. Good. His skin, now protected from the drying wind, would take on the light color of the cloth, close to the color of the female being. And the hood would hide his face. Perhaps it was his face she had found so alarming.

What if she had gone to alert others of her kind? Scorpio, dressed in the cowl of a Benedictine brother, set out across the field to collect the orb. It was time to find water, and to search for this Palace of the Popes.

He gently scooped up the orb and his dejection lifted as, briefly, his face was bathed in its amber light. His determination renewed, Scorpio concealed the orb in the sleeve of his robe, and set off in the direction of Avignon.

Cosily tucked away, the orb dimmed to a dark, burnished bronze.

By the time she neared the outskirts of the city, Leah had convinced herself she had had an elaborate hallucination, based on her anguish over Aimeric. But if she could face a demon, she decided, she could certainly confront a lowly mortal, and a lout at that. She would meet with Aimeric, and demand his apology.

Chapter
3

*T*he Rhône had darkened to the rich blue of tempered steel by the time Leah started back across the half-mile span of St.-Bénézet's Bridge. On the opposite shore, wan and regal, the Palace of the Popes rose from its throne of rock. Already the afternoon had peaked. Leah would have no time to watch reflections in the glassy river, nor could she slow her pace to study the assortment of travelers who streamed across the bridge in both directions. Today she would even forgo her customary game of counting, as she moved from pier to pier, the twenty-two stone arches that supported the famous Pont d'Avignon.

As the only bridge across the Rhône between Avignon and the sea, St.-Bénézet was a major thoroughfare. Merchants traveled to and from the seaports to the south, where they sent shiploads of Provençal goods, herbs and chestnuts and coral, to all parts of the world, and returned with exotic imports to delight the courtiers at Avignon: cinnamon, vanilla, perfumes. Tradesmen trundled cartloads of cloths and dyestuffs, leathers and wines out of the papal city to the great fair at Beaucaire, to sell or exchange for soaps and pottery, pipes and knives. Local traffic was heavy, for the bridge connected the papal city with Villeneuve-lès-Avignon, the cardinals' suburb on the western bank of the Rhône. Squires, clerks, nuncios and messengers attached to the Holy See crisscrossed St.-Bénézet daily, as numerous as mice in a night kitchen.

Normally Leah was entranced with the variety she observed on the bridge. It seemed as though the entire world found its way to St.-Bénézet. Arabs and Africans, peddlers with donkey carts, prostitutes in their evening finery, adventurers fleeing their creditors, courting couples, escaped prisoners seeking sanctuary, lawyers sated from a day of bargaining, servants leaving the palace for the day, troubadours readying for the night's entertainment, knights and penitents, foreigners and foot soldiers—to Leah, in the clear light of late afternoon, all of the myriad faces and costumes of humankind looked equally safe and familiar; for she was haunted by her vision of the demon Scorpio.

She could not rid herself of the memory of his face, his changing demonic face: curious and avian, frightening and reptilian, strangely, undeniably human. She tried to rehearse the excuses she would make to her grandmother, but soon her mind would again replay her encounter in the field. She could see herself stamping her foot, freezing with terror, running into the forest. She could hear the demon's watery, wheedling voice, calling her name. And always, finally, her thoughts would return to the pulsing ball of light. Again she would recall its uncanny warmth, and again she would be suffused, just for a moment, with an overwhelming sense of the miraculous.

Leah turned her thoughts to the nature of miracles. The Torah contained many references to demons and angels and miraculous events. Were miracles always accompanied by angels? She had no doubt that angels existed, and as for miracles, why, the very cobblestones beneath her feet were evidence that miracles occurred. She knew the story of St.-Bénézet's Bridge by heart.

Since the time of the great Roman engineers, a bridge long enough to span this wide, wild stretch of the Rhône was thought to be an impossibility. Everyone agreed it could not be done. Nontheless, work on the Pont d'Avignon was undertaken in 1177 by the Frères Pontifes, a company of bridge-building monks who believed they were obeying a direct order from God. The heavenly message had been delivered to them by a twelve-year-old shepherd boy named Bénézet.

Bénézet heard the voice of the Lord call to him three times as he tended his flock, commanding him to build a bridge across the untamable Rhône. Though he was just a humble shepherd boy, Bénézet set out to inform the Bishop of Avignon. On his way, he met an angel who showed him the spot where the bridge must stand. Young Bénézet ferried across the river to relay the news to the bishop. But the bishop was annoyed. He disliked having his time wasted, and assumed the boy was mad. Bénézet became a laughingstock—until he was able to perform a miracle to prove his claim. The boy lifted a stone that was thirty feet long and seventeen feet wide, and carried it with ease, trailed by a stunned and rejoicing populace, to the river's edge, where he marked the very spot the angel had shown him. And there the impossible task was begun.

Well into its second century in 1351, the Bridge of St.-Bénézet was still considered a wonder of its day. The story of its divine inspiration was a staple among the Avignonese—particularly among a local group of thespian street urchins known as the "players of St.-Bénézet," budding young swindlers whose enterprise was tolerated, for a small consideration, by the keepers of the tollgates.

Leah, her mind on miracles, paused to watch one of the players ply his trade. The boy adopted an expression of the most angelic charm. His costume was artful: he had adopted the sheepskin vest of a rural shepherd, though it was likely he had never been farther from the city than the western end of St.-Bénézet. His mark, a gawking traveler, was unmistakable.

"Excuse me, sir," the boy began modestly, "but you appear to be new to our city. Allow me the honor, then, of acquainting you with the tale of the Miracle of St.-Bénézet Bridge!"

The visitor, ruddy and well fed, dressed in a new mantle and road-worn boots, was perhaps a burgher from a provincial town. His mouth had dropped and his eyes filled with delight at his first sight of the city with its imposing palace, just waiting for him beyond the bridge. Exhilarated by travel, interested and polite, he was pleased to listen to such a friendly youth.

"Sir, it is God's truth that this miracle was enacted by a shepherd boy no older than myself!" the player continued. Without missing a beat, he launched into a spirited and pious account of the miracle, complete with dramatic gestures and a small chorus of *oohs* and *aahs* from his confrères, who soon gathered with well-rehearsed spontaneity.

Leah had seen many newcomers to Avignon regaled in this fashion. Today on the bridge it was business as usual. The traveler was impressed with the hospitality and civic pride of the young Avignonese. The player finished his piece, and

paused while the traveler complimented him. Then he extended
an insinuating hand to collect his "gratuity."

The visitor noticed for the first time that he had been herded
against a narrow cast-iron railing by a band of smirking urchins.
Beneath him, placidly waiting, was the Rhône. Bewildered and
hurt, he fumbled for his purse and withdrew a coin. It was a
handsome purse of soft velvet, fastened to his belt by a flimsy
cord.

Leah caught the swift glance that passed between the player
and his partners. One of the smallest ran off immediately.
Everyone knew that the players made most of their living by
selling tips as to the size and location of a visitor's purse to
the pickpockets who worked the tollgates, and to the "false
beggars" who arrived for work at the bridge chapel each morning able-bodied and sighted, put in a full day of begging,
blindfolded or strapped to a wooden leg, and nightly performed
miracles of their own by regaining their eyesight or resprouting
missing limbs.

Experienced travelers always had their tolls ready—four de-
niers for a wagonload, two for a horse and rider, one for a
donkey, half for a man on foot and half that again for a pig—
and strode purposefully past such entrapments with their purses
well hidden.

Leah clutched her coins in her fist and hurried on her way.
She felt a pang of sympathy for the newcomer. He was sure
to have his purse cut before he was ten yards from the bridge.
Previously she might have judged him naive and foolish, might
have admired the wolfish art of the players. But today she
suddenly grew angry, and all thoughts of demons and miracles
flew from her head. She remembered instead a conversation
she had had with Aimeric.

"The players are masters of allegory," Aimeric had pontif-
icated. "Nothing could be more amusing than to observe their
miracle play turn to a morality play. For beneath the surface
of this holy city, at its very heart, do we not find corruption
and greed? Do the players not provide a fitting baptism for
outsiders entering the papal city, then? Indeed, do they not
provide a service to these unwary newcomers—relieving them
of their illusions as well as their purses?"

Allegorical the players may be, but did that make them
admirable? At the time, Leah had found Aimeric's insights

brilliant and poetic, and she had adopted his reasoning as her own, for she had wanted nothing more than to share in the views of the sophisticated Avignonese courtier. But were they sophisticated? Or was jaded perhaps a better word? How foolish and naive she herself must have appeared to Aimeric and his friends. Did they see her, too, as a tidy allegory?

Here she was thinking of Aimeric again. Her vision of the demon must have shaken something loose in her! For today she did not enjoy her role as a knowledgeable insider; rather, she found herself seeing Avignon through the eyes of a visitor from another place. Today a newcomer's unguarded delight at his first sight of St.-Bénézet's Bridge had moved her; and she was sickened by the casual ease with which a far from innocent urchin had exploited this moment of joy, and ruined it. Today she felt oddly impelled to act, as though she was driven by a secret strength, a warm ball of light.

Leah tarried until she was walking apace with the traveler. She would have to take care that none of the players noticed her—noninterference was an unwritten law on St.-Bénézet's Bridge. An opportunity presented itself soon enough. She was jostled by an overburdened coal porter, who in turn had stepped aside to avoid a fat cardinal, red-robed with a furred cloak, who rode a prancing steed home to his mansion in Villeneuve.

"Hide your purse well, sir," Leah mumbled, bumping against the beleaguered newcomer. "There are pickpockets about. And don't give alms to the beggars at the chapel—they are false." And with that, she hastened on her way to the tollgate, filled with a happy sense of accomplishment, and inspired to set the world to rights.

In the waning light of late afternoon, Leah headed for the Papal Palace to look for Aimeric de la Val d'Ouvèze. If he could not be found in the palace courtyard, he would undoubtedly be at his favorite post just outside the quarter, skulking near the gate in the rue Jacob.

Fresh from the countryside, Leah approached the palace with another of her senses grown as acute as a newcomer's. The eyes report beauty, she thought, but the nose tells quite another story. Even the elegant courtiers who climbed the stone staircase to the great arched portal held pomanders to their nostrils or scented silks to their mouths.

Leah watched a group of three merry ladies making their way to whatever banquet or entertainment was planned for the evening. Up the steps they fluttered like a trio of rare birds, multicolored, their fur-trimmed sleeves drooping almost to the ground, their headdresses decorated with feathers and pearls. Their laughter was cultivated, their gowns refined and their bosoms fashionably bared. How they could glide in their soft satin shoes, so self-assured! Leah imagined them seated at table, listening to poetic lyrics, perhaps, or enjoying sparkling conversation; drinking fine wines from crystal goblets, their long fingers plucking flirtatiously at grapes or spicy morsels. They would discuss the affairs of the world. Each guest would be served on his or her own golden plate. . . . Leah's confidence faltered as she sighed enviously. She suddenly felt very tired and drab. Perhaps she had best just go home.

Aimeric was stationed outside the quarter, casually scanning the street. It was almost sundown, and the gates to the quarter would be closing soon. Leah saw him first and withdrew into the shadow of a side alley, her heart pounding and her resolve melting. Why must he be there? How could she face him in her dusty clothes, with her headdress of twigs and her brooches of tiny sticks and leaves, with jewellike clumps of ivy root poking through her mud-stained apron?

Aimeric was dressed for a night at court, his wavy golden locks lightly brushing an ermine collar, his long legs encased in hose of sapphire blue, his hips just covered by a short, tight-fitting doublet of sky-blue brocade shot with shimmering silver threads. Leah watched him from her hiding place; he looked more gallant than ever. Bowing nobly, he spoke to a passerby, a stout woman who giggled and wagged an admonishing finger as she bustled home to her bread and soup. Leah felt an unexpected and uncontrollable surge of jealous anger. Was it all just a game to him? Would he flirt with anyone in a skirt? Pouncing from the shadows, she steeled herself to tell him goodbye once and for all.

When Aimeric saw her, his face lit up.

"My sweet Leah!" he cried joyfully. "You have come to meet me, after all! I feared I was never to see you again, and here you are at last. My love, why have you kept yourself from me? Do you not know that I wilt, I perish?'' Aimeric grinned and clutched at his chest as though his heart would burst through his sumptuous doublet.

Leah faced her suitor, her eyes flashing. ''I am not a ripe fruit to be plucked,'' she stated vehemently. Aimeric stared at her as though she had gone mad.

''A ripe fruit?'' He frowned, confused by her tone. Then quickly his face relaxed, and he grinned again. ''Ah, it is a riddle. You are jesting with me!''

''I heard you yesterday in the rue des Marchands, bragging to your friends,'' Leah continued, wishing she had the nerve to slap his face. Her eyes were starting to sting, but her voice did not waver. ''You have toyed with me unkindly. I have no intention of being sampled, then cast aside.''

Aimeric's expression grew gentle. Surely this young girl had not taken his overtures seriously!

''I have no memory of any such words,'' he said, laughing lightly. ''But if you overheard me with my fellows, why, you heard but strategies in the game of love. Mere thrusts and parries, challenges that pass between rivals. Meaningless trifles!''

Leah's eyes narrowed in speechless fury. Would he not answer her accusation, then? Did he think her so stupid? Her anguish was growing. But coupled with the pain was a hint of scorn, a scorn tinged with pity for the shallowness of this too-handsome man.

Aimeric, unused to coldness from women, was fumbling for words. What had she said about fruits? He mustered his charm and quoted from the *Roman de la Rose*. ''To pluck the fruits of love in youth is each wise woman's rule, forsooth . . .'' he tried. The raven-haired Jewess was staring at him with undisguised rage. He laughed nervously. Women were such moody creatures. Why, she was acting just like a woman of the court!

''Surely you don't think I flatter you falsely?'' Aimeric whined coyly. ''Do you reject me now as a ploy to drive me mad? Indeed, you have become a queen in the court of love!''

Leah had heard that one already; desiring to hear no more, she turned and fled into the security of the quarter.

''Wait, come back, my beauty, my only love. . . .'' Aimeric's enticements followed her through the gate and into a narrow, twisting alley. Once out of earshot, Leah leaned against a gloomy doorway and let her tears flow into her sleeve. How guileful her elegant courtier turned out to be; how easily he lied! Only his riches separated him from the lowliest player on St.-Bénézet's Bridge, she thought bitterly. And the urchins must earn money for bread. But Aimeric—Aimeric seduces for sport.

Beyond the gate to the quarter, Aimeric shrugged. There was no understanding womankind and their whims—and it seemed the enchanting Jewess was like all others of her gender, at least in this respect. But was it not that blend of the familiar and the exotic he found so intoxicating? She was as mysterious as the most practiced of courtesans! How could a girl with her medical knowledge of the bodies of men be so naive in matters of love?

Aimeric shook his head. He would miss his little Leah. He was aroused by her unkempt beauty and amused by her thirst for learning; not least, he was flattered by her obvious admiration for him. But he truly had wounded her, it appeared, and this he regretted, for he had cherished a vague hope of bedding her. Perhaps another day . . . but tonight he would wait no longer. There was to be a feast at the palace!

Leah indulged herself in a last muffled round of sobs. If she didn't hurry, she was sure to be seen. In the Jewish quarter, everyone knew the business of everyone else. There may have been more space since the Black Death had carried away so many of their number; still the quarter was crowded and intimate. Her tears subsiding, Leah walked along winding cobbled alleys hemmed in by stone houses with red-tiled roofs. At least the stench was not as terrible as in the rest of the town. Here, the privies were emptied frequently; carters kept the open street sewers from overflowing; and the people often bathed. Leah dried her eyes and emerged in a small square near the temple, the well and the baths. She called a greeting to the butcher's wife and nodded to M. Emmanuel, the cloth-dyer, who waved back with purple-stained fingers. She would be home in time to help Grandmère prepare the evening meal.

The two-story house that Leah shared with her father and grandmother was larger than most of the others in the quarter.

The rabbi's house was by necessity the largest, as he was
obliged to entertain numbers of visiting scholars. But the de
Bernays had four rooms altogether, not counting the cellar.
Upstairs, a low-ceilinged loft had been divided in two. On one
side, Leah shared a bed with her grandmother, while her father,
so often called away in the night, slept alone on the other, a
very great luxury even in the wealthiest of families. On the
ground floor the doctor had his study, and the family had their
common room and kitchen.

Leah crossed the patch of kitchen garden at the back of the
house, pushed open the heavy wooden door, ducked her head
beneath the low stone lintel and entered the toasty kitchen.
Already a broth was simmering on the hearth, fragrant with
rosemary and onions. Grandmère Zarah was seated on a bench
at a long wooden table, her back to the firelight, deftly plucking
a partridge in the near-darkness.

"I'm back, Grandmère," said Leah softly, reaching above
the table to light the oil lamp. "I've brought ivy root for your
eyes." Watching her grandmother work so patiently, Leah
regretted that she hadn't returned sooner. She knew she was
spending much of her time with her father and his patients,
just when Grandmère most needed her help. But the more she
learned of medicine, it seemed, the more there was to know.
Must she choose between Grandmère and her studies?

Once, the de Bernays had kept a serving girl to help with
the household chores. But she, like so many others, had met
with the Black Death, and the family had learned to manage
alone. It was time that Leah speak to her father about hiring a
new servant. Then she could devote her energies completely
to medicine and become a renowned female physician. She
would be respected worldwide. Welcomed at court. That would
show the Aimerics of the world!

Leah passed through the kitchen to her father's workroom.
It was her favorite room in the house, carpeted, with a little
leaded window and a door that opened to the street. There her
father's patients came to call, bearing their flasks of urine like
the most treasured of perfumes, nestled in padded wicker baskets.

Leah unknotted her soiled apron and arranged the crumpled
roots and sprigs of herbs in a wooden tray that had been specially made to fit in the top of a large ebony chest. Beneath

the tray, wrapped in paper or linen cloth, stored in beakers or metal boxes, were the powders and balms, preparations and ingredients her father prescribed for his ailing patients. The pharmacy chest had been a gift to Nathan from an Arab physician with whom he had studied at university, and it was carved with exotic designs that Leah loved to trace. Later, she would return to sort her findings, separate the roots, leaves and seeds, crush and dry them, grind and pound them, boil and strain them, as required by the recipes in her father's cherished books. But now she went directly to the kitchen to help her grandmother. There was a pile of turnips to be peeled.

"There's no hurry, child," Grandmère Zarah said as Leah slid into her place at the oaken table. "Your father has been called to the palace—an emergency, said the young page. One of the cardinals was suddenly taken ill, and the court physician is indisposed as well."

"He's gone to court?" Leah wailed. She wished she could pound her fists on the table. If only she had come home sooner! Perhaps she could have gone with her father and had a glimpse of the banquet. She thought miserably of the reason for her delay: Aimeric de la Val d'Ouvèze. Damn him, after all! Leah choked back her anger and searched the shadowy room in sudden panic. She really must gain control of herself, lest she call forth the demon again. There was no sense blaming Aimeric for this anyway, she thought. Her father would never have taken her on a call to a cardinal. Besides, she'd have her own day at court soon enough, when she became a great healer in her own right. Wasn't Nathan always comparing her to Trotula, the famous woman physician who wrote medical treatises and taught at the university in Salerno? "You see?" he would say to Zarah. "She's another 'Dame Trot'! " Grandmère would always just shake her head.

Her reasoning had worked, it seemed. There were no demons in Grandmère's kitchen. Breathing deeply to calm her nerves, Leah noticed that her grandmother had ceased her plucking and was squinting at her in the darkness, waiting for her to continue.

"No doubt Father will cure both the cardinal and his physician at once," Leah remarked, a bit hysterically. "They will see how brilliant he is, and reward him. And he'll teach me his arts, and I'll become a great doctor as well, and travel the world!"

Grandmère Zarah was not to be fooled; something must have happened today. Leah was on the verge of tears.

"So, we're no longer in love?" she prodded gently. "Ah, well, it is probably for the best. First choices are always bad luck, you know. Did I ever tell you about the first suitor my father picked for me?"

Leah shook her head and bit her lip.

"His name was Samson," Zarah intoned ponderously. "He was so handsome! He was a good deal older than I, with a deep voice and a big beard, so manly and sophisticated!" She sighed girlishly. "I thought I was in love! How I cried when I learned he was to marry another! He was betrothed to Jobine de Troyes, who was rich and plump, before my father could come up with a bride price. That's because Samson was arrogant, he wanted a fortune!" Grandmère Zarah laughed, waving the partridge, now fully plucked, over the table. "Luckily, it turned out, because just two years later, he was so much older, his ears drooped from his head like wings and his teeth dropped like petals. He grew fat!" Zarah held the back of her hand over her mouth and dropped her voice to a whisper. "And his smell was very bad!"

Zarah hooted to herself as she felt around the wooden table for a paring knife. Leah began to laugh too. The light came back into her eyes and she felt a rush of warmth for her grandmother. Zarah hadn't demanded to know where she'd been or reprimanded her for running off in the morning. The loss of her vision must be frightening, yet she never complained.

"But you know, child, these men are not all so bad," Zarah concluded. "Look at your grandfather, rest his soul, and your father. Soon we'll find you a good husband, and you'll be happy."

Leah felt her face flushing red and her temper rising, suddenly uncontrollable. "I don't want any husband!" she screamed at Grandmère. Toppling her bench, she heaved a turnip to the floor and stormed from the room, aching from the strain of the day, frightened of demons, mourning the loss of her first love. In the heavy silence of her father's workroom, Leah was overcome with shame at her outburst. What could have come over her to shriek at Grandmère that way? Zarah's story had been meant to cheer her. She just didn't understand, that was all.

Filled with remorse, Leah returned to the kitchen. It had grown late. Zarah had finished preparing the partridge and was absently stirring the kettle on the hearth.

"Grandmère, I'm so sorry," Leah said, retrieving her bruised turnip. "I meant no disrespect."

"We'll talk more some other time," Grandmère Zarah said quietly. "Now ready the supper things, for I hear your father's footsteps outside, and it sounds as though he is bringing someone with him."

Chapter 4

Scorpio had not ventured far into the forest before his fear and exhaustion all but dissolved. In their place he felt a confidence and energy that seemed to come from somewhere beyond him. From beyond him, yes—but from somewhere within him as well. *The orb?* The question formed in his mind, and as quickly disappeared. Traveling in the direction the girl had run, he made his way through the green woodland with a sense of calm that was enlivened by moments of pure rapture; for he was enchanted with the beauty of the unknown planet on which he had landed.

He had never imagined an interplanetary journey before, though of course he knew it was an everyday occurrence for the Hunter folk and their many visitors. His own people rarely left their aquaglobes and hydrogardens. How limiting, he thought. This was exhilarating! Everything was new. Already he had noted several kinds of songbird, and a few small mammals and insects. These he found interesting. But the variety of vegetable life filled him with reverence. There were so many strange species! And the forest through which he was passing seemed to have developed at random, obedient only to its own forest laws—unlike the strictly ordered and painstakingly cultivated plant life on Terrapin. Here were pines and oaks, shrubs of myrtle, lowly ferns, ancient trees and slender saplings, all growing companionably in one place!

Scorpio sighed. Much as he loved his homeland, its liquid gardens and its water-filled globes, there was a familiarity to this foreign wilderness that pained him. Had Terrapin been like this once, before the Hunters? Scorpio suddenly knew that it had. He knew it with a certainty he had no need to question, and the knowledge made him heartsick. How could his people have forgotten how they once lived? How long had it been since the wildlife on Terrapin was truly wild? Since the fish had been permitted to breed freely, the mammals to mate unwatched, the plants to root where they may?

He must tell them on Terrapin. He must remind his people of the old ways.

In the relative safety of a grove of trees, Scorpio removed the darkened orb from his sleeve, turning it, prodding it gently, studying its marbleized skin. "Take me to Terrapin," he willed it, resting a hand on its leathery surface. He concentrated, he spoke the words aloud, he prayed. But the orb appeared to slumber, its inner light dormant, its mysteries sealed within.

Scorpio was forced to give up. *Water*, demanded his brain with a primal urgency. His senses were alert to the sound of it, the smell of it. Drawn to a cool running brook, he bathed and drank his fill, and emerged refreshed, the water streaming from his limbs in sparkling ribbons. His cetaceous skin was once again glossy and soon paled to a mottled ivory beneath the Benedictine habit. The scratchy garment, bloused at the waist and secured with its knotted cord, afforded a pocket where the orb could rest. There the dim ball, held snugly against the cavity of flesh beneath his rib cage, generated a cosy warmth.

He would have to find help to master its powers. With renewed resolve, Scorpio continued on his way to the city, descending a hillside when the forest thinned. At the foot of the hill, a man-made orchard of olives and figs marched away in tidy ranks that seemed almost homelike after the undisciplined forest. There was no one in sight between the neat rows of trees. Drawn by a strong smell of water, Scorpio aimed eastward and soon emerged on an unpaved road that bordered the western bank of the Rhône. The breadth of the river took his breath away. And with the recognition of unlimited water there came joy. He would not have to worry about lack of moisture, that was certain.

Alert! Scorpio drew back into the orchard. There were travelers on the road. Moving toward him, two couples led primitive wooden carts drawn by stocky beasts. It was the custom of these people to be clothed, he could see. The men wore knee-length tunics and thick leggings, leather boots, and loose hoods that bunched into cowls around their shoulders. Their wives wore simple dresses with the hems tucked up at the waist to reveal contrasting underskirts of gold or blue, and head-coverings of plain white cloth. The men walked together in weary silence, while the women trudged behind, talking in high, flat voices, like the girl Leah's.

Following some distance behind the couples was a trio of men, all with a curious circle of fur circling their bald heads, dressed in brown frocks not unlike Scorpio's own. Their voices were lower. From the safety of the orchard, Scorpio studied their slow but steady progress, their hooded heads angled downward, their arms crossed in front of them, their hands invisible, each hidden away in the opposite sleeve.

The travelers all walked in the same direction. Scorpio looked to the north. On the horizon he could see a stone bridge that split the sparkling river like the scalloped fin of some mammoth silver fish. On the east bank, blurred by distance as though it were under water, a city like a crowded reef climbed a rocky hillside. Houses roofed with rounded clay tiles, red, brown, orange, clustered together like so many snails, and gray stone buildings clung to the rock like barnacles. Barely visible, topping the craggy mound like a colony of sea urchins, was the largest building of all, a pale stone palace with crenellated turrets and two piercing spires.

Avignon, thought Scorpio. The home of the girl Leah, and the dwelling place of the supreme ruler of this world, the Pope. The watery image of the city in the distance pleased him.

In imitation of the travelers he had seen, Scorpio pushed his hands into the sleeves of his habit and emerged onto the road with his eyes cast downward. The posture had its merits. With his arms crossed before him, he could both support and conceal the bulge of the orb at his belly. His peripheral vision suffered with the peaked cowl pulled forward, but his face was fully shadowed. Taking slow, measured steps, he fell into line with the traffic, too far from his fellows for conversation, but close enough to avoid a conspicuous solitude.

Scorpio attracted little notice on St.-Bénézet's Bridge; travelers in clerical garb were by no means uncommon. So far he had seen only one species of cognizant, though they varied greatly in detail. There was a marked diversity of physical stature—in this, they were more like the Hunters than his own people—as well as differences in costume and coloration. They were quite noisy. And their odors were strong: heady, or perfumed, or foul. Many of the men had hair growing from their faces as well as from their heads. All of them had the same formation of cheek and nose as had Leah, the same outlined mouth and lidded eyes. Scorpio found them rather awful—and so, presumably, they would find him. It was no wonder that Leah had been alarmed.

By the time Scorpio reached the gatehouse, Avignon loomed invitingly ahead and the Palace of the Popes was a crisp silhouette against the evening sky. His quest for help was almost at an end. Once off the bridge, the palace couldn't be more than a few minutes' walk away. Scorpio patted the orb at his belly, looking for all the world like a roly-poly friar who had just had a full meal. He started for the gate. But a problem presented itself. People were offering small bits of metal to the gatekeeper, some sort of coinage, it appeared.

Scorpio backed away from the gate, searching for a quiet place to consider his plight. He paused at St.-Bénézet's Chapel, a small stone building with a vaulted ceiling that was built onto the bridge, supported by one of the pilings. Just beyond the chapel was a group of men who appeared to have stopped for a rest. Two of them were lying on the cobblestones. They were all variant types, Scorpio noticed. There was a man with only one leg, and another with bandaged eyes, and yet a third, made crooked by a hump on his back, who supported himself on crutches and held out a quavering hand to passersby.

Squatting gratefully a short distance from the hunchback, Scorpio could watch the travelers line up at the gatehouse to pay their tolls. He could jump into the river and swim to shore, that was one solution. But he would certainly be noticed. And he didn't want to risk harming the orb. It was growing darker. Perhaps a wooden cart would join the line; he could cling to the rear, or conceal himself inside. Searching the distance, he thought he could see a wagon or two making their way across the bridge. He would just have to wait.

A shadow fell over him. "Do you need help, Brother?" asked a voice. Forgetting himself, Scorpio looked up, directly into the face of a black-robed monk who had just finished his evening prayers at the chapel. As their eyes made contact, the monk recoiled. Then, gesturing quickly from head to chest to shoulders and muttering wildly, he hurried away. Scorpio drew the hood of his garment further forward and hung his head. His face frightened and repulsed these people, of that he no longer had any doubt.

Behind him, the hunchback brandished a crutch and called out angrily, "Begone, interloper!" But Scorpio was oblivious to the threat. The shadow was back. Scorpio watched the hem of the black garment as it brushed the ground before him, but he did not look up again. "God be with you, Brother," said the voice. A coin dropped into Scorpio's palm, and the black robe hastened away, murmuring, "Have mercy on his pitiable soul. . . ."

Scorpio suspected he had been the object of charity. Turning the coin over in his hand, he silently thanked the Deity for using his plight to provoke a blessing from the black-gowned man. For were not acts of kindness a balm to the soul? Perhaps there were more similarities between his own people and these long-robed folk than met the eye. With his faith renewed and strengthened, Scorpio waited for the monk to disappear, then hurried through the gate to Avignon.

Behind him, the hunchback adjusted the ball of rags strapped between his shoulder blades and breathed a sigh of relief. "Who let that leper among us?" he demanded of his companions. "Even the truly blind and legless couldn't compete with that. Why, he was as wasted as Lazarus himself!"

Scorpio had found little to complain of on this new planet—until he encountered the overpowering stench of Avignon. So much compost going to waste! There it was, clogging the riverbanks, floating in roadside gutters, fertilizing cobbles and brick. But, Deity be thanked, even the smell worked to his advantage. For just as few residents ventured far without a cloth of some kind to cover their mouths and noses, so Scorpio could walk with his head erect, eyes exposed, though shadowed, holding the roomy cowl across his face.

The city struck him as both quaint and forbidding. Most of the dwellings were single-storied, though crammed together along muddy streets. Everything was made of wood or stone. There was no noise from pumps or generators, and none of the piercing metallic whirs of Terrapin's industrial centers; but the river roared and people shouted, cart wheels trundled through cobbled alleyways, and the din was as ferocious as any Hunter stronghold.

Overlooking it all, the Palace of the Popes topped the gray stone boulder on which it was built like a bronze crown on a dowager queen. Hugely scaled, with walls nine feet thick and towers some 150 feet high, it dwarfed the little houses that proliferated in its shadow with barely an alley's width to separate them. The facade was so plain as to be almost barbaric, broken only by the narrowest of windows, peaked and trefoiled in the Gothic style, and by two slender spires that framed the main gate like devil's horns, the sole ornaments on an otherwise impenetrable exterior. The gate itself, a cavernous opening, was the height of three men, carved and arched and guarded by men-at-arms.

Scorpio tried to squelch a wave of dread as his mind spewed forth the image of Chanamek. For a moment he could almost see it superimposed on the Papal Palace, an implacable steel ziggurat with a soaring central tower and corona of snoutlike telescopes that continually searched the night. The Palace of the Popes was primitive by comparison, though no less imposing. It was not the home of a man with no enemies, Scorpio reflected, but rather the citadel of one who commanded all the power in his realm, and yet feared to lose it. This was a fortress, built to endure. Like Chanamek.

For all its austerity—and unlike the Hunter citadel—the Pope's palace seemed open to any and all who wished to enter. A constant and varied stream of people disappeared through the gate, among them, Scorpio noticed, several men wearing light-colored habits very like his own. Even as he spied on the fortress in the gathering darkness, two boys in matching livery emerged to light torches against the evening's gloom. The orange firelight reflected dully in the chain-mail armor of the palace guards, who stood at attention as yet another lively crowd passed through the gate. There were no coins exchanged that Scorpio could see. No one was questioned, no one turned away.

Emboldened by his observations, Scorpio adjusted his copious hood, placed a steadying hand on the orb at his waist and, trailing a boisterous knight and his squire, walked quickly between the unflinching guards into a dim vaulted passage beyond the gate.

In a burst of torchlight at the end of the passage, the Palace square opened to the night sky, bounded on all sides by stark, soaring walls. But within the walls, the enormous courtyard was a pool of color. Guests posed or strolled in merry groups, sporting a rainbow of finery, trimmed with wafting plumes and fluffy furs, yards of silk or filmy gauze. Here and there a figure in a pearl-white robe would move through the company like an egret among peacocks. To the right, musicians ringed a large stone well. To the left, like a fountain, a wide stone ramp overflowed with courtiers whose voices swelled above the strains of song and festive laughter that drifted to the courtyard from some inner banqueting-place.

Scorpio, undaunted, threaded his way among scurrying servants and chattering courtiers, up the ramp and through another gaping arch, to the north wing of the palace. The spill of guests thinned to a trickle for the length of a lofty, pillared promenade with a massive wood-beamed ceiling. One side of the promenade opened to an unlit cloister, its thick low hedges lending texture to the blackness. At first glance, Scorpio thought the cloister deserted. But as he followed the walkway, he gradually became aware of muffled whispers and mysterious squeals emanating from the hedgerows. High above the cloister, from a brilliantly lit second-story gallery, banqueters leaned through pointed windows, hooting at the figures hidden below.

Was it a game? Were they watching his progress as well? Scorpio nervously hugged the shadows, his confidence beginning to wane. Images of the Hunter stronghold flicked at his memory, accompanied by faint impulses: *Run! Flee!* Rounding a corner, he gasped in fright; an equally startled pair of lovers popped apart at his approach. Averting his face, he hurried on, wondering at the choked guffaw that followed him. "Good evening, Brother," called the young man, hushing his paramour, who had dissolved in a rippling peal of giggles.

Scorpio's confusion mounted. Did the beings taunt him? Had they recognized him as an outsider? They couldn't have seen his face. But perhaps his behavior was incorrect. Had he violated a custom? His black-robed benefactor on the bridge had also called him "Brother," he recalled. Next time, he would reply to this greeting in kind.

Scorpio paused to collect himself at the foot of an immense staircase. But his mind still churned out haunting images of Chanamek, and his sense of foreboding increased. He had found his way to another mighty fortress; but who were its architects, if not crude giants? There was, as yet, no sign of an advanced technology, no evidence that any of the cosmic energies had been harnessed, no indication that interplanetary travel was practiced. Nor had he seen representatives of other cognizant species. Although the girl Leah had distinguished her own people from those ruled by the Pope, the distinction seemed to be merely tribal.

Could he expect these beings to accept his presence, understand his tragedy? Come to his aid? What if they feared him, just as his own people in their aboriginal tales, centuries old now, had feared the developing Hunters? Would this Pope be a leader wise enough to have intuited truths beyond his species' present capabilities, that there existed other beings, other worlds? And what world had he come to, where was he? Where Terrapin?

Scorpio was panicking. His mind issued orders to *breathe. The orb!* He groped for the orb; it had slipped forward over his belt and pulled at his front like a pendulous tumor. Breathing deeply and cradling the orb beneath his habit, tightening his belt and securing it in place, Scorpio struggled to regain his focus. How easy it was to lose track of his purpose. His imagination had gotten the better of him; but the plight of his people had to be his primary concern. For now, the orb had not yielded its mysteries. His next hope was to find Pope Clement VI.

Scorpio proceeded up the broad staircase, attracting little notice among the clusters of guests who conversed on the landings. The young lovers he had disturbed scampered past him hand in hand, not giving him a second look.

He emerged before a crowd of revelers who filled the colonnaded loggia that overlooked the cloister far below. Both the surge of guests and a lilting music seemed to originate from a doorway midway down the corridor. Over the throaty voice of a perfumed and buxom lady of the court, Scorpio could distinguish the tinkling of crystal and the clanging of platters, the odors of roasted meats and wine.

"It's too tragic," the young woman asserted, waving a ring-laden hand in a mink-trimmed sleeve. Her golden hair, bound in a silken net, was held in place by a simple jeweled fillet from which fluttered a lacy veil. "He is the cardinal I most favor. So cultivated and kind. It was his heart, they say. You should have seen him, the poor man! He was as green as the *sauce verte*."

"Let us pray he recovers, Lady Isabeau," said her companion, a stout auburn-haired lady encased in brocades, whose large rolled headdress was spotted with pearls. "He must be strong of heart. For it's said the Cardinal de Gascon is as generous as he is kind." She raised an insinuating eyebrow.

"Oh, he is, madam," said Lady Isabeau sweetly. "*Very* generous. Second only to the Pope himself!" She coughed slightly, then added gravely, "As befits his station, of course."

All at once a strident fanfare was sounded and cymbals clanged. The guests began to herd toward the doorway at the center of the corridor. One red-faced gentleman lurched the wrong way, halting to clasp the pudgy hand of Lady Isabeau's companion.

"Clement VI lays a fine table," he announced, jovially slurring his words, "but I'd rather romp with you, my pheasant, than taste the sweetest of subtleties!" He stooped unsteadily to kiss her hand.

"You'll have to romp alone," the lady replied, snatching her hand away, "for I'm returning to the Grand Tinel. The next course is about to begin, and its subtleties are a fairer attraction than you, sir! Why, the Pope has promised a miracle!"

Scorpio followed the two ladies excitedly. He was learning much from their conversation. A cardinal, it seemed, was second-in-command to the Pope. And the Pope performed miracles to entertain his guests!

The Grand Tinel, as he expected, was a mammoth dining hall, five times longer than it was wide, paved with stone and hung with paintings and tapestries. The ceiling, barrel-vaulted for its wondrous length, was covered in blue fabric studded with golden stars, and soared as high as a Hunter launching silo. Many of the decorations showed figures with golden discs behind their heads. Could they represent orbs? Perhaps these people did know of interplanetary travel—was it possible?

Increasingly jostled by the crowd, Scorpio trailed the ladies around the perimeter of the immense hall. The lengths of the Grand Tinel were lined with guests' tables that stretched from a raised dais at one short end to an overflowing sideboard at the other.

Some of the servants at the sideboard—carvers of meats and panters who sliced trenchers of bread, the almoner who kept the crusts and the servers who delivered the delicacies—were dressed in light-colored robes like his own. But all of them bore a knife or a platter, a ewer or tureen; Scorpio, empty-handed, noticed he was out of place at the end of the room closest to the dais, where the two ladies settled into their seats. Bowing his head even further and securing a place against the wall behind them, he searched for a break in the traffic so he could slide back to the great open door.

"It's a shame the Pope has retired to his quarters before the subtleties he planned," said Lady Isabeau as, with a flurry of trumpets, a stream of servants marched from the kitchen four abreast, bearing enormous confections of bread and sugar in lively colors, cleverly constructed in the shapes of entertainers, a juggler and a dancing bear, musicians and jesters. The guests oohed and gasped, laughed and applauded as figure after figure was paraded the length of the great hall.

Lady Isabeau's doughy companion squealed with delight at the sight of the edible sculptures. "It is a shame," she agreed. "No doubt he was very shaken by the illness of Arnaud de Gascon. These are the most magnificent of subtleties! It is truly a miracle what can be created out of simple sugar and paste. My mouth waters at the sight of that marzipan knight! Is he not handsome?" She tittered flirtatiously.

"On the contrary, my mouth has gone rather dry," Lady Isabeau replied, evidently bored. "You, there, butler—" She waved a hand at Scorpio.

Scorpio started in surprise.

"Butler, please see that our wine ewer is refilled," she continued, thrusting an elaborate silver pitcher backward over her shoulder, not bothering to look in his direction. "Just take it, there's no need to come all the way around," she remarked, then turned languidly back to her conversation.

Grabbing the ewer by its single, ornate handle, Scorpio took the opportunity to escape the banquet. He had no wish to be discovered as an imposter. Exiting the Grand Tinel, he chided himself for expecting a miracle of an interstellar nature! Clearly, he had allowed his hopes to lead him astray. Correcting his course, he set off in search of the Pope's private quarters. If this palace adhered to the logic of a Hunter citadel, the Pope would surely occupy a tower. The largest tower was at the opposite corner of the cloister, clearly visible through the openings in the colonnaded loggia.

Retracing his steps, Scorpio descended the grand staircase and crossed the darkened cloister garden. Opening a door in the base of the corner tower, he once again began to climb. A stone ceiling spiraled above him, supported by bleached bone-like ribs. The only light was afforded by torches, and the stairwell smelled of smoke and oil. Emerging at the top, he was in yet another long, narrow corridor that led to another, and another. The corridors were all of stone, some of them guarded by sleepy men-at-arms, others cold and deserted. Scorpio avoided the guards and wandered, searching for an unguarded doorway, perhaps a service entrance, that would lead him to the papal quarters. But it was difficult to distinguish one corridor from any other in this mazelike fortress, and he soon found himself, he thought, back in the hallway at the top of the stairs.

The corridor was interrupted at intervals by heavy wooden doors, arched and pointed, all identical. Scorpio was halfway down the hall when one of the doors behind him creaked open. He drew back against the wall as an elderly, white-robed monk exited the chamber nearest him and glided away in the direction of the tower stairs, his leather sandals swishing on the smooth stone floor.

Through the open doorway, Scorpio could hear snatches of a heated conversation.

"He can't last much longer," said a man's voice, silky and reassuring.

"We must pray he recovers," another said solemnly.

"Who's to say if this physician will be able to save him?" squeaked a third, agitated voice. "What if—"

"Our own Gisnard de Carliac has drunk himself into a stupor!" the first speaker interrupted. "We've fetched the nearest doctor we could find, the most famous physician in the Jewish quarter—and they're all renowned, as you well know." An imposing man, clean-shaven, wearing a bloodred robe, poked his head out of the doorway and called sharply to the monk, who had almost reached the staircase.

"Brother Celestine! Make haste with that water the physician asked for—His Eminence is failing fast!"

The voice was that of the first speaker. Scorpio froze, hoping he would be camouflaged against the ivory-colored stone. But the elderly monk must have spotted the glints of light on the silver ewer Scorpio still carried, and beckoned urgently.

"Hurry with that water, Brother," he hissed. "Didn't you hear Cardinal Signac? His Eminence the Cardinal de Gascon is dying! In here!" The monk disappeared into the chamber closest to the staircase.

Scorpio hesitated. He peered into the ewer. It held but a few drops of red wine. *Run! Flee!* cried his senses. But he would have to pass both chambers to reach the staircase to the cloister.

The ancient monk beckoned again from the sickroom. "What is keeping you, Brother? *Hurry!*" he croaked insistently. His eyes had widened in panic, but not, Scorpio thought, from the sight of an alien face. He doubted Brother Celestine had even registered his features. Something else had frightened him, something in the dying man's chamber.

Scorpio slid past the chamber in which the cardinal called Signac spoke with his associates. A glimpse inside revealed a cluster of figures, all in red. He continued stealthily to the sickroom door.

Suddenly two figures emerged. One was the elderly monk, his hood pushed back from a wrinkled scalp, his sleeves rolled up to his bony elbows, his face pale. The other was a middle-aged man in a flowing gown of dark red, with undersleeves of indigo and a black headdress made from yards of wrapped cloth. His trim, pointed beard was brown, as were his calm hands, compared to the monk's white, clammy forearms.

"The Cardinal Arnaud de Gascon is dying," said the doctor, clasping the monk's arm gently. "He's been poisoned. I've done all I know to do. You must fetch your superiors to administer the last rites."

Brother Celestine nodded weakly as the doctor returned to his patient. "You keep watch here until I return with Cardinal Signac," he ordered Scorpio numbly, "and ask the doctor if he still needs the water." He shuffled slowly down the hall.

Scorpio peeked into the sickroom. It was a small chamber, dominated by a narrow bed. Arnaud de Gascon, the dying cardinal, was lying on his back, straining to breathe with horrifying whimpers, his lips curled back from his teeth in pain. His unfocused eyes stared blindly at the ceiling. Pasty and sunken against the vivid scarlet of his gown, his face was twisted, though the muscles appeared to be frozen in place and his expression did not change. The exhausted doctor stood by the bedside, helplessly awaiting the inevitable.

Scorpio's mental messages had taken an uncharacteristic, though no less compelling turn. *Help him!* his mind cried. *Heal!*

The physician barely took his eyes from the patient as Scorpio entered the chamber.

"Take his hand and pray for him, Brother," he said quietly. "You can do little else, for he is fast dying. He has been purged and bled as well, but the poison was strong, and paralysis sets in. Soon it will reach his heart, and he will be free of his pain."

The physician stepped back as Scorpio approached the cardinal's bedside and leaned over the dying man. Arnaud de Gascon showed no reaction.

"He is blind," added the doctor. "It always goes thus with aconite. It is close to the end."

Turn him on his stomach, press the small of his back, came the unfamiliar messages. An irregular, rattling noise began in the cardinal's throat, and his face began to turn a sickly purple.

"Please allow me," Scorpio said to the doctor, dropping the ewer to the floor. "We do it this way where I come from." Grasping the cardinal by the shoulders and heaving mightily, he rolled him onto his belly so his face, now deepening to fuchsia, hung over one side of the bed. In a single, forceful movement, Scorpio threw his weight onto the cardinal's back and pushed.

Suddenly Scorpio felt a tingling heat beneath his ribs, as though the orb, secured beneath his robe, had become a living, moving thing. *The orb!* The messages must have come from the orb!

The sensations of heat and movement intensified as Scorpio pressed the hidden globe to the base of the cardinal's spine. It felt liquid, like a globe filled with water, but fiery, like the sun.

The doctor stood nearby, too stunned to protest, as the cardinal stirred and groaned. The dying man's lungs began to swell and his limbs to tremble. With a tremendous gathering of force, his head lifting, his eyes near to popping, he suddenly seemed to explode, expelling the contents of his stomach through his mouth, sending the foul matter fully across the small bedchamber. His body twitched, then relaxed to a calm, regular breathing.

Scorpio, who had struggled to maintain his position on top of the bucking cardinal, relaxed as well. As the heat from the orb abated, he climbed down from the bed and gently rolled the patient onto his back again. The cardinal's eyelids fluttered shut, and he slept peacefully, his face a slightly flushed but healthy pink.

Scorpio was well pleased. The orb had many powers, it seemed. It must have repaired his wounds from the Hunter laserfire, and now it had healed the cardinal as well. But had it responded to the cardinal's need? Or to Scorpio's empathy on seeing the cardinal in pain? And how had it engineered the messages he had received? Thus preoccupied, it took him several moments to notice the speechless physician, who was staring at him with a mixture of wonder and fright.

"Who are you?" he finally whispered. "And how . . . ?"

Run! Flee! Scorpio, alarmed, heard the approach of the other cardinals in the hallway. He mustn't be trapped here with the orb. This time he would obey his instincts. *Go!*

"Farewell, Doctor, a blessing on you and your patient," he blurted, and bolted from the bedchamber to the stairway, through the cloister, and down the monstrous corridor to the palace courtyard, where he concealed himself, breathless, behind the great stone well, his search for the Pope temporarily suspended.

In the bedchamber of Arnaud de Gascon, the Jewish physician, Nathan de Bernay, was trying to hush the incredulous cardinals as they crowded around the sleeping man's bed. In the putrid-smelling corner, a saintly Brother Celestine set to work with a bucket and scrub brush.

"You are a talented doctor indeed!" remarked one of the prelates, a short man with a squeaky voice. The others added their accolades.

"Cardinal de Laval, I thank you," said Nathan, "But I beg

you, allow the patient to sleep. The poison has taken a great toll on his energies, and he must rest."

"Poison? Preposterous!" said Bertrand Signac angrily. "Who would dare to poison a cardinal? Doctor, you are undoubtedly a fine physician, but it is obvious that this man is the picture of health. He has had nothing more than a touch of indigestion."

Nathan de Bernay let the cardinal's protest pass. He had no wish to involve himself in the politics of the Papal Palace, nor did he care to tangle with Bertrand Signac, whose machinations were known to encompass more territory than the Pope's own, whose control had infiltrated the lives of kings and commoners alike, whose power had extended from Naples to Britain, from Spain to the kingdoms of the East, and whose displeasure was to be feared.

"Naturally, I give only my opinion, sir," said Nathan respectfully. "Perhaps I am mistaken."

"Undoubtedly," answered Signac. "There must be no talk of poison!" His voice took on a silken tone. "We don't want to panic several hundred banqueters!" He chuckled as if the entire idea was ridiculous. The other cardinals tittered nervously in agreement.

"Indigestion!" the Cardinal de Laval summarized the matter.

"The cardinal's health is restored," said Nathan, "and that is all that is important. But you must thank one of your own brothers for his help—for it was the strange Benedictine who healed the cardinal, even as he lay on the brink of death. Who is he—the deformed one? And where did he go? I would like to confer with him, for he has studied techinques I have never seen, and surely he has the healing touch! He left this ewer. . . ."

Cardinal Signac snatched the silver ewer from the doctor's hand and strode from the chamber, just in time to see the hem of an ivory-colored habit disappear down the great stairway.

"Brother Celestine!" The elderly monk reappeared in the corridor, holding a bucket and scrub brush at arm's length. "Who was the brother who fetched the water?" demanded Signac.

"I don't know, Your Éminence." Brother Celestine bit his lip. "I've never seen him before."

"Well, find him and bring him to me!" Signac commanded, shoving the ewer at the trembling monk. "He dropped this vessel, perhaps he's returned to his service at the banquet. Go *now!*"

Nathan de Bernay exited the bedchamber with the other cardinals, closing the door behind him.

"I'll take my leave now, my lords," he said firmly. "The Cardinal de Gascon should be given milk and honey when he wakes, to soothe his stomach. His diet should be mild. Just the blandest of cakes, perhaps. I am gratified he lives."

"As are we all, Doctor," said Bertrand Signac graciously.

"Where are you, Brother? Cardinal Signac calls for you!"

Scorpio cowered behind the well as the elderly monk breathlessly crossed the courtyard, the silver ewer dangling against his pale habit. Brother Celestine shuffled painfully to the gate and searched the darkness beyond the palace, then returned to the courtyard and sighed. The crowd had thinned, but music and laughter still echoed from the Grand Tinel, less dense but increasingly raucous as the last of the banqueters drank and reveled into the night. From the shadows a nobleman and his lady staggered across the courtyard and out the gate. "All those stairs," the old monk whined tiredly. Then, resigned, he set off once again for the great banquet hall.

Scorpio waited for several minutes, until he was sure the monk had gone, then emerged from his hiding place.

"There you are, Brother!"

It was the Jewish physician. *Flee!*

"Please don't run away—I only want to thank you for your help. You are a great healer! Do you not know that Cardinal Signac seeks you? Why do you hide from a fellow member of your order?"

"I am not what I seem," replied Scorpio cautiously. The doctor's voice was warm and kind, and Scorpio's fear abated.

"Do you mean that you are not really a Christian brother?" asked Nathan.

"I am not," Scorpio admitted. "But I seek the Pope. I must see him."

"I understand," said Nathan sympathetically. He felt a wave of pity for the courageous stranger. What an odd, warbly speech he had. The poor man must have lived his entire life as an outcast, due to his terrible deformity. Probably he hoped that Clement VI could cure him. Was it leprosy? Or a defect of birth? Nathan would have to examine him at closer range to be certain.

"I am not sure that the Pope can work the miracle you seek," he said gently. "But *you*—you are a most talented healer. Are you from an Arab land? Would you could teach me your methods. I have studied with Arab physicians myself, you know, though never have I seen such a cure! But come. You will be in danger if you are discovered in the palace, impersonating a Christian brother. Perhaps you can arrange for an audience with the Pope on one of your feast days. In the meantime, why not stay with me? I have need of an assistant, and I can offer you shelter where you will find some degree of acceptance."

Scorpio was in no position to refuse help now that it was offered. But how could the physician know what he sought from the Pope? Was it a miracle he needed?

It felt as though eons had passed since his ordeal on Terrapin. The orb had cooled, and dragged heavily against his robe. Too tired to think clearly any longer, he gratefully followed Nathan through the Papal Palace gate, and then through the gate of the Jewish quarter. Soon he could sleep.

Chapter
5

"**M**y house is yours." Nathan de Bernay ushered Scorpio into his cosy study and consulting room. He stowed his leather bag of tools and preparations in a wooden cupboard and lit a lamp with the candle that had been left burning to welcome him home. "Please rest yourself while I inform my mother and my daughter that I've brought a guest."

Scorpio waited patiently, glad of a few moments alone. The room was simple and pleasant, and sized at a comfortable scale compared to the Pope's palace.

Nathan went to the kitchen where Leah ladled an aromatic stew from the hearth and Grandmère Zarah was adding an extra place at the table.

"I see you have heard the tread of my guest!" said Nathan heartily. "I am sure you will enjoy him. I know little of the young man myself, except that he is a great healer, from foreign parts. Unfortunately, he has suffered some sort of calamity and his face is much deformed. Not the leprosy, so I judge, have no fear. But though he is not a Christian brother, he wears the garb of a monk to allow him free passage and to conveniently hide his face. His knowledge is uncanny! Tonight he cured the Cardinal Arnaud de Gascon of a deadly poison—indeed he brought him back from the very brink of death. I have asked him to stay with us for a while, and work as my assistant."

"Father!" Leah's outburst was pained and indignant.

"Leah, I am hoping to relieve you of some of the burdens you carry," said Nathan gently. "This way you will be able to study and help me at home, and aid your grandmother as well. You are needed here. Soon you will marry...." At Leah's stricken look, Nathan broke off. "We will discuss the arrangement later, daughter," he continued. "You, too, will be able to learn much from our guest—more than I could teach you alone! So be kind to him, for his road has been an arduous one."

"I will, Father," Leah promised. How generous of spirit was her beloved father. She could refuse him nothing. But she was not about to be replaced by a stranger, nor would she agree to remain always at home while this mysterious young man traveled freely with her father.

Nathan disappeared into his study for a moment, and returned proudly, leading a slight, hooded figure.

"May I present Master Scorpio," he said. "Scorpio, my mother Zarah, and my daughter Leah."

Grandmère Zarah beamed delightedly at the newcomer and bade him sit down, warm himself at the fire, take a meal. She could just make out his shape, a milky figure in a peaked hood. She couldn't see if he was ugly—but that would be just as well if they were to have a young man living under the same roof as Leah. She was thrilled that Nathan had found a new assistant. At last he was coming to his senses! Now she could concentrate on finding her granddaughter a husband.

Leah felt faint and her mouth hung slack. Her father had brought the demon into their house, to live with them, he'd said! She couldn't wrench her eyes from Scorpio's face. He was staring at her with those wide, buglike eyes of his, and his lipless mouth had opened like a slash, then closed again in a short, tight seam. Why, if she didn't know better, she would swear he was as surprised as she! What kind of trickery was this? What did he want with her, with her family? Did he plan to harm them? Had she brought him forth? And what was he doing disguised as a Benedictine, of all things?

"Try not to stare, Leah, it's rude," Nathan whispered, seating Scorpio across from his daughter. He passed a bowl of scented water, that all might cleanse their hands. He said a brief blessing, and insisted on serving his guest himself. "This young man is a miracle worker," he told Zarah enthusiastically, serving Scorpio a portion of turnips.

Of course he works miracles—he's a demon! Leah's thoughts

were racing. Her father seemed so happy. How could he be so impressed?

Nathan continued to chat graciously, occasionally shooting his daughter an encouraging glance. But Leah, wavering between terror and guilt, anxiously prodded her food. Periodically she would glare at Scorpio, willing him to return to his own demonic realm. But the creature refused to meet her eyes, and at length began to eat as though he hadn't seen food for days.

Grandmère Zarah was gratified to see her supper so enthusiastically consumed. The young stranger was attentive, too, and she hadn't felt so amusing in years. She told several cheerful stories of her youth, and found the newcomer's rippling voice to be soothing and pleasant. But how silent Leah is, she thought. Could her granddaughter be attracted to this quiet young man? Or is she finally learning the proper modesty for a young girl? Either option would be satisfactory, of course. All in all, Zarah could not have been more pleased.

As Leah numbly cleared the remains of the dinner from the table, Nathan relaxed and spoke of his days at university. There was something about the young stranger that made him feel nostalgic for his youth. Zarah had felt it too, he noticed. But his guest was painfully self-conscious and reserved. Probably he was not accustomed to feeling accepted. They must all do their best to make him feel at home.

Scorpio was worried about the girl Leah, who seemed about to explode with tension. That she feared him was clear, but he hoped she would soon understand that he meant no harm. Warmed by the hearthlight and stimulated by the fragrant smell of stewed herbs, he found himself deeply interested in the lives of this close-knit hairy family. It was a privilege to dine with them, he felt, for who else among the Aquay had ever supped with another species? Although he was careful to keep his remarks to a minimum, he responded gratefully to their kindnesses and stories, and, as the girl stayed silent, he began to eat hungrily. He listened to the doctor's tales, and finally a sleepiness stole over him that even the orb, nestled warmly at his belly, couldn't dispel.

Nathan yawned, as did Grandmère Zarah. Leah glowered at the demon with narrowed eyes.

"Fix Scorpio a pallet in my study," Nathan bid his daughter. "It seems we all need our beds."

"I will see to our guest." Leah uttered the first words she had spoken since the demon had come into her house. She had never felt more enervated, sapped of all strength and reason. Fear propelled her as she waited for her father and grandmother to retire. Fear and fury. She would have to keep her voice down, for her father would still be awake and at his prayers. She whirled accusingly on Scorpio.

"You were supposed to possess Aimeric, not me," she hissed. "What are you doing here? Why do you torment me? You cannot stay—I will tell them you are a demon, and no physician! Why, you are not even powerful, you told me so yourself. What trick did you perform and call a miracle to seduce my father? Do not think that you will seduce *me*!"

Scorpio roused himself to confront the troublesome girl. What must he do to soothe her fears?

"I performed no miracle, it is true," he said wearily. He raised beseeching eyes to the girl's angry face. "Please listen, for I tell you the truth. Have no fear of me. I am not a demon. But neither am I of your world. I am simply a lost traveler from a galaxy distant from yours." He paused and sighed. The girl was staring at him blankly. "Yours is not the only planet that is populated with beings who can speak and think. You will have to use your imagination to understand. Think of me as a foreigner from an undiscovered land, if you will."

Leah regarded the demon skeptically. Were there madmen among demons? Perhaps he had been expelled from his own world, perhaps he was a demon with delusions. But he spoke as guilelessly as a child, and seemed neither evil nor dangerous. And he had healed a man.

The orb.

"It was not I who healed that man."

The demon had spoken as though he could read her thoughts. Leah suddenly pictured something, something she had dreamt, perhaps, a ball of light.

"It was this—it was the orb,"

Briefly turning his back on Leah, Scorpio withdrew the instrument from beneath his robe and held it forth for her to examine once again. The orb glowed dully. Leah cracked a shy childlike smile, as if greeting a well-loved, but distant, memory.

"You know I seek to discover its powers, to learn how it

works. Tonight I sought the Pope, not your father. We met only by chance. It may have been the orb that led me to the sick man, I do not know. But I learned that it can heal.''

As it had in the field, Leah's mood again mellowed as she watched the orb, its faint orange light slowly swirling, warming her complexion and the demon's like a fading fire. From upstairs, her father's pious chanting reached the study. She felt protected by his prayer. Maybe this is all a dream, thought Leah finally. I must sleep.

"Please, I must sleep."

There, that was the proof. Leah was startled from her reverie. The demon echoed her thoughts, he must be of her own creation. But how to explain the compelling and glorious mystery, the orb? Probably it was nothing but a bladder with a candle inside, a cheap magician's trick.

"I must conceal the orb in a safe place," said Scorpio. "Your father has never seen it, nor has any other. Only you. Will you help me to hide it? Just for this night. Then I will be gone. Please, for I must rest."

Leah was too confused to fight any longer. The creature seemed genuinely weak, more tired even than she. Well, even magicians and madmen had to sleep. "I will help you hide your magic globe for one night," she conceded, "and tomorrow you will go. We suffer no demons on the Sabbath. Do you agree?"

Scorpio nodded. Leah led him to a large ebony chest. Beneath the carved lid, a deep tray was filled with the drying herbs she had gathered that morning. As lovingly as one might cradle an infant, Scorpio laid the orb amongst the herbs and closed the chest. Then, as Leah departed, he spread his blanket on the deep red carpet and slept.

Leah's fear of the demon had abated. He had made no move to touch her. Surely he would not come near the bed she shared with her grandmother. He seemed to want only shelter, for the present. But she could allow no harm to come to her family. If she did conjure him, she must also watch him. Skirting the stairwell for the blackness of the kitchen, she lit a candle and settled down at the empty table, a troubled, wakeful guard.

❧   ❧   ❧

The candle guttered and Leah jolted awake. It was not yet dawn. She had better get to bed before Grandmère Zarah discovered she had spent the night in the kitchen. She tiptoed toward the stairwell. A sickening memory of the previous night's dinner crept over her. Had the nightmare been real?

In the dim light of her flickering taper, she could see the figure of the demon magician huddled on her father's prized carpet. Stealthily, silently, she moved to the herb chest and cracked the ebony lid. A golden glow suffused the room and a fresh, spicy aroma wafted from the chest. In the colors of spring, green and violet and buttery yellow, her herbs had started to flower.

Chapter
6

*B*efore breakfast on the morning of the Sabbath, Nathan de Bernay cheerfully gathered his family together and attended services at the synagogue. Scorpio had declined to accompany them as Nathan's guest, saying that there was something he must do. Nathan was secretly disappointed. He would have liked to show off his new assistant and introduce him to the community. But he understood. Scorpio would not be comfortable as a center of attention.

It was unfortunate, Nathan thought. Such a fascinating young man, though full of contradictions. Scorpio was a puzzle, to be sure. For one thing, he claimed to be widely traveled. But his grasp of geography seemed to Nathan to be rather fuzzy. And while he said he had never taken religious vows, yet he appeared to own nothing but the threadbare Benedictine habit he wore. He seemed to have a vast knowledge of plant lore, judging from the little conversation they'd enjoyed last night. Scorpio had listened with great interest as Nathan described the symptoms of aconite poisoning he had observed in Cardinal de Gascon. But the few plants Scorpio had mentioned Nathan had never heard of. They must be terribly obscure. Exotic.

Come to think of it, Nathan never did quite pinpoint where Scorpio had come from, or where he had studied medicine. He only had the sense that it must be unimaginably far away—Cathay, perhaps? Would Scorpio be an idolator, then? Nathan did find it curious that one with such a seemingly empirical turn of mind would fall prey to superstition where his own misfortune was concerned—did he truly believe the Pope could cure him? But perhaps in Scorpio's situation, one would try anything, cling to any hope. Such a horrible deformity. What could the Creator have been thinking of?

Nathan, catching himself, silently apologized to God for doubting His wisdom. Sighing reverently, he fastened his eyes on the conical glass lamp that burned perpetually before the holy ark and rejoined the men at their prayers, calling the responses he had committed to heart since his boyhood.

From behind the wooden grille that screened the narrow women's section from the rest of the temple, Leah listened to the service with her eyes tightly closed, fervently praying that the demon be removed from their midst. But she soon found it difficult to concentrate.

"They say he is stern, and also spoiled," whispered a voice next to her.

"Silly, you will soon cure him of that! Now find one for me!"

"There he is! Can you see him?"

"I think he's handsome—how lucky you are!"

It was Félicie and Jacobine Morel. They were discussing the various attributes of Daniel, the rabbi's son, who was to wed Jacobine. The bride-to-be was peering through the latticework and studying the boy's every move with an intensity he must have found unnerving, for now and then he would look over his shoulder as though he knew he was being watched.

Grandmère Zarah leaned across Leah's shoulder to shush the two girls. But she smiled tolerantly, and shot Leah a meaningful look, as if to say that the synagogue was as good a place as any to shop for a husband.

Leah rolled her eyes and looked disgusted. She had spied through the wooden slats many a time, and knew what she would see: the same boring boys she had grown up with, surreptitiously scratching their backsides or wiping their noses, lost in prayer or shifting from one foot to another, it didn't matter. There wasn't one she would care to take for a husband.

Leah tried to fasten her mind on worship. But thoughts of Scorpio intruded, intertwined with an angry vision of Aimeric de la Val d'Ouvèze. She was amazed to realize that she hadn't given Aimeric a thought since the demon's arrival last night. She was strangely grateful for the respite. Now that she really considered it, the demon had done no real harm. So far he had provided her with the courage to face up to Aimeric, and he had helped her father to heal an important official at the papal court. She had no doubt that the orb was something special; not after seeing her neatly tied bunches of wilting herbs revived as though she had placed them in water. Magician or madman, monster or monk? If he disappeared as he'd promised, she might never know. And if he was a demon—well, she decided he must be a good demon, after all.

Scorpio needed to find a hiding place for the orb. He had seen the look of wonder on Leah's face when, in the darkness of pre-dawn, she had lifted the lid of the herb chest and gazed at its spectral light, how the light of understanding had dawned in her eyes. Early this morning, Scorpio himself had gazed with a mixture of horror and awe at the budding blossoms and newborn florets on the marjoram and lavender, savory and sage. It was wearying to be the custodian of such power. It would be better if the orb was hidden until he could find someone to help him use it well.

He had promised Leah he would leave her house once he was rested, and although her father had been generous and kind, Scorpio would soon be called upon to explain his miraculous medical techniques. It would be best if he left. He would search for a hiding place where he could come and go, someplace that reminded him of home. Later he would return to thank Nathan and Zarah, and to bid Leah farewell.

Thus resolved, Scorpio set off for the river. But suddenly changing his mind, he set off for the palace first. If he did get to see the Pope, he would want to have swift access to the orb. Perhaps the well in the courtyard would do?

Much to his disappointment, the great openwork gate to the palace was shut, as was a wooden barrier behind it. Scorpio could hear men's voices, droning together in a low and hollow chant that echoed from somewhere beyond the walls. He followed the sound along the narrow alley that fronted the palace, uphill to the source of the song.

The voices were coming from Notre-Dame-des-Doms, the huge cathedral that flanked the Papal Palace. Scorpio had noticed the building earlier, because its slender belfry almost matched the height of the Pope's greatest tower. But beyond the cathedral was something he hadn't noticed: a garden.

Drawn to the greenery, Scorpio climbed a steep embankment and found himself in a vast park on the palace grounds, high atop a rocky hill. Up here, the wind was crisp and cold. All of Avignon stretched below him, the flat blue ribbon of the Rhône, and the undulating sea of houses, jammed together in crooked rows and roofed in rippling tiles of red and rust. Up here, above the city, were the barns and the henyards, the orchards and vegetable gardens that supplied the Pope's table. Here Scorpio felt almost at peace.

Scattered throughout the park, workers, male and female, weeded flower beds and planted seedlings, tended animals and pruned shrubbery, as deer and peacocks roamed freely among the trees. Here and there a gardener in tunic and breeches would look up from his work to wonder why a thin Benedictine brother had chosen to skip his morning's prayers and wander in the garden. But most found it no mystery.

Scorpio watched one of the workers, a portly man in a hood and leather apron, as he strode purposefully to a well-trodden path and disappeared, whistling tunelessly, into the trees. He had been carrying an implement that was strangely familiar, though long obsolete on Terrapin. It was a sort of mesh bag, fastened to a long pole. A net.

The path led, as Scorpio had hoped, to an oblong pool set among slender trees. A fishpond. The workman skillfully swept his pole through the waters, and departed with a thrashing netful of silver.

Peering over the edge of the pond, Scorpio longed to join the variety of fish within. The water was clear, but the pond was deep and lined with weeds; he could not see to the bottom. It was perfect. He released the orb from the confinement of his robe and tenderly dropped it into the water. There the orb floated for a moment, a summery golden yellow, then drifted to the center of the pool and gently sank.

The service was over and, as was usual on the Sabbath, Nathan was hungry for his breakfast. Joining Leah and Grand-mère Zarah outside the synagogue, he was proud to lead his two ladies homeward, one on each arm.

The de Bernays were surprised to find the door to Nathan's

study ajar when they arrived home. Who would disturb them on the Sabbath?

"Perhaps our guest has returned from his errand," said Nathan hopefully. It would be pleasant to talk with him over a long morning meal.

As they entered the consulting room, an agitated papal messenger jumped to his feet.

"Excuse me for intruding, sir," he said. "But you are the physician, Nathan de Bernay?" At the doctor's nod, he continued. "It's the cardinal, sir. Arnaud de Gascon. He's taken ill again, sir, and my master asks that you come right away."

"It is my Sabbath day, as you know," said Nathan politely. "But I will send my new assistant—he tended your master last night, and cured him well. Scorpio!"

"I'll look for him, Father," said Leah, hurrying to the kitchen, and checking the rooms upstairs. On her return to the study, she quickly peeked into the herb chest. The orb was gone. He had kept his word. "Scorpio has gone, Father," she said softly, relieved.

"My master asked for you, sir," the messenger persisted. "He said to fetch the Jew physician, Nathan de Bernay."

Nathan frowned. This messenger did not wear the arms of Arnaud de Gascon. "Your master—do you wear the livery of Bertrand Signac?"

The messenger nodded nervously. "He said it was most urgent."

"Is his own physician still indisposed, then?"

The messenger wiped sweaty palms on his haunches, still nodding.

Nathan sighed. "Very well. Cardinal de Gascon is now one of my patients, and I must go. Daughter, fetch my bag from the cupboard."

Leah regarded her father oddly. Couldn't he see that his bag was sitting in plain view, right on the table?

But Nathan was preoccupied. He had no love for Bertrand Signac, and it was well known that Cardinal Signac had no love for the Jews of Avignon. Nor did he wish to be involved with a poisoning. And Nathan was certain that de Gascon had suffered from aconite ingestion, for the symptoms were unique. The old Benedictine who had tended him, Brother Celestine, had reported the cardinal's alarm at the tingling in his body, and the distinct feeling that his hands were made of fur. By the time Nathan had arrived, de Gascon was racked with agonizing pains in the head and chest. He complained that his vision was souring, that everything was turning a yellowish green. And then he had descended into delirium and blindness.

Nathan had never known anyone with symptoms so advanced to be cured. By all of the laws of nature, paralysis should have stopped the cardinal's breathing and arrested his heart. If it hadn't been for Scorpio—where was Scorpio? Could he heal a dying cardinal twice?

Nathan pushed aside his trepidation. Probably de Gascon was only suffering from minor complications following his ordeal. It would be only natural. And if the symptoms were the same as last evening's, Nathan could turn him on his stomach and imitate the maneuver that Scorpio had used.

"Shall I go with you to the palace?" Leah asked eagerly, handing her father his bag. What was wrong? Her father seemed so troubled.

"Not on the Sabbath, Leah," said Nathan shortly. "And certainly not to tend to a cardinal. I want you to wait here for Scorpio, and if he returns, tell him what has happened. It is his help I might need."

Leah nodded. Her father thought he needed Scorpio, but what he really needed was the magical ball. And now she had sent Scorpio away. Well, it was all for the best. Father was the finest doctor in Avignon, with or without that orb. And of course her father was right, a cardinal's bedside was no place for her. She was sure the cardinal would recover. Father would become a famous healer at the palace, and . . . Would she ever get to see the inside of the Papal Palace?

As Nathan hurried into the bright Sabbath morning with the messenger, Leah comforted Grandmère Zarah, who had fallen to trembling, though she couldn't say why.

Chapter
7

*A*rnaud de Gascon was already dead, and had been so for well over an hour, Nathan judged. Even from several yards away, at the entrance to the small bedchamber, he could see that the pupils were fixed and dilated, the mouth motionless and slack, the skin a pallid gray. About the eyes, though they may have been blind before the end, there remained a suggestion of terror, as if to say, "Lord, no, not this again."

On either side of the narrow bed, long-faced cardinals stood solemnly over the corpse as Bertrand Signac completed the rite of extreme unction, dipping his thumb into a small pot of waxy balm, anointing the forehead, closing the eyes, marking the ears, nostrils, lips, hands and feet of the deceased, asking for absolution of his sins.

Nathan bowed his head respectfully for the duration of the sacrament; the room filled with the sickly sweet odor of the balm.

"I regret to see that I have arrived too late to be of service," he said when the ministrations had ended. "Please accept my condolences."

"You hardly look surprised, Doctor," said Bertrand Signac. The malice in his tone was unmistakable. Slowly wiping his oily thumb on the inside of one scarlet sleeve, he challenged Nathan de Bernay. "Do you suppose this to be another case of poisoning?"

"Has he eaten or taken any fluids?"

"He seemed well this morning," a quavering voice piped

up. The tremulous speaker was Brother Celestine, the elderly monk who had attended de Gascon so faithfully the day before. "He was exhausted, but cheerful, and woke at dawn. He took tea and a little cake—a poppy seed cake, his favorite, specially prepared for him this morning. I took it in to him myself and—"

"Silence!" ordered Signac. "I would hear what our famous physician has to say."

Nathan, taken aback at Cardinal Signac's vehemence, was nonetheless reflecting on the similarity between poppy seeds and the tiny seeds of *Aconitum napellus*: monkshood. Still, he couldn't be sure that a second dose had been administered to the deceased.

"His first ordeal left him in a greatly weakened condition," he ventured cautiously. "It's possible that, as a result, his heart has failed. If you'll allow me . . ."

"Don't let him touch the body!" Signac commanded.

Nathan jumped backward, startled, and collided with the messenger, who blocked the doorway.

"*You* are responsible for the death of our lamented cardinal, Arnaud de Gascon!" Signac lowered an accusatory finger at Nathan. "Do not try to deny your guilt—yesterday's 'miracle cure' was just a ruse, was it not? An excuse to plant *this*!"

Reaching under the pillow of the dead cardinal, Signac extracted a reddish object, which he held up to a stunned group of cardinals, then brandished in the incredulous face of Nathan de Bernay.

It was a wax doll, crude and lumpish, with the crown of its head flattened into the shape of a cardinal's hat. Through its heart was a single bronze pin.

"Last night you planted *this* in his bed!" Signac cried triumphantly.

Nathan was reeling from outrage and shock. The heat in the small room and the overpowering smell of the sacramental balm were making him nauseous. He breathed slowly to steady his temper, all the while chiding himself for having broken the Sabbath.

"It's the same kind of doll you Jews make. We know about your invidious sorcery! Why, a Jewish doll like this one was once used in a plot to murder the Pope himself!" Signac was raving. The shortest prelate, Cardinal de Laval, looked at Nathan with a combination of disgust and fear. The expressions on the faces of the other cardinals ranged from doubt to boredom.

"May I examine the doll, if you please," requested Nathan quietly. He turned the waxen image over in his hand, then nodded curtly and passed it back to Signac. "It is true that some of my people have made such dolls . . ."

"Aha!" shouted Signac.

". . . .but they are used only to divine the location of lost objects. I do not hold with such superstitions. I am a physician, sirs, and know nothing of sorcery. Furthermore, the plot against the Pope you speak of occurred over thirty years ago. You may recall that the dolls used against John XXII were made to order for one of your own bishops, who was later hanged!"

Signac bristled as several of his associates chorused their agreement that Nathan's memory was, indeed, correct.

Nathan's dignity had been restored. "I am an educated physician, a man of medicine," he asserted. "You called me in yourself. Why would I want to murder a cardinal, a man whom, until last night, I had never even met?"

The prelates nodded, and looked questioningly at Signac. The physician's reasoning was sound.

"Perhaps he owed money to one of your kind, eh? To one of your relatives?" Signac grew increasingly venomous.

"I assure you, that is not the case," replied Nathan.

"Then you deny the charge of murder by treachery?" cried Signac.

"Most certainly."

"Search his bag!"

A quartet of guards had materialized in the doorway. One of them stepped forward and emptied Nathan's leather bag on the cold stone floor. Surgeon's tools of iron and brass tumbled forth, clanking atop the soft packets of herbs. Small glass cups, used for bloodletting, clinked against the wooden boxes of salve. A bit of cloth drifted silently to the floor, a scrap of cloth that Nathan did not recognize. Signac bent down to pick it up, and withdrew, meticulously, ten tiny objects one by one, letting each fall to the floor with a metallic ping.

"You see, my lords," said the silky voice, "how the Jew carries with him brass pins?" He paused. Then shouted. "Pins! Like the needle that pierces the very heart of this waxen doll!"

Nathan's protests were ignored.

"I want this Jew's house searched for instruments of sorcery! Guards!" Signac was in his glory. "Take this self-styled physician to his dwelling place and conduct the search in his very sight!"

Signac had trapped him, whatever the reasons. Even had he kept the Sabbath, the outcome would have been the same, Nathan could see that now. Falling silent, he turned his thoughts to God.

Chapter
8

*S*corpio, unencumbered, slow-
ly returned to the Jewish quarter from the palace gardens. His
steps dragged, for without the orb he felt heavier rather than
lighter, as though the force of gravity had increased, and his
plan of action, conceived in optimism and previously so clear
and simple, now seemed cloudy and full of holes.

The morning was warm, and the deep Benedictine hood was
beginning to itch his head. How he wished he could move
about freely, with his face turned to the sun. But so far Nathan
and his sightless mother were the only beings he had encountered who didn't find him entirely repulsive. Nathan was tol-
erant and kind, Scorpio reflected, and he seemed to be a learned
man. He decided to risk Leah's anger to speak to her father
just once more, to learn what he could of this powerful Pope,
and of the planet and its ways. It looked as though he might
have to spend some days on this world, and he didn't even
know its name.

No one stopped him at the gate in the rue Jacob, though a
lone Benedictine was a less than common sight in the quarter.
Everyone, including the gatekeepers, was hastening to the
scene of a commotion in the public square before the synagogue. Scorpio stopped short. Nathan de Bernay was being
marched through the square in the custody of eight armed
guards.

Filled with confusion and horror, Scorpio stayed at the back of the crowd. What could this mean? Could it have anything to do with him?

"Stand back, on the orders of Cardinal Bertrand Signac!" the captain of the guards shouted, pushing at the crowd.

A tall, commanding man swept into the square. He wore a dark green overtunic, and his thick black hair and curly beard were both neatly parted in the middle. He was followed by several other men of similarly dignified appearance.

"I am Rabbi Isaac de Lunel," he announced to the guards. His tone was friendly, but firm. "Evidently you have made a mistake. Nathan de Bernay is a renowned physician and a most respected member of our community. It is unthinkable that he would commit any crime. I demand his release. Please ask Cardinal Signac to submit his complaint to my authority, and we shall certainly take action in our own court, as is our custom, if it has any merit."

"This exceeds your authority, Rabbi," replied the captain, an officious youth who was evidently much enjoying the proceeding. "The doctor is accused of murdering Cardinal Arnaud de Gascon, and we are ordered to search his house."

An outcry went up from the crowd as the guards dragged Nathan across the square in the direction of his house. Scorpio pushed forward. On the opposite side of the square, he could see Leah, a stricken look in her eyes, clutching her grandmother's arm and backing protectively toward their doorway.

"Go back to your houses," the guards shouted at the crowd. "Keep back! We won't tolerate any disorder in here!"

At the rabbi's signal, the crowd fell back and parted, creating a path to Nathan's door. Nathan turned, as though to reassure his neighbors. But his eyes suddenly locked with Scorpio's. Never had Scorpio received a clearer message. *Run! Hide! Now!* Scorpio obeyed, and ran from the quarter, his hood flapping loosely away from his face.

One of the guards, following Nathan's gaze, caught sight of the fleeing Benedictine. "Stop that monk!" he shouted, grabbing another of Signac's men and breaking into a run. "It's the Jew's accomplice! The leper! The Jew hired a leper to lay his hands on Arnaud de Gascon!" But somehow the crowd seemed to thicken around them, impeding their progress, and the mysterious monk vanished into the maze of alleys that was Avignon.

• • •

By the time the two guards returned to the house of Nathan de Bernay, bewildered, empty-handed and panting for breath, the search had turned up a cache of reddish wax and a crucifix belonging to the dead cardinal.

"You knew right where to look, didn't you? Your own messenger put them in the cupboard himself, this morning," Leah shrieked furiously at one of the guards. "He was sweaty and nervous, and now we see why. My father's bag was removed from the cupboard and left on the table. It was tampered with, can't you *see*?" She turned from one guard to the next, all of whom avoided her eyes with the exception of the young captain, who smirked.

With Leah wailing and Grandmère Zarah pleading piteously, Rabbi de Lunel trying to reason and the inhabitants of the Jewish Quarter heaving insults in their anger and outrage, Cardinal Signac's honor guard bore a quietly defiant Nathan off to prison.

Chapter 9

*P*ope Clement VI was enjoying fish for dinner again. The firm white flesh was moist and springy, and perfectly garnished with a syrup of ginger-spiced wine. The fish had been particularly abundant lately, according to his chief cook, and, Clement observed, unusually tasty as well. He must make a note to congratulate his kitchen staff.

How lovely it was to dine alone in the comfort of the papal apartments. Clement savored the last of his meal and called for a flagon of Châteauneuf, newly arrived from the papal vineyards north of Avignon, to be sent to his study. He moved from his private dining room through the robing room, where, for once, no ambassador awaited a private audience, no cardinal came to complain of another, no communication from the *camerarius*, the much-needed and equally dreaded minister of finance, urged him to curb his spending or threatened to disturb his sleep.

Clement exchanged his vestments for a nightgown and cap of whitest linen and a roomy, ermine-lined overrobe. His soft, pinkish skin thus swathed in white, his bald head safe beneath the prophylactic cap that outlined rosy cheeks, puffy eyelids and full, pursed lips, Clement resembled nothing if not a huge and sensuous infant, or perhaps the man in the moon.

Dismissing his chamberlains, he climbed the stairway to his bedchamber, which occupied the entire fourth story of the Magna Turris, the Great Tower. Here, more than anywhere else in his palace stronghold, Clement felt secure. The tower walls were ten feet thick, built to protect his holy person and, no less significantly, the library and two treasuries that sandwiched his bedchamber. On the sixth story, some one hundred fifty feet above the Great Courtyard, sergeants-at-arms guarded the peace from a crenellated turret.

By day, Clement VI excelled in his role as Pope. His legal and political experience was as broad as his theological knowledge, for he had served as chancellor at the French court before advancing to a cardinalship. His eloquence was as renowned as his elegance. His court was magnificent and his expenditures lavish. He was a king of kings. But his duties were demanding and public. He reserved his nights for the enjoyment of the finer things.

From his bedchamber, the Pontiff followed a narrow connecting passage to his study, a small room housed in a secondary tower he'd had erected adjacent to the Magna Turris to expand his personal apartments. Above him was his private chapel; below, two stories of wardrobe rooms and, on the ground floor, a private steam bath of which Clement was righteously proud. But the study was his haven, and he looked forward to an evening of solitude, with no thoughts of the eternal squabbles between England and France or the troublesome wars in the Papal States, no worries about his flagging plans for another Crusade, or this unfortunate business of Arnaud de Gascon. Eagerly he anticipated the flavor of the full-bodied red wine, heady, like his reading, and warm going down.

Settling comfortably at his reading table, Clement wrapped a long but pudgy hand around the jeweled goblet that stood, brimful, waiting for him, and drank. There began the stirrings of profound satisfaction. He considered with ever-deepening pleasure the frescoes that adorned the study walls, frescoes he himself had commissioned as a respite from the scenes of angels and martyrdoms that covered the rest of the palace. Here were secular scenes of worldly delights, hunting and falconry, women bathing and children playing, scenes of forests, orchards, birds and beasts, all on a background of rich dark green. At the top, a frieze of wildlife on a ground of red marched merrily beneath the wood-beamed ceiling that was itself covered with patterns and florets. Only in the study, buried in the center of an impregnable tower, were the artworks peopled, not with saints, but with noblemen and servants gracefully engaged in outdoor pursuits, all painted to order for a Pope who was too often confined by his own enormous power.

Clement looked wistfully at a dreamy, yet animated scene of a brown-hooded hunter in a forest of evergreens, setting his ferret after a hare. Then his attention was captured by a portrait of the papal fishpond. The pool held all manner of swimming things, pike and carp, and ducks and a dolphin, while men at the water's edge fished with a long-handled net and a weighted cast net, and a hook and line. The scene, like the others in the study, had been painted by the court painter, Matteo Giovanetti di Viterbo. Ah, the Italians. Perhaps, thought Clement, pausing to drain his goblet, he should invite Matteo back to add more fish to the fishpond, considering their recent plenty.

Clement saw patronage of the arts and letters as one of the duties, and delights, of rulership. His mind on inspired Italians, he opened a volume he was curious to examine, an edition of new works by the diplomat and innovative poet Francesco Petrarch, recently returned to Avignon from his native Italy. Clement hoped to attract Petrarch to a position at court. The poet had already turned down an apostolic secretaryship, having no desire to be distracted from his writing, he claimed. Perhaps a bishopric? But Clement was aware that Petrarch found the court at Avignon to be corrupt, even dissolute. The Pope couldn't comprehend the poet's thinly veiled disgust. Petrarch simply refused to separate his vision of the papacy from the reality of Clement the man. But was the poet not a man of the world? No one had written of love of woman with more passion than he; he had worshipped his idealized Laura above all others, and his lines since she had been taken by the Black Death were nothing less than sublime.

> She used to let her golden hair fly free
> For the wind to toy and tangle and molest;
> Her eyes were brighter than the radiant west.
> (Seldom they shine so now.) I used to see
>
> Pity look out of those deep eyes on me.
> ("It was false pity," you would now protest.)
> I had love's tinder heaped within my breast;
> What wonder that the flame burned furiously?

She did not walk in any mortal way,
But with angelic progress; when she spoke,
Unearthly voices sang in unison.

She seemed divine among the dreary folk
Of earth. You say she is not so today?
Well, though the bow's unbent, the wound bleeds on.

The wound bleeds on. Sublime. Clement sighed. He couldn't help but think of Cécile, the raven-haired Countess of Turenne. Perhaps he should have invited her for the evening. She must visit again soon. Come to think of it, it was unfortunate that Petrarch had encountered the countess, dressed as a man, waiting to be admitted to the papal chambers. What thorns in the side these Italians could be to a French Pope! Take this matter of the strife between the Visconti of Milan and the Florentines! But as artists they were unsurpassed, such sentiment, such command of the lyrical. . . .

All the same, it had been a stunning disguise. Clever, even titillating. In truth, it disguised little. Emptying the flagon into his goblet, Clement let his thoughts drift back to the challenging advantages of the Countess of Turenne.

The very thought of her brought stars to his eyes. Clement VI pressed his eyelids to clear them of the oddly flickering lights that swam in his vision. Eyestrain, he didn't doubt, caused by reading with such concentration. As he blinked, the lights began to coalesce. The flickering steadied and leveled into two pinpoints of light that hovered near the ceiling. With them Clement could hear the murmur of voices, as though there were watchers in the rafters. Were there spies in the chapel above him?

"Guards!" called Clement assertively. But his command came out in a strangled cough, as, instantaneously, the lights grew blindingly bright, and two red devils popped into his study.

They wore long black gowns that fell from the shoulder, leaving their crimson arms bared. Their leather skullcaps were also black, with openings for two goatlike nubs on the forehead, and spiraling ram's horns that swept backward and pierced the air above their heads. Their faces were hideous, birdlike, with elliptical eyes as black as their gowns and a sweeping cheekbone that crossed from ear to ear, creating a beaklike point where the nose should be. One of the devils was large and well muscled, and exuded the cleverness and agile strength of some mountain-dwelling beast. The other was also tall but elastically thin, with a regal bearing and piercing stare. The thin one held a small glowing ball that swirled with golden light of a wondrous intensity.

Clement VI crossed himself repeatedly and recited prayers in Latin. He was stupefied, even frightened. But a good part of him was already dumbfounded by wine, and his own self-regard afforded him additional protection from stark terror. For who should have visions, if not the Pope? He was to be tempted, it was clear. The devils had probably divined his reverie about the Countess of Turenne. Perhaps it was a trifle immodest, perhaps—

"You are the leader here?" It was the thin one who spoke. His voice was reedy and resonant, like the sound of an organ as tenor notes issued from its pipes.

"I am Pope Clement VI, representative of Christ Our Lord on Earth." Clement replied with poise, then intoned: "I adjure thee, O serpents of old, by the Creator of the World who hath power to cast into Hell, that thou depart forthwith from this house, in the name of our Lord Jesus Christ, Amen!" Devils must be respected, of course, but one must hold one's own ground.

"We care nothing for your God. Our business is with you, Clement VI."

The Pope balanced slightly, but his voice remained firm. "You have come to tempt me, then? I will never succumb to your invitation to Hell!"

"We invite you nowhere."

The Hunter assassin spoke patiently. First encounters on new planets were always difficult. And he was pressed for time, so, perhaps unwisely, he had omitted the usual formalities.

"You are here to torment me, then," cried Clement, his mood abruptly conciliatory. "I confess my sins freely. For must we not sin to overcome sin? Must we not experience temptation in order to reject it?"

The two Hunters eyed one another sourly. Foreigners were so unpredictable.

"We did not come here to bargain," the assassin stated

flatly. "Listen closely, Clement VI. We are here to find another of our kind, an Aquay. He is bearing an orb, one of these."

Clement stared, mesmerized, as the devil held forth the beautiful ball. Light swirled about its surface like firesmoke.

"We know he has it, and we know he is nearby. He is called Scorpio. Do you know of him?"

Clement shook his head, distracted. What a curious thing was this ball of light. Could it be a trick of Satan's?

"I have never seen another like you, nor such a wonder as this orb," he replied. "What does it do?"

"It has many powers." The muscular devil seemed about to say more, but he was hushed by his companion, who withdrew to the corner of the study. There the two held a whispered consultation.

"He obviously knows nothing." Lethor the Assassin held the orb away from his body and noted the information relayed from the sensors at the front of his helmet. "There are more of these beings nearby, we must make haste now. Besides, my skin burns and pinches in this humidity. Scorpio must have buried the orb, or ours would have led us directly to it. Therefore, Ardon, we will have to track Scorpio himself."

"When we find him, Scorpio is mine," said Ardon the Stalker, flexing the scarlet skin that tightened over his biceps. "But we can use this Pope being to draw him out. He is the ruler of this planet, is he not? He must have a network of spies and informants like any leader."

"We must guard against the error that the Pope himself makes, Ardon," said Lethor. "We must not form conclusions based on our experience of our own world. We don't know the extent of his power, nor by what right he rules. Nevertheless, your idea has merit. For the Pope concludes that we have come to cause him torment, and we frighten him."

Clement VI felt annoyance bubbling inside him like an impending belch. How dare these devils consult behind his back!

"Return and face me!" he bellowed.

"Certainly," said Lethor, turning to the Pope. His tone was syrup, wicked. Brandishing the orb in the face of the astonished Clement, he hollered back. "You will search for Scorpio! He has stolen that which is ours! Use every means that is available to you, O Great One. For if you do not find Scorpio, we shall return to torment you. We shall cause you unending pain such as you have never known, nor can you imagine such torture. You have one week. If you fail to find Scorpio, your future is agony and anguish."

Turning to face one another, the devils grasped the glowing ball of light between them and vanished.

Clement was spent. His hands trembled and his face was as white as his ermine robe. He clutched at his heart and searched the shadows. Could it have been the wine? He quickly regained his composure as four guards tromped into the room. It would be unseemly to appear so vulnerable in front of subordinates. What did they want? Had he called for them?

"We heard shouting, Your Eminence," said one. "As did the chamberlain working in the wardrobe beneath you. But it seems we were mistaken. Please excuse our intrusion."

"You saw nothing?" Clement asked, forcing a casual tone.

"No, Your Eminence. Nothing." The guards were obviously confused.

"You are very alert. For there was nothing there! I was rehearsing a sermon, and I am afraid I was carried away with my own oratory. But please, wait without until I dismiss you."

Clement moved to his spacious bedchamber. A fire crackled brightly in the hearth. But even with his guards posted just beyond the doors, even in the elegant turquoise chamber, painted with golden vines and arabesques, songbirds and squirrels, he no longer felt secure. Beneath the down-filled covers on his great bed, he resolved to examine his situation with as calm a wit as he could muster. Had the chamberlain and the guards heard the devils too, then? Or was it his own shouting they had heard? The creatures may have been real. Or they may have been a nightmare, brought on by thoughts of Petrarch and too much wine.

If he ordered a full-scale search for a devil, he would be thought mad. But what if this Scorpio was real? And what of the treasure the devils were after—what of the orb?

Clement was haunted by his vision of the orb. Could it be he had seen the Sacred Orb of the Pantocrator? Perhaps this Scorpio was the angel who controlled it. Perhaps with such power, no devil could harm him. Perhaps . . .

The connoisseur in Clement began to overshadow his fear, and even his awe. What a coup it would be to own such a relic. How he would like to procure such a piece! Not at the price of his eternal soul, of course. No, he would have to find this Scorpio and buy the orb outright.

The court illuminator, a weathered artist of advanced years, was up all night with an agitated Clement VI. By morning, he had produced a portrait of the devils the Pope claimed to have seen in a vision of Hell. One of the likenesses, a tall, thin, red devil, held a glowing ball of fiery orange.

Clement VI had pronounced himself well satisfied. He, too, had been awake until dawn, composing the sermon he intended to preach at the morning's High Mass at Notre-Dame-des-Doms, describing his terrible temptation, and how he had overcome it by shouting down the demons and invoking the Name of the Lord.

Quietly, but insistently, he had slipped the portrait of the devils, not yet dry, to a select few of his private guard, with orders that they should search far and wide for such a one, and bring him to the palace.

And, mad popes being no great rarity in anyone's experience, the guards had hurried off to do his bidding, no questions asked.

Chapter
10

Grandmère Zarah perched stiffly in Nathan's narrow, straight-backed armchair, thin-lipped and silent. Leah bustled around her, sobbing mindlessly and picking through the disorder Cardinal Signac's men had left in their wake. Manuscripts and instruments were scattered across the floor, herbs and powders had been ground into the precious carpet, flasks were broken and liquids spilled. But the chaos was a needless blind, Leah knew. She had watched the captain of the guards signal his men to cease the wrecking. Then he had walked purposefully to the corner cupboard, wrenched it open and withdrew the evidence that damned her father.

"A crucifix, of all things!" she shouted bitterly. "What would a Jewish physician want with such a thing? How stupid it all is! It's just not fair!"

Zarah made no response. At last, overcome with frustration and misery, Leah threw herself at her grandmother's feet and whimpered, "Oh, Grandmère, why is this happening? Where have they taken him?"

And at last Zarah stirred from her chair. Pulling her shawl tightly around her shoulders, she drew herself to her feet and spoke with steady resolve. "Our people have long been persecuted," she told Leah. "We have been driven into exile and our temples have been destroyed. We have been named as witches, slaughtered and burned. Even here, in the safety of Avignon, we have been confined to this quarter and banned from the guilds. Perhaps it is God's will that our love for Him be tested through trials that never change.'' She gripped her granddaughter's arm and fastened her dim eyes on Leah's own. ''Heed me well, child. Your father is an innocent man. Like so many of our people who have gone before him, he has been falsely accused. But God's will will be done.

''I go now to find Rabbi dé Lunel, to ask him to intercede for the life of my son. He will help us as best he is able. You, Leah, must put our house in order. You must pray to God that He imbue you with the dignity of Esther and the patience of Rachel. And tomorrow you will visit your father and find out what you may.''

It seemed that all of Avignon was buzzing with talk of the Pope's morning sermon. People swarmed through every lane and alley, returning from High Mass at Notre-Dame-des-Doms. Gathering in groups of four or six, posing to show their Sunday garb to best advantage, they gossiped and speculated, expounded and twittered, as though they all had taken an excess of angelica. No one was discussing the death of Arnaud de Gascon, Leah noted wonderingly. Nor did she catch her father's name. How could they all go about their lives so blithely? Didn't they know that Nathan de Bernay was confined to a prison cell, accused of a sorcery? What could people be talking about that was more scandalous than murder?

Leah paused to eavesdrop on an agitated couple, perhaps a merchant and his wife.

''Only Pope Clement would banish not one but *two* devils from his sight!'' said the man, a gaunt figure in a suit of russet and indigo. ''I suppose he's seen the last of them!''

His wife, outfitted in saffron trimmed with vair, wrung her hands and searched the windows above the street. ''We must be on the lookout for devils ourselves, he said. They come from above and appear when you least expect it. He said we are to appeal to him directly for salvation if we are visited. We must be ever vigilant, he said!''

The woman hurried into one of the choicer lanes of the city, pulling her husband after her.

More devils? thought Leah. Had Scorpio gotten in to see the Pope, after all? She had thought she was finally rid of him. But the merchant had said there were two devils. Were demons and devils the same? What if Scorpio was one of them? Could he be a Christian devil, after all? He had never seemed to be evil. He had even kept his word and disappeared the morning the cardinal died, just as he had promised.

Leah gasped aloud with the sudden realization: Scorpio could have murdered Arnaud de Gascon and implicated her father! Was it her own willfulness and disloyalty, then, that had brought disaster on her family? The thought was unbearable. She must find a way to save her father. Fervently she prayed to be granted all of the virtues of the matriarchs, Sarah, Rebekah, Rachel, and her namesake, Leah. Please, God, grant me the fortitude of Leah!

The dank prison was filled with drunkards and cutthroats of the worst sort. They jeered at Leah as she passed, their emaciated fingers wagging through small barred openings in heavy wooden portals. Nonplussed, an unkempt and unshaven gaoler conducted Leah to the end of a corridor.

"It's not often that we have a lady in here," he stated. "Your father's just around the corner. We kept him separate, you know, him being a sorcerer and all."

Leah opened her mouth to protest, but the gaoler held up an admonitory hand.

"Don't waste your breath, girl. I make no judgements one way or the other. I just lock them up, and sometimes I let them out. Here we are, then. I'll be back for you in a half hour's time."

Leah embraced her father, tears pooling in her eyes. She handed him his well-worn prayer shawl, and a loaf of bread, specially baked in the quarter in the great oven under the synagogue, that she had smuggled under her cloak. Aside from the dark circles that bespoke a sleepless night, he looked well enough. His mixture of joy and anguish at seeing her was evident.

"We have little time, daughter," Nathan began. "You must listen while I tell you what I know. My trouble is deep. For I believe it was Cardinal Bertrand Signac who had de Gascon killed.

"The night I was called to the palace, Signac had expected his own physician to attend. But Gisnard de Carliac was drunk. Perhaps it was Signac who made him so, to fog his judgement.

Or perhaps he would have lied on behalf of his patron, this I cannot know. But my colleague took too much wine and slept like the dead, and I was called in. The nearest Jew.'' Nathan paused to collect his thoughts.

"The poison causes heart failure, it is easy to mistake. But I had the misfortune to recognize the symptoms. I have no doubt it was aconite—monkshood. You know the plant?''

Leah nodded.

"I am not certain, but I believe de Gascon must have been given a second dose, perhaps on a poppy seed cake he took for his breakfast.''

Leah could hold her tongue no longer. "But, Father, could it not have been Scorpio who poisoned the cardinal, and allowed them to blame you? He was there, as were you. You know so little of him, after all. . . .''

"No, Leah," said Nathan firmly. "You must trust me and put such thoughts out of your mind. Scorpio is difficult to look at, I know, and a foreigner with mysterious ways. But he is a good man, a great healer, and we will need his help.''

"But—"

"Hear me out. The story becomes clear. Do you not know that the Pope is supposed to be at war with the Visconti family of Milan?''

"Those they call the 'Vipers of Milan'? But why—"

"The dispute is over territory in the Papal States. It is said that negotiations are under way for a treaty with Giovanni Visconti, the Archbishop of Milan. Such an alliance would replenish the papal coffers—Clement's treasury has dwindled and he borrows heavily to finance his wars and his lavish court. And you must know as well that such an alliance would replenish the fortunes of the cardinals, from whom he has borrowed, for they divide among them fully one half of the Church's revenues!''

"But I still don't see—"

"Now I shall tell you, daughter, that Arnaud de Gascon was known to be in the pay of the Florentines, the archenemies of the Visconti. De Gascon was working against the treaty, and he had Pope Clement's ear. While Signac, rumor has it, is nothing less than a Visconti spy.

"Arnaud de Gascon was meant to die the night I was called. But Scorpio healed him, and I was foolish enough to opine aloud that the cardinal had been poisoned. Signac had no choice but to do away with me and the cardinal both."

"So Scorpio has done you harm!" Leah cried. "Oh, Father, I must tell you—"

"Scorpio has done no harm," said Nathan, shaking Leah by the shoulders. "They would have arrested me on the first night, had the cardinal died. My fate was sealed the moment I mentioned poison in the presence of Bertrand Signac.

"Listen, now, for our time is almost up. You, Leah, must find Scorpio and beg him for his help. You must search for evidence to clear my name. First, you must contrive to examine de Gascon's body and confirm that it was poison that killed him. Look for the seeds of the plant from which aconite is drawn."

"Monkshood," said Leah, nodding. She had seen the plant with its purple bell-shaped flowers growing wild in the environs of Avignon.

"Perhaps, with your knowledge of herbs and Scorpio's knowledge of medicine, you will find a way to tie the poisoning to Signac. If you do, you must ask Scorpio to appeal to the Pope himself. In Christian law, the word of a Jew is never to be taken above that of a Christian. But Scorpio can speak in my defense. For he is not a Jew."

Leah left the papal prison with an aching heart. She would carry out her father's wishes, of course. But no judge was likely to listen to a leprous-looking demon, Christian *or* Jew. Besides, she would have to find a hundred Christians to testify for her father to outweigh the word of Bertrand Signac. Leah beamed hopefully. What of her father's patients? How many of their lives had he saved? Surely they would do him this service.

She decided to pay a visit to her favorite patient, Mme. Roussillon. Hadn't she always been kind to Leah, and spoken to her of poetry and art as if to an equal, pressed upon her little books to read and encouraged her to broaden her interests? Surely such a cultured lady, with her passion for the chivalric ideals not just of courtly love, but of loyalty and justice, honor and truth and defense of the oppressed, would come to the aid of her esteemed physician, Nathan de Bernay. Mme. Roussillon would probably welcome the opportunity to offer Leah counsel, and might even contact her influential friends at court.

And if Aimeric was at home—Leah's stomach churned miserably at the thought—why, she would just ignore him.

Mme. Roussillon was embroidering linens in her small but elegant quarters. Her health appeared much improved, Leah observed. She stood and turned to receive Leah, and blinked with surprise, as if she were not sure whom she was addressing.

"It's Leah de Bernay, madame. The doctor's daughter."

Mme. Roussillon crossed herself rapidly and took a step backward.

"Well, so it is, and it's lovely to see you, my dear." Mme. Roussillon pressed a hand to her ample bosom. "You haven't brought more of the valerian decoction, I trust? For you can see, I am so much better now, and I hardly think I'll be needing . . ."

"I've come on behalf of my father," Leah interrupted.

"I quite understand that he won't keep our appointment, dear, you needn't have come. I was terribly shocked to hear what has befallen your poor father. Such a kind man, and an excellent physician. He must have been possessed by the Devil himself to have murdered a cardinal. I never would have thought . . ."

"Please, Mme. Roussillon, I have come to ask you—"

"Not after what has happened, I'm afraid. It would be quite out of the question." The matronly lady turned her back to Leah and wiped at her brow with a delicate linen square. "I'm just not looking for household help at the moment, dear, I'm sorry."

Leah choked back her anger and spoke steadily. "None of it is true, you know. He is no sorcerer, nor a murderer. You must know!"

But Mme. Roussillon had beckoned for her maidservant to show Leah the door. "You were always so like him," she muttered, backing toward her bedchamber. Her look held genuine pity, but it also held fear.

"Leah." The voice was soft, even sympathetic. So Aimeric had been at home. He must have followed her to the sheltered courtyard of his aunt's apartments, where Leah now stood, her shoulders slumped, her head bowed.

"How naive you are, after all." Aimeric was matter-of-fact. "It has nothing to do with the truth, you see. The situation is a matter of politics. Bernard Signac has found his scapegoat. What everyone knows to be true, none will speak. Not even I, should you grant me all your favors."

Leah shot him a furious glance. "You are all cowards," she hissed.

Aimeric shrugged, in no way insulted. "Cardinal Signac is a formidable enemy. My uncle, the bishop, fears him. Even the Pope would be wise to fear Signac." Grasping Leah by the shoulders, Aimeric gently lifted her chin so he could meet her eyes. "I have never meant you harm, Leah. Please believe that I am trying to help you now. And I am telling you that you'd best make your peace with your father."

Chapter
11

*L*eah's disappointment in Mme. Roussillon was as bitter as gentian; but Aimeric's dispassionate words held a ring of truth. She had tried to help her father in her own way, and it had not worked. Now she would respect his wishes. For it seemed there was no help for her father in this world.

Before the gates of the Jewish quarter were locked fast for the night, Leah slipped from her father's house. Embracing Grandmère Zarah at the threshold, she reassured the old woman that she was doing Nathan's bidding. Then, armed with a small oil lamp and a loaf of bread, she set off across the Pont d'Avignon to seek Scorpio.

Already there were stories being circulated in the quarter about the mysterious monk who had fled at Nathan's signal; of how the people had swarmed the cardinal's guards and allowed the stranger to escape; and how they had known him to be Nathan's new assistant, a foreigner of hideous aspect, but with unusual talent. He had not been seen since he disappeared into the rue Jacob. Leah prayed that he would have returned to the field where they had met.

Scorpio was her last chance. She knew not what he was, nor where he had come from. But she would appeal to him to help her: it was her father's will. Perhaps Scorpio could use his powers on Nathan's behalf—the powers hidden in the shining ball of light.

● ● ●

Deep in the darkening forest, Leah turned up the wick on her lamp and held it, swinging gently, at arm's length. Shadows danced around her like ghostly marionettes strung from twisted tree limbs. The night was cold, and the silence was deceptive, a velvety quietude brushed with little noises, close and subtle. Leah felt the nocturnal eyes of a thousand secret watchers; yet she had never felt more alone, as if she were the only living creature in an endless forest, and the rest of the world had disappeared.

With the descent of night, before the rising of the moon, the space around her seemed to thicken. Soon the yellow lamplight only served to render the blackness beyond its small aura all the blacker. Her crackling footfall sounded as loud as the din of the market at Prime. As she advanced, her presence seemed to generate a flurry of woodland night noise, hooting and scurrying, screeching and flapping. Leah's mind began to fill with images of spirits and demons, carnivorous beasts and birds of prey. Despite herself, she began to run, slowly at first, shielding her lamplight, and then more steadily, ignoring the brambles that pulled at her cloak, until she emerged, panting, at the edge of the fields of Montmajour Abbey and stopped short, witlessly dousing her carefully guarded wick in a single, violent sloshing of oil.

All it takes is a moment's negligence and the light can be lost forever. Leah sunk to her knees and wept, holding her face above the thin plume of smoke that snaked from the spout of the lamp. She wept in frustration and in despair; for fear of the dark and for love of her father. She cried in self-pity, and vowed to remain in place where she sat and never move again; and she cried for relief that the forest was behind her and now she could move on.

By the time Leah had done with her tears, the moon had risen, wrapping sky and earth in a wafting gray gauze. Leah ventured to the edge of the field, to the three stone gardener's huts where she had last seen Scorpio. The huts hunkered in the field like a row of sleeping bears. No movement came from within.

"*Scorpio!*" Leah whispered. No sound. Feeling for the cold stone openings, she whispered three times in succession. From each doorway, there came no reply, only the echo of desertion.

Leah tried again. She had been so sure she would find him here. This time she stood full in the doorway of each hut, searching the inky darkness for some sign of the demon or the glow of the orb.

This time she was rewarded. In the last hut she saw a shape, a patch of something less than black. Feeling her way in the darkness, knocking her shin against the edge of a wooden bench, Leah plucked at the warm scratchy softness of a Benedictine robe and tugged gently. "*Scorpio!*" But the empty garment came away from her hand and slid into a heap at her feet.

Bundling the habit under her arm, Leah strode purposefully back to the middle of the field. "Damn you, Aimeric de la Val d'Ouvèze!" she tried, stamping her foot. Scorpio did not appear.

All alone in the center of the field, Leah began to feel frightened again. The earth felt suddenly cold and damp. A layer of mist was beginning to form, blurring the edge of the world in reflected moonlight. On the farthest horizon, atop its craggy hill, the Abbey of Montmajour loomed, remote and spooky. Leah fell still, straining to identify the noises of the night. She realized that she had been listening all along to a sound that resonated from the trees behind the gardener's huts. It was a shrill, rhythmic chirping, multilayered, like the song of a hundred katydids. But it was much too cold for crickets. And there were variations in the sound, alternating with the chirping: two low warbling tones that overlapped like a hollow chord.

Despite her apprehension, Leah was drawn to the sound. She found it unlike any she had ever heard, and strangely beautiful.

Perhaps she had suspected all along that the source of the sound would be Scorpio. He had discarded his Benedictine robe and climbed into a tree, where, crouching low along a heavy limb, he raised his head to the stars and chanted. His coloring was dark and mottled. His huge eyes were open to the starlit sky, the brilliant moon reflected as a pinpoint in their midst. He made no sign that he was aware of Leah, and his chanting rose and fell.

Leah was frightened. Scorpio looked unhuman, like a salamander, or some tailless basilisk. But as she stood beneath him, silently awed, she was reminded more than anything of her father as his lips moved in candlelit solemnity, lost in prayer. Scorpio's song was such a reverie, comforting and sad. For the briefest of moments, Leah felt a stirring of mystical communion. Then, fearful, or perhaps unwilling to succumb, she withdrew from sight and waited for Scorpio at the base of a nearby tree, moved and lulled by his eerie song.

In the dead of night, Scorpio climbed down from the oak. Leah silently handed him his robe. Out of respect for the aftermath of prayer, she did not speak. Scorpio appeared to have found some comfort. But above all, Leah thought, he looked miserable and lost.

"Thank you," he said simply, and slipped into the robe. Almost immediately his skin began to pale. Leah, too, blanched as she watched the process.

"I have come on behalf of my father," she began, gathering her courage. "He is accused of murdering the cardinal you healed. We beg you to help us. If you have not the powers of a demon, perhaps your magical ball can help?" Scorpio listened, unblinking and still, fading from charcoal to smoke to an ashy gray to the palest eggshell brown. "Tell me again what you are," Leah whispered, "for you are so like us and yet so unlike us."

"I am of an outcast race on my own world," Scorpio began. "My home is called Terrapin, and we are known as the Aquay. My goal is to rescue my people from oppression and carnage, just as you now fight to save your father."

"There are outcasts even among demons, then?" Leah asked wonderingly.

Scorpio sighed. It mattered little what she called him, after all. It had taken courage for her to seek him out; he couldn't help but admire her for that. For the first time, albeit from need, she was willing to trust him. And she had requested, rather than demanded, his aid. Without the orb, he felt bereft, and in need of a friend on this backward planet. Maybe he and Leah could help one another.

"A demon I am not," he reiterated. "I am not yours to command, nor have you created me. But our paths continue to cross, it seems. So we must try to understand one another." The girl accepted this overture with a nod. But where to begin? "Tell me, Leah—what do outcasts do on your planet?"

If Leah was surprised by the question, she did not show it. She answered thoughtfully. "They band together, as have my people. Or they are doomed to wander alone."

"I am such a wanderer. It was the orb, you see. It carried me here—perhaps to you. Perhaps together we may find out why."

Leah looked confused, but she waited patiently for Scorpio to continue.

"The orbs have many powers," he explained slowly. "I don't yet understand how they work, or all that they can do. But I know that I somehow used the orb you have seen to travel to this place, and I believe it helped me to understand your speech. I know that it can heal, and we both know it helped your herbs to sprout."

"By magic?" ventured Leah timidly. So Scorpio had seen her in the study, after all.

"Does your sun shine by magic?"

"Not by magic, no. I believe that God has made it so."

"I don't know who or what created the orbs," said Scorpio. "But I believe they are more like little suns than like tools of magic. I think in some way they are of the natural world. Like the sun, they seem to have potential for great good, and also to do ill. But maybe they can be controlled by a master magician. Maybe they are magical, yes." Scorpio smiled ruefully. Despite his knowledge of interplanetary travel and hydroglobe technology, the power of the orbs seemed as magical to him as it must to Leah. But it occurred to him for the first time that perhaps the Hunters had not yet mastered all of the possibilities of the orbs. Did they know the orbs could heal? Scorpio wondered. Leah interrupted his thoughts.

"There are more than one of these orbs?"

"On Terrapin, there were three—three orbs." Scorpio's tone was musing and slow. "Our enemies, the Hunter folk, found one in their travels, then another and a third. Perhaps they used the first orb to lead them to the rest, I do not know. But the orbs embued the Hunters with overwhelming power. And they used this power to enslave the Aquay. Those who protested were slaughtered. They seemed to know the ones who would be driven to organize resistance."

The Aquay paused, then spoke with urgency. "They were going to kill me anyway, you see. They had murdered my friend. Leandro was his name." He met Leah's gaze. "That day, something inside me snapped. I chose, alone, to steal an orb and bring it to my kind. I thought with an orb I could restore some of the balance. But it has brought me here. Perhaps they will follow me, I don't know. I begin to weary of the chase."

Scorpio leaned against the massive oak and drew his knees to his chest.

"Who will follow you?" prodded Leah. "These Hunters?"

"Ardon," said Scorpio, a faraway tone overtaking his liquid voice. He closed his eyes.

Leah looked into his seamless, eyeless face.

"I must have angered Ardon," Scorpio said suddenly, emitting a bubbly rill.

Surprised and intrigued, Leah recognized the gargling sound as laughter.

"Something had snapped, you see. Leandro was gone and I was alone, poised at the edge of a solitary pool and ready to dive beneath the water, when I looked into the face of death itself: Ardon is his name. Tall and rugged. Handsome, even, as Hunters go. He squatted down and greeted me by name. 'Just a formality,' he said politely. 'The honorable Stalker always appears to his prey.'

"How fortunate for me, I thought, to have a Hunter *of honor* assigned to my personal execution. Is it preferable to be slain by a man of honor, do you suppose? But, after all, it was his honor that cost him his quarry—me! For the Aquay are good-mannered, and not likely to resist. So as expected, I nodded courteously and slipped meekly beneath the water. 'Until tomorrow, then,' he responded, and hunkered down at the edge of the pool to wait out the night.

"It was just as he expected. He planned to doze, and kill me in the morning. Until I slapped the water like a whalefin! Sent out a sheet of water like a wall of glass! Splashed him all over!"

Leah was taken aback. Scorpio was laughing, and could barely speak. As his watery peals grew stronger, their force almost tickled. Soon, she too was laughing until her eyes teared.

Scorpio struggled to regain control of his senses. He must have been very tired and overloaded for his brain to have triggered an emotional release of such force. *Laugh!* The command continued to squirt through his consciousness, and his body obliged. And now Leah was laughing too, with droplets running from her funny fringed eyes. How silly she looked, with her face so contorted. But her laughter was companionable and bubbly, and made him want to laugh all the more.

"B-but why is it so f-funny?" She managed to sputter. "He wanted to *kill* you!"

"It-it's the Hunters, you see," said Scorpio giddily. "They cannot tolerate the water, it burns them, and their skins shrink! But what's funny was, *oh, me*, it was his face! He was so surprised!"

They laughed until the convulsions wound down. Leah sobered first. She had earlier found release in a satisfying jag of crying. Scorpio soon followed suit. After his bout of laughter he felt energetic and cleansed. He was recalling the rest of his tale.

"I didn't stay to watch his skin turn red," he went on at length. "How he howled! It was a chilling sound, but I let him shriek. By the time I heard him blasting the water with his treacherous beam I was well away. And by then the next step seemed so simple. They were going to murder me anyway. So I stole into the stronghold of Chanamek, and I made off with the third orb."

Leah listened, rapt, as Scorpio described the terrors of Chanamek. He spoke of the Hunters, and of the Aquay and their ways. There was much she could not believe was true—Hunter weapons that shot forth beams of light, ships that traveled to the stars. Often, she told herself that Scorpio was mad, that he had dreamt a dream that he believed was true. But always she would remind herself that she, too, had seen the orb of light, and she, too, had witnessed its power.

As the night lifted to a pre-dawn gray, Leah gently interrupted.

"Scorpio, you have told me all I can comprehend in one night. But I must ask you—what has become of the orb?"

Scorpio sighed. Leah had been a patient listener. She had told him much as well. There were no other species of cognizants on this green planet. The people simply called their earth "earth." They knew nothing of its shape, or of its position in the galaxy. And he was still lost.

"The orb is hidden at the Palace of the Popes," he said. "I must return to Avignon to retrieve it. My quest is to master its secrets, and nothing less."

"But the cardinal's men hunt you in the city," said Leah anxiously. "And there has been more talk of devils—two devils. The Pope has vanquished them, it is said!"

Could the Hunters have come for him so soon? Scorpio wondered. How could they have found him? And had the Pope really bested them? If so, he was a powerful ruler indeed, and may yet be able to help. Maybe he should still consult the Pope. Or was this simply a superstitious land, ruled by sad tales of demons and sorcery?

"Scorpio, my people will protect you as best they are able. And I will help you to retrieve your orb, if you in turn will help me to prove the innocence of my father."

Scorpio found Leah's reaction to her father's imprisonment both poignant and practical. Nathan had been kind to him. And Leah had responded to his need with an offer of help, even as she had asked for his. "It is urgent that I find a way to return to Terrapin," he answered. "But if I cannot rescue my own kind at this moment, surely it is better that I detour for a short time to help another. I will do what I can."

Leah nodded and offered Scorpio a tired smile. "Even without your orb, you have special talents," she said. Scorpio acknowledged the irony with a watery trill. "I have thought very carefully," Leah continued, "and I believe I have a plan."

Chapter
12

*T*he sun rose, casting an autumnal orange glow over field and forest, like a low fire at the edge of the world. Leah was wide awake and filled with a hopeful excitement that overlaid her exhaustion from a sleepless night. She and Scorpio would save her father. She wanted to begin at once.

"I will tell you my plan on our way to Avignon," she said. "Let's be on our way, for the longer we delay, the more likely we are to be noticed by the brothers on the hill at Montmajour Abbey." Even as she spoke, the first faint intonations of the Benedictines at Prime carried across the valley. "If we are seen, they will think one of their novices has sneaked away to meet with a damsel near the gardener's huts, and send someone after us!"

Scorpio was able to laugh at Leah's little jest. The previous night she had explained to him something of the Church and its structure, and of the significance of the habit he was wearing. Despite his initial confusion, he was beginning to understand some of the complexities of earth society. There was such diversity, such a multitude of factions! One could be of the same race but of different nations; of the same nation but of different religions; of the same religion but of different races and nations. And the differences were so subtle! Physically, the people were all the same!

Among his own people there were differences in talent, in temperament, in personality. There was a class structure, to be sure. But the divisiveness on Terrapin was between the two species of cognizant, the Aquay and the Hunters. Their differences were clear; indeed, they were genetic! How could it be otherwise?

It would be amusing, Scorpio thought, if the squabbling earthlings had to cope with more than one species of humankind! As it was, they may as well have had dozens, considering the high seriousness with which they approached their differences. However, he reproached himself, it was absurd that he should be critical of a skirmishing planet, while full-scale genocide occurred on Terrapin. And he could little afford to indulge in nostalgia for the days when the two cognizant species on his own planet worked in symbiotic accord. He would do better to devote his attention to setting things right.

This morning, Scorpio too was filled with an energy born of renewed hope. He was eager to do what he could for Nathan. Then he would concentrate on mastering the secrets of the orb. He set off into the forest with Leah, listening intently as she recounted the conversation she had had with her father, detailing his suspicions of Bertrand Signac. She then proceeded to explain her plan.

"Father says we must search for evidence to clear him. But evidence will do us little good unless we can tie the murder to Cardinal Signac. Perhaps we can get a look at Arnaud de Gascon's body, to prove it was poison and not sorcery that killed him. For now, I have searched our house and found this. It isn't much, but it is a place to begin." Almost apologetically, Leah pulled a chunk of purplish wax from her apron. "Signac's men left this behind. It's a sample of the wax from which that cursed doll was formed."

Scorpio examined the wax. He looked at Leah questioningly.

"It's the color, you see. In the Jewish quarter we commonly use tallow—a wax made from animal fat. The color is a grayish white. Or we might use more costly beeswax candles. They are more sweetly scented, and are colored a tawny golden yellow. Sometimes the two are mixed together, or there may be herbs mixed into the tallow to improve the smell. But this wax has an unfamiliar texture and a strange, fruity odor, and it has been colored with some dyestuff I don't recognize. It is not used in the quarter, and is certainly not from our house. So I suggest we try to trace it. Let's go first to the marketplace. The merchants there supply the townspeople, including the courtiers and all their households. We shall pay a visit to the waxmaker's stall.''

The road was crowded with marketgoers, and the Pont d'Avignon even more so. Leah cautioned Scorpio to follow behind her at a discreet distance—it wouldn't do for a Jewish girl to be noted traveling in the company of a monk—and to keep his cowl well over his face. Cardinal Signac's men were still prowling the city on the lookout for Nathan's assistant, the escaped ''leper.''

''There may be some danger to you once we are at market,'' Leah added. ''There, as on the bridge, everyone observes everyone else. If you are noticed, you must flee from the marketplace to my grandmother's house, and she will hide you well. You will be safe among my people.''

Scorpio nodded obediently and trailed Leah into a dense maze of streets and alleys, many of them paved with cobbles or brick, all of them lined with busy shops and open stalls, makeshift booths and moving carts. Marketers haggled with vendors over wares of every description: meats and salt, butter and cheeses, honey, oil and spices, cloths and dyes, hatchets and knives, wines and beers. There were goldsmiths and blacksmiths, ironmongers and fishmongers, cobblers and saddlers, drapers, an armorer, and a wandering singer with a dancing bear on a leash. Hawkers shouted the prices of eels, of milk, of coal and bundles of faggots, of baskets, wineskins, crockery, cauldrons, of combs and needles and scents. Wheels squeaked, buyers bargained, children darted among the stalls, whetstones whirred, cleavers chopped, and pigs and fowl squealed at the butcheries.

Scorpio was overwhelmed. His mind was telling him to *Flee!* But where was the danger? He didn't see any of the cardinal's guards. *Flee* the noise and chaos, he assumed; it must be an instinctive agoraphobia that he'd never experienced before. It took all of his powers of concentration to override the unexpected panic and keep Leah in sight. So he did not notice the pair of flickering lights that tailed him, hanging behind and just above his head, weaving even as he did among the crowd.

Nor did Leah notice the lights in the air, so ubiquitous were the sparkling scissors and flashing scythes that were strung across the shopfronts, and the glinting signs and banners that swung above the stalls. At intervals, briefly, she would glance behind her to pick out the bobbing Benedictine hood from the crowd at her heels. Occasionally she would pause to finger a bolt of cloth or sniff at a jar of dried lavender, waiting for Scorpio to catch up.

At length she stopped at a chandler's stall. It was situated at a narrow crossroads, in an area of specialty shops that were stocked with costly goods and patronized by the attendants of the nobility. Well-dressed ladies with shopping baskets on their arms sniffed at the perfumery and bargained for trinkets, while skinny youths in the liveries of the finest houses juggled more bulky parcels and straggled homeward with the most burdensome purchases.

The chandler occupied a well-positioned corner stall. He had open counters on two sides, and the whole was canopied in bright, striped cloth. Behind the counters, vats of animal fat and melted wax bubbled on low wood fires. Rows of finished candles were arrayed on the counters, long and short, scented and plain, twisted and straight. There were bundles of tapers hanging from a rafter, and a fringe of long wicks made of various fibers, and ceramic pots holding oils for lamps.

In a neighboring stall, a metalsmith sold ornate candlesticks and candelabram, mortars and kettles, engraved vases and oil lamps. How pretty they are, Leah thought, fingering the simple lamp she still carried in her pocket from the previous night.

Craning her neck, she searched the crowd for Scorpio. Across from the chandler, a breeder of hunting dogs exhibited his wares for all to inspect. The elegant animals were chained in a row to a horizontal beam, each collared in studded leather, each with its own piggin of water. Opposite the houndsman, on a diagonal from the chandler, was a falconer's stall, open at the front and back but canopied and curtained on two sides. The birds displayed were hooded and still but for one huge raptor, chained at the ankle, who tore at a reddened piece of meat.

Leah caught sight of the bobbing cowl. Scorpio had reached the back of the falconer's stall, where the falconer tethered his horse. The horse whinnied as Scorpio passed by, shuffling and flaring his nostrils. Leah waited until she was sure Scorpio had seen her, then turned to the chandler with her question.

The waxmaker was a cheerful fellow with a large square

face, flushed almost maroon from tending his cauldrons of boiling oil and wax. "My wife is usually here to help," he explained to Leah, giving one of the vats a vigorous stir, "but today she does her own marketing! Now, how can I help you?"

"What can you tell me about this kind of wax?" she asked as Scorpio joined her, his hood pulled well over his face.

The waxmaker turned the chunk of purplish wax over in his palm, smiling with recognition. "You didn't buy this from me, did you?" he asked. "It's rather exotic, you see. And as far as I know, I'm the only person in these parts to make it. It's a special mixture of beeswax with a bit of tallow for body, and my secret ingredient—a sort of mulberry. Gives it the color, you see. Different texture and scent, too. It's very expensive. Does the cardinal want more of it so soon?"

"The cardinal?" asked Leah, nudging Scorpio. She blinked and rubbed her eyes. She must be tiring, for she was starting to see little dots of light when she turned her head quickly. But she was too excited by the waxmaker's words to pay much attention to anything else. As it was, she had to strain to hear him above the din of the barking dogs. What could have set them off so? One would think there was a bear running loose through the marketplace!

"Cardinal Signac, of course," the waxmaker was saying. "Are you newly in his employ? I stock this wax for his household alone, for he prefers the color to any other, and claims that the scent reminds him of his boyhood. Didn't you come to market with his young butler and the guard over there?"

Leah looked behind her and turned away again with a jolt. Three of the cardinal's men were patrolling the marketplace. And they were accompanied by a young man in the cardinal's livery—the "messenger" who had been nervously waiting for Nathan's return on the morning of de Gascon's death!

Leah quickly concealed her face in the hood of her own cloak. "Scorpio!" she whispered. "Keep your face hidden and walk away from me, for the cardinal's men are about!" Was it her eyes? No! What were those lights that were flickering near his head? Her alarm doubled. "And look out for the little lights!" she urged, waving them away from Scorpio's face. Her hand seemed to pass right through them!

Scorpio dodged and ducked, batting at the lights as though they were biting flies, slapping at the air, trapping his sleeves in the long strands of wick that hung from the chandler's stall.

"Careful, there, Brother!" called the waxmaker as Scorpio tangled his tidy rows of wicks.

Scorpio tried to drag the clinging wicks from his sleeves as the lights spiraled closer. Catching his peaked hood in a row of hanging tapers, he struggled to pull free and whipped sharply toward the marketplace, yanking the disguising cowl from his head.

The waxmaker gasped as Scorpio's face was revealed.

Leah bent to help her friend, pulling at his hood and hitting away the whirling lights. But their intensity only seemed to grow.

"What *are* they?" she cried.

Attracted by the disturbance, the cardinal's men turned their attention to the waxmaker's stall.

"It's the leper!" shouted the captain of the guards.

"He's buying more wax! To murder another!" yelled the youthful butler. "Grab him!"

The cardinal's men strode purposefully to the waxmaker's stall, their weapons drawn, as Scorpio struggled to his feet. The lights dimmed and hung unmoving, one on either side of his head.

"Ho, there, sir!" the waxmaker cheerfully greeted the cardinal's young butler. He never liked to miss the opportunity of a sale. "More of the cardinal's special wax for you today?"

His words were cut short by a singing hum in midair, followed by a sickening thud. The waxmaker pitched forward, gurgling with blood, an arrow from a tiny assassin's crossbow neatly embedded in his throat.

Leah felt a scream rising in her lungs. "*Run!*" commanded Scorpio, shoving her out of the way. Grasping her sample of wax, Leah stumbled across the alley to the falconer's stall as the cardinal's men advanced on Scorpio.

"Take him!" commanded the captain of the guard.

The butler, satisfied, tucked his little crossbow back beneath his vest.

Leah watched in horror as a crowd gathered around the waxmaker's stall. Several of them moved to restrain the waxmaker's wife, just returned from her shopping, who wailed in anguish at the sight of her slain husband.

"This leper has murdered the waxmaker!" announced Signac's butler.

"Kill him!" came the response from the crowd.

One of the guards raised his sword, then lowered it, its tip poised at Scorpio's throat, to await the order from his captain.

The crowd, as one, sucked in its breath. Every eye sparkled with anticipation.

Soundlessly, in two explosive flashes of light, two red devils materialized from thin air, flanking Scorpio.

The crowd, as one, shrieked in terror.

"It's the devils! The leper commands the devils!" Some ran, some were frozen to the spot in horror and curiosity. Those who remained crossed themselves and clutched their neighbors, murmured prayers and peeked at the scene through squinted eyes. The waxmaker's wife screamed and tried to throw herself at their feet, begging for the soul of her husband.

Scorpio understood that the Hunters had found him at last. He didn't recognize the thin one. The other, strong and deadly, was Ardon the Stalker.

The devils frowned and pointed at the cardinal's men, swiftly, one by one. A spattering of thin, white beams of light sliced through the air, and the cardinal's men slumped to the ground, their mouths open in surprise, their eyes boggling and dead. There was a chorus of gasps from the terrified crowd.

Scorpio recognized the Hunters' weapons, delicate daggers that spit out white-hot beams of light. They were secured, like decorative spikes, at the bearers' wrists; so it was that it appeared to the assembled crowd as if the guards were felled by a mere devil's gesture, collapsing with steaming holes in their foreheads.

Stunned and fearful, the crowd backed away.

The Hunters grasped Scorpio between them, leveling their weapons at his chest, and hissed, one into each ear: "Where is the *orb*?"

Unable to let the matter rest, the breeder of hunting dogs, once the waxmaker's closest friend, shouted angrily from the safety of his stall. "The leper has summoned devils to do his dirty work! Witch! *Kill him!*'' Setting loose his dozen well-trained dogs, he stood back to watch the results of his life's work.

Barking and yowling with no thought of light beams or devils, the first pair of dogs attacked, leaping onto the two scarlet-skinned black-robed Hunters and sinking their teeth where they landed.

Again, death beams skewered the air and the two dogs fell howling, only to be replaced by their slavering kin.

Scorpio, momentarily ignored in the melee of gnashing teeth and laserfire, slipped through the tangle and left his captors to their fate. He slithered over the counter into the waxmaker's stall, unnoticed by the maddened crowd, who reveled in the fight and shouted with bloodlust like drunken peasants at a bear-baiting.

Scorpio made a sorrowful gesture of respect to the wax-maker's corpse. Then he slid through the side entrance of the stall, free to disappear into the streets of the marketplace. Where was Leah?

"There he is! After him!" Scorpio recognized Ardon's voice. Looking across the open corner of the waxmaker's stall, he could see the two Hunters, still held in their tracks by a handful of dogs. Four beams of white light shot past him as he ducked across the alley. In the waxmaker's stall, the laserfire split a vat of boiling oil, which spilled onto the wood fire burning below. Instantly, with a wavelike roar, the shop burst into a wall of flames, fueled by oils and animal fats. The wooden counters caught first, then the hanging wicks and tapers; finally the body of the waxmaker was buried as the canopy of the fabric roof collapsed in a sheet of blazing stripes.

Panic swept through the crowd. Devils be damned—a fire could destroy the entire marketplace. "He's set the stall on fire!" screamed the falconer. "Water!" was the cry.

Already roused to activity, the houndsman gathered up his piggins of water by the armload and heaved them on the flaming stall, splashing the devils in the bargain. The devils shrieked and flapped their wet robes as their skins took on blotches of crimson.

From every direction, merchants and townspeople came running with buckets of water to douse the flames. The dripping

Hunters howled like ferocious infants. With the discovery that the same water that would quench an earthly conflagration could immobilize the devils with the pains of hellfire, the townspeople soon were pouring more liquid on their former tormentors than on the burning chandler's stall, satisfied to sacrifice more of their marketplace in order to gloat as the Hunters turned a fiery fuchsia.

Scorpio felt someone grab him from behind. "Stop struggling, it's me, Leah!" Leah scowled at him as though he had been very stupid.

"Why are you still here, so close to the flames?" She was struggling to control a frightened horse. "I'll stay to watch those devils. You must get out of here! I've unleashed the falconer's horse—now ride him to safety! My grandmother will hide you!"

With no further urging, Scorpio mounted the falconer's horse, who chose a direct route away from the marketplace and galloped as far from the fire as it could go.

Leah returned to her post behind the falconer's stall to watch the aftermath of her plan go up in flames. The devils were still howling for Scorpio, and screaming with pain as people drenched them with water. The waxmaker was dead and could no longer testify to help her father, and now Scorpio was accused of murder as well! The fire was almost under control, and the Pope's own soldiers, wearing shiny breastplates emblazoned with the six red roses of Clement's arms, had arrived to clear the market.

"It's the devils the Pope described!" shouted one of the soldiers, staring in wonder at the infernal scene.

The Hunters struggled to their feet. They were surrounded by some thirty men in primitive metal armor. Scorpio had escaped.

"You're under arrest," said the leader of the soldiers, nervously eyeing the pile of dogs and cardinal's guards lying at the devils' feet. The crowd was silent, and a smell of singed flesh and burning fur mixed with the oily smoke from the chandler's stall.

The Hunters looked wearily at one another and nodded.

There was no sense killing unnecessarily. Their skin was the color of red grapes and beginning to blister.

Lethor removed a glowing amber ball from the depths of his robe. He and Ardon grasped it between them. They held it lightly, in cupped hands, with arched fingers. Locking eyes, they nodded slightly and vanished.

In their wake, an astonished and hysterical crowd picked its way through the smoldering marketplace.

Leah, stunned and discouraged, slowly made her way back to the Jewish quarter, unnoticed and unremarked upon. But she nurtured a small joy: for she now recognized the devils as the Hunters Scorpio had described; she had seen another orb; and she had observed how they had used it.

Chapter
13

Grandmère Zarah shook her head grimly as she daubed at the smears of soot on Leah's cheeks and brushed the ashes from her hair. The milky gray cloud that obscured her vision seemed to grow denser day by day. Still, peering at her granddaughter's shadowy face, she could tell that the dark circles beneath Leah's reddened eyes would not wash away.

"You've had quite a time of it, my girl," she remarked. "You smell like a smokehouse."

Leah coughed, and grunted in shame. How would she explain to her grandmother that she had nothing more to show for all her trouble but the same lump of wax she had left home with the day before? Nathan was still in prison, and Scorpio was missing.

Zarah finished her ministrations and gave Leah a reassuring hug. "Never you mind. The healer is safe."

"So you have seen him!" Leah perked up at the news. "But what of the guards?" Zarah shrugged. Leah could see that the cardinal's men had already come and gone, searching for Scorpio. They had done their usual damage. In the kitchen alone, the wooden benches were overtuned, a heavy cupboard had been moved away from the wall, a barrel of grain emptied onto the floor.

"It's good that you are a girl," Zarah stated flatly. "No one thought to ask after you." Then her mood lightened, and she gave a wicked little laugh. "But young Mossé led those ruffians a merry chase on the falconer's horse! Scorpio was already hidden away by the time Signac's men arrived. While they were here making a mess of things, Mossé put on Scorpio's habit and galloped past our door as boldly as you please! One monk looks so much like another—you should have seen the cardinal's men run!''

Leah laughed. Then she lifted her eyebrows questioningly.

''The rabbi has hidden him in the cellar of the temple, where he can rest.'' Zarah was firm. ''Now you will rest as well. And then you will have a bath. Later you can join Scorpio if you wish. He has already told us of the fate of the waxmaker.''

Leah felt too full of sorrow to speak.

''It was not of your doing, granddaughter, you were not to blame. And do not lose hope. There is much we can do to help your father. Tonight, after dark, we will meet in the bread bakery. You had said that your father wished you and Scorpio to examine the body of Cardinal de Gascon. So, while you were off burning down the marketplace—''

Leah looked up sharply, ready to protest. But she could see that her grandmother was smiling gently, perhaps even with pride.

''—the rabbi and I have been hatching a plot of our own.''

Her grandmother's plan was clever. Leah smiled as her head touched the pillow. She slept deeply and woke with a start. She had dreamt that her father was calling her name. It was late afternoon, already dusk, too late to visit him today. But soon, she promised herself, she would bring him the news that he longed to hear, that she and Scorpio had found a way to set him free.

Rising quickly, Leah made her way to the women's bath-house in the public square. She left her clothing with an attendant in an anteroom, and hurried barefoot across the cold stone floor of the steamy bath chamber. Studiously ignoring the curious stares of the other women in the large wooden tub, she lowered herself into the hot, soothing water and closed her eyes. The women around her drew away as though she bore a communicable curse, and whispered among themselves.

Leah knew she was an object of gossip, that they longed to question her about the cardinal's murder, about her father's mysterious assistant, about the fire in the marketplace. Since the first day she had left the quarter to assist her father, the other women had treated her with a mixture of disapproval and envy. But something in her tired expression must have moved them to tact, for they were solicitous rather than malicious, and let her be.

At first, Leah was grateful to be left alone, excused from their questioning. If the truth be told, she had always encouraged the other women to see her as somehow apart from them, as a girl with aspirations. Different. Perhaps even better, she admitted, suddenly ashamed. For as she sat naked in the bath, one woman among others, she experienced a feeling of profound isolation. How comfortable these women were with one another, she thought wistfully, listening to their easy chatter and sympathetic laughter.

No one asked her anything. She had rejected their society and they had respected her choice. Some had shunned her, others were polite. But she was lost to them, and they to her. Leah had always assumed they were jealous of her learning and her small freedoms. Today in her loneliness, she was surprised to recognize in their expressions only pity, frank and resigned.

Leah understood that these same women offered unwavering sympathy to Grandmère Zarah. They wove themselves together as a safety net, stretched across the great pit of despair into which each of them might otherwise fall. Just as each of them had in her turn, they saw that Zarah had suffered a hard life; she had lost a husband and then a daughter-in-law; she had no grandsons, and the granddaughter was a problem, not yet married, such a disappointment; and now the tragedy with the doctor. . . . The women would visit Zarah, shoulder some of her grief, add their strength to hers, gather round. For the first time Leah understood her grandmother's pain on her behalf. She understood that the women pitied her for losing her way. For losing them.

But self-pity was an unproductive luxury, and Leah would not allow herself to wallow. Not today. Not as long as her father was a prisoner.

It was growing dark when Leah let herself into the synagogue. The square stone building, the hub of all community activity, was curiously quiet tonight, its special meeting rooms deserted. There were no groups of boys reciting their lessons, no gossipers or storytellers, no family gatherings or wedding preparations. It was as though by some mysterious signal the Jews of Avignon had agreed to avoid the temple, while the rabbi and the councilors of the quarter met among themselves. Only in the temple proper were there voices to be heard: Rabbi de Lunel conducting an evening service, joined by the singsong cant of the other men.

Leah made her way directly to the dark stone staircase leading to the cellar, hoping to have some time alone with Scorpio before the rabbi and the others arrived. Scorpio was something she had that was special, she thought. Something apart.

She pushed open a heavy wooden door and breathed deeply. Leah had always loved the low, vaulted chambers beneath the temple, with their mixed odors of stone and mortar, smoky oil from the flickering lamps, cold spring water and baking bread. For here were the great community bread ovens, where Jewish bakers fashioned the round or braided *challot* loaves for the Sabbath, and baked the flat, unleavened *matzoh* bread for the eight days of Passover. Families who had a feast to prepare, or those too poor to have ovens of their own, came to the synagogue to cook their meals. In yet another subterranean hall was the deep stone tub where the pious carried their dead to be cleansed. And beneath it all, down another long flight of steps, was the underground pool of the *mikvah*, the ritual bath, cool and dark, that rose and fell with the swelling of the moon, fed, as it was, by the sparkling waters of the Fountain of Vaucluse.

Torches had been lit along a narrow corridor that led toward the farthest reaches of the cellar, where the bread ovens were built into the thick stone walls. Leah peered into every chamber along the way, searching for the unlikely figure of a Benedictine monk in a Jewish synagogue. There was a sound of dripping water, and she followed it.

Scorpio lay naked, faceup, in the coffin-shaped stone tub reserved for the dead. His eyes were closed and his waterlogged skin had turned a chalky gray. He lay in the water with his arms floating at his sides, his tiny nostrils and bony knees just breaking the surface. A trickle of water dripped rhythmically from a stone spout at his feet, sending a shallow spiral of ripples along each thigh. Near his head, folded neatly as a pillow, was a white shroud.

They've drowned him, Leah thought dully. She let out an anguished groan and fell to her knees at the edge of the tub. Her eyes welled with tears, but she made no other sound. For some minutes she wept in silence with her head bowed. Please don't let this be happening, she prayed. She could not bear to look at him. She wanted to protect him. He was her friend, she realized with the first flush of grief. He was her friend, and still she found his appearance grotesque. She would have to pull him from the tub and dress him, then wait for the others to come.

Leah lifted her chin and prepared to undertake the job at hand.

Scorpio rose from the tub with no help from Leah, water cascading from his skin in sheets, and opened his eyes.

Screaming in abject terror, Leah backed away from the rising demon. He hadn't been breathing, she could swear it. Now he lived. His face showed fright almost equal to hers, changing to almost obsequious concern. She watched, frozen, as Scorpio, with excruciating politeness, lifted the shroud and slipped it over his head. The garment, she could see, was nothing more than a white baker's smock, two sizes too big for him, dusty with flour and dotted with bits of dough.

"I-I thought you were dead," she managed to croak, still trembling. "Th-this is where we wash our dead."

Scorpio's eyes seemed to widen, and he lifted a hand to his mouth. Then he made the peculiar warbly sound that Leah recognized as laughter.

Leah's temper flared. "What a fright you've given me! How could you just float there like that?" she scolded, even as she was flooded with relief. Scorpio's skin, as white as his apron, began to glow like pearls.

Scorpio swallowed his mirthful trilling. "I am sorry," he said contritely. "I needed water, and I was sleeping."

"I have *news*," Leah continued impatiently. "After you fled, the townspeople practically boiled your Hunter friends with buckets of water. And then the Pope's men arrived and tried to arrest them!"

Scorpio let out a peal of gargles.

"They were very angry that you'd gotten away!"

Scorpio knew he should be worried, but the thought of the Hunters thus foiled filled him with heady delight. This peculiar planet seemed to inspire him to extremes of emotion. He must try harder to keep himself in check!

"They had another *orb*!" Leah insisted. "I saw them use it!"

"You saw how it worked?" Scorpio sobered at once.

"I'll show you," said Leah. "In the bakery. We'll wait for the others." Scorpio skipped eagerly ahead of her, his baker's smock flapping around his skinny ankles. She would never have imagined that a demon could be so silly. With a deep sign of cheerful hope and fond exasperation, Leah followed him to the basement chamber that served as a bakery for the thousand Jews of the quarter.

The cavelike room was still warm from the day's baking. Indeed, with its low, barrel-vaulted ceiling and arched walls of grainy stone and brick, all bleached white with a dusting of flour, the room both looked and smelled like the inside of a loaf of bread. On two sides of the room, thick stone slabs served as worktables. The larger of the tables, made of a dark, slate-colored stone, was built against an outer wall of the synagogue. At the back of the table was a polished wooden post pinned to an iron swivel, a permanent rolling pin that stretched diagonally to the ceiling, where it rested in a great iron hook like the mast of some stranded ship. At the very top of the wall, night air filtered through a grilled window that opened to a cobbled courtyard behind the temple.

Climbing onto the table, Leah stood on tiptoe and peered through the iron bars into the night. The courtyard was deserted. Scorpio pulled a wooden bench to the center of the chamber as she clambered down again.

"They held the orb between them, like this," Leah whispered, seating herself. She cupped her hands, arching her fingers so that the tips defined the shape of a small sphere. Then she dropped her hands and shrugged. "That's all. They stared at one another and nodded, and then they vanished."

Scorpio looked puzzled. "It doesn't sound very mysterious, does it? But I will try it. Perhaps there are pressure points on the orb I hadn't noticed before."

"They killed a lot of people," Leah said reproachfully. "And they would have killed you. How did they find you, these Hunters of yours?"

"I don't know. But I will have to move quickly, before they

find me again, and before I become the cause of more deaths. They want only me. But they care for no one."

Leah had no doubt that Scorpio—demon, angel, or whatever he might be—was in the gravest of trouble. She had witnessed the ferocity of the Hunters, and had felt for herself the power that emanated from the ball of light. "Scorpio, you must not be seen in Avignon," she began slowly. "You are hunted by the marshal for the murder of the waxmaker, and for setting fire to the marketplace. The cardinal's men are after you, and the Pope's men too."

"I must leave this place."

"I know. I will find a way to fetch your orb. In return, I am hoping you will agree to the plan my grandmother and the rabbi have conceived to help my father."

"And a good plan it is, too!" Mossé de Milhans, the man Grandmère Zarah affectionately called "young Mossé," strode into the bakery. He was a strapping man of thirty, a successful textile merchant admired for his forthright manner, a quality that was enhanced tenfold by his cheerful temperament. A widower of two years, he had also lost three of his four children to the Black Death. But he was known to rejoice that he had been spared to care for his only son. And it was very well known that Mossé de Milhans was in search of a new wife.

"Hello, Leah." Mossé's greeting was warm, and his smile was genuine. Leah smiled back, but her greeting was formal. She liked Mossé very much—who wouldn't?—but she knew that Zarah had been practicing her matchmaking skills, and she feared Mossé was responding. He would make a perfect husband, Leah admitted. He was hardworking, kind and devout. But it was out of the question. He would soon have her mothering a houseful of children, and, while he might be proud of her learning, he would never allow her to continue. And what did he know of the world, of poetry and courtly manners?

Leah caught herself and turned away, blushing. She had been staring speculatively at Mossé de Milhans, and he had gazed back, a puppyish look in his eyes.

"Here is a present, Scorpio the Healer." Mossé broke the awkward silence, tossing a bundle to Scorpio. Scorpio unrolled a crisp new monk's habit and slipped it over his head, pulling the cowl as far forward as it would go.

Mossé waited respectfully. He supposed the Healer must be

accustomed to the shadowy hood; no doubt he had suffered countless taunts and persecutions. The disfigurement was horrible, even he had to admit. Perhaps the Lord had burdened him in proportion to his gifts. Young Leah was certainly showing her backbone, working with such a frightening figure to save the good doctor. She had strength and beauty both.

Rabbi de Lunel arrived, escorting Grandmère Zarah on one arm. He was followed by a thin man in his twenties who carried a bag of carpenter's tools on his shoulder and a short wooden bench under his arm. Leah rose to sit with her grandmother, and the four men occupied the longer bench.

"So, Mossé," began the rabbi, "you must tell us of your adventure with the falconer's horse."

Mossé beamed delightedly. "The guards chased me through the streets of the quarter, out of the gate in rue des Marchands and almost to the river. Then I led them right back into the marketplace. Such a maze! 'Now we'll have him!' shouted the guards. But never has a monk ridden so wildly! The market had been cleared of buyers for the day, and was still smoldering. I galloped through the streets until I could see the guards were ready to trap me—they split into two groups and set out to head me off. Before they could get ahead of me, I took a corner sharply, so I was out of their sight. Then I hopped from the falconer's horse, doffed the habit, draped it over the poor steed and spurred him on his way. Then I hid in an empty shop. Half of the guards pursued the riderless horse, who trotted home to the falconer's stall, for there I saw him, munching on smoky hay, as I made my way home."

"But didn't they search the shops for Scorpio?" asked Leah. "And didn't they find the Benedictine habit?"

"You are quite right to ask," Mossé said admiringly. My, the girl was intelligent.

Leah winced as Zarah's elbow nudged her ribs.

"The guards searched the shops," Mossé went on. "They found me right away—for I ran from the shop and summoned them myself. 'The leper!' I cried. 'I saw him ride past my shop on a horse, and then he seemed to disappear into thin air!' We all ran together to the falconer's stall, and there stood the horse, with Scorpio's old habit draped over its back. Naturally they searched. High and low. But they found no sign of a naked leper." Mossé looked at Scorpio apologetically, but the Healer seemed to take no offense, so he continued. " 'He's disappeared, all right,' said one of the guards. 'Those devils must have come for him,' said another. So the guards took the habit back to the cardinal, as evidence that the culprit had simply vanished!''

At this everyone in the room roared with laughter.

"You are brilliant, Mossé," said Zarah, her elbow busy at work again.

"The Christians have gone devil-crazy," said the rabbi, shaking his head in wonder.

"Everyone is having visions of red devils and the fires of Hell," said the carpenter. "They talk of nothing else."

"They may be ridiculous, but they are dangerous," said the rabbi. The group nodded soberly.

Scorpio felt strangely, sadly, at home among this small group of earthbeings. He was reminded of the secret resistance meetings that had taken place on Terrapin, gatherings of the hurt and frightened, who faced their oppressors as did this group, with courage, hope and humor. They had thought of themselves as a gathering of gnats, insignificant one at a time, effective as a missile in a swarm. But the Hunters had killed the Speakers among them, one by one, and the swarm had never congealed into a missile, or even into a pellet. Who is left to defend the Aquay? Scorpio wondered bitterly. Now there may be just me. Scorpio the tenacious gnat.

". . . the habit?" Leah was saying. "Didn't you bring Scorpio a new habit?"

"I am a textile merchant, am I not?" said Mossé, his eyes twinkling. Again, the group laughed.

"We must hasten to business," said Grandmère Zarah. The gathering fell respectfully quiet. "Rabbi de Lunel and I have devised a way to smuggle Scorpio into the Cathedral of Notre-Dame-des-Doms, where they have taken Cardinal de Gascon's body. No one here can doubt the innocence of my son Nathan in this ghastly death. But before we take action to accuse another, my son wishes us all to be certain in our own hearts that the cardinal's death was caused by poison—a dose of poison administered by one of his own kind. Because it is Nathan's wish that Leah also inspect the corpse, she will go as well. And I pray, Rabbi, that it will be with your blessing."

Rabbi de Lunel rose to speak. "It was Zarah who brought

to my attention some of the assets of our community that we tend to overlook. It is well known, for example, that Jews are forbidden to join the trade guilds, or to practice crafts that the Christians wish to keep for themselves. But it is also known that in practice, Jews are permitted to patronize their own tradesmen within these walls, and that some of our most talented tradesmen are frequently commissioned to do specialty work for Christian clients—as long as the transaction is arranged through a Christian guild member.''

"And as long as the lion's share of the profit goes to the Christian guild member!'' added the carpenter.

The rabbi laughed ruefully. "Salomon, here, our most renowned cabinetmaker, recently received a shipment of wood from his cousin, a timber merchant. It is the finest mahogany to be found in all of Avignon, sent here from distant North Africa. And Salomon, as Zarah pointed out to me, had just ordered a quantity of plush crimson satin, cloth of the heaviest weight, from our friend Mossé. We put two and two together. And so we have brought Salomon here tonight to ask him if perhaps he has received an interesting commission from the Christian Carpenter's Guild.''

"Indeed I have,'' said Salomon, his eyes twinkling merrily. "For there is no one else in all of Avignon who could build a box as fancy as mine.'' Beckoning to Scorpio, he pulled a set of measuring sticks from his carpenter's bag. "But what is *most* interesting is the fact that I received the commission *before* our last Sabbath—the day *before* the banquet at the palace. *Two* days before Arnaud de Gascon died!''

"To ensure the effectiveness of Zarah's ruse, we must gather every bit of evidence we can,'' Rabbi de Lunel added. "Leah has already uncovered the truth about the wax. She and Scorpio will identify the poison that was used. And Salomon will try to discover who placed the telltale order with the Carpenter's Guild.''

"Excuse me,'' Scorpio ventured. "But why I am being measured, I don't understand. What did the messenger order from Salomon?''

"Forgive me for my bad manners, Master Scorpio, I thought you knew,'' said the rabbi. "Scorpio the Healer, allow me to present to you—Salomon the Coffinmaker!''

Chapter
14

The coffin was a work of art, superbly crafted and elegantly shaped. The dark grain of the African mahogany had been rubbed and polished to bring out its plum-colored highlights. Inside, a sleek satin lining of the brightest cherry red, lightly cushioned and embroidered in golden threads with the crest of the de Gascons, perfectly complemented the glossy wood. On either end, the gilded handles were decorated with finials in the shapes of the winged evangelists, a lion, an eagle, an ox and a man. Each of the figures had jeweled eyes, subtle points of bloodred ruby. It was just as Salomon had said, Leah thought, running her hand along the smooth contour of the gently swelling lid: no one could have made a better box.

She tugged uncomfortably at the vest she wore over an unfamiliar tunic and breeches, and checked that her hair was hidden beneath the workman's cowl that framed her face. Straining anxiously, she tried to catch a last glimpse of her reflection in the coffin's sheen as Salomon and Mossé tossed a simple tarpaulin over the weighty container and tied it to the two-wheeled handcart on which it lay.

"You look fine, Leah," said Mossé reassuringly. "No one would ever suspect you are not a boy." Not unless they notice the rather too-large eyes, he thought, the full lips and soft cheeks. . . . Mossé quickly checked his impure thoughts. Flushing deeply, he kicked at the wooden wedges that held the cart wheels immobile, and threw his weight against its two long handles. Salomon steadied his masterpiece from the back, then shifted to take his side of the handcart as it began to roll.

"You will walk behind us, Leah," Salomon directed. He grunted as he and Mossé pulled the handcart between them. "You are my new apprentice, and your name is—what *is* your name for the day?"

Leah bit her lip and tried to choose a boy's name for herself. She followed the two men out of the shop and into the narrow lanes of the quarter, observing how they struggled when their way was rutted or rough.

"I am your apprentice, correct?" she said finally. "So you would just call me 'boy.' And I should help you push." Bracing herself against the back of the cart, she added her weight to the undertaking.

Mossé and Salomon exchanged a look of dismay.

"Leave it to us, boy!"

Leah heard an angry, warning edge to Mossé's command. It wouldn't do for her to take her disguise too seriously, he seemed to say. The men were putting themselves in great danger to help her and her father, and they were already pushed to their limits. Wisely, she backed off and walked behind the cart in as servile a manner as she could muster.

"That's better." Mossé was appeased.

In the streets closest to the palace, the cart rolled more smoothly. But as they approached the Cathedral of Notre-Dame-des-Doms, the two men seemed to bristle with tension.

"Here comes the Christian carpenter who will act as broker," Salomon whispered to Leah. "His name is Séguret. He is a high-ranking member of the Carpenter's Guild. Don't worry, he'll have little interest in a lowly apprentice."

Leah hoped that Salomon was right. The man striding toward them looked like a successful tradesman, but the fringe of fur that trimmed his goatskin hat bespoke a conceit not quite fitting to his station.

"You're late," began M. Séguret. Salomon tightened his grip on the cart.

"I see you've brought my casket," Séguret continued, as if to take possession not only of the object but of its creation as well.

Salomon was a patient man. But, although he was secure in the knowledge that his skill and talent were superior to the cocky guild member's, it rankled that M. Séguret would make more money for little more than an hour of his time than would Salomon, who had labored tirelessly for a week to finish the casket by the appointed hour. It rankled even more that Séguret would take the credit as well. But for Nathan's sake, it was important that all should go well.

"It's a terrible thing about Cardinal de Gascon," Salomon remarked casually. "But how fortunate a coincidence that such a casket as this was almost completed on the day he died. I am honored to know that such an illustrious personage as he will go to his rest in *my* handiwork."

Séguret took the bait at once, and glowered at Salomon. "It was indeed fortunate, was it not, that Cardinal Signac had commissioned *me* to supply him with a handsome casket of the finest wood? The cardinal has been exceedingly generous, in my opinion. Do you know that he had ordered this casket for an elderly member of his own family, who, God be thanked, still lives? But when Signac heard of the fate of his dear colleague, Arnaud de Gascon, he immediately donated this casket to his memory. And of course we appreciate your contribution, Salomon. After all, it's the least that *you* people can do, seeing that it was one of your own who murdered de Gascon!"

"Why, you—" Leah caught herself and clamped her mouth shut.

"Why, let's make haste to the sacristy, then," Mossé interjected cheerfully, hauling with renewed vigor on the heavy cart.

The Cathedral of Notre-Dame-des-Doms soared above the city of Avignon from its favored site on the rocky precipice of the Rocher des Doms. The building was insulated by the Palace of the Popes on its southern flank, and the gardens and stables of the Papal See on the bluff to the north.

Breathing hard with effort, Salomon and Mossé began the climb to the cathedral. For the last stage of the journey up the steep hill, they rested a moment, then changed positions. Mossé applied his shoulder to the back of the cart and pushed, while, under the watchful eye of M. Séguret, Leah took her logical place next to Salomon at the front of the cart and pulled.

"Something of a weakling, that apprentice of yours," Séguret observed to Salomon as he strode authoritatively ahead, making no effort to help.

Salomon rolled his eyes at Leah, his lips curling with amusement. Then he heaved, guiding the cart toward the rear of the cathedral, where a small wooden door led directly to the sacristy. So far, all had gone well.

It was cold in the sacristy. Leah held the door ajar, shivering, as Salomon and Mossé unfastened the tarpaulin, slid the mahogany coffin from the cart and gently deposited it on a wide stone slab at the center of the floor. Although there was incense burning in all four corners, the vaulted chamber smelled of death.

Near the casket, on a stone bench along one wall, the cardinal's body had been laid out, ready to be prepared for burial. The corpse was covered with a cloth of white linen that was embroidered with an ornate cross and neatly tucked around the head and feet. On a table next to the remains were a robe and hat of cardinal's red, and the brocade vestments dotted with pearls, the sapphire ring and coral rosary, the jeweled cross and jewel-encrusted prayer book that de Gascon would bear as he lay in state, waiting to be laid to his eternal rest.

Leah shuddered and bowed her head, dreading the job that must follow.

"You are an artist indeed," M. Séguret said grudgingly, patting Salomon sharply on one shoulder. "The casket is as beautiful a one as I have ever seen." Despite himself, Salomon looked pleased. "If you two will come with me, we shall attend to the financial transaction," Séguret continued. "Your boy can wait outside with the cart."

Leah shot a panicked look at Mossé, who shrugged and followed the others back outside the sacristy. Leah had no choice but to join them as well.

The three men disappeared in the direction of the palace, and Leah was on her own. The door to the sacristy was guarded by an indifferent-looking monk who nodded as she settled down on the cart. She had to think of a way to get back inside, and quickly.

"It's a terrible tragedy, the cardinal dying so suddenly," she said in a gruff, low voice.

"We all must meet our Maker," the monk responded patly.

"If it would please you, Brother, I'd like to give the casket a final polishing. It's made of mahogany, come all the way from Africa!"

"You don't say? That's a kind offer, boy, especially coming from one of your kind. Come with me, then. I'd like to see this fine casket myself!"

Leah groaned inwardly. Now how would she get rid of him?

"They'll be coming to dress him soon, so you'll have to hurry." The monk led Leah down the short corridor that led to the sacristy. "And I'll have to get back outside. I'm supposed to be guarding the robes and jewels, you see."

Good, he would only stay for a moment. Leah removed a soft cloth from her vest and slowly began to polish the lid of the already radiant coffin. "I won't be long if you have to get back outside," she said.

But the monk seemed to be in no particular hurry. "So this is African mahogany," he said, circling the casket. "It's so shiny!" He ran a hand along the glossy wood. "Seems solid enough!" He knocked three times on the fitted lid. "What's it like inside?"

But Leah was pressing down on the lid in horror. Three knocks—that was the signal!

The lid thumped under her hands.

"What was that?" gasped the monk, pulling Leah away from the coffin. As they both stood back in horror, the lid of the coffin slowly raised, and an apparition stepped forth. It was a bright red figure in a white Benedictine robe.

The monk froze, a whimpering quaver rising in his throat. Then he bolted from the sacristy, screaming in terror. "A devil! Another devil, come to take the cardinal! And he's right in the cathedral!"

Leah, too, was horrified. Scorpio's face and hands had turned a flaming crimson.

"I've taken on color from the satin lining, you left me in there for so long," Scorpio said between deep breaths of open air. "Don't stare like that, we've got to hurry now!"

With trembling hands, Leah drew back the snowy cloth from Cardinal de Gascon's face. The sickening sweetish odor of decay was strong, and already the face had begun to blacken.

"I cannot look," she faltered, pulling away. She hadn't had

to look into the face of death since the Black Plague had swept off northward, two years before. She wasn't sure she had the courage to look again. "Please, will you examine his eyes," she asked Scorpio beseechingly. "The pupils should be fixed and dilated. I'll check the fingernails for any seeds or bits of foodstuff that might have lodged there." She felt along the linen shroud, locating a stiff hand. A new wave of nausea struck.

"Sit down next to the table," Scorpio directed firmly. "Just tell me what to do. The pupils are greatly dilated. What does that mean?"

"It's consistent with my father's diagnosis of aconite poisoning—but it could mean many other things as well. Is there an odor of almonds about the mouth?"

Grimly determined, Scorpio opened the cardinal's mouth and pushed down gently on his chest. A slight puff of foul-smelling air escaped the purpling lips. But it told him nothing.

"Check the chest cavity," Leah whispered. "Quickly!"

Scorpio drew the sheet away from the body. "This man has been embalmed," he said quietly, "and disemboweled. The stomach cavity is stitched up and empty. We will find no evidence here."

"Inside his mouth!" Leah urged. "The last thing!"

Holding his breath, Scorpio turned his face away and searched with his fingers in the dead man's mouth. The teeth had been neglected. Several were loose. One of them, a lower rear molar, came away in his hand.

"We've got it," he said, fighting disgust, willing a feeling of triumph to overtake him. Embedded in the rotten tooth was a single black seed, like a poppy seed, but slightly larger.

Leah had recovered sufficiently to look. "Monkshood!" she whispered. "Now there can be no doubt! But we'd better get out of here before we're accused of defiling a corpse!"

Scorpio handed Leah the tooth and covered the cardinal, tucking the linen neatly back in place.

Leah closed the lid of the coffin and watched while Scorpio washed his hands in a font of carved stone. Then, as Scorpio's color faded from pink to peach to the familiar Benedictine white, she had an idea. Grabbing the cardinal's plain red hat and robe, she concealed them under her tunic.

There were noises coming from the doorway that led into

the cathedral. "He's in here, I swear to you, he climbed right out of the coffin," the monk was babbling. He was answered by the sound of tromping feet and rattling swords.

Scorpio and Leah raced for the corridor and out the sacristy door, where Salomon and Mossé were anxiously waiting. Scorpio dove under the tarpaulin that lay in a heap on the cart, and the three Jewish carpenters trundled safely away.

Chapter
15

Would he be there? Aimeric could hardly be considered dependable, Leah thought as she slipped quietly through the darkened alleys of the quarter. It was the dinner hour. Here and there small windows glowed with golden light, broken by the shadowy movements of the families gathered within. Leah felt a pang of longing as sharp and debilitating as a sudden wound, a longing for a family dinner taken at hearthside. She pictured just such a dinner as those she used to find so dreary, with her grandmother humming, her father at prayer and herself staring into the firelight and dreaming of—freedom from such dinners.

Leah bit her lip and hurried through the darkness, wondering how many other ways she could find this night to prove herself a fool. She must have been mad to think Aimeric was interested enough in her welfare to help. But if he wasn't there to meet her, she had already decided she would go on to Villeneuve by herself. She was little concerned with her own safety, not with her father in such desperate straits. If anything should happen to her, Grandmère Zarah would be well taken care of by her friends in the quarter. And Scorpio was safely hidden in a chamber beneath the synagogue, in hope that the Hunters would have a harder time finding him if he stayed underground. If she was caught, Mossé could fetch the orb for him, wherever it was.

Leah had seen her father late in the afternoon. The change was alarming. He looked weak and sallow, and his garments had hung on him, rumpled and limp, as though he had suddenly shrunk. He had not been allowed to leave his cell, nor had it been cleaned. The odor was terrible. He had apologized for it, tried to disguise his shame, told her that one got more accustomed to it after a time. He said he had been eating and sleeping, and that he was hopeful all would be well. But his eyes were sunken, and there were bruises on his face and arms. Leah knew he was lying to spare her pain.

"I have encouraging news," she had said, describing the rare wax and the tiny seed from the monkshood plant she and Scorpio had discovered in de Gascon's tooth. "There can be no doubt that Signac was behind the poisoning." But the wax-maker had died in a fire in the marketplace, she had explained; and even if they admitted despoiling the corpse of a cardinal to obtain the tooth, they couldn't prove that the seed was embedded in the tooth when they found it. Still, it was something.

Leah had carefully avoided any mention of devils. How could she explain that Scorpio was pursued by scarlet beings who could kill with beams of light? Nor did she detail the plan she had concocted, for how could she tell her father that Scorpio could change his skin? She wasn't even sure what she thought of these things herself. For now, she was simply proceeding on faith.

But Nathan was filled with new hope. "Some of the guards seem to fear me," he remarked. "It seems all of Avignon is seeing devils. Even the Pope! But the visions are working to my advantage, for the uproar is so great that they've neglected to set a date for my tribunal in the Consistory. I guess I have the Devil himself to thank!" He had winked at Leah, and she had managed a weak smile.

"In truth, I thank God for the delay, and I believe he answers my prayers," he went on. His tone had grown serious, but not somber. "Now we have our proof! I couldn't have made that doll. You needn't show the authorities the tooth. We can tell them of the wax! You did well to find Scorpio, daughter. And the knowledge that your grandmother and the rabbi, and Salomon and Mossé, all of you have worked so cleverly on my behalf—it fills my heart with hope. Have you looked for the baker of the fatal 'poppy seed' cake? All that remains is to find a way to tie the poison firmly to Bertrand Signac."

Leah sighed. They would say that her father had conspired with the waxmaker, and that Scorpio had murdered the wax-maker to ensure his silence. That the baker was in Nathan's service. That Signac's order for a fancy casket was a happy coincidence. Their evidence proved nothing. But she kept silent. Nathan had confirmed what Leah had already planned to do next. She would pay a visit to the household of Bertrand Signac. She would have to go alone, for it was dangerous for Scorpio to risk being seen. And neither could she risk being seen, or her plan would be spoiled, so she would have to go by night.

"Keep us all in your prayers, Father," is all Leah had said. "For I think we have devised a way to assure that the true murderer is revealed. If we are successful, the Pope will hear the confession of Bertrand Signac himself!"

After dark, Leah knew, the Pont d'Avignon was the province of thieves and cutthroats, prostitutes and drunkards. For a young girl crossing alone, the danger would be great. Even if she dressed as a man, it was likely she would be accosted if she traveled on foot. Leah needed an escort. Someone with a horse. Someone at home in the night world of the bridge, who wouldn't much care that she thought it necessary to sneak into a mansion in Villeneuve-lès-Avignon. Someone with a few loose scruples, but who might feel inclined to do her a favor.

The solution was painfully obvious: Aimeric de la Val d'Ouvèze. She would have to swallow her pride and face him once again. Leah agonized over how she would convince him. Must she humble herself and beg? Embarrass him into a chivalrous position? Join him in his bed?

When finally she located him, browsing, she presumed, for the tastiest "fruits" in the fecund little square off the rue des Marchands, she decided on a direct appeal. Aimeric had looked up with satisfaction at her approach, as if he'd know all along that she must find him irresistible. But she thought that his greeting held a grain of honest pleasure as well.

"I need your help to get into Bertrand Signac's mansion," she had said. "Just a ride across the bridge, and perhaps a little distraction at the gate." Much to her surprise Aimeric de la Val d'Ouvèze had required no coaxing.

"Truly you *are* a sorceress, little Leah," he had answered.

"Though your plan is likely to fail, you know—for you are no match for the wiles of Bertrand Signac. But when I am with you, my judgement seems to melt like butter. You have such loyalty! Coupled with such passion! Of course I will help you. I am at your service, fair maiden, in this your time of travail."

In fact, Aimeric had been as surprised as Leah at the quickness with which he had acquiesced. But there was something about her he found compelling. Perhaps it was the way she had called him a coward at their last meeting; or maybe he was just a little sorry he had hurt her feelings, and sorry that her father would be executed, as surely as the sun sets. Her beauty moved him, and he liked her. He knew he shouldn't waste his time on a Jewess. But he especially liked her when she needed him. How could she be so naive as to think she could bargain with Bernard Signac? He'd just go along for protection—and besides, he was bored.

Leah realized with shocked amusement that Aimeric must think she intended to throw herself at the cardinal's mercy and plead for her father's release, perhaps sacrifice her virtue in exchange for a pardon. Or even that she intended to murder Bertrand Signac in his bed! Why would he risk an involvement in such a scheme? But Leah did not question Aimeric's motives. She was fortunate to have caught her former suitor in one of his more courtly moods. "I shall be ever in your debt," she had said graciously, not missing the twinkle of acquisitiveness that flashed across Aimeric's visage.

"You may have scorned my advances once; but it pleases me that you do not find me completely without advantages," Aimeric replied.

"I merely intend to search for a way to prove my father's innocence," Leah had ventured. "Or Signac's guilt."

Aimeric had shrugged noncommittally. "I have no love for Bertrand Signac. Besides, as posts are vacated at the top, more positions open at the bottom. Everyone advances when cardinals fall." So that was it! Leah wondered if her surprise showed. She had never thought of Aimeric as a man with ambition. Was he hoping for an appointment at court? "My uncle, the bishop, would then be in line for a cardinalship," he'd continued. Ah, that explained it: his ambition was not for himself, but for his guardian. "And if you are caught, they would never associate me with you," he'd added wryly.

Leah had disregarded that remark. In fact, she was grateful that it was true. Even such a rake as Aimeric would be unlikely to be gallivanting about the mansions of Villeneuve in the dead of night with a Jewess. But she had no wish to endanger him, and it was reassuring to know that, should anything go wrong, Aimeric would be protected by his noble birth. If it pained her to accept that Aimeric's motives were less than altruistic, she hid it well. She had gone on to explain the details of the night's foray. She needed to get into a downstairs chamber, and she needed to search the garden.

"You'll have to distract the dogs," Aimeric noted. "Signac is known for his stables and his kennels."

Leah had been pleased that Aimeric was showing an interest in her plan. But she was frightened as well. She wouldn't have thought of the dogs. There were bound to be other dangers she hadn't anticipated.

She must have looked stricken. "Don't worry," Aimeric had said at once. "I'll bring meat. This is beginning to sound like quite an adventure! Perhaps you will be so grateful to me that you'll—"

Aimeric had broken off. He had meant his remark to be taken lightly. But it seemed he was always putting his foot into his mouth with this strangely fetching girl. Would he never remember that she just didn't know how to flirt?

"Anything," Leah had muttered. "I'll repay you in any way I can. But not until my father walks free."

Aimeric had rolled his eyes. "I may have to wait forever, then."

Leah, stirred at last to anger by Aimeric's calm conviction of her father's doom, lifted her hand to slap his face. But, anticipating her fury, he had grabbed her hand in midair and pressed it to his lips, as though he had realized his tactlessness. "I will meet you tonight, then," he said with a flourish, "under circumstances I, for one, sincerely wish were other than they are!"

Then Leah had watched him stride off down the rue des Marchands, feeling as flustered as a schoolgirl.

Leah paid the guard at the gate in the rue Jacob, slipping him something extra to let her through. "I know it is after dark, but one of my father's patients—a lady who wishes to remain anonymous, you understand?—is having the pains of labor two months before her time. I have some tea for her, to ease her pain.''

The guard winked knowingly. This was gossip-ridden Avignon, after all, where an early birth meant the lady had been entertaining while her husband was away at war. So the doctor's daughter had a baby to deliver, what business was it of his? "Discretion is everything, is it not, mademoiselle?"

Leah walked through the gate and into the night. In the deep shadow of a deserted alley, Aimeric waited impatiently, shifting from one foot to the other and twisting the leather reins of his horse into a sweaty knot. By the time Leah rushed up to meet him, she was slightly out of breath and flushed with excitement.

"Let's go!" she whispered. Aimeric lifted her onto the horse, then mounted himself, so that she was sitting sidesaddle in front of him. His arms encircled her, and as he leaned forward to adjust the reins, he could smell the hair that was bound at her neck. He breathed deeply and tightened his hold as he kicked his brown mare and broke into a sudden, bounding canter toward the Pont d'Avignon.

Leah drew in a sharp breath and struggled to maintain her composure as she jounced against the padded saddle on the horse's broad back. Aimeric held her steadily against him, and she could feel his breath in her hair. She fastened her gaze on the route ahead and tried to concentrate on her plan for the night. But what could she do about the alarming warmth that was invading her limbs, bathing her skin like a hot salve? Something was stirring her, as though her body was a cauldron, as though her blood was slowly boiling on the hearth.

So this was what it was like. The heat rises, the will dissolves. One urgency is replaced with another. She would have to ignore it, this feeling, she thought. Or tonight her greatest danger would come from herself. Please hurry, she prayed silently. And don't let me want him like this.

As if in answer to her prayer, Aimeric spurred his horse past a tattered beggarwoman with a squalling infant in her arms and started up the ramp to the gatehouse of the Pont d'Avignon. He had to release her to pay their toll, and she drew the hood of her cloak securely over her head.

Aimeric took the bridge at a decorous trot, not wishing any

more than she to call attention to themselves. Leah could only stare with a mixture of fascination and shock. She had always thought of herself as somewhat world-wise. But she was little prepared for the sight of the night creatures who haunted the Pont d'Avignon.

There was the usual assortment of beggars and cutpurses, of course. She had expected that. No doubt a sinister figure or two could be found hugging the shadows of St.-Bénézet's Chapel. But most of the people on the bridge were women. They stood in pools of torchlight, calling out to prospective customers in raucous voices, some of their invitations sharp and clever, others slurred by drink. Their clothing was colorful, if not always clean, and their loose, disheveled hair fell unleashed about their shoulders. Here and there a breast popped gaily from the confines of a bodice, or a skirt was tucked up to reveal a fleshy leg. There were many soldiers and guards among them. But they were not patrolling to keep the peace; they were there to sample the wares.

The noise was cacophonous. The conditions were miserable. But the participants, for the most part, seemed to be good-natured. Where Leah had expected secrecy and stealth, there was instead a lively boulevard as public as the marketplace.

"Are you rich, handsome?" A plump red-headed tart grasped the bridle of Aimeric's horse, her hips swaying as she walked next to them.

"Not anymore," Aimeric answered, grinning. "My lady here has soaked me for every cent!"

At the sight of Leah swathed in her dark cloak and glowering even more darkly, the woman wandered away, winking broadly at Aimeric and giving the mare a slap on the rump.

Aimeric seemed quite at home on the bridge, Leah thought glumly. How easily he had spoken to that woman.

"Don't let them upset you." He spoke close to her ear. "We are almost through this part. They only gather at either end."

Aimeric spurred the mare onward. For a short distance beyond the torchlight, couples grappled in the shadows, moans peppered the thin moonlight, men and women laughed and argued, coins changed hands. Soon they rode into the long stretch of darkness that spanned the Rhône, toward the lights that beckoned from the cardinals' mansions in Villeneuve.

They had indeed passed through a secret world, thought

Leah, but one in which the mysteries belonged as much to women as they did to men. Did they feel powerful? she wondered. Or were they afraid?

Leah was only vaguely aware that she had been insulated by her father's wealth, protected by the tenets of her faith, by her sheltering community. For too long she had regarded these things as restrictive. So it was that she also failed to see a group of women enslaved by an irreversible poverty. Leah saw only their apparent range of choices, and a freedom that was unavailable to respectable women.

Riding through the darkness with Aimeric, she felt wild, separate from any world she had ever known and very far from home. There was nothing but the rhythmic movement, the odor of the horse, the river, the leather reins, the riders. There was the relentless heat, strangely thrilling.

The ladies at the Villeneuve end of the bridge were of a more exotic mold. They posed together in suggestive tableaux, their perfume wafting like clouds of mist on the cool night air. They were elegantly dressed in low-cut gowns, in fur-trimmed hoods, in veils that promised untold beauties beneath, in jewels, in single pendant pearls suspended like milky droplets between inviting cleavages. There were several boys among them, their loose shirts open to reveal doeskin chests; and an African in a brocade robe languishing at roadside as though he lay on the thickest of carpets.

In contrast to the aggressive hawkers at the Avignon end of the bridge, these haunters of the night were suggestively silent, as though their very existence was inducement enough.

"They are expensive amusements," said Aimeric, "for that cardinal or bishop who might be struck with a flight of fancy on his way homeward. That one, for instance, the golden-haired angel in the gown of yellow velvet, is a boy no older than yourself, famed for his beauty."

Leah's mouth dropped. "You mean he *chooses* to be a woman?"

"Are you so unhappy with what you are?" asked Aimeric gently. He spurred the mare and cantered up a winding ridge into the hills of Villeneuve.

Leah's heart was in her throat. It was time for the night's work to begin. So soon. ● ● ●

The mansion of Cardinal Bertrand Signac was situated on a rocky cliffside overlooking the Rhône. It was hidden from the road by a high stone wall, and bounded by forest on either side. The torchlit gate was guarded by two men-at-arms who chatted in the bored tones of watchmen who have nothing to watch.

Aimeric harnessed his mare to a tree well off the road on the near side of the property and walked with Leah into the dark wood. Together they emerged at the edge of the forest and studied the house in the moonlight.

The mansion was built of thick blocks of stone, buttressed at the sides and roofed with tiles. The lower floors were served by plain, rectangular mullioned windows, but the facade was embellished on the third and highest floor with narrow trefoil windows topped by crosses, in the ornate style of the Palace of the Popes. The entrance, a great pointed arch, opened onto an inner courtyard. It was protected by a portcullis, tonight half open like the mouth of a waiting mastiff.

"That's a good sign," Aimeric whispered. "It's likely the cardinal hasn't returned yet from the palace. But I see no way for you to get in. You can't just walk across the courtyard and through the door."

Leah was ready to strike out on her own. "Wait with your mare," she said. "If you hear any commotion, go back to the bridge. And if I fail to meet you there, return to Avignon. And Aimeric—I thank you."

"Good luck, then, Leah." Aimeric hesitated. Then, thinking the better of whatever gesture he may have been about to make, he disappeared back into the forest.

Leah shouldered the sacks of meat that Aimeric had handed her. "The dogs will be at the back of the house, near the stables," he had told her. "If you don't go near them, you may not even need this." But his words had given her an idea. There were other features at the back of the house. There would be the cliff, leading down to the water. Surely, somewhere near the sheer drop to the water, there would be a latrine. And it would most likely be in sight of a rear entrance to the household. Once inside, she would search for more of the wax needed.

Leah crept silently through tangled foliage. The latrine was simple to find. The odor emanating from the crude stone hut was distinctive, and recent deposits were strung behind it like a slimy tail just visible in the moonlight where a drainage pipe emptied onto the rocky cliff below. Inside, the hut was probably nothing more than a board with a hole in it. Even in rich men's houses, people still got splinters in their behinds. Leah had watched her father remove many a one. The servants got them, anyway, she amended. Probably the cardinal had his own polished privy somewhere indoors that would be emptied by a servant into the same accommodating Rhône.

As Leah expected, the hut was located on a direct line from the kitchen entrance at the back of the house, where the great chimney was still smoking and a single torch burned at the wooden door.

Leah waited patiently, breathing through her mouth, and was soon rewarded. A kitchen maid, her hair pulled back under a crisp white cloth, came out to use the latrine. The girl lifted the torch from its bracket and hurried through the kitchen garden as though her need was urgent. As soon as the girl was settled in the stone hut, Leah leapt through the darkness and slipped through the kitchen door.

She was in a gray stone vestibule with a small domed ceiling. Three wooden doors framed in pointed stone arches opened ahead of her and to either side.

"Is that you, Marie? Back so soon? Did you bring the herbs I asked for?" The shrill voice must belong to the cook, Leah thought. It was coming from the door to the left, from the side of the house where she'd seen the great chimney. Leah tiptoed to the door ahead of her. It creaked as she pushed it open.

It opened onto a dining hall. The room was long and narrow, and the walls were hung with tapestries that fell almost to the floor. The floor was tiled with multicolored squares, in softly glazed designs of birds and florets arranged in a pattern as artful as an oriental carpet. A huge table, draped in white cloth embroidered at the edges, and benches of polished oak ran the full length of the room. Against one wall, a sideboard was heaped with treasures to rival the Pope's: etched silver platters and knives with jeweled handles, mazers of silver, ewers of crystal, goblets of gold. At the head of the table, a carved high-backed armchair, canopied in red, awaited the master of the house. Before his place at table stood a miniature silver ship, a jeweled *nef* castled fore and aft, bearing a cargo of salt and spices.

Near a second door at the front of the house, a low fire flickered in a stone hearth. Oil lamps cast a warm glow on the sideboard. But the *nef* gleamed in a brighter light. Next to the cardinal's place at the head of the table, in an elaborate golden candelabrum with three curving arms, burned three fruity-smelling candles of rich maroon wax.

Eureka! Leah licked her thumb and forefinger and extinguished the candles, each with a satisfying hiss. Pulling them from the little spikes that held them in place, she stuffed them down the front of her dress and headed for the wooden door that would take her back to the vestibule and then to the kitchen garden. But someone was coming!

The door flew open and the cook strode into the dining hall, her hands on her broad hips. She wore the habit of a Benedictine nun, but both her demeanor and her speech had more in common with an overworked countryman's wife.

"Marie, where are you, you lazy girl?" she demanded. Leah cowered behind the door, willing herself invisible.

"Just look at this table! I thought I told that strumpet to fix new candles in here. She's left bits of wax from the old ones about, like a rat leaves crumbs. Useless girl!"

The woman bustled out, leaving the door wide open. Leah did not move. Soon the cook returned with a fistful of candles, which she lit at the hearth and jammed onto the candelabrum one by one. "Hmmph!" was her remark. She returned to the kitchen, pulling the door to the dining hall shut behind her.

All was quiet. Leah crept from her hiding place, her heart pounding, and opened the door a crack. The cook was bustling noisily in the kitchen. Leah slipped into the vestibule, toward the garden door. But again someone was coming. Marie!

The third door in the vestibule was her only choice. Leah ducked inside. She found herself in a huge pantry, dimly lit by a single small lamp.

The wooden shelves on the stone walls were stocked with dried foods of every kind. There was a great barrel of salt and jars of grains, kegs of flour and crates of dried fruits and nuts. In one corner there were spices, in another soaps and oils, and in a third . . . Leah almost groaned aloud at the irony. There

were dozens of candles, all made of fruity-smelling maroon
wax.

Hiding two more of the candles in her bodice with the others,
she lifted the oil lamp from its hook in the wall and listened
for sounds from the kitchen. Then, shielding the lamplight with
her cloak, Leah slipped back into the kitchen garden.

That was easier than it might have been, she thought, breathing a sigh of relief. But how was she to find a patch of monkshood in the dark, in a garden as large as the square outside the
synagogue?

Suddenly the vestibule door swung open again and a grumbling Marie emerged, grabbing the torch. "And don't you
forget the savory, neither," the shrill voice followed her into
the night. "It's in the section next to the sage!"

Leah threw herself flat on the ground beside a row of over-
grown squash. The vegetables would have been harvested some
weeks before, but Leah was grateful for the generous ground
cover the huge leaves still provided. Marie was at the other
end of the garden, tsking and whining to herself. "Call me a
useless cow, will she? And me suffering from the bellyache!
What am I to do? I bring her the marjoram, I bring her the
basil, and now she wants savory. And soon we'll be bringing
them all in to dry, she says. I never could tell a sprig of parsley
from a thistle bush! Which one is this, then?"

Leah breathed slowly, the candles pressing into her chest.
She'd been a fool again, she realized. The cardinal would never
grow monkshood in his own garden, where it would more than
likely wind up in his own dinner! But with the understanding
came disappointment. She would have to return to search the
woods by daylight. Where else would one cultivate a poisonous
plant? They would have to delay their plans—for a sample of
aconite was a crucial ingredient in the plot she had cooked up
with Scorpio and Zarah.

Marie took her doubtful finds back into the kitchen, and
Leah began the precarious journey back to the forest. She didn't
want to cross the garden, in case Marie reappeared. It would
be best to cross the darkest expanse of yard to the latrine again,
then skirt the cliffside until she reached the forest.

Halfway across the yard the barking began. Two enormous
mastiffs bounded around the corner of the house. Trailing
their leather leads loosely behind them, they made a beeline

for Leah. The moonlit dogs, huge black snarling shapes in spiked collars, their teeth dripping wetly like bloodied daggers, looked like they could tear a horse in two. They must smell the meat on her! Dropping her lamp with a strangled cry, flinging the sacks of meat into the garden, Leah raced for the latrine and slammed the door, the slavering beasts close on her heels.

"Herod! Samson!" The voices of two men-at-arms followed on the heels of the dogs. "They've trapped someone in the latrine again," said one. "Probably Marie," guffawed the other. "She's been in and out of here all day! Ho, Marie, is that you?"

"Who else would it be?" called Leah in a whiny voice. "Get them beasts out of here, or I'm never coming out!"

The mastiffs barked wildly, sniffing the ground outside the latrine, jumping up against the stone hut, snorting and growling.

"You dropped your lamp, Marie," the first soldier called. "It's still lit, though. I'll put it on the ground outside, you can pick it up when you're done."

"Thank you—oooh, what gas!" Leah groaned, and made a rude noise.

"Let's get out of here," said the second soldier, holding his nose.

"Aye, before Sister Stewpot comes scolding at us for chasing one of her girls. Herod, down! Samson!"

Grabbing the protesting dogs by their collars, regaining control of their leather leads, the men-at-arms hauled them away.

When all had fallen silent, Leah found she was trembling. She could have been mauled to death, or perhaps worse, captured as an intruder. What could she have been thinking of, coming here like this? Peeking from the latrine, she was strangely touched by the pale light glowing from the little oil lamp the kenneler had placed against the side of the hut. And then she fell to her knees in the damp mud and wept with joy. The dog's claws had raked the earth at the foundation of the hut, tearing loose the clumps of plants that grew there. Uprooted and mud-spattered, cast against the latrine wall and outlined in the light of the lamp, was a stalk of monkshood.

Aconite. The spindly plant was growing on both sides of the

latrine. The heavy purple flowers, climbing the stalk like a clothes tree hung with cowls, were just finishing for the season. It made perfect sense, Leah thought, almost amused. What better place than a latrine to grow the deadliest of blooms? No other place could afford such a constant stream of high-quality manure, yet be so rigorously avoided by anyone who had no need to be there. Surely no one lingered here to admire the flowers!

Leah gathered several plants, then sped into the forest to search for Aimeric. It hardly mattered to her to find that he wasn't there, and the mare was gone. Wearily, she began the walk in the dark down the hillsides of Villeneuve-lès-Avignon toward the Bridge of St.-Bénézet.

"Psst! Leah, is that you?" She had only gone several yards when she heard the familiar voice and a faint whinny. He was waiting for her, after all. "I heard the dogs and thought I'd better move to a safer place. Are you all right?"

Leah nodded, allowing herself to be lifted into the saddle and delivered to the bridge. It was very late. The colorful denizens of the night had long since dispersed. She was suddenly so very tired. Aimeric's arms around her felt safe and good.

"You were very brave to do what you did," Aimeric was saying.

"Hmm?" She must have fallen asleep. She and Aimeric were at the center of the Pont d'Avignon.

"But we'd best get rid of this." Aimeric took the little oil lamp that had been swinging gently at the mare's side and flung it into the night. They watched it until it was swallowed by the silent river somewhere far below.

The darkness was complete. They were utterly alone. Leah felt the creeping warmth again. Aimeric was holding her very close.

"Did you find what you were looking for?" he murmured, pressing her to his chest. Leah nodded dumbly, her mind whirling. His breath was on her face, his lips were on her cheek, at her neck. She had told him she would do anything to thank him—maybe it wouldn't be so bad. The heat was swelling in her belly like a wave.

"What's this?" Aimeric sounded annoyed. The hard wax

candles in her bodice were digging into his ribs.

Leah withdrew one of the candles. "It's to make a doll," she said.

"A w-wax doll? Like the one in de Gascon's bed?"

"This one's for Signac," said Leah dreamily, pulling him back to her. "I needed special wax."

Leah felt Aimeric stiffen and then thrust her away, as if with an effort of will.

So he is a virtuous man, after all, thought Leah, making no protest. It was for the best. It was just the night, the fear, the proximity of a handsome savior. She might have succumbed. But Aimeric had behaved well.

They rode back to Avignon in silence, Leah satisfied and relieved, Aimeric almost frozen with terror. So she was a sorceress! Soon she would practice her fiendish art on Bertrand Signac. And he was all alone with her in the night! She must have put him under her spell, he could see that now. It's a good thing he hadn't coupled with her, or he'd be in her power forever.

Chapter
16

On the night of the following day, Scorpio waited patiently in his place of concealment behind a floor-length tapestry in the darkest corner of Cardinal Bertrand Signac's dining hall. He was sorry that Leah could not be here to watch what was to come. But it wouldn't have done for the cardinal to think the de Bernays were in any way involved.

Like most of the high-ranking courtiers in Avignon that night, Cardinal Signac was dining on fish, a gift from Pope Clement's own kitchen. He signaled for his favorite servitor, a long-lashed boy of almost indecent beauty, to deliver his covered dishes from the sideboard and to pour him a goblet of wine. But the cardinal preferred to dine with no distractions, and the boy soon withdrew.

The soup was fine and the fish was delicious. The cook had outdone herself tonight, he thought. What could this be? Chewing greedily, he pulled the next dish toward his place. He lifted the ornate domed cover from the silver trencher, smacking his lips in anticipation.

Scorpio watched triumphantly as the cardinal grabbed at his throat and made a choking noise. As the cardinal began to splutter, unable to speak to call for his men, Scorpio swallowed his own mirth and practiced a fierce expression.

The cardinal's face had purpled in horror. Silhouetted on the platter, artfully arranged on a bed of aconite leaves, was the chubby figure of a red wax doll in a little wax cardinal's hat, holding a sprig of still-flowering monkshood, fashioned with loving glee by Grandmére Zarah.

Scorpio stepped quietly from his hiding place and into the candlelight at Signac's elbow. The cardinal, who had been unable to take his eyes from the offending dish, looked up at the appearance of the rustling red gown.

"*Aiieeeeh*!" The screech of terror would surely be heard throughout the household. Soon the men-at-arms would come running. The cardinal fell to quivering, whining in Latin in a sniveling voice, making the sign of the cross in Scorpio's direction. Scorpio knew what Signac must see: a fearsome devil of the brightest red. For, attired in the round, flat hat and scarlet robe that had once belonged to Arnaud de Gascon, his skin had changed to match.

Scorpio stepped forward and spoke to the cardinal in his watery voice. "Tell your household not to be alarmed. Send your men away. *Now*!"

Scorpio withdrew into the shadows as clomping footsteps resounded from the front of the house. An armed guard pounded at the wooden door and marched into the dining hall.

"E-everything is fine," croaked the cardinal. "I-I thought I saw a rat. Wait outside until I finish my meal."

The guard turned sharply on his heel and left the room as a nervous servant peeked through the door at the kitchen end of the house. Before he could speak, he, too, was waved away.

"So, Bertrand Signac, do you see this?" Scorpio emerged from the shadows, brandishing a stalk of the poisonous monkshood plant. "I do hope you have enjoyed your delicious dinner. I learned the recipe from you—the very recipe you so thoughtfully passed on to Arnaud de Gascon just before he, er, came my way."

The cardinal clutched at his throat and gagged. "Devil! Begone!" Staggering backward from his thronelike chair, he thrust a finger deep into his mouth and tried to eject his dinner.

"I see you are familiar with this plant," Scorpio continued smoothly. "But look closely. Do you not recognize me? I can cure you of the effects of this poison, just as I did for Arnaud de Gascon. Don't you remember?"

Signac froze and peered closely at Scorpio.

"I only ask a simple favor of you," said Scorpio. "Unless, of course, you prefer to die in agony, as did your victim, whose death throes you yourself witnessed in their entirety."

Signac fell to his knees and moaned, as though he could see Arnaud de Gascon before him, screaming in pain, writhing in delirium and finally rattling in a burst of terror as his spirit escaped him.

"I see you remember," said Scorpio. "You would do well to hurry, for you have but two or three hours before the poison takes you. You'll know the sequence when it starts, of course. The tingling sensation all over your body, the feeling that your hands are covered with fur." He paused. "Then the chills and shivering, as though you had snow in your veins instead of blood. There is the agonizing pain, naturally. Inability to move or escape. The madness, the yellowing of your vision that leads to blindness. And finally, sweet death, delivering you to my care forever."

Scorpio was quite enjoying his acting job. He wished the de Bernays could have witnessed the fruits of their scheme. The cardinal was in tears on the floor.

"Heal me, Satan," he pleaded. "What would you have me do? I will do it."

Scorpio drew himself to an imperious height and held the sprig of aconite over the cringing cardinal. "Call for your finest horses and carriage. Your time runs short. Together we will visit Pope Clement VI." Signac looked up at Scorpio beseechingly, whimpering and nodding obsequiously. "You will confess to the Pope the murder you have committed for which an innocent man has been doomed," Scorpio commanded. "If you do this, you will live."

Chapter
17

"**P**ssst! Your Holiness!"

The Pope groaned.

"Forgive me, Your Worship, for rousing you at this late hour, but it is a matter of the utmost urgency."

Scorpio watched with satisfaction from a shadowed corner of the papal bedchamber as Bertrand Signac, now close to panic, struggled to awaken Pope Clement VI. From his great bed the Pope, swathed in white linen, drew a coverlet of fur over his head and snored, flopping onto his stomach like an Arctic seal.

"Your Holiness, *please*!" Signac grasped the holy shoulders and shook.

The Pope rolled onto his back and pulled himself up into his pile of bolsters and cushions, grumbling and rubbing his eyes. He seemed taken aback to see Signac; as his mouth opened in a surprised "O," an extended, almost melodic burp emerged, and with it the faintest odor of the evening's wine.

"Bertrand, what in blazes are you doing in my bedroom in the middle of the night?" The Pope hauled himself fully upright and pursed his lips. Cradled in a sea of covers in his close-fitting white nightcap and gown, his features pink and puffy with sleep, Pope Clement VI was hardly the authoritative imperator Scorpio had expected. At this moment he resembled more a royal piglet, irrationally swaddled and all too vulnerable. Could this be the man whose wisdom and might could unravel the mysteries of the orb?

"Forgive me, Most Holy Father," Signac entreated, falling

to his knees at the edge of the bed and kissing Clement's doughy hand. "I have been visited by a devil, and I must do as he says, or I shall die."

Clement's aspect changed, and Scorpio decided his first impression may have been hasty. Fully awakened, the Pope was commanding and assured.

"So they're back, are they?" he demanded, throwing his covers aside and displacing Signac in the bargain. "Hand me my robe, I shall be but a moment." Accepting the ermine robe that Signac proffered from the end of the bed, Clement disappeared into his study.

Signac paced nervously, wringing his hands and wiping the sweat from his brow. He looked terrible, haggard and unshaven, his usually elegant features collapsed, his pallor death-like.

"Already I am chilled to the bone," he whined, addressing the shadows where Scorpio stood motionless. "I will tell him as soon as he returns, you can be assured. I beg you, remove this curse from me!"

"Until you confess your crime, you are doomed," Scorpio replied evenly.

Signac crossed from the bed to the hearth, where he warmed himself at the low fire, then back to the bed again.

"Bertrand, are these the devils who visited you?" The Pope returned from his study with a small painting. "Did they carry with them a glowing ball?"

"Only one visited me," Signac stammered. "And he is—"

Scorpio shook his head and Signac caught the cue.

"—and he has poisoned me, *just as I poisoned Arnaud de Gascon*! There, I've said it. Forgive me, Your Holiness, but I must speak quickly, or I shall die as well, poisoned by the devil who haunts me."

"Then speak, by all means!" Clement waved a hand in alarm.

"He has bade me to make a full confession to you."

The Pope looked confused, but agreeable. "Very well, Bertrand, if it will ease your soul. I will hear your confession. Shall we adjourn to the chapel?"

"If you please, I must do this now, without delay."

The Pope signaled that the cardinal should continue. Signac's words came in a rush.

"Forgive me, Most Holy Father, for I have sinned. I took the life of my brother Arnaud de Gascon while in the pay of the Viper of Milan."

Pope Clement VI looked angry and weary. Signac took a breath.

"As *you know*," he continued pointedly, "Arnaud de Gascon was critical, even rancorous on the subject of the Archbishop of Milan. He had gone so far—too far, many thought—as to recommend that Giovanni Visconti be excommunicated." Signac paused. The suggestion was not without reason, he knew. It was said that the Archbishop of Milan had only celebrated Mass once in his entire life, and on that occasion he had dropped the Host! But the power and riches of Giovanni Visconti could not be ignored, even if he was a poor sort of churchman. It was the survival of the Church as an institution that mattered, was it not?

"Visconti controls Bologna now," Signac continued, his words tumbling forth as he raced to excuse himself, even as he hastened to save his own life. "Without the Milanese, we will lose all control in the Papal States. The Holy See is already living on loans, there is the Crusade to worry about, and this endless war between the English and the French, not to mention the expenses of the court..."

Clement waved his hand impatiently. He had to listen to enough of this sort of talk from the *camerarius*, without hearing it from a confessing cardinal.

"... in short, without the revenues of the Visconti, our own treasuries will be exhausted. Information came to me that de Gascon was in the pay of the Florentines, the enemies of the Milanese, that he was spying on their behalf..."

Signac's words trailed off. He mopped his brow.

"And since you are in the pay of the Visconti, the unpleasant necessity of removing de Gascon fell to you?" prompted the Pope.

Signac hung his head.

"Are you not aware that I have entered into negotiations with the Visconti?" demanded Clement. "It was unnecessary, this murder! The Florentines have made their objections well known to me. But last year, when we needed their help to combat the Visconti in Bologna, they refused. They thought they could triumph over the papacy and the Milanese both. Now they fear that the Visconti will devastate Tuscany! Arnaud de Gascon was a foolish man. But *you*, Bertrand—you have been more foolish still!''

The Pope sighed, then focused his attention on Signac again, as though he had suddenly remembered that he was hearing a confession, not leading a political discussion. ''And you have committed a grave sin.''

Clement and the cardinal prayed in Latin, and the Pope gave Signac his blessing. ''We will speak again to determine your penance,'' said Clement. ''But there is more I would know. This devil you speak of—there was just one?''

''Only one, Your Worship. His coloring was red, but his face differed from the devils in your painting. And he carried no such ball of light.''

''You must have seen the third demon, the one whom I seek,'' the Pope said smoothly. ''If you see him again, tell him I would speak with him.''

Signac clutched at his throat and looked anxiously into the shadows.

''As I would speak with you, Your Holiness,'' said Scorpio, stepping forth. The startled Pope made a sign of the cross in the air before him, but quickly regained his composure. Scorpio made similar motions as he circled the pathetic figure of Bertrand Signac, who was complaining of the pains in his chest. What a weakling this murderer is, he thought, and what a powerful force is a guilty mind. He and Leah hadn't poisoned him, of course. But Signac looked as though he might obligingly curl up and die if left to his own imagination.

''Aconite, begone,'' Scorpio pronounced. With a grateful little yelp, Signac grasped the hem of Scorpio's robe and made as if to kiss his feet. Scorpio wrenched his robe from the cardinal's hand and stepped backward. ''The curse is lifted. You will live.'' He waved Signac away. The cardinal breathed a great sigh of relief and stood erect, his features regaining a measure of rather sullen dignity.

''We will meet again by day,'' Clement said graciously. ''You are no doubt in need of rest. And Signac—I am obliged to you for delivering this, er, gentleman to my presence.''

Signac nodded and fairly flew from the chamber. At last

Scorpio would have his audience with the Pope.

"You must be Scorpio," the Pope began, turning to fetch the painting he had commissioned. "I have met two of your friends. Do you recognize them?"

Clement VI studied Scorpio as Scorpio admired the painting of the Hunters. This devil was shorter and slighter than the other two, and different about the face somehow. Less predatory. But he was costumed in cardinal's red, the same color as his skin, and Clement took the message as a powerful *memento mori*—even the officers of the Church could be condemned, he was reminded. But Clement had made his own confession, and his conscience was clear. His gluttony was well under control—he wasn't that fond of fish—and he hadn't been with a woman since the other two had visited. There was certainly no sin in trying to win the Orb of the Pantocrator for the Holy See.

"They want your ball of light, your orb," Clement added.

"So that is why you have set your men on me. They have threatened you unless I deliver the orb?"

Clement VI declined to respond.

"These others are evil," said Scorpio. "But I seek knowledge of this orb. It is said that you have such knowledge."

So, the orb did exist! Clement's eyes glinted greedily. What a coup it would be to own such a treasure! And then he would vanquish all three of these damned devils—it couldn't be too difficult, judging from the reports his men had brought him from the marketplace.

"Bring the orb to me," Clement commanded regally. "Then you shall see what I know."

"I will bring it to you tomorrow," said Scorpio. He was beginning to worry that if he stayed in one place much longer, the Hunters would locate him. It was time to finish his business and flee back into hiding. "I will bring you the orb after you free Nathan de Bernay, the Jewish doctor who was falsely accused of the murder of Cardinal de Gascon. I will bring his daughter to witness your act."

Scorpio was pleased. He had kept his part of the agreement with Leah, and Nathan would be freed. It appeared the Pope had some knowledge of the orb and its workings. Perhaps he would soon be on his way back to Terrapin.

● ● ●

Pope Clement VI was less than pleased. He had sympathy for the Jew, but he could hardly accuse one of his own cardinals of murder. The scandal would be enormous, and his court was riddled with scandal enough. The Jew was convenient.

Why should the devil care for the Jew, anyway? Unless he was a Jewish devil—could that explain why the other two were pitted against him? Could that be why Scorpio didn't seem to know how his own orb worked?

Clement's mind was racing. It could be that he was witnessing clear evidence of a new spiritual truth: As above, so below. As on earth, so in Hell. Perhaps even in the underworld, the souls of the Jews battled with the souls of the Christians. Of course, it was hardly likely that a Jewish devil would appeal to the Pope. Then again, Clement was known for having protected the Jews during the Black Death, provided them a haven from persecution in Avignon.

And what of the orb? Clement had stared at the painting of the Hunters for hours, ignoring the devils and trying to recapture in his memory the hypnotic intensity of the beautiful, swirling light. How could such beauty reside in the underworld? It was a thing of Light.

Clement VI was stumped. No matter how he posited the relationship, he couldn't decide how Scorpio and the Jews and the other two devils were connected. But he was certain of one thing. The two devils would be returning for Scorpio, and he would be pleased to deliver him. But first, before they showed up, he would take possession of the Sacred Orb. It belonged with the Vicar of Christ on Earth: the Pope. Its place was in the Light.

Chapter
18

*L*eah couldn't remember when she had been happier, or more nervous. She had barely slept, or been able to sit still, since Scorpio reported the news of Signac's confession. Today her father was to be freed, and at last she would have her day at court. Afterward, there was to be a celebration at the synagogue. All of the Jews of the quarter had turned out to wish her well, for they felt that the cardinal's confession had vindicated not only Nathan de Bernay but all of them.

Leah was wearing her best clothes for the occasion; everyone had agreed that she couldn't have looked more beautiful. Her gown was the color of sunlit amber, and was trimmed in sapphire brocade. Suspended from an embroidered headdress that was dotted with tiny pearls, a delicate veil fluttered lightly about her face, and settled like a cobweb on her long black hair. Her mantle was velvet of a rich forest green, bordered with marten's fur of golden brown.

Beneath the cloak, Leah was perspiring. She and Scorpio were to be received at court by Pope Clement VI himself.

As she followed Scorpio through the broad arched gate of the Papal Palace, Leah held her breath in anticipation of her first sight of the Palace Square. She breathed outward in awe. The crenellated walls, turrets and towers were positioned just as she had expected them to be. But even though she had watched the newly finished wing being built, even as she had seen the walls rise to fill the sky above Avignon, still she had not imagined the overwhelming power of the space the walls must contain.

An elegant squire, one of the hundred or so attendant to the Pope, hurried forward to meet them. Bowing courteously to Scorpio and Leah, but unable to hide a flash of curiosity, as though they were honored ambassadors from an exotic land, he indicated they should wait and disappeared through a gaping arch in the massive wall to the right. Above the arch, overlooking the courtyard from its lofty second story, was the Pope's Indulgence Window, a lacy rosette supported on spindly columns through which the faithful could be blessed.

Leah's awe was tinged with satisfaction. The palace was even more glorious than she had imagined. It positively soared. Of course, this was not the way she had imagined she would see the Papal Palace—accompanied by a demonic Benedictine at whom everyone stared openly with thinly disguised fear. Leah was not unaware of the steady, surreptitious trickle of chamberlains and chaplains, couriers and curates who seemed to have arranged that their duties would take them through the corner of the Palace Square where she and Scorpio waited.

Leah watched as Scorpio, once again pale beneath his Benedictine habit, adjusted his cowl to cover his face. She was as happy for him as she was for herself. He would accompany her to the Audience Hall, and would stay to secure the release of her father. Then, together, he and the Pope would examine the orb, and if all went well he would find a way to return whence he came.

Leah smiled. Scorpio had been so kind to Grandmère Zarah this morning, regaling her with the tale of Signac's fright, praising her waxen handiwork, teasing her gently for worrying, reassuring her that Nathan would be at home in time for the Sabbath. "The cardinal found your culinary masterpiece irresistible," Scorpio had told Zarah. "Never have you prepared a finer meal! That grinning—or should I say grimacing—little doll was the perfect main course. And the garnish! Flowering monkshood, rather than parsley—a most creative touch!" It had been good to hear her grandmother laugh again.

How terribly she would miss him, Leah suddenly realized. For all the fury he could evoke in her, and for all of the miseries for which she couldn't help but blame him, he had taught her much, and been a better friend than any other she had known.

The squire returned. "I am to escort you to the Hall of Great Audience," he announced. "You are to have a private audience with the Pope." He inclined his head respectfully toward the deeply shadowed arch. "Few are so honored."

Leah resisted the urge to take Scorpio's hand as they were ushered across a dimly lit passage. Master porters stood aside to let them pass at the entrance to the Hall of Great Audience. They descended a flight of stone steps. Each step was circular, each wider than the next, so that they seemed to spread into the chamber below like a wave. Leah felt dizzy, and vaguely diminished, as though she had shrunk to the height—and been beset by the fears—of a four-year-old.

The Great Audience Hall looked to Leah like a forest of stone, vast, yet oddly intimate. Although it ran the entire length of the new wing, the space was divided into a series of bays, each with its own recessed window, and the whole was supported by a line of scalloped columns, their ribs splayed like the branches of thick, sturdy trees to form the peaks and arches of the ceiling. The ceiling itself was relatively low, its sections jointed like the wings of bats, as though a man-made cavern had been chiseled into a mountain of rock, with one side opened to the light of day.

At the far end of the hall, enclosed behind a circular barrier of masonry and regally enthroned upon a carpeted dais, Pope Clement VI awaited their progress. The Pontiff was resplendent in embroidered cloth of gold that hung from his shoulders in stiff, pyramidal folds, and he wore a miter that echoed the shape of the arches behind him, as if man and building were one. He was flanked by a sparse semicircle of various retainers, none of whom Leah recognized. A few of them appeared to be barristers, and several wore cardinal's red. Signac was not present; and the room was guarded by a ring of sergeants-at-arms. But for the most part, the wheellike arrangement of benches that were normally filled by the tribunal body known as the Rota were empty.

Leah and Scorpio approached the judge's dais and Scorpio pulled the cowl from his face. But if Clement was disconcerted by Scorpio's change, both of complexion and habit, from cardinal's red to gardener's beige, his expression showed only a slight, possibly even amused, lift of an eyebrow.

We must look as insignificant as insects to him, Leah

thought, squaring her shoulders and tilting her chin proudly
upward to face him. But before she could speak, the Pope
raised a single pink hand. He had spared her embarrassment,
Leah realized. It would not have done for her to speak first.

"Allow me to confirm what your companion"—the Pope
nodded to Scorpio—"has undoubtedly told you. I have heard
the confession of a murderer, a personage of noble birth, who,
by virtue of the sanctity of the confessional, I will not name.
But be assured that the murder of Arnaud de Gascon weighs
heavily upon his soul. No doubt the injustice of a false accusation weighs similarly upon your father, child. I will see to
it that he is freed at once."

Leah turned to Scorpio with tears of gratitude in her eyes.

"And now, sir," continued the Pope, "I believe we have
an urgent matter to discuss. Perhaps the lady will await you
outside?"

Leah, elated, curtsied deeply to the Pope and whispered her
heartfelt thanks. She wanted nothing more than to rush to the
prison, to embrace her father as he walked through the gate.
But she couldn't bring herself to leave without saying goodbye
to Scorpio. She walked the length of the Great Hall of Audience
as if on a cloud, admiring the painted frescoes and the carvings
of fabulous beasts that crouched beneath each cluster of spring-
ing ribs. What a magnificent room it was! How could she have
found it intimidating? By the time she reached the circular
steps, Scorpio was hurrying to join her.

"I have told the Pope that the orb is on his own land."
Scorpio's flutey voice held an edge of excitement Leah had
never heard before. "He is eager that I should fetch it at once,
and return with it to this chamber." He paused, as though he
had been selfish in thinking of his own triumph first. Then,
pressing Leah's hands between his own, he looked into her
eyes. "Thank you for your help," he said. "I don't believe
the Pope will go back on his word. Your father will be freed."

Scorpio's hands were warm and firm, like the hands of any
man. And he had thanked her, when she felt nothing but gratitude toward him. Leah felt a pang of loneliness, as though
Scorpio had already gone. She searched for a way to tell him
goodbye. "Shall I come with you to fetch the orb?" she asked,
suddenly shy. She pulled her hands away, hoping for a reprieve.

● ● ●

Clement VI waited until he was certain the smug little devil, the leper-healer, the demon sorcerer, or whatever he was, was out of earshot. "Follow him, and bring me the orb," he ordered the captain of his private guard. "When you have it, you can kill him, but be neat about it. All of Avignon will want to see the body of this devil laid out in the Palace Square. And you may as well pick up the girl while you're at it. She's obviously learned her sorcery from her father."

"I would like you to come with me," Scorpio replied simply. He turned and walked up the rounded steps. Behind him, two flickering lights gradually grew brighter.

"Scorpio! The Hunters!" Leah screamed in horror and raced past Scorpio for the archway, pulling him into the passage that opened to the Great Courtyard beyond.

The lights seemed to leap in the air, and the Hunters materialized in the center of the Palace Square, blocking the exit to Avignon. There they stood, their crimson faces grim and determined, their arms crossed fiercely over their chests, their black robes settling around their ankles as though the cloth had been lifted by some spirit wind.

"This way!" Scorpio clutched Leah's hand and dragged her back into the passageway. "Run!"

A long, narrow corridor spanned the outer length of the Audience Hall. A short distance along the corridor, a stairway led upward.

Tiny beams of light, like the reflections of pins, flashed against the stone wall behind Leah's head, leaving crumbling hollows in the block. Leah and Scorpio flew up the spiraling staircase to emerge on the floor above the courtyard. One wall danced with the afternoon shadows of the pierced rosettes in the Pope's Indulgence Window. Opposite the window was yet another arch, a magnificent arch with a monolithic lintel, carved on the left with angels leading souls to Heaven and on the right with the damned in the fires of Hell. A pier at the center of the arch held a statue of Saint Peter, who separated a pair of gargantuan wooden doors.

Scorpio pulled Leah through one of the doors, the door on the angels' side. It closed with a resounding roar.

"Oh, God," Leah cried weakly. They were in a chapel, a

space more vast than the Cathedral of Notre-Dame-des-Doms, as long as the Audience Hall and three times as high, an airy space filled with miraculous sunlight. Their footsteps echoed to the Gothic heights as though they were dancing across a skin drum. On the walls were tapestries, none of which reached to the floor, and a simple stone altar faced rows of wooden pews, carved and low. There was no place in which to hide.

"This door," insisted Scorpio, pulling Leah onward. A small tierce-point door opposite the altar led to a sacristy. "You must get away, or they will kill you. They only want the orb."

"No, they want *you*—they also want *you*!"

The Hunters burst into the chapel as the sacristy door swung closed. From the sacristy, a very long, narrow corridor, unlit and windowless, led to the private apartments of the Pope. Scorpio pushed Leah ahead of him. She felt herself running, running. In the distance, as if through thick stone, she thought she could hear the barking of dogs.

The corridor hooked sharply to the right and Scorpio and Leah emerged in the Pope's private dining room. Two doors opened on the far side of the room. Scorpio looked through one, and exclaimed with recognition.

"This is the robing room! I passed through here with Signac last night. The Pope's bedchamber is just beyond it. You must hide in there. You'll be safe. I'll take the other doorway. I think I can find my way out of here. Adieu, Leah!"

Leah turned desperately to Scorpio. How could she leave him like this? They would kill him! She could hear the Hunters in the narrow corridor. Soon they would both be caught.

"Go! There is no time!"

Leah turned toward the robing room as Scorpio had ordered.

"There they are! After them!" A contingent of the Pope's men-at-arms appeared in the robing room. "You're ordered to kill the leper on sight!" barked one. "And beware of the devils he commands. But take the girl prisoner!"

Again, Scorpio pulled Leah into a narrow passageway to safety. "Betrayed!" he whispered bitterly, running, running.

"Wait!" hissed Lethor, freezing at the entrance to Clement's dining room. "The Pope's men will capture them for us!"

Waiting for the guards to thunder through the chamber, the Hunter commander beckoned to Ardon the Stalker to follow.

The maze of corridors ended abruptly. There were no doors, no windows, only a stone wall leading to nowhere.

Leah clutched Scorpio, shielding him with her body. Six of the Pope's men-at-arms advanced on them. The men took their time, swaggering as they walked, their weapons drawn, but casually lowered.

"His Holiness Clement VI had several dead-end corridors constructed to foil would-be assassins," leered the captain of the guard. "Luckily for us, you've found one of them. Saves the breath."

Leah's eyes widened in terror. Behind the Pope's guards, the Hunters were silently advancing. They smiled grotesquely with each unhurried step they took, their faces a patchwork of raw, peeling flesh and sutured scars, souvenirs of their skirmish in the marketplace. Ignoring the guards, they looked only at Scorpio.

"Take us to the orb!" commanded the thin one, his words spitting forth in a snakelike hiss.

The Pope's men whirled on the Hunters, uttering cries of alarm. The devils were back, this time in the Pope's own palace! The captain charged, brandishing a sword at the heftier of the two, the one Scorpio knew to be Ardon.

In seconds, the captain of the guard was felled, a tiny hole smoldering in his metal breastplate. *Flash! Flash! Flash!* The devil had hardly seemed to lift a finger. Three more of the soldiers died instantly in brilliant bursts of light. Like magic, slender trickles of blood pooled at a throat, a forehead, in an eye socket. The final two soldiers collapsed to their knees, crossing themselves and praying.

Leah squeezed her eyes tightly shut, waiting for a piercing pain, for death to overtake her. Her head was filled with a rush of noise, as though her blood was gathering behind her ears. All at once she knew the sound: it was the barking of a pack of dogs, and the clamorous footfall of armed men.

Pope Clement VI, tall, lordly and angry, strode into the corridor and faced the scene. He was surrounded by a phalanx of guards, a many-layered human shield. The men in the foremost ranks could barely restrain their yapping dogs. The second rank held buckets of water at the ready. It was obvious that the Pope had been well briefed as to the scene in the marketplace.

Clement VI drew himself up to his most regal height.

"The Orb of the Pantocrator is the rightful property of the Holy See," he intoned. "Devils, I banish you from my sight!"

Ardon and Lethor backed toward Scorpio and Leah until they stood possessively, one on either side of their quarry. Leah held her breath and Scorpio quivered as Ardon extended the daggerlike spikes at his wrist and pointed at the Pope.

"Loose the dogs!" commanded Clement.

"There is no more time for this nonsense!" hissed Lethor. Whisking an orb from beneath his robe, he and Ardon quickly encircled Scorpio and Leah.

Leah stared at the small, glowing, radiating haven of light.

Raising the orb above their heads, Lethor arched his fingers and pressed gently, as Ardon laced his fingers through Lethor's own.

In a blinding flash of sweet golden light, all four were gone.

Leah felt a feverish wave of heat engulf her, and a heady calm, as though she was stilled amidst turbulent motion. Was she in darkness or light?

Opening her eyes, Leah was petrified with disbelief. She and Scorpio were alone with the Hunters on the Rocher des Doms, the rocky cliff beyond the cathedral, near the gardens and the stables of the Papal Palace. How could they have gotten here? *The Hunters' orb.* In the distance, through her terror, she could hear the commotion of a gathering army, and the maddened frenzy of a pack of hunting dogs.

Ardon the Stalker held Leah from behind, his bloodred arm stretched across her throat like a slashing promise.

"Now, Scorpio," said the thin Hunter. "You know Ardon will kill you when he is ready. But I, Lethor, Assassin of the First Rank, tire of this planet and its inhabitants. I am prepared to spare the life of your little friend if you will lead us to the orb with no further resistance."

Guards and dogs were pouring from the palace. Ardon tightened his grip around Leah's neck and extended the stiletto lasers at his wrists.

"I will take you there." Scorpio met Leah's eyes, his look expressing the hope and the sorrow of frank defeat. Then he broke into a run.

Through flower gardens and vegetable patches, orchards and wooded trails, past the stables and the henyards, Scorpio ran with but one thought in his mind. *Reach the orb*! As he ran, his strength seemed to grow. There were wings sprouting from his ankles; he could almost feel them beating against the lovely humid air of this green planet.

Behind him, the Hunters followed briskly, their skins enflamed from their exertions in the moist atmosphere. Leah was with them; he could hear her light breath mingled with the Hunters' huffing. Not far behind them came the army of the Pope on the heels of their own stalkers, the highly trained dogs whose flaring nostrils, exquisitely sensitive, picked out the odors of the black-robed devils and hounded them hungrily.

Scorpio ran to the far end of the fishpond and stopped. Close behind him, the Hunters reached the pond and looked at one another in dismay. The pond was overflowing with shiny silver fish. Thousands of fish. They jumped from the pool like excited molecules and disappeared again below its surface. The water churned.

Ardon and Lethor fell to their knees, searching the pool for a glimpse of the orb, calculating whether a dousing of this magnitude would kill them, wondering to which of them the task should fall. At any moment the dogs would reach them. They must decide.

Leah stood at Ardon's side, momentarily forgotten. The fish flapped and splashed at the surface of the pool, their scales glittering in the sunlight. A clattering contingent of the Pope's men-at-arms charged into the clearing and made to loose their arrows at the Hunters. Light glinted from their armor, flashed from their swords.

In the split second before the lasers fired, in the briefest of moments before swordplay echoed through the papal clearing, Leah's eyes met Scorpio's. The look they exchanged was silent, mutual and instantaneous. With no hesitation, with the grace of diving birds, they plunged through the crowded, silver-packed waters to the bottom of the pond.

Chapter
19

"*S*wim, Leah, there is no turning back. Swim, now, like an Aquay!"

"Scorpio, I can hear you, I am swimming toward the orb. *The orb.*"

Their minds locked together in silent calm, Scorpio and Leah dove toward the vibrant light that glowed from the depths of the papal fishpond. Their arms, like wings, propelled them downward through a tangle of fins and gills. Schools of fish parted before them to open a path, then closed again to fill the gaps. Above them in the world of air, the water frothed with laserfire gone astray, with spears and arrows released by frantic crossbowmen, with wounded soldiers twitching at poolside, to die among asphyxiated fish.

Leah expelled the last of her air in a tiny stream of bubbles. Her black hair drifted around her in an inky cloud. She and Scorpio briefly watched the bubbles float upward. Above them, in a distant world, a battle was raging. Here and there a fish would explode like a silver wine vessel split at the seams, spilling its crimson innards in a burst of slick streamers. *Like comets*, thought Leah. *Like rockets*, thought Scorpio. The surface of the pond darkened with blood.

At the bottom of the pool, the water was stained a delicate pink. It filtered downward in rosy striations, illuminated like watered silk by the light of the orb. Scorpio and Leah reached forth as one. The orb seemed small, as though all but its core had dissolved, leaving just a ring of filmy light where once had been solid matter. But as their hands passed through the honey-colored corona, as their fingers interlaced and arched against the orb's leathery surface, as they felt the pulsing leap of energy travel upward through their limbs, there was no denying its life-giving power.

Is this what death is like? wondered Leah. Is there a future, where time stands still.

Leah opened her eyes. They were still at the bottom of the pool. Seconds must have elapsed, but nothing had happened. She felt as though her lungs were about to burst.

Leah pushed upward toward the surface of the pool. The water was clear, and there were few fish. Next to her, Scorpio, too, was rising. Her eyes were closed and his cowl spread peacefully about him like the gown of an angel. Leah could just see that he held the orb close to his body, tucked under one arm.

Gasping for air, Leah dragged herself from the pool and rolled onto her back on the ground. Her clothing clung to her like a liquid stone, and her muscles ached with tension. But the air felt balmy and sweet.

Scorpio's head bobbed to the surface and he floated serenely for some moments. Then he swam, one-armed, to the edge of the pond as a fish darted merrily in and out of his wide, Benedictine sleeve. He seemed to be as at home in the water as the fish, Leah observed. She looked about the clearing in confusion. They were quite alone at the pond. The Hunters were gone, as were the Pope's men-at-arms. There were no barking dogs or clanking swords. Even most of the fish had disappeared.

"Are you all right?" Scorpio clambered from the water. "I thank the Deity you are safe."

"What has happened?" Leah examined their surroundings with mounting anxiety. "Everyone is gone. But we are still here, at the pond. I thought your orb would take us to a different place, just as the Hunters' orb somehow moved us from within the palace to without."

"I don't know," said Scorpio, studying the clearing. Something did seem different. The smell of the air. Or the trees, perhaps. He concealed the orb beneath his habit. How good it felt, the warmth, the weight. If only he could keep it with him always. He was pleased that Leah was unharmed. Perhaps her presence had somehow tied them to this planet. But no doubt Ardon and Lethor would come for them again. It was time to see her safely home, and then—on to Terrapin.

"I must go to my father," said Leah. "I must know that he is safe."

"But the Pope has ordered your arrest as well as mine." Scorpio lowered his voice, searching the trees for guards. "He betrayed us both, do you not remember?"

Leah hung her head. "Our plan has failed." Idly she began to wring the water from her dripping skirts.

"After dark, I will see you back to the quarter," said Scorpio. "Then we will find out what we may. You may have to hide, as I did, in the synagogue. Or even leave Avignon for a while. But I shall trouble you no further. The orb will take me where it takes me."

Leah nodded. She felt drained and defeated. Scorpio was right.

"We'd better conceal ourselves until we dry," she said. Her voice was flat. "There is a rocky ledge behind that stand of trees. We can sit there and catch the wind from the river."

Scorpio watched sadly as Leah disappeared into the trees. They *had* failed, and he might have gotten her killed besides. He should never have become so involved with the beings on this planet. And Leah's questions were bothering him. Why *hadn't* they been transported out of Avignon? Where had all the soldiers gone? And why were there *buds* on the trees?

Scorpio! Leah let out a terrified shriek.

Scorpio left the fishpond and hurried to Leah's side. She was sitting on a ledge of rock on a steep bluff. The view stretched beyond the Bridge of St.-Bénézet, across the sparkling Rhône to the hills of Villeneuve-lès-Avignon.

"What is it? What's wrong?"

"The walls—look! Avignon is surrounded by ramparts, *huge* stone walls, with turrets and gates—it couldn't be! They were not there this morning. It takes years to fortify a city so!" Leah turned to her companion, terror-stricken and trembling. "Oh, Scorpio, what is happening? Do you see them too? Am I mad?"

For Scorpio, what had begun as a faint suspicion was now confirmed. "It was the orb," he answered softly. "We *have* traveled, Leah. But we have not traveled in space—we have traveled in time!"

Leah's eyes widened, and she shook her head vigorously. "That is not possible. This cannot be happening. It is a dream." Suddenly she grabbed Scorpio's shoulders and shook him as hard as she was able. "Take me back! What have you done? *Take me back!*"

Scorpio was as stunned as Leah. He did not doubt that time travel was possible. But he felt more lost than ever, and overwhelmed by questions. How far forward had they come? If the orb allowed one to travel in time as well as in space, had he traveled in time when he left his own planet? What year was it now on Terrapin? Was he perhaps in earth's future, but Terrapin's past? Or vice versa? The questions wouldn't stop. How did the orbs work, what were their limits, had the Hunters mastered all of their powers, how had they used them to enslave his own people? Was he lost in time?

Leah stopped shaking Scorpio when he let out a prolonged, pained wail. But she remained seated with an arm about his shoulders. That he was as frightened and confused as she, she could see. Strangely, Scorpio's pain was almost a comfort to her. She was reminded again, and at last began to believe, that he was neither angel nor demon, but a being perhaps as unfathomable as her present situation was inconceivable.

Leah made an effort to face what she could see. Scorpio held back no secrets. He was lost. Therefore, they must unravel the mysteries of the light-filled ball; and she was as likely as he to find a way to do so. It seemed that fate, for whatever reason, had thrown them together, so together they would seek the answers they needed. If this was the future, so be it.

Leah's terror was gradually giving way to a curious excitement. None of the other girls in the quarter had had such adventures, of that she was certain.

"Let's do what we are able, one task at a time," she said to Scorpio. "Are you dry? No? Then let's stand on the ledge and study this new city." Helping Scorpio to his feet, Leah held her skirts and her hair to the wind. It must be early spring, by the feel of it, she thought, with just a hint of sun-warmed air blowing up from the river. It's afternoon, judging from the sun. She turned her back to the wind and looked toward the Palace of the Popes.

"Clement must have died," she remarked. "There is a new pope. Do you not see the arms on the banner that flies from the highest turret?"

Scorpio looked admiringly at Leah. Her approach to life was practical, he thought. The unanswerable she simply put aside, and her acceptance of the evidence before her allowed her great flexibility. If only the Aquay had been so clear-eyed! He watched as Leah scrutinized the view. Her curiosity and thirst for learning seemed to mitigate her fear of the unknown, though there was no doubting her courage. She had recognized his despair and had been sympathetic. She made no recriminations, and was patiently waiting for him to recover. To his surprise, Scorpio realized that he was describing a good friend.

"You have been very kind," said Scorpio. "Thank you."

"I am sorry to have shaken you. I was frightened. But now you have your orb back, and we have learned one way to make it work! You'll soon find your way to Terrapin." Leah's face was once again bright with hope. "I must look for my father. Perhaps things will be different now if Clement is truly dead. I say we should venture into town and find out what year it is. We can pretend to be travelers from a distant land."

As perhaps we are, thought Scorpio grimly. But he agreed. If they hadn't come too far in time, Leah could return to her home and he would be on his way. He would miss her.

Leah braided her hair and smoothed the folds of her skirt, brushed the velvet of her cloak and pressed the brocade edges of her sleeves. The soaking in the fishpond had done her finery little good, but she was presentable. Scorpio, his habit still damp and smelling like a wet sheep, looked as shabby as ever. That was perfect. He would be taken for a country priest come to seek benefices in Avignon.

Together, the unlikely pair descended from the Rocher des Doms.

"Excuse me, sir." Leah stopped an elderly gentleman just outside the cathedral, while Scorpio pretended to rest nearby. "I wonder if you could tell me how long the city walls have been here. I lived in Avignon as a child and have recently returned, but I don't remember them."

"You're quite right, girl," replied the man. "We've only had the ramparts, let's see, five years now. They were started in 1357, after the truce."

Leah did a quick calculation in her head, then glanced furtively, panicked, at Scorpio. It was 1361. They had jumped ten years. But the old man was looking at her strangely. She must conceal her shock. "T-truce?" she managed.

"The truce of Bordeaux, girl, between England and France. Put all of those Free Companies of mercenaries out of work, and now they're ransacking all of France. Isn't that why you're here? Taking refuge from the pillage? The villains!" The old man shook his head. "I see you've got all your finery on your back—you're lucky you got through at all. No wonder you're a bit addled. Why, the White Company is camped just south of here. If Innocent VI doesn't pay their ransom . . . ."

The old man broke off. "There, now, girl, don't look so alarmed. There are patrols of the Pope's men everywhere, and more wooden barricades going up. You can hear the noise all over the city. You'll be safe enough in Avignon."

"I hope so, sir!" Leah answered. "But it's not the glamorous place it was in Clement's day, is it?"

"No, indeed!" The old man's eyes twinkled. "Those were the days—music, banquets, artists, ladies. Now, Innocent—he'd like nothing better than to finish his days in the monastery he built across the river, the Chartreuse. He'll get there soon enough, too, he's as old as me!" The old man cackled mischievously. "But Clement ran his court like a king! Cost him, too. . . ."

Leah left the old man to his ruminating and rejoined Scorpio. "It's been ten years," she said. "Shall I say I've been in hiding? In prison? How have I survived? How is it I haven't aged? Scorpio, how can I go home?"

All the while she was questioning, Leah was walking resolutely toward the Jewish quarter. She paused at the gate. That, at least, had not changed. Her face registered joy, and terror, nostalgia and resignation, all in a matter of seconds. At last she turned to Scorpio and embraced him briefly, ignoring the astonished stares of passersby.

"Scorpio, will you wait for me? I fear what I will find inside, but I must go by myself. Please, if I am not back in an hour or two, I hope you will find your way to what you are looking for.''

Leah slipped through the gate in the rue Jacob and disappeared into the winding alleys of the quarter. They seemed as crowded as ever, dark and smelly. She avoided the square and the synagogue, and entered the back garden of her father's house. A lamp was lighted inside, and the smoke from a cooking fire rose into the dusky sky.

Leah was not certain why, but she felt compelled to knock. Footsteps hastened to the back door.

The door was opened by a woman in her mid-twenties. Leah recognized her only with difficulty. She was Félicie Morel—a grown woman. She held an infant on one shoulder, and a small child clung to her skirts. At the sight of Leah she blanched as though she was seeing a ghost. Leah understood.

''Please forgive me for arriving unannounced,'' she began, ''but I am a relative of the de Bernay family, seeking news of my relations. I was told they lived here?''

''Forgive me! Come in.'' Félicie introduced herself as Leah sat on a wooden bench near the fire. The kitchen looked almost the same. But new benches had been placed around the table, which was covered with a fine linen cloth, and a curtain of a crisp green fabric covered the tiny window that overlooked the garden.

''It's j-just that you look so much like one of the de Bernays. Her name was Leah. . . .''

''She would be my cousin, I believe,'' Leah said. ''My mother and her mother were sisters.''

''I had no idea Madame de Bernay had a sister,'' replied Félicie. ''She's been dead these many years.''

''What happened to the rest of the family? My cousin?''

Félicie looked stricken. ''It is a tragic story,'' she began. ''And you have traveled such a long way. Perhaps you would like to see the rabbi?''

''I am staying with my husband's family,'' Leah said. ''We are only passing through on our way to Carpentras. But please, if you could tell me. . . .''

''They are all gone now, I am afraid,'' said Félicie. ''The doctor, Nathan de Bernay, was executed ten years ago for the murder of a cardinal under Pope Clement VI.'' She paused as Leah turned pale. ''Don't be ashamed. We all knew he was innocent. It is said that another cardinal was the true murderer. But of course, the Pope would never have allowed such a scandal to become public, not when there was a scapegoat handy. The Jews were bitter, and there were protests, of course. But the Church prevailed.''

Leah choked back angry tears. "And my cousin?"

"Leah." Félicie shook her head in wonder. "Her death is surrounded in mystery. The way the story goes, she was drowned with a mysterious stranger on the grounds of the Papal Palace. Her body was never recovered. Some say she was a sorceress, and that devils took her! Others say she was eaten alive, that Pope Clement kept sharks in his pond. You can see where she drowned still. There's a fishpond in the Pope's gardens. In Avignon, some people say they've seen her, and the stranger too, a monk, floating at the bottom of the pool, just faint, like shadows. People tell such stories! Am I frightening you?"

"No, please go on," Leah urged.

"Well of course, some say that Leah ran off with this monk, who was a leper, to live in a leper colony! She wanted to be a doctor, like her father, you see. And others say she didn't run off with a monk at all, but with a handsome young Christian knight!"

"A knight?"

"A nobleman's son. He went off years ago to join the Crusade. He used to court all of the Jewish girls back then."

"How do you know of all this? Did you know her?"

"A bit. She was a little older than me. She was standoffish, and had too much book-learning for her own good. But she loved her father, that's what my husband says. He knew her. He says she was slaughtered by the Pope's men-at-arms, and that it was as simple as that." Félicie shrugged. "My husband was a widower and a friend of the family's. He moved into this house to look after Nathan de Bernay's mother, Zarah. She would have been your grandmother too, I guess. What a pity you lost touch with the family! After the son and the granddaughter died, there was no one left, you see. Zarah was old and blind. She's gone too, about six years now. She was grateful for the help and the company, and spoiled my husband's older boy! She deeded the house to my husband.''

Félicie's voice grew brighter. "You must meet him. Will you stay for supper? Mossé will be home soon."

Leah's heart was breaking. She no longer had a home. Her family was gone, she had failed to save her father, and now she must leave the quarter, quickly and forever, for if Mossé recognized her he would be terrified.

Should she go upstairs for her clothes? But of course they would all be gone. Would they still have her father's herb chest? But there was no way she could carry it. Leah wrenched herself from the fireside and clasped Félicie's hand.

"Thank you for your time," she said warmly. "I wish you and your family all happiness. But I am afraid I must be on my way."

"I wish you a good journey, then," said Félicie. "You'd best hurry, for the gates close at sundown. It is a shame my husband couldn't have met you—you look so much like her."

Leah smiled and took her leave. Félicie's voice held a trace of honest regret. But her expression was one of unconcealed relief.

Once outside the quarter, Leah allowed herself to cry. Her grief came in waves, as the understanding of all she had lost became more and more real.

In a dark alley, on a filthy side street near the Pont d'Avignon, Scorpio held her by the shoulders and murmured words of comfort when he could. Toward morning, the orb grew warm at his belly and he pressed it gently against Leah's back.

Gradually, as dawn broke, Leah's sobs subsided. "If you'll have me, I'd like to come with you," she said to Scorpio. "We are both lost now, it seems." She began to walk.

Scorpio walked next to Leah in companionable silence. She seemed calm enough this morning. But she would have more grieving to do, he was certain, and drastic adjustments to make as well. He hoped they would soon find a place she could safely settle. Now, with the orb tucked warmly against his midsection, he felt the urgent call of Terrapin. He could never bring her with him. Or could he?

"You don't know how to work the orb well enough to predict

where we'll land,'' Leah said gently, as though she had read his thoughts.

Scorpio the Aquay turned to face the human creature, Leah de Bernay. Their eyes, separately, told stories of mingled despair and hope. Their eyes, locked together, found a mutual reserve of joy. This world they were in, this place in time, they rejected. Together they would reach for the future.

"Where shall we jump from?"
"How about the bridge?"

With the night sky still an inky indigo at their backs, Scorpio and Leah walked east across St.-Bénézet's Bridge, into the pink-washed dawn.

SCORPIO RISING

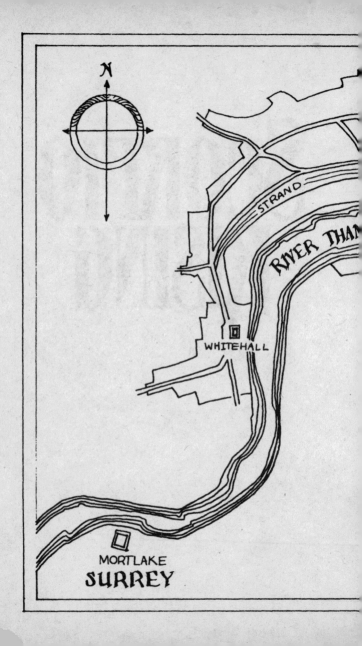

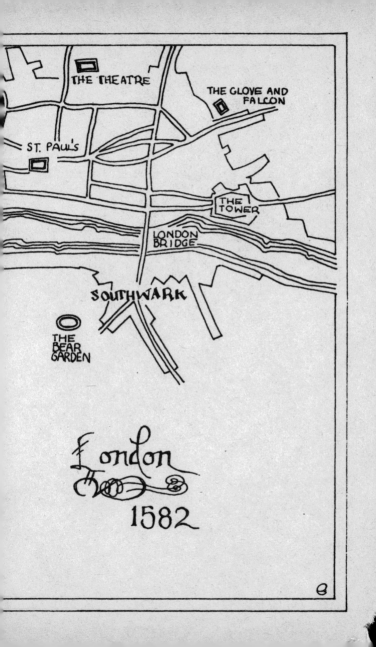

Prologue
Between Worlds

*A*drift.

I know that I occupy a pocket of warmth and safety where there is no sense of movement or the passage of time. Yet something in me says I'm adrift. A castaway from everything I've known. At times, the all-pervading warmth here makes me dream that I'm an infant in the womb.

Yet I don't think an infant has as many memories as I.

I have no body that I can feel, yet I know the physical part of me is safe, cared for. I can take my identity out, turn it in my hands like a burnished coin.

Leah.

Leah de Bernay.

Daughter of Nathan de Bernay, renowned Jewish physician of Avignon.

Sometimes the memories form pictures: the turreted bridge of St.-Bénézet at morning, crowded with lumbering carts, plodding peasants as unaware as their overworked and bony beasts, aggressive street merchants already beginning to cry their wares in raucous voices. A fine lady and gentleman richly attired but holding perfumed kerchiefs to their noses against the pervasive stench of the close-packed city. Fourteenth-century Avignon was a dirty, sprawling, endlessly fascinating place, with the court of Pope Clement VI as its social center. Famed artists and scientists, as well as

1

ecclesiastics, were drawn by Clement's generosity as a patron.

I'll admit it; I was as blinded as any young girl by the pomp and glitter of the papal court. In my own sheltered, strictly monitored life in the Jewish quarter, I dreamed of what it might be like to live as the courtiers did, freely and with passion. With these stars in my eyes, I was almost seduced by one of the courtiers, Aimeric de la Val d'Ouvèze. He was so different than the boys I knew. They were all boring, serious young men that appealed, no doubt, to Grandmère Zarah, but not to me. I learned in time that Aimeric, like many of the young men of the court, was faithless and trifling. He thought of me only as a possible conquest. I even overheard him say as much to one of his friends. I hated him then, but his handsome roguish face appears before me, and I doubt if I'll ever be able to forget him entirely.

The Plague.

No, I don't want those memories.

Bodies piled up in the streets, and rank smoke from hasty funeral pyres. There was fear in the Jewish quarter then, as rumors were spread that the Jews had poisoned the wells. It was as if they thought placing blame for the Plague would somehow make things better. Grandmère Zarah had often told the story of the goat sent into the wilderness bearing the sins of the Hebrew people—the scapegoat. I understood that story perfectly now.

And my mother went out to nurse a sick friend and never returned. No, I don't want to remember that, but it was important. During the Plague no young man wanted to be apprenticed to a physician. I was the only one who could help my father, and he began to teach me his skills.

Exposed to his knowledge, something happened to my mind. I had been sheltered and lulled into the acquiescence expected of a young woman. Before that time my life had been completely planned. A husband, chosen by my family, of course, and if all went well, children. That was all. Most women thought it was enough, but something snapped, and suddenly I had a thirst, more, a lust for knowledge. I wanted to know about everything in this world and worlds beyond.

I didn't realize how much I'd changed until one day when I joined the women in the public bathhouse. They were a closed circle to me; their lives intertwined because they did the same things, believed the same things. I couldn't imagine my own life conforming to the pattern of theirs, and they seemed to know it, too. I could see in their eyes that they considered me different—possibly even scandalous. That look in their eyes still haunts me. It's as if they wanted to tell me something.

So it was when I encountered the demon in the wood outside the city, I did not run away as others in my place might have done. Ever since I was small, I had heard tales of *shedim,* demons both evil and benevolent, and this certainly seemed to be one of that breed.

When I first saw Scorpio, I was stunned. I stood there paralyzed with fear, trying desperately to convince myself that this was an illusion—only a trick of the hazy light filtering down through branches above. I had almost convinced myself, too, when the thing spoke in an eerie warble, as if someone were trying to sing underwater.

Then I had to admit that it was real. It appeared to have substance; the trees behind it weren't visible through its grayish, vaguely manlike shape.

I wonder now why I didn't run screaming from this apparition. It's one thing to be told as a child that *shedim* exist; quite another to meet one face-to-face in the woods. Yet there was something about Scorpio, something hard to define. His expression seemed to say he was lost, vulnerable, far from his home.

I can hear Scorpio's high-pitched burble of laughter as I think of demons. I remember that I'm not alone in this dream womb. He and I are twins, despite our differences. We're so close here I can feel his presence; sometimes we seem to sense each other's thoughts. He doesn't consider himself a demon, but a person, like myself. He calls the place he comes from Terrapin and talks of it as if it were as real, as substantial as Avignon, his people the Aquay, as mine are the Jews. He said that his people were being murdered by another race, the Hunters, and that an assassin had been sent to kill him. I saw these Hunters and hope never to see them again. I suppose they're no stranger looking than Scorpio at first glance, but they are evil, and he is not. I can't explain it any better than that.

Yes, I know, all this is hard to believe, even for me, and I'm here. Wherever that may be.

He told me he had come to my world by means of an orb, a small, glowing globe. At first when I saw it, I thought it must be a trick, a bladder with a lamp inside, but the steady golden light emanating from it drew my concentration and lulled my fears. I discovered that while the orb was a power, it was one that Scorpio didn't wholly control.

After that first meeting with Scorpio, my life began to unravel, though none of it was his fault. By chance my father was called in to treat a cardinal, Arnaud de Gascon, and in making the diagnosis, let slip the unwise remark "poison." Indeed it had been poison, administered by another cardinal, Bertrand Signac. It hadn't been all that difficult for Signac, in his position of power, to throw the blame onto my father and have him sent to prison.

I can still see my father in that filthy cell. His face was bruised, but he put on a hopeful expression and talked about how I could prove who the real murderer was. Now I think only meant to keep my hopes up, but I was self-important then, eager to try and prove his innocence, full of plots and plans.

And with Scorpio's help, how we plotted and planned. I can hardly believe now the risks I took. The women would have been even more scandalized had they seen me skulking about Signac's house, hiding in a latrine when the guards came too close.

Scorpio and I finally tricked Signac into confessing his crime to Pope Clement, and I was promised that my father would be freed. I really believed then that all would be well, and my life would return to its normal course. We didn't realize that the Pope coveted the golden orb. He wanted to have it for himself, and a strange being and a young girl didn't seem such a high price to pay. Scorpio and I found ourselves trapped between the Pope's guard and the Hunters, with only one possible escape. We realized it at the same moment and grasped the orb together.

It moved us, somewhat in the way we're journeying now. Although there was no feeling of movement.

We were surprised to find ourselves in Avignon again, though there were details about it that had changed, and I had the impression that time had passed. Thinking to greet my father, I rushed home.

What we hadn't understood was that Clement didn't want the scandal of one cardinal murdering another. Grandmère Zarah would have said he wanted a scapegoat, and my father was perfect. He had been executed.

Ten years ago.

I heard the news when I returned to my home and found it occupied by a former friend of mine. She told me about the death of my father, and some years later, of Grandmère Zarah. It was strange to hear from her lips that she believed Leah de Bernay had been dabbling in sorcery, like her father, and so had been slaughtered by the Pope's men-at-arms. So I was dead, too.

It no longer seemed a great adventure. We humans know what it is to move through time day by day and eventually see all that we have loved and known pass from us. But we were *not* made to take ten years at a leap. Scorpio tried to comfort me, and the orb had a healing touch. Otherwise, I don't think I would have wanted to live.

When I was healed, Scorpio told me he was preparing to journey on. He wanted to find a place and time where the workings of the orb could be explained. Once he gained control of its powers, he hoped to return and save his people. On impulse I asked if I might go with him. There was no one left in this world that I could care about, and though it sounds strange, I felt closer to Scorpio at that moment than to any human being. So we left.

I can't say that this is a long journey, but surely there's plenty of time to wonder if perhaps I made a mistake. Avignon was a place of foul smells, of restrictions, of plots and conspiracies, but no matter what its drawbacks, I knew it. Even though Scorpio's was the only familiar face, it was not a human face. I can't be sure that the motives I give him are true ones because he's still an "other."

But I still have to admit that being between worlds is exciting. Even if I were offered the chance to go back to that circle of women and live my life according to their pattern, I don't know if I could accept. What is scandalous is now second nature.

All that I do know for sure is when the journey is over, when I'm decanted from this womb, I can't go trustingly forth into the world like a newborn babe. I'm no longer easy prey for an amorous stare and a vapid, handsome face. I'll no longer take the word of popes and princes on faith.

I think the journey may be nearing its end. I feel a whirling sensation, a pressure, as if my body were being squeezed over all its surface, blood rushing to fingertips, toes. I feel memory slipping, but I struggle to hang on to it. I must try to take something of my heritage, my identity, my memories into the next world.

Whatever sort of world it may be.

Chapter
1

*D*r. John Dee, Astrologer
Royal to Her Majesty Queen Elizabeth I, sat at a writing
table in his chambers at the Palace of Whitehall. For long
moments he stared into space, and then his quill would
return to the paper again to make quick, nervous notations.
A fire burned in an immense fireplace before him, the heat
searing his lined, ascetic face even as drafts of cold air
buffeted playfully at vulnerable spots where bony ankles
emerged from large, fur-lined slippers. Cold rain occasionally tick-tacked against the mullioned windowpane. When
he looked up from his work, he could see the fragmented
image of Westminster Abbey. Gothic arches and pointed
towers made it seem, for all its bulk, to yearn toward the
heavens, though the sky was drear and colorless this November day.

A servant trained in unobtrusiveness had come and gone
like a wraith, leaving a tray of victuals, cold fowl, pasties,
a goblet of claret. The chamber was large and sparsely
furnished, though what furnishings there were had a pon-
derous ornateness, and hardly a wooden surface was without
its carvings of strapwork, cartouches, grotesque birds and
animals, the wood polished to a gloss by generations of
willing hands. The mantelpiece rose almost to the ceiling,
every inch of it embellished until it resembled a fantastic
gatehouse or garish Sicilian tomb. And as if this were not

decoration enough, here and there the carvings had been accentuated with bright touches of color. The tester bed, almost large enough to become a room in itself, had a headboard of wainscot and hangings of brown velvet and gilt fringe. Firelight glinted off threads of silver and gold worked cleverly into tapestries that softened the walls, an unending display of scenes of the hunt and of battle, rich with symbol and muted color. The room's whole aspect was of a heavy-handed opulence.

At the moment, Dee seemed oblivious to his surroundings, although, in truth, he was merely deep in concentration. There were many benefits that came with his position. Who would have thought that befriending a bastard princess with no claim to the throne and casting her horoscope would lead him to such a high state. He paused, thinking that it had nearly led him to the scaffold in those unsettled times. But he'd had no reason to regret his acts. Not only had the Queen proven herself surprisingly adept at statecraft since she gained the throne, she was loyal as well. Many of those who now held high places in her court had been with her from the beginning.

Still, he grumbled to himself, things were seldom perfect. Elizabeth called him her Merlin, but now, as then, astrology was a suspect science. It went against the doctrine of free will, the fools said, to think the future was foretold by the stars. He sighed hugely. So much ignorance in the world, when there was so much to know, so much joy in the learning.

When he set his quill to dancing over the paper again, he realized that it had dried out and paused to dip it into the inkwell. It would seem that after the honors he had earned as a geographer and mathematician, with his contributions in navigation and optics, the Queen could find a better use for him than playing at a common game of spies!

Even so, he had to admit he had felt a certain sense of

importance earlier that day when he was told that two "gentlemen" wanted to confer with him. He knew that the gentlemen in question were Lord Burghley and Sir Francis Walsingham, two of the Queen's top-ranking advisors with whom he'd been on intimate terms for some years. He rather liked William Cecil, Lord Burghley, with his open countenance, lined forehead, and pale eyes which seemed to take in every detail. Even in the elegant, dark-colored padded doublet and trunk hose, a huge starched ruff flaring about his face, Burghley had the mild-mannered air of a very efficient clerk. As the Queen's Minister of the Treasury, he had proven his efficiency when his monetary reforms stabilized the country's finances. His political ambitions, however, belied the impression of a humble clerk. He had made no false steps in his rise to power. Walsingham, on the other hand, with his heavy-lidded eyes and smoothly trimmed beard, seemed sleek and complacent, a man who knew secrets. A staunch Puritan, he had served a lengthy term as Her Majesty's Minister of Intelligence and had uncovered more than one popish plot against the realm.

"As you may know, the Duc d'Alençon is in the Netherlands, pursuing his military campaign," said Burghley, who seldom wasted time on social amenities when there was a job to be done, "but his representative de Simier is presently at court."

Dee knew that the seventeen-year-old d'Alençon, brother of the King of France, was the latest of Elizabeth's "suitors," rather a mismatch for Elizabeth in her forties, though romance had little to do with it. Throughout her reign the Virgin Queen had held out the hope of a royal marriage to the heir of this or that powerful country. To choose among them would probably have led to factionalism and thus to war. Never to choose . . . yes, that was what kept the balance of an uneasy peace. He wondered how a mere woman could have thought of it, and then decided that perhaps *only* a woman would have thought of it. It would seem likely that such a game would wear thin after so many years, but that was only the greater tribute to the spell of enchantment Elizabeth could weave about herself when she chose. Something of a magician herself was the Queen, Dee thought with amusement.

Dee nodded, saying nothing. He knew they would get to the meat of it directly.

"When we told him of your occult studies, he was intrigued about your experiments with scrying," said Burghley.

"He wishes, as we had hoped, to attend a séance at your home," Walsingham continued.

"All will be in readiness for him," said Dee. "My assistant, Edward Kelley, is in residence there. He has displayed a genuine talent for reading the future in crystal. *Monsieur le duc* will be amazed."

"I'm sure your assistant has many *talents*," said Walsingham with a cat-licking-cream smile. "His reputation is not exactly spotless."

"We'd be pleased if, during the séance, de Simier was led to give us information about d'Alençon's concerns," said Burghley, getting back to the subject in his direct way.

"I can do no less for my country and my liege," said Dee, politely stifling a yawn. These were duties he'd performed before, many times. He knew his friends were far more interested in whatever secrets he could pry out of his guest than in any demonstration of magic, genuine or not.

"And in turn, we're willing to impart certain information regarding Elizabeth's state of mind that may be passed on to de Simier. Her Majesty is singularly taken with young d'Alençon's charms; this must be made clear. She is eager for this wedding to take place, joining the fates of these two great nations."

"Might it not be beneficial if the marriage were foretold

in the heavens?'' asked Dee dryly. "I can arrange it.''

There was a pause as Burghley shot a knowing glance at Walsingham. He was recalling a conversation the two men had had earlier over dinner.

"I wish we didn't have to rely on Dee so much,'' Walsingham had said, thrusting his knife toward his plate to spear a last sliver of pheasant. "The man worries me.''

"He's rendered good service to us in the past,'' replied Burghley. "And of course he's brilliant. Mathematician, geographer, expert in navigation, astronomy and optics. When he read his preface to *Euclid*, I was told that the hall was so full, people had to stand outside, peering in through doors and windows to hear him.''

"The people gathered not to see a scholar, but a magician. Scientific studies are not the full extent of his learning. He studied under Agrippa and styles himself the Magus of Britain.''

"I know. The Queen calls him her Merlin, but she is taken with pageantry, and I think Dee has a certain flair for the theatrical himself. I don't believe it does any harm.''

"Not if it were all merely show, but you've heard the rumors: that he talks to unnatural beings through the device of a crystal. That he and his assistant went to a graveyard at midnight to resurrect a corpse so that it might speak to them.''

"Pious men know that the world of spirits exists,'' said Burghley.

"I say he takes these notions of spirits too far for his own good. Fear of witches and black magic is widespread. Our own plans could be jeopardized if Dee's experiments bring the wrath of the ignorant down upon him.''

"Come now, you're speaking of an old acquaintance who has been quite useful to us in the past. We can't judge him by the gossip of dullards. They confuse the line between science and superstition.''

"So does John Dee."

His thoughts now returning to the present, Burghley saw that Dee was looking self-satisfied after his jest of controlling the future through his knowledge of astrology. Could he think he had been taken seriously? Burghley could see how someone who dabbled in magic might very well become erratic. Walsingham trusted no one, of course; that was just one of the endearing traits that made him such a good Minister of Intelligence, but it was not Burghley's way to be hasty. As usual, he would bide his time, and watch, and plan.

After further consultation the two men rose to go, their business concluded.

"Have you forwarded my request to Her Majesty for funds to further my research into the spirit world?" he asked, since the time seemed propitious.

"Your petition has been heard and will be dealt with anon," said Burghley in his earnest manner. "You do understand that word of these dealings must be kept secret."

"The times are rife with talk of witchcraft," said Walsingham. "In the common view your studies are suspect. If you continue to work with us, you'll be rewarded in due course. In the meantime I know that your undying devotion to Gloriana will suffice."

Dee smiled, a mere twist of thin lips half hidden in his beard. It was often noted that Gloriana took full advantage of her subjects' devotion, while the lid to the royal coffers remained closed.

A branch of burning wood crackled, awakening Dee from his reverie. How bright the flames were, how hypnotic their silken movement. He stared into the brightness, trying to achieve a trance state and see images instead of random patterns. No visions appeared, and the glare only made his eyes burn and water. If only, he thought, I had psychic talents myself, instead of having to rely on others. My assistant, Edward Kelley, is a true seer, no matter what others say about him. I know that his fits of temper sometimes make him the very devil to deal with, but no one else has given him a chance. They think because he's had a few scrapes with the law his trances couldn't be genuine. But I've been there, and I've talked to . . . I don't know, beings from the world of spirits. Angels. Why shouldn't we try to contact these all-knowing beings? Imagine it, a world where all knowledge, all learning, could be held in common and available on the instant, rapid as a flash of light!

Carried away by his own imaginings, Dee had to rise and pace about the chamber to calm himself. The melancholy comfort of the well-appointed room now weighed more heavily upon him than before. Elizabeth and her ministers, for all their wisdom, contented themselves with prying into the dirty little secrets of princes. When I attempt to unlock the secrets of worlds unseen, Dee grumbled to himself, they say, "Some magics are too dangerous to know." While I search for a route to Cathay, whence ships could return laden with gold and jewels, the monarchs squabble among themselves over their tiny holdings.

For a moment he was angry at his surroundings. All of this finery was merely borrowed. Despite his years of devotion to learning, he had only a pittance he could call his own to pay for his research. If only I could convince the Queen that my dialogues with the spirits are real, he thought, that the angels are good entities and could make of her realm a true Golden Age if we listened to their wisdom. If only . . .

Since there seemed no practical point in continuing this line of thought, he returned at last to his writing table, where a draft had tumbled the papers. Carefully, he began to put them back into order and to occupy his mind with the task at hand. Walsingham, knowing Dee's facility in cryptography, had requested a new system of cyphers for use in espionage.

Dee's studies of the Kabbalah, a book of Jewish mysticism, had led him down some interesting byways. As a mathematician, he found it fascinating, for instance, that every Hebrew letter had numerical value. This gematria seemed to suggest an idea for a code, and he'd been working on it for some time. As he rearranged his papers, his eye noted a Kabbalistic symbol, the tree of life with its ten spheres, or *sephiroth*.

By concentrating on this symbol, one was supposed to ascend from the world of matter through worlds of spirit. He had been using the image as a part of his code, but now he fixed his attention on it wholly, wondering if there was really anything to it. He began to control his breathing. Human breath was composed of fire, air and water and was a potent means of inducing a trance state. By ascending through the spheres, one ultimately reached the crown, the topmost aspect.

As he stared toward the window, the symbol seemed to have left the paper, for the highest sphere now hovered in the air outside and glowed with an inner radiance that was almost blinding. "My stars, it really works!" he gasped, as his vision swam with afterimages that made him imagine the ball of radiance encompassing a human figure. A man. Or was it a woman?

No, impossible, he told himself, realizing that he was not in a trance state, but was wide awake. And he could still see the globe, hovering like a soap bubble outside the window, its contours shivering in the wind.

Getting off his stool so rapidly it fell behind him, he leapt to the window just in time to see the luminous object drift past the window and down into the courtyard beneath. As it touched the earth, there was a blinding flash, and then the light began to fade. Dee watched it go with an aching sense of loss, as if he'd seen one miracle and there would not be another.

But all evidence of his vision hadn't yet disappeared, he realized. Not one, but two humanlike figures stood motionless in the courtyard until the light had dimmed. Like two statues, they stood, as if entranced and unaware of the cold, the drifting streamers of rain. After a moment they began to move sluggishly and to look about themselves in wonder.

"Angels!" thought Dee with excitement. "This time *my* meditations have summoned them!"

Dee burst from his rooms unmindful that he was dressed only in the loose garment he affected in private moments and his wife called his wizard's robes. His slippers flopping with every step, he began to run through the palace toward the courtyard.

Chapter
2

*L*eah hugged her arms about her body as cold rain lashed her. She had almost forgotten what cold was like, but the rain was an effective reminder. The memories of the orb voyage were fading fast. Soon she would remember nothing of being between worlds.

She and Scorpio huddled close together and looked around bemusedly. The sky looked the same, what they could see of it. The walls of an immense stone structure surrounded them, but of course they had no way of telling what it was built for. Certainly, it was larger than any individual's home needed to be. The many-paned windows, some shining gold where lamps were lit behind them, made the place glitter like a fairy palace. Glass had been a rarity in her world, and never had she seen it used so lavishly. The elegance and beauty impressed her, until she remembered that Clement's gorgeous palace in Avignon had only masked the treachery which sent good men to their deaths for no reason. But this was another world entirely, she told herself. Maybe it would be better.

Before they could become acclimated to this new place, they heard footsteps and turned to see an apparition hurtling toward them. It appeared to be a madman in frowsy robes of rusty black, disheveled hair and beard, and slippers that flapped at every step. Before Leah could attempt to address him and ask where they might be, he had prostrated himself before them on the wet stones.

Scorpio and Leah exchanged looks of puzzlement as the man groveled before them. Leah was beginning to know Scorpio well enough to know how he reacted to new experiences: with utter panic. She saw his eyes bulge and the muscles of his face tense, as if every fiber of his being urged, *Run away! Hide!*

The man lying before them was speaking incoherently. "Welcome Uriel! Welcome Soror Mystica! I, too, am a seeker after truth, a student of the crystal, seeker of light!" If he was out of his mind, he was crazy with joy, Leah thought. Then she realized that he wasn't speaking French and that she could understand most of his individual words, if not his meaning.

"I have long awaited this meeting," he said, rising to brush at the muck on his garment, as if he had just now remembered his dignity. "I did not think it would come so soon."

"He has been waiting for us?" questioned Scorpio in a whisper only Leah could hear. "How did he know we were coming when *we* didn't know?"

"I am Dr. John Dee, Astrologer and Magus to Her Majesty Elizabeth I."

Leah understood his words and recognized the language as English. Scorpio seemed frozen with fear. Leah opened her mouth, closed it again and then spoke.

"This is Scorpio of the Aquay and I'm his companion, Leah. Please, sir, may we go inside? Your climate is most intemperate." Amazingly the English equivalents of her thoughts formed themselves in her mouth. The sound of it was alien to her as the words emerged, but the man seemed to notice nothing amiss.

"Of course. What am I thinking? Angels decide to visit

the planet and I keep them standing out in a drafty courtyard.''

This was all very mysterious. Then Leah remembered
that she had understood Scorpio, too, when he first appeared
to her in Avignon. She recalled that the orb had seemed to
take away her pain when she grieved for her lost family,
and reasoned that the orb must have prepared them for this
destination. Of course, this was a different world, and many
concepts were new to her; occasionally, Dee's words were
only a blur of sound. After she was exposed to the concepts,
Leah supposed, the words would again make sense. She
eyed the disheveled figure that led them toward a huge
carven door and wondered whether it was a good idea to
be entering an unknown dwelling with a madman as guide.
But a welcome after their long journey was more than they
had expected, and they followed willingly.

Leah got a clear impression of elegance as they were led
through one room and into another. Heavy furniture carved
with bizarre patterns. Candelabra of glass reflecting a blaze
of candle flame. She marveled to see a vast, open staircase
with carven banisters; most of the staircases in the dwellings
she had known in Avignon were spiral and enclosed.

Dee caught the look of awe on her face. ''Don't they
have stairs in the celestial realms—'' he began, and then
remembered how they had come here. Of course, those who
flew rarely had need for stairs.

Dee shoved the two of them into a curtained alcove when
a servant with a tray crossed the room. ''Quick, you mustn't
be seen.''

''Do you think it's possible that he knew we were
coming?'' asked Scorpio, finding a voice at last.

''I'm afraid our guide may not be sound of mind,'' Leah
said gently. ''Keep your hood close around your face. It
would probably be best if you did not speak; he had a wild-
eyed look when he first saw you, and the sound of your

voice might make him abandon us altogether. Right now we need him, lunatic or not.''

Dee had been careful that no prying servant would see the two strangers he conducted to his chambers; there was a great deal to do, and he wanted to keep this discovery strictly to himself, at least for a time. Here in the palace, where rumor was second nature, he had little chance of keeping secrets.

Only when he had them safely in his own rooms did Dee breathe deeply again. The two slight figures made for the fire immediately. ''The celestial plane has a climate warmer than that of our Isles, I take it,'' he said, though it shook him a little that angels should seem to cling to the baser comforts.

Still, at least one of them was like nothing that had ever been seen before on this earth. There was something frightening in the wide, bulging eyes above a beaklike protuberance. A monkish robe hid the rest of the creature from view, possibly for the best. The being held in one hand a strange sphere that seemed to radiate its own light. Dee tried not to stare at the sphere, but it drew the eye. Possibly a symbol of power, he thought.

The other looked for all the world like a human woman, with an intelligent brown-eyed face and a shining fall of dark hair that she fluffed dry before the fire. Although, Dee realized, for all he knew, the form these visitors took could be one of their own choosing. Even as he observed her slight, womanly shape limned in damp clothing, he imagined the outlines moving . . . twisting . . . becoming something altogether different.

That made him uncomfortable, so he began to question his visitors again, switching languages, a kind of test. He asked Leah, ''Have you come a long way?''

''It feels like we've come a very long way,'' said Leah,

smiling and looking toward Scorpio, as if for his approval. Her studies with her father had made Latin familiar to her. There was not the same discomfort she felt in speaking a language she didn't think she knew. When he switched over to Greek a few sentences later, she followed him easily.

There was no question, Dee told himself. Only angels could speak all languages at will. He went to his writing table and brought over the page he had been meditating on. "You might wish to know how you were summoned," he said.

Although the female star-dweller glanced at it with interest, she immediately handed it to Scorpio. Evidently, the ugly one was of superior rank. Perhaps the one that looked like a woman was only a celestial interpreter.

"I was meditating upon the topmost *sephirot*, the *kether*."

"Yes, the crown," said Leah. "That's from the Kabbalah. A book written by my people."

"Your people? The angels? Oh, I see, you mean the book was divinely inspired. I've often thought so."

Leah gave him a puzzled look but held her tongue.

"When my mind was fully engaged with the idea of perfection, your craft appeared outside my window. I called you, and you arrived."

This disclosure seemed to excite Scorpio, but Leah motioned for him to remain silent. Dee was certainly learned if he knew the Kabbalah, and with his hair and beard smoothed and the mad light of joy somewhat tempered in his eyes, he didn't seem quite so much like a madman as he first had. But Leah was still suspicious.

"Yes, we have arrived, but, er, astral travel is somewhat disorienting and I am not quite sure where or when we are," said Leah.

"This is England, of course, the realm of Her Royal Highness Elizabeth I, and the year is one thousand five hundred and eighty-two in the year of our Lord." Dee now spoke directly to Scorpio, inclining his head deferentially and mouthing the words in slow motion.

Leah was silent. She had already lost a great deal, but it shook her a little to have her own world and all she'd known relegated so certainly to the dusty past.

"Who is King of France?"

"Henry III is King of France."

"Does the Pope still rule?" she asked, knowing that though Clement would be dead by now, a successor, no doubt, followed in his corrupt footsteps.

"Not in England, my lady," Dee said frostily.

"Thanks be for that," said Leah. "We've had enough of tyranny."

Dee grew even more excited, thinking, My stars, the angels must be Protestants! Her Majesty will be doubly pleased.

"You said Elizabeth I was Queen of your land, but who is King?" asked Leah.

"Why, there's no King; the Queen is our sole ruler, and a great one she is."

Leah stood silently, trying to digest this. She saw nothing wrong with a woman becoming a physician, but a woman in charge of an entire kingdom? It awed her. Somehow she wasn't ready for this idea.

"I've heard that you star-dwellers have all knowledge of the past and future," said Dee. "Can you tell me aught?"

"We can but try," said Leah nervously.

"I have had a vision," said Dee, "of a world-spanning British Empire based on navigation and exploration. I have seen an armada of commerce: gold, spices, silk, jewels. Did I see this truly?"

"This will come to pass," said Leah, smiling behind her hand. The Britain she knew of was a tiny half-island filled with barbarians. To her mind they had as much chance of founding a world empire as men did of . . . walking on the moon. But it didn't seem politic to say so under the circumstances.

"Thank you, thank you," said Dee, bowing so low before Scorpio that he almost scraped the floor.

It hadn't escaped Leah's notice that Dee couldn't keep his eyes off the glowing orb that Scorpio still held. "I see you have an interest in our device," she said. "Do you have knowledge of such things?"

"Most certainly," said Dee. "We have discs and orbs as a means to divine the future, though ours are of polished crystal and yours seems to be of liquid gold." He tried to get as close as possible to peer at the orb in Scorpio's hand, but his nervousness at the strange appearance of this spirit kept him too far away to get a good look.

"Do you know how it works, then?" asked Leah.

"I understand how it works, but it takes a special talent to use it. As it may be with you. My lord"—again he inclined his head to Scorpio—"is in possession of the device and so he must have the talent to use it. I myself have no aptitude for such things, but my assistant communicates with such as yourselves almost daily. Perhaps you know Madimi, or Medicina?"

Leah pretended to search her memory, then shook her head.

"I'll take you to my home at Mortlake to meet my assistant if you wish. It is a quiet place, where no one will disturb us as we confer."

The ugly one seemed beside himself with excitement, yet he still didn't speak. "We would be delighted to go," said Leah. Dee busied himself with making more notes and left the angels to finish drying themselves by the fire. Now I have proof for Her Majesty, he thought. I can present these creatures at court! What a stir we'll make, especially when they see the beaked one with the glowing sphere. The royal coffers will stand open to me. Perhaps the star-dwellers will even let me examine their celestial crystal. The discoveries I'll make! My wildest dreams were only the beginning!

"He said that he called the orb here, with that diagram," said Scorpio excitedly at the fireside.

"But by the way he looks at the orb, he's never seen such an object in his life," said Leah.

"Since we know nothing of how to control the device, can we be so certain that he did not use it to bring us here? The people in this time may have advanced knowledge."

"And I suppose the folk of Avignon were dullards by comparison," said Leah frostily.

A silence built between them. "I meant no offense," said Scorpio.

"I know you didn't," said Leah with a sigh. "I only meant that we don't know enough of these people as yet to know if they can truly help us. Do you remember how this one acted when we first landed? He also called us angels."

"What are angels? Is that something like your *shedim*?"

"Yes. No. In truth, they are opposites. Angels are creatures of goodness and light. Demons are wicked, contentious creatures." She said this last with a direct look at Scorpio.

"Those are only words to describe what you do not understand," he said.

"I'm too weary to argue theology with you now."

"Perhaps the orb has brought me to the very man who can teach me its secrets," continued Scorpio, as if Leah had not spoken at all. "If I don't trust him, I may never find out."

"We should be cautious in our dealings with him, but I don't see anything wrong with accompanying him to his house, for our own purposes. We'll be safe there while we learn more about this time we've traveled to. It does seem . . . somewhat advanced," she added grudgingly, thinking about developments in architecture and about a queen who sat by herself on the throne of a kingdom. ''This must be a kind and gentle time, indeed, if a woman can rule,'' she observed.

Seeing the tray of victuals the servant had left, Leah remembered how hungry she was. Dee idly reached over to it for a drumstick and proceeded to chew away noisily. When he saw her watching, he only continued eating until he chewed the fowl down to the bones and then devoured the pasties until only a few crumbs remained.

Manners have certainly gone out of style in this age, Leah thought. Here we are starving, and he doesn't even offer us a bite.

As it grew late, Scorpio and Leah leaned together sleepily, on a bench before the fire, exhaustion making them forget their quarrels. Scorpio felt hopeful for the first time since he left his own world. Leah mistrusts the man, he thought, but even though he did stare at my differentness, he didn't seem so alarmed as others have. It seemed he *expected* me to be different in some way. And he said his assistant often talked to beings such as myself. Think of it, beings like me! I've almost forgotten what it's like to look into a face that isn't alien.

He felt Leah breathing deeply beside him. She was almost asleep. Responsibility for her hung heavy on his mind. He wished, for her sake, that she had never gotten involved in his search, but he had to admit it would have been a lonely journey without her. This was still her world, and the chances were that somewhere in their travels she would find a suitable place to make a home, and if all went well, he would be going back to Terrapin.

Soon, he hoped. The anxiety that had built up within him was now dying away. He looked down at the orb, lying in a fold of his robe. It did not look as full and glossy as heretofore, but as if it, too, needed rest. It glowed dully, like light inside a leather bladder, the skin grown dry and flaky. Even its magic grows weary, Scorpio told himself as he secreted the orb in a leather pouch he wore attached to his belt. He heard the *scratch-scratch* of Dee's quill over the paper and then nothing at all. He welcomed sleep, knowing that in his dreams he would go home.

Chapter
3

*L*eah stepped down from the carriage with a great deal of relief. Between the rutted roads and the crude springs of the vehicle, she had had a severe shaking. The leather coverings of the windows had also let in the rain and cold wind. Scorpio was looking frightened again, his wide eyes taking in everything, and she moved closer to reassure him, though she had no idea of how his mind really worked. For all she knew he was repelled by her gestures of friendship.

Dee's home was much humbler than the palace, of course, but she liked it. It sprawled in all directions, Dee evidently having built onto it at various times in various styles. The structure reflected dully in the small stagnant lake alongside it, flanked by a few leafless trees.

"We must make haste," said Dee, putting a hand on each of their backs and pushing them forward. "Jane, my wife, loves company, but I didn't quite know how to announce the two of you, so perhaps it is best if she doesn't know, at least for now."

Leah found the interior of the dwelling neat and tidy, if not elegant, the floor softened with a layer of rushes. "Hmm, what's that good smell?" she asked as a scent of roasting meat wafted through the house.

Dee looked at her curiously. "Why, my wife is preparing dinner. She would be upset if she knew we had guests and she was not allowed to offer them our hospitality. She would never understand when I told her our guests were angels and that they had no need for worldly sustenance.''

''No need for—'' Leah could feel her mouth water, remembering how long it had been since her last meal.

''Come. Quickly, or one of the servants will spy you.'' Dee conducted them to a large room with shelves jutting out from every available wall. Leah caught her breath. On the shelves were more books than she had ever hoped to see in a lifetime. She remembered her father carefully guarding his small hoard of volumes like a treasure. How he would gape to see this array!

''I'm, um, something of a collector,'' said Dee modestly, though he moved among his shelves with a sense of pride. ''After Henry VIII declared the country Protestant, I hate to say it but many irreplaceable books in the monasteries were actually burned. I did my best to save what I could.'' He walked along the shelf indicating: ''Aristotle, Plato, Agrippa, Paracelsus, Homer, Vergil—near four thousand, the fourth part of which are written books.''

''I don't understand,'' said Leah. ''This many books. How could this many books be copied? It would take *armies* of monks and scribes.''

Dee smiled and brought down a volume near at hand. Leah marveled at the small uniform characters.

''I imagine you of the celestial plane don't need printing,'' he said, ''since telepathy is no doubt common among you. But it's been a great help in the spread of knowledge among humankind.''

''Then this is not done by the human hand?''

''It is done by a machine called a printing press.''

Leah thought about that a moment. It staggered her imagination. Books that were not one of a kind, copied painstakingly by hand. Knowledge that was there for the taking, for *anyone*. It seemed impossible, outrageous.

Scorpio was entranced by two large, prominently displayed spheres. ''Those are the globes given to me by Mercator,'' Dee explained. ''They are images of the earth.''

''Where are we now?'' asked Scorpio. His thin, bubbling voice startled Dee, who had been treating Scorpio like a visiting potentate who didn't speak the language.

But Scorpio's obvious curiosity made Dee bend over a globe and place his finger on a spot. ''We are . . . here!''

Leah tried to consider the world as a globe. If that were so, then some people were walking upside down, like flies on a ceiling. She snickered. This was too much for her, so as Scorpio and Dee conferred over the globes, she wandered about the room. On a table she saw an amazing array of toys made of metal: a bird in a gilt cage, a knight on horseback, a long-legged mannikin.

''This is another of my hobbies,'' said Dee, catching sight of her interest. He hurried over and touched something and the bird began to flap its wings. Leah caught her breath, so real was the effect, but after a moment one of its wings fell off.

''I have a little trouble with that sometimes,'' said Dee. ''Never mind, watch this.'' The knight on horseback jounced up and down.

''It's wonderful,'' said Leah. ''How can you make them move so? Is it by magic?''

''A kind of magic.'' Dee beamed. ''He's propelled by a clockwork mechanism.'' He showed her where the toy was wound up and placed it on the table. The little man actually walked, putting one foot before the other with an internal clicking sound, as Leah stared.

''Would you like to take one of them back to the celestial realms?''

''Could I?''

''Of course. I can construct more.''

It took Leah some time to decide which toy she wanted.

Finally she chose the mannikin and placed him carefully in the pouch she wore at her belt.

Dee excused himself, leaving them alone. "Imagine it, a room whose walls are lined with knowledge," said Leah. "And toys that move. I'm afraid I've underestimated Dr. Dee. If he's mad, it's a divine madness, and the world would be the better to be infected with it."

"I had the feeling that I came to the right place this time," said Scorpio.

When Dee returned, he brought with him a hulking companion dressed in a doublet of greasy leather, stockings all awry on beefy legs. He had a broad face, a ruddy complexion, and though he combed a tangle of rust-red hair forward to either side of his face, it was immediately apparent that, for whatever reason, he was lacking both ears.

Dee's assistant, Edward Kelley, swaggered into the room, bravado covering a sense of unease. He knew that Dee was often angry with his fits of temper and his scapegrace ways, but his ability as a medium had always kept him his job. Now who were these two interlopers cutting in on his territory? What—one of them a wench! And a comely one at that. But swounds, where did Dee find that other one? That face—ugly as a boggart he was. A freak of nature or—he made a sign to ward off evil—maybe nature had nothing to do with it.

". . . my trusted assistant and a gifted trance medium," Dee was saying, which made Kelley puff out his chest. He looked large enough already, since his doublet, sleeves and trunk hose were stuffed full with bombast. And, as Leah would learn later, so was the wearer himself.

Leah thought that his red-cheeked appearance made him look like a grouse in the mating season. She hadn't enjoyed the look he gave her when he came in. She fancied it was similar to the way she'd drooled over Dee's cold fowl. In the next moment, as her stomach lurched, she wished she hadn't thought of food.

"Our visitors were conducted here by means of a golden crystal," Dee told Kelley. "An orb filled with light."

Kelley looked at the two again. Some sort of cony-catching scheme, he thought, though he had not heard of this one before. He was too smart to believe these two were truly celestial travelers. Scorpio was only a horribly deformed man. But that shape—long, skinny, like an eel. Kelley shuddered. Now that the hood of the robe had fallen back, he saw (and this interested him most) small, irregular holes where the intruder's ears should be. Kelley touched the side of his head without realizing it. Some years ago he'd been put on trial for forgery and had paid the penalty of losing both his ears. It was true that he had done the crime, but he'd done so many worse things for which he'd never been punished that he had a feeling of injustice about this. It did not make him any less attractive to the ladies, he knew, but it made him feel imperfect, all the same.

"I'd certainly like to see this otherworldly crystal—if our visitors are willing," said Kelley to Scorpio.

"I'm afraid the device has lost power because of the long journey," said Scorpio lamely. "Perhaps I will demonstrate it for you later." He didn't trust this man and was glad to keep the orb safely in its pouch. It did interest him to find another being who had no external ears. He had assumed that everyone on this planet had the same ugly swirls of flesh sticking out from the sides of their heads. It seemed to him like a deformity. "I'd be interested in seeing your crystal device," he said.

Dee led them to a small room that abutted the library. It had only one narrow window which let in a shaft of light that fell directly onto a table covered in red silk. With an air of pride, Dee stepped forward to withdraw the silken coverlet. "Here is my magic mirror of cannel coal," said

Dee, "where I have oft contacted the celestial beings." The table was painted in brilliant colors, its sides covered with arcane writing in bright yellow. "Under the feet of the table are seals of wax inscribed with Kabbalistic symbols as protection against evil entities," said Dee. A heavy disc of polished obsidian was placed on another large wax seal on the tabletop. Light from the window fell directly upon it and shimmered mysteriously in its somber depths. Leah had to admit that it was an effective display.

"The angel Uriel instructed me in how to construct the proper setting for my showstone," said Dee. "But I do not know if my assistant is prepared for his tasks." He turned to Kelley.

Kelley knew that according to Dee, magic should only be performed when one was "pure," meaning having abstained from all the pleasurable vices and being clean in body and spirit. Kelley had never abstained from anything in his life, but he had found that regular attempts at hygiene and confident lies usually met with the old stargazer's approval.

"I'm at your lordship's service," he said, seating himself in the sole chair and leaning over the glowing crystal.

Kelley was ambivalent about using the crystal. Although he loved the power over others that he gained when he pretended to go into a trance and prophesy, on many occasions something had happened when he looked directly into the crystal. It was as if he were drawn out of himself, and it scared the hell out of him. Dr. Dee could always find a way to pressure or flatter him into looking into the crystal, and though Dee was always careful to refer to those they contacted as angels, Kelley was not so sure. He had learned to direct his vision toward the tabletop in most cases, rather than into the heart of the crystal; it was safer that way. And anyway, he had so many unsavory secrets in his past that falling into a trance state during which he might confess one of them did not seem a particularly good idea.

By now, Kelley was adept in simulating such a state. After a moment he let his head fall back, eyelids open to show the whites. Polysyllabic sounds began to pour from him, as if he had no control over lips and tongue. To Leah and Scorpio, the noises were pure gibberish.

"He speaks in 'Enochian,'" explained Dee. "But, of course, I don't have to explain that to you. It's your native tongue."

"I, um, understand it well," said Scorpio, pretending to listen carefully. "He is, er, congratulating us on our safe journey."

"And telling us to cooperate with you in every way," added Leah.

At last the charade was over. Kelley began to revive by slow stages, looking about wildly and adding an overdramatic "Where am I?" for good measure.

"They understood you perfectly," said Dee.

"Eh?"

"Every word," said Scorpio. "A very interesting discourse."

Kelley looked at them through narrowed eyes. At that moment a bell rang.

"My wife announces dinner," said Dee.

"Dinner," said Leah in a plaintive echo.

"We would be pleased to join you," said Scorpio. "You see, even though I am obviously of the spirit realm, my traveling companion is like yourselves. And I am also allowed to eat and drink while in my carnal form, although, of course, I do not enjoy it. I go along with it, out of duty." He sighed as if in resignation to the inexplicable customs of mortals.

Leah looked at him sharply. It seemed that Scorpio was learning a great deal from humanity. All the wrong things.

"Of course. Give me a moment to break the news to my wife."

Leah and Scorpio were conducted to the dining hall, where they were treated to the sight of a table laden with all kinds of foods: chickens, rabbit, veal, along with salads and several huge, round loaves of fresh-baked bread. Leah was hungry, but this was ridiculous. There was the little matter of her own dietary taboos, and obviously, everything here hadn't been prepared in what her family would consider a proper way. However, the Jewish religion was nothing if not practical, she thought. One was never expected to actually starve in order to observe dietary laws.

Leah gathered that those at the table made up an extended family, which included some of the Dees' grown children and a few other relatives on either side of the family. There was a great deal of lively conversation and debate. Mistress Dee held forth at the head of the table as if she entertained angels every day of the week (one never knew when married to Dr. Dee). Leah saw her look curiously at Scorpio now and then and wondered how Dee had explained their presence. Scorpio was filling his mouth with roast lamb in sauce with such gusto that Leah had to quietly remind him he wasn't supposed to be enjoying it.

Mistress Dee was a tall, handsome woman, who told them she had once served as a lady of the Privy Chamber. She seemed proud to admit that Elizabeth chose only the most attractive people to attend her. Leah was awed by Mistress Dee's gown of saffron satin, the sleeves encrusted with brightly colored stones. The skirt was immense and by some means made to stand away from her hips. The chair she sat in had no arms, which was a lucky thing or the wide skirt would not have been accommodated. The collar was of several layers of stiff material, plaited to stand out in a wheel-like effect. The fashion made Mistress Dee seem a figure larger than life.

"Your ladyship," said Edward Kelley as he took his place, making a low bow, as if he imagined himself cutting a dashing figure.

Mistress Dee looked at him as if she had seen a toad or other loathsome reptile, then coolly continued her conversation.

Mistress Dee's fine attire made Leah uncomfortable about her own garb. The gown she was wearing was one of her favorites, but travel and rough usage had left it a wrinkled and faded mess. Before long, however, the camaraderie and lively talk made her lose her self-consciousness about her lack of fine clothes.

"In my country, before I left to travel with Scorpio, there was a great fear of sorcery," said Leah to her host some moments later. "Do your occult studies put you in danger?"

"My quest for knowledge has always been misunderstood," said Dee. "Even in my early days. At Trinity I produced Aristophanes' *Pax*, which included the performance of the *scarabaeus* flying up to Jupiter's palace with a man and his basket of victuals on his back. The ancients had many clever devices, and by dint of my studies and my mechanical skills, I made a beetle such as Aristophanes would have been proud of. The wings went like this"—he moved his hands up and down to simulate flight). "Three stout lads hoisted it with ropes and pulleys, cleverly hid. The audience was astounded, and for months afterward there was a great scandal, and rumors were spread that the machine's rising was done by sorcery!"

Leah noticed that Mistress Dee laughed as loudly as the rest, though it seemed obvious that this story wasn't a new one.

Later the candles had burned down and the tone of the

conversation became more serious. Dee began to talk of his antiquarian studies.

"According to the legend, King Arthur did not really die, but awaited the time until a Welshman should ascend the throne," he said. "The Tudor line fulfills this prophesy, and we all consider the Queen the living embodiment of Arthur in our age." Others at the table offered their assent.

"I've heard all the tales of Arthur dismissed as mythical," said Kelley.

"Nonsense. He is well documented as a historical figure. Why, I know for a fact his carcass is buried at Glastonbury, along with those of many other mighty princes. We also know that Arthur made voyages of conquest, to Iceland, Greenland and to Atlantis—"

"The new lands to the west are most commonly called America," said Kelley. "After their discoverer, Amerigo Vespucci."

"This effrontery is uncalled-for at my table, sir," said Mistress Dee sharply.

"Arthur made many voyages and sent colonies thither," continued Dee, "thus establishing his jurisdiction. Through these same conquests, Elizabeth has the right to much of Atlantis, and since other Christian princes do now make conquests upon the heathen people, we must do so as well. History demands it of us. The Queen was very receptive to the documents I presented her proving her right to claim the new lands."

The snubs by Mistress Dee having penetrated even his thick hide, Kelley fell silent and glanced surreptitiously at Leah and Scorpio. If these interlopers are presented at court as celestial travelers, we're likely to be accused of sorcery again, he thought. And the penalty for that is the stake. He touched the side of his head again, without knowing it. Dee has led a sheltered life, him with his wife from the palace with her lah-de-dah airs. She is a beauty, though. And for all her rough talk, I think she could fancy me a little.

Scorpio probably lied about having a powerful crystal; I haven't seen it yet. Maybe I ought to slip into the freak's room in the night and *gkkk*—he made a twisting motion with his hands beneath the tabletop. That would solve the problem. I can think of a better fate for the other one. He snickered to himself. She's a pretty little thing.

But if I go along with Dee, maybe the blame will fall upon him alone. I'm just his humble assistant following orders. If he's locked up in the Tower, that leaves me free to become a famous medium in my own right.

Or if it turns out that Dee is covered with glory, I can always claim it was due to my psychic powers. And after we're all a great success at court, maybe I'll seduce the wench, convince her to run off with me. Too bad I don't have time to pursue it further tonight, but I've got an appointment with de Simier's houseman. A small gift should loosen his tongue about his master. I don't need much, just a few bits of information for use in the séance. The duke will be amazed when I read his mind. A lucky thing people are so stupid. I wouldn't be able to make my way otherwise.

Chapter
4

*A*fter the meal was over, Mistress Dee showed Leah and Scorpio their accommodations for the night: two large, adjoining rooms, each with its own fireplace and lavishly appointed bed. There were no corridors; each room opened onto the next. Leah didn't worry about privacy when she saw that the bed was almost a small, separate bedroom within a bedroom, hangings of heavy golden damask screening it on all sides. Mistress Dee swept the hangings back so Leah could see the richly embroidered coverlet over a thick mattress and plump pillows. It looked inviting to Leah, who was exhausted.

Before leaving, Mistress Dee said, "I could not help seeing that you came without baggage. I wonder if you would like a few things to wear."

"I would appreciate it," said Leah, who thought coming without baggage was something of an understatement, under the circumstances. Mistress Dee led the way to her own chambers and knelt before a trunk. "My sister was about your size. She died last year of the ague."

"I'm sorry."

"Do you want to try this on?" Mistress Dee held out a gown of yellow silk with embroidered flowers of all colors.

"Yes, it's beautiful."

The garments were all quite mysterious, but Mistress Dee explained everything patiently. There were wooden busks to shape the bodice, a partlet to cover neck and shoulders, petticoats, and the farthingale, a skirt with hoops of cane in a cone shape to make it stand out. Leah turned this way and that, admiring how the skirt bloomed around her like the petals of a tulip.

"The farthingale is the latest in fashion. You should see the skirts of those at court, every woman vying to have a grander skirt than the other until they can hardly walk through a room side by side without upsetting the furniture. Of course, Her Majesty must always have the grandest of all. It goes very hard with a lady who tries to outdo the Queen. I've seen her tear a sleeve right off an offending lady's dress."

This sounded strangely petty to Leah, who had imagined Queen Elizabeth as a wise, stately ruler, but she decided she should say nothing about it to Mistress Dee.

"Now these." Mistress Dee handed her two strange-looking wrinkled tubes. She had to indicate Leah's feet and legs before Leah knew what she was supposed to do with them. The stockings slipped onto Leah's legs easily, showing the contours of calf and thigh. "Oh, they feel—"

"Quite sensuous. Possibly even sinful? You must have come from a backward land not to have knitted stockings, my dear. Wait, you must have garters to hold them up. And don't forget shoon." She brought a pair of yellow leather slippers from the trunk.

To complete the costume, Mistress Dee fastened a small set of ruffs edged with lace around her throat and topped it off with a necklace of amber beads.

"Now you can go about in style," she said. "I'm afraid that no amount of finery will disguise your unfortunate friend. Is his deformity an accident of birth?"

"Uh, yes, I'd say so," said Leah, thinking that Scorpio had definitely been born that way. It was a new shock every time Scorpio's appearance was mentioned; since she had grown so close to him, she no longer found him ugly. At first his body had seemed a skinny travesty of the human shape, but once she realized he wasn't human, she gained perspective. Muscles lay along bones in another, not necessarily displeasing way. He could move more easily and flexibly than most human beings, she'd noticed. "Was Mr. Kelley born with his defect?" she asked.

"You mean the defect of being a great rogue and scoundrel?" said Mistress Dee with a laugh. "Oh, no, he's had a number of years to practice that. Oh, if you mean his lack of ears, he got in a scrape for forgery and—" Here she waggled her fingers and made snipping sounds.

"That seems cruel," said Leah. Penalties had been harsh in her own time. Somehow she thought men could have learned by now not to mutilate each other in the name of justice. Her father had explained that the ancient law of "an eye for an eye" was only meant to be a metaphor for equity, not a spelling out of correct punishment.

Mistress Dee looked surprised that anyone would question the penalty. "I'm aware of a few things our Mr. Kelley has done that would earn him a worse punishment, had he been caught. Lucky is what he is. And lucky I'm not the one who carried out the sentence." She snipped with her fingers again. "I wouldn't have stopped with the gentleman's ears!"

Leah and Mistress Dee laughed heartily together.

"But seriously, my dear, I think you should avoid him as much as you can. I don't know how John puts up with him. I've asked him many a time to let the man go, but he says he can't replace him." She sighed. "I'm proud of my husband's accomplishments, but sometimes he undertakes experiments that aren't prudent. As to the truth of what he told me about you and your friend—"

"What did he tell you?"

"That you materialized from a glowing ball of light and

are emissaries from another world. Well, perhaps, and perhaps not, but we have had a pleasant talk, so I will not question.''

By now Leah was nearly dropping off to sleep where she stood. "I'll not keep you up any longer," said Mistress Dee, rummaging in the trunk again. "Here's a rail, a nightdress, and a small bottle of scent." Leah was to discover that both the men and women of fashion in this age drowned themselves in perfumes and colognes, a variety of scents from floral to musk. The sweet smells were usually used to mask the fact that bathing was an infrequent occurrence for most people. However, Avignon had been no rose garden, so this usually did not bother her.

When Leah returned to her room, she tried to walk quietly, thinking Scorpio must be asleep. But she heard voices, and, going to the half-opened door, she saw Scorpio seated before the fire with Dr. Dee, deep in conversation. Her first impulse was to join them. Scorpio had knowledge of a sort, but he was too desperate to solve the mystery of the orb, and altogether too innocent when it came to dealing with humankind. He needed her protection and guidance whether he would admit it or not. Still, all that she had been shown in Dee's study impressed her greatly. Dee was not a charlatan, as she had first feared, but a wise and learned man. The orb was so incomprehensible it would be a sore test of even Dee's knowledge.

All Scorpio had was the hope of someday returning to his own world with the means of saving his people. Seeing the two of them there, so intent on sharing knowledge, she didn't have the heart to interrupt. Even if Dee eventually disappointed Scorpio, it couldn't hurt to let the being have his hopes a little while longer. Not to mention that weariness, caused by all the new sights and sounds and sensations, was lapping over her like a warm tide. It didn't seem to bother Scorpio that much, but such a leap in time as this was exhausting. She silently closed the door.

She had changed to her nightdress and had just pulled back the bedcurtains and was preparing to test the softness of the thick mattress when a silent-footed chambermaid came through the door. The maid was holding a strange, long-handled device, and without a word of explanation pulled back the bedclothes and thrust the device into the bed, pushing it down toward the foot. Leah almost cried out. She had seen faint wisps of smoke coming from the device and feared that the careless servant was about to set the bed afire.

With a curtsy the maid withdrew, and when Leah slipped into the bed, she felt a comforting warmth. Rope supports beneath the mattress cradled her. This world might have its drawbacks, she thought, but the people in it certainly knew how to sleep.

To Dee, Scorpio's voice sounded like the cool splashing of water in a fountain. He was even named for a sign of the zodiac; to an astrologer, that was certainly portentous. It was not like talking to the spirits through a trance medium, though he had reams of notes taken from scrying sessions with Kelley. He felt that if he could understand even half of what the star-traveler told him, he would have such knowledge as no man had had before.

But it was all so curious. Scorpio was trying to explain about an aqueous race that created farms from grasses and plants that grew in water. Hydro. Ponics. He wondered if this were only a retelling of Plato's "Atlantis." There was another race, the Hunters, red-skinned creatures spawned on the deserts of Scorpio's world, who hated the water and those who lived in it. There had been a conflict, though it was one-sided because of the Aquays' natural lack of aggression. The orb, with its magical powers, was contested by both races. Could this be a metaphor for the war between the Sons of Darkness and the Sons of Light? From the being's tale, it certainly seemed as if Darkness had the upper hand. And as above, so below. Lord knew, there were evils aplenty on the earth.

Scorpio listened attentively to Dr. Dee hold forth on his theories of the occult and the things he'd learned from conversations with angels. He seemed wise and beneficent, quite unlike Pope Clement, who had promised much and delivered little. And he had a magic mirror to communicate with other realms, much like Scorpio's own orb. The assistant, Kelley, had seemed to be shamming with his language of gibberish, but perhaps Kelley wanted the black glass for himself and didn't want its full potency known. "It was your powers of concentration that made the orb appear in this time period," said Scorpio. "Please, I need to know how to control it, so I can return home and save my people from the Hunters."

"But I thought you were in charge of the craft and decided to come at my call," said Dee.

"Quite the opposite," said Scorpio. "I know the orb has great powers because I have seen it work, but I have no control over it."

"This is strange," said Dee. "Great magic without a magus. Well, I'm called the Magus of Britain, among other names. Perhaps it was not just chance that brought you here. Perhaps I can help."

The following afternoon Scorpio, Leah and Dee gathered in the doctor's study. Kelley had gone off on a mysterious errand, and Leah was glad. She had not liked his curiosity about the orb, and after what Mistress Dee had told her, she was not of a mind to trust him.

Scorpio untied the thong that held the pouch to his belt and brought out the orb, laying it on a table before them. The rest and darkness must have renewed its energy, for it glowed against the dark wood of the tabletop with a luster that made them all regard it in awed silence. To Leah, it seemed somehow alive. To Dee, it resembled that acme of the alchemist's art, the philosopher's stone. To Scorpio, it was an enigma, and one which he must soon solve, if he wanted to end his exile.

"Perhaps it's only a matter of mind control," said Dee, putting both hands out over the orb. "Rise . . . Rise!" The orb lay quiescent on the tabletop, though Scorpio thought it pulsed a little with what he almost imagined was a kind of laughter of light.

"I had a vision just before you emanated," said Dee at length. "It may be important. It was Elijah's Chariot of Fire."

"I know of this symbol," said Leah. "The *merkabah,* the Throne of Glory. It's a way of approaching God, not in the usual way, by prayer and patience, but directly, through intuition. My father and—uh, we often conversed with the Kabbalists in Provence."

"What were you thinking just before we transported?" Scorpio asked Leah quietly.

She tried to recall. "I had knowledge of the symbol," she admitted. "It may have crossed my mind by accident."

"The chariot symbol," continued Dee, "has been the subject of much debate among scholars, but its true meaning remains veiled in secrecy. I don't have the knowledge, but I do know one man who may know of it. He is a Jew, a Kabbalist most ancient and secretive."

Mention of Jews made Leah feel suddenly guilty. It was true that no one here had asked her if she was a Jew. Earlier she had almost said, "My father and the rabbi often conversed with the Kabbalists," but something had stopped her.

Dr. Dee had simply assumed that she and Scorpio were otherworldly. She hadn't lied or denied her heritage, but she had the feeling she wouldn't have been welcomed here as a guest if she had announced the fact. Knowing something of the endurance of her people, she wasn't really surprised that there were Jews in this time, but she wanted to know more.

"Tell me, what does it mean, 'a Jew'?" she asked.

"Oh . . . well, a kind of religion," said Dr. Dee, who seemed not to have thought much about the source of his own Kabbalistic learning. "Another reason for men to divide and struggle against each other. The Jews were all expelled from England around 1290, I believe."

"If they were expelled, how can they be here now?"

"There has been a slow influx since that time, and Her Majesty doesn't concern herself overmuch with the way a man worships once the doors of his house are closed. There's an occasional flap; rumors of a conspiracy, and then a few of the more prominent Jews are expelled, which quiets everything down again, and the colony continues to grow."

"But we were talking about the Kabbalist who may know something that will help," said Scorpio.

"Yes, his name is Jacob Auerman, and he carries an untranslated and unpublished text from the Book of Enoch in an amulet he wears around his neck. He has refused to reveal its contents to another living soul. Perhaps it holds the key to your mysterious orb. I've never met him, actually, but I'm sure that if I approached him as a fellow mage, he'd be glad to help us."

"When can we see him?" asked Scorpio.

"I suppose it would be possible to undertake such a journey tomorrow, if you like."

Leah began to feel happy, imagining Jacob Auerman as a kindred spirit. They would have a great deal to discuss, she knew, meeting across the years.

Chapter
5

*T*he horses' hooves clopped on the cobbles as Dee's carriage took them into London's Jewish colony. "There are still walls," she said, though these were of wood and not half so sturdy as the walls in Avignon. "Did your Queen cause the walls to be built?"

"There have always been walls, I believe, ever since the colony was established," said Dr. Dee, "but as to who might have ordered their construction . . ." He spread his hands in a helpless gesture. The gate stood open, and there was no gatekeeper to ask their business or collect a toll. Leah hung in a window, watching the scene pass: closely packed houses of wood along a narrow, winding street. In the ghetto of Avignon, land had not been made available for new building, so living space to accommodate the growth of population had been created in the form of precariously perched third and fourth stories. New building looked similar here, though considering the open gate, Leah was not sure whether it was because the colony hadn't been given leave to expand outward or because tradition was just being followed blindly.

The dress and manner of the people in the streets were familiar to Leah, as if these same people might simply have been picked up in Avignon and set down in London. She saw boys yelling and scrapping on their way to the *yeshiva*, prim housewives carrying baskets with produce and meat they had scrupulously inspected according to ancient law, and two elderly men in sidecurls and fringes conferring sagely on a street corner, as if they endlessly debated some commentary of the Talmud. She had been impatient with Grandmère Zarah when she answered every question with, "It's tradition." Yet, someone adrift in time could appreciate customs that had stayed the same for thousands of years.

Nothing changes here, she thought, and was amazed to think that with her background she could probably create an identity and blend in, despite the fact that she came from one hundred years in the past. For a few moments it was tempting to contemplate such an idea.

At last the carriage drew up before a narrow house of darkly weathered wood that looked as if it creaked and groaned as it jostled for position among all the newer structures around it. A withered serving woman opened the door and looked sharply at the three, her gaze pausing at Scorpio. She gave a faint gasp.

Dee introduced himself and asked to see Jacob Auerman. The woman withdrew, only to return a moment later to say, "He will see you in his study. This way, please."

Auerman's study was not nearly as impressive as Dee's, but the room exuded an atmosphere of great age, with its smells of moldering paper and dust, darkened wood paneling and furniture of ancient design. A collection of human skulls in a glass case had evidently not been cleaned off for some time, if spiderwebs and the remains of desiccated insects were any indication. For that matter, the man himself seemed unimaginably old as he hobbled about the room leaning on a gnarled walking stick. His posture was stooped, and when he looked up, it reminded Leah of a tortoise peering out of a shell. He had the same tight slash of mouth and tiny, squinted eyes.

Auerman peered up at the three of them. He had heard

of John Dee and had read Foxe's depiction of him as the Great Conjuror, but his own idea was that Dee was rather a Great Charlatan, using magic for his own political ends rather than in a pure quest for knowledge. The other one—his eyes were drawn to Scorpio's face, since he could see little else in the enveloping garment, though there was also something frighteningly wrong with the shape of his body—this one gave him a chill. It looked for all the world as if God had made a serpent walk upright again as in elder times. He avoided looking into those hypnotic eyes, and his hand sought the amulet around his neck for comfort. The third one was ordinary enough, a dark-haired young woman in the scandalous garb of the times. A woman should be modest enough to keep her place at home with father or husband, not be traveling about with a court-appointed dabbler and this . . . monster, he thought.

"Good day, Grandfather," said Leah politely in Hebrew. Surprised at Leah's greeting, Auerman answered her and drew her out, to see if she was like the talking birds they'd brought from the New World. They, too, could learn a few phrases, but that did not mean there was a brain in their heads. He discovered that she could speak Hebrew as well as himself, although her syntax was of an antique variety, as if someone had taught her the language from old books.

As Dee began to tell his story about how two angels had appeared to him from a shining craft, Auerman saw Leah lingering near his desk, her eyes on a parchment. She seemed almost to be reading it, though he knew that was impossible, since girls were never taught to read.

He moved it closer to her. "Can you tell me what it says?" he said challengingly.

With horror he listened to her read it aloud and then look up as if for his approval. He considered this outrageous. Studies for women would destroy the social fabric, create freaks who belonged nowhere. He pulled the paper back so quickly it tore. "There, look what you have done," he said. Though she had done nothing, Leah felt humiliated. Dee looked peeved that his story had been interrupted.

"But what is it you want of me?" asked Auerman, wishing the interview were over.

"The *merkabah* symbol may be the key to controlling the shining orb-craft, which resembles a fiery chariot," said Dee, "but we must know more about it. You are the only one who has such knowledge."

"Yes, many have come in quest of my secret," said Auerman, "but you vain, shallow seekers after personal gain always go away again empty-handed. Your tale of angels is ridiculous. You are a credulous dilettante, sir. Not only do you use magic for your own political gain, but in your misguided experiments in the occult you play with fire. I would not be surprised to see you burned."

"But what is the point of wisdom, if not to teach it to others?" asked Leah.

Auerman averted his gaze as if he had not heard her. A woman debating matters with men was simply unthinkable.

"The Kabbalah is not for amateurs. The paths to the Secret Garden are fraught with peril. From the darkness of the mind strange creatures materialize: the *chayot*, vibrating living beings composed of pure energy, and the wheel-shaped *ofanim*. A man can go mad from the visions. Certainly, such studies are not meant to entertain the Queen on an otherwise dull day. I'm afraid I must declare this interview at an end."

Disappointedly, the three turned to go. Upon seeing Dee's crestfallen face, Auerman felt a twinge of remorse. "I understand your thirst for knowledge, Doctor, but you cannot divide your forces between what is right and what is expedient. A true Seeker follows the narrow path and eschews fame and fortune. It can be no other way."

• • •

In the carriage on the dispirited return trip, Leah said, "I'm sure he has the key to our problem. What can we do?"

"We must prove our sincerity," said Scorpio. "I am sure if he knew that my purpose was to save my people from destruction, he would be more willing to help."

"Even if you told him, I doubt you would be believed," said Leah. "His mind seemed closed, except to what is in his dusty old books."

"Perhaps we could bribe him," said Dee.

"We came here empty-handed," said Scorpio. "And even if we had something your kind would consider valuable, it would not help. You heard him say that magic should not be done to gain fame and fortune."

"We could always beg," said Dee ironically. "Or ask to borrow it."

"Or steal it!" added Leah, surprised to hear the words come from her lips. Even if she were so inclined, she realized she would have little idea of how to go about it. If she did know how, she wouldn't hesitate. It seemed unfair. He had heard her speak Hebrew, and rather than embrace her as one of his own, he had simply snapped his tortoise mouth shut and acted as if she didn't exist.

"You don't know how it was on Terrapin when we had to live as fugitives, in our underwater hiding places," said Scorpio. "The children could no longer frolic amid the waterweeds. We dared not laugh or speak or make sudden movements. A living death. My people are still living it, even though I escaped. I dream of the danger sometimes: dark, menacing shapes casting shadows on the water. The fear. I wake up with my heart pounding and tell myself I am safe. But I still feel the fear because I know the Aquay feel it. The Hunters will hound my people until not one remains. It's not even malicious, just their way. I thought

I could do something to help, but now I begin to wonder. It may already be too late."

"With the orb there is no such thing as too late," said Leah. "We know what wonders it is capable of. We simply have to find a way to use it."

That night, Leah paced before the glow of embers in her fireplace. Earlier, when she had looked into the next room, she had seen that the bedcurtains were drawn and supposed that Scorpio must be peacefully asleep by now. However, she was too angry to sleep, remembering how Jacob Auerman had rebuffed them. He had had no respect for her scholarly achievements; he acted as if she were some outlander, with strange ways, rather than one of his own. She racked her brain to think of something she could tell him that would make him give up his secret, but she was unable to come up with anything.

The house was silent at this late hour except for the whistle of the wind along the eaves. A noise made her pause to listen. It sounded like stealthy footsteps in the next room. A board creaked and the footsteps stopped. If Scorpio was abroad, why should his steps sound stealthy? She opened the door very slowly and peered into the darkness. The banked fire in Scorpio's hearth gave a faint light, and she could make out a bulky shape moving about the room. Shadow made it look even larger and more threatening, and she had only one thought—Hunters! How did they follow us here? she wondered.

But as she watched, she saw with some relief that the shape was human, at least, and as it crept about the room, searching, she thought she might have an idea of who it was. In fact, it could be only one person in this household. She decided she'd wait and see what his intentions were.

The intruder moved along the side of the bed and at last seemed to find what he was seeking: Scorpio's garment with the pouch still tied to the belt. The thief fumbled and the orb spilled from the pouch to bounce onto the floor in a pool of golden radiance.

As the figure leaned down as if to retrieve it, in the witchlight of the orb Leah recognized Kelley's face. Just who she thought it was. He stood there half crouched, as if entranced by the orb's glow but afraid to grasp it.

While he stood transfixed, Leah walked up behind him and laid a hand on his arm. The effect was startling. The man nearly jumped out of his skin.

"I—you—he—" Kelley got out in a stuttering gasp, but seemed incapable of saying more.

"Don't be alarmed," said Leah. "I was only . . . admiring the way you crept in here so stealthily."

"That thing—that thing that glows. What is it?"

Leah picked up the orb and quickly put it back in its pouch, throwing the room into darkness. Kelley's presence was more threatening now. There was no movement from the bed; Scorpio must still be asleep. She spoke quickly to cover her nervousness.

"There must be an art to stealing. To creep in past all barriers and bear away the treasure. It seems so exciting. It is a talent I've often wished I could cultivate."

Kelley was silent a few moments as if he were trying to figure out whether she was speaking truthfully or just playing with him before turning him in. At last his ego won out. "Well, most of it just comes naturally to me," he said. "Been practicing this particular art since I was a boy. But I know that everybody doesn't have such a talent. There's a place to learn it, if you're really of a mind."

"Could you tell me about it?"

"It's a place run by an old friend of mine, Lord Foistwell by name. I could set you up there, easy. It's a school, kind of. A school for thieves."

Chapter
6

Scorpio was silent as Leah packed her few belongings into a valise Mistress Dee had loaned her, but it was a silence filled with unspoken questions. She tried not to consider how vulnerable she would feel when she was truly on her own in this strange world.

"I'll be back soon, after all," she said finally when the silence had grown too uncomfortable to bear.

"But you haven't told me anything of your plans. Is it because you don't trust me to keep them secret?"

"Of course not," said Leah. She hadn't told Scorpio her plan because if he heard she was going to go among thieves and scoundrels for his sake, he might try to put a stop to it. Or so she told herself. "There may be a means by which I can discover the secret that Jacob Auerman is hiding in his amulet, but this is something I have to do alone."

"But if there is danger—"

"We took risks when we solved the mystery of the cardinal's murder in Avignon, and if you'll remember, I did my share."

"That was different. You were in your own time then. You knew what to expect. You wouldn't be here if it weren't for me, and—"

"I asked to go along."

"On impulse. How could you know what you were leaving behind?"

"I left nothing. Everyone I cared about was dead. Including myself." Leah paused. She had spoken sharply, causing Scorpio to fall silent. "You aren't to blame for that," she continued more gently. "If I belong anywhere, I belong here and now. And you will simply have to trust me."

"I suppose I can do nothing else, for now."

"While I'm gone, keep a wary eye on Edward Kelley. I think it would be a good idea to find a hiding place for the orb. Kelley has been itching to lay hands on it."

Scorpio didn't look any happier, but he seemed resigned, so she took her leave. Mistress Dee and Edward Kelley were waiting downstairs, sitting opposite each other and looking daggers, as if they'd been doing this for some time.

"I hate for you to go so soon," Mistress Dee told Leah.

"I have no wish to leave your hospitality," said Leah, embracing the woman, "but my Master Scorpio has bid me to see and study your city of London and its inhabitants. Looking as he does, he's loath to mingle with folk, so he is sending me."

As a parting gift, Mistress Dee gave Leah a small purse of perfumed leather with a few coins in it.

"I put her in your protection," said Mistress Dee sternly to Kelley, as if insinuating that things would go badly for him if he broke this trust.

"Madam, it is not a duty I take lightly," he said with a clumsy bow. "She is in the best of hands." He smiled at Leah in a proprietary way that made her skin crawl. Despite her earlier bravado, she began to wonder about the wisdom of going off on her own among rogues and scoundrels, but if there had ever been a time to call a halt to her plans, that time had passed.

As the Dees' carriage set off down the road on a cool yet brightly sunlit morning, Leah's mood lightened. The day seemed bursting with a feeling of adventure and discovery.

The only thing that threatened to spoil it was Kelley's presence. He kept trying to catch her eye, so that he could smile fatuously. He obviously thought she was charmed.

"Since we've been given the use of the carriage for the day, I'll be glad to show you a bit of London before we go to Lord Foistwell's school," he said..

Leah was glad of the chance, though she would have chosen other company.

Leah was amazed, as they approached the city, at how the volume of traffic swelled. She had never seen so many carriages, drays, carts and litters all fighting for space in narrow streets that had evidently not been designed for such a crush. Those on foot added to the confusion, but of necessity gave way to the vehicles. Avignon's streets had been narrow, too, she remembered, but only on market day and during the fairs was there such a volume of traffic as this. She noticed stone uprights erected before many of the buildings, and Kelley told her they were there so that the jostling of wheeled vehicles didn't destroy the houses.

Many of the houses had a striking black-and-white appearance. The framework was made of upright timbers strengthened by horizontal and sloping beams, the interstices filled in with lath and plaster. Each story bellied out over the one below it, causing the narrow streets to be gloomy, even by day. There was a great deal of filth and offal splattered on the cobbles, which made her believe that slops were emptied from stories above. A drainage channel of sorts ran down the middle of the roadway. She reminded herself to watch carefully should she have to walk along any of these thoroughfares. She saw a man shoveling dung into a small handcart, and Kelley told her there were several of these "scavengers" hired to clean the streets. Evidently, there were not enough of them to make a great difference.

Shops were often on the street-level floors of the houses

and consisted of a shutter which let down to a counter. Signs hanging above denoted the trade, usually a guild symbol or other pictograph, identifying the shops for those who could not read. Leah noticed that a great many of the same types of businesses would cluster on one street. Kelley told her that it was only sound business. A customer could then look over the wares of a variety of goldsmiths, for example. With many shops to choose from, one wasn't likely to go farther afield to buy. He said that this usage had caused the naming of various streets, such as the Poultry and Grocer's Court.

What struck her most was the variety and quantity of goods for sale. And the merchants and peddlers, not content to let the passersby simply look at the goods, plied their trade by means of their voices. "Mistress, would ye have any fair linen cloth? I will show you the fairest linen cloth in London."

"Hot apple pies and hot mutton pies, fresh herrings, fine potatoes."

"Swepe chimney swepe, mistress, with a hey derry swepe from the bottom to the top."

"Ha' ya any corns on your feet or toes?"

The messages, shouted or sung in a variety of voices from musical to rasping, made the streets echo with an unending cacophony.

At the heart of this city of bustling commerce, Leah discovered, was the River Thames. She was fascinated by its dark expanse, the wharves on which jutted the stark silhouettes of cranes, awaiting the loading and unloading of ships. Small, brightly decorated craft called wherries were everywhere. She saw people on the wharves shouting, "Westward ho" or "Eastward ho", and Kelley explained that considering the condition of the streets, many Londoners preferred to do their journeying by boat, and by their shouts, they hailed a boatman going in the desired direction. He said that some liked to ride the wherries as a diversion.

She thought that sounded exciting, but didn't say so, since the prospect of being alone on a boat with Kelley was not appealing.

The river was spanned by a single bridge, supported by stout arches and enclosed on either side by rows of splendid houses and shops and roofed above. The actual roadway was a narrow one. About midway across, Leah saw a gatehouse tower which guarded a drawbridge. Atop this tower was a series of metal spikes, each topped with something round. To her disgust, she saw that they were human heads, in various stages of decomposition, all the way from fresh to shriveled leather and a hank of hair on a skull.

"What's the purpose of those," she said with disgust.

"Why, those are the heads of criminals," Kelley answered as his hand went protectively to where his right ear had been. He didn't seem aware of the gesture. "Displaying the heads is a good object lesson to those considering a life of crime, of course," he said. "Everyone knows that."

Leah did know. In Avignon the authorities had often done something of the same sort; only she had expected more of this time. "Does the Queen know this is done?" she asked.

Kelley laughed. "It's done by her law, so I hardly think she can be ignorant of the process."

"But she's a woman."

Kelley shrugged. "I suppose so. But she's also the Queen." That seemed to settle it for him, though it made Leah uneasy. Taking a person's life was an awful responsibility. She had never thought about it before, but in her own role as a physician, she might be called in on a case where a life hung in the balance. The lives of the women she'd known suddenly seemed terribly safe. No wonder many were content in it.

The carriage rolled on, and they approached an immense structure, built in a series of arches, ornamented with airy turrets, every line so obviously pointing toward the heavens that she half expected it to take flight for all its size. "That's St. Paul's Cathedral," said Kelley. "It was a deal grander than this, but the steeple caught fire and burned some years ago and it was never replaced."

Are we going to attend a service? she thought with a certain amount of alarm, surprised that Kelley should think of such a thing. She wondered what excuse she could give.

As they came nearer, Leah saw that along one wall, boys with catapults were trying their luck at the pigeons that flew about the ancient building. Quite a few people were coming and going from the cathedral, and they didn't seem to have piety on their minds. She was surprised to see that some tradesmen had even set up temporary stalls in the churchyard and were selling their wares. In spite of her shock, she was fascinated by the products on display, because most of them were books and pamphlets. It had been astonishing to see so many books in Dr. Dee's study, but she had accepted that because they were all in the charge of a learned man, but to have knowledge laid out on a counter for any passerby with a few pennies in his pocket—

A wizened little man approached Kelley and Leah. "Would the lady enjoy the ballad of the hanging of the notorious highwayman Tom Howe?" He brandished a sheet of paper.

"The lady would not enjoy hearing that," protested Leah. But the balladeer continued to push the paper at her, until Kelley stepped toward him. Immediately, the little man scuttled away.

She didn't feel insulted for herself, but felt that all the reverence her father had had for the written word was somehow debased by a writing on such a vulgar subject as the hanging of a thief. She wondered if this was what happened when writing and printing became available to all.

As they entered the cathedral, all about them, fashionable gentlemen and bold-eyed courtesans paraded in the latest

fashions. Prosperous merchants in long robes trimmed with
fur conferred gravely. Young apprentices scuffled, snatching each other's hats. Others exchanged jests and anecdotes.

"I thought you called this a cathedral," said Leah.

Kelley laughed. "Oh, I don't think of St. Paul's as a
church," he said. "It's more of a meeting place. It's where
half the business deals of the city are made, and if you want
a job, just wait at a certain spot and pretty soon a prospective
employer will come by to look over the crop. Down on
your luck and can't afford to eat? Wait at the tomb of Duke
Humphrey and before long an old friend will come by and,
seeing you there, will extend an invitation to dine. It's also
a shortcut for porters carrying casks of beer and loads of
fish and vegetables between Carter Lane and Paternoster
Row.

"And in the evening a different sort of enterprise will be
going on, if you get my meaning," added Kelley with a
wink.

After a time the carriage drove alongside a crumbling
stone wall that looked out of place in the modern city. Kelley
told her that the Romans had built it centuries ago, and
though it hemmed in the city on three sides, London was
burgeoning, and new growth was spilling outside the walls.
Leah watched it dwindle with distance, feeling a little, herself, like an antiquated object that the events of time were
overwhelming.

The carriage driver shouted down that his horses were
tiring and that it was time to put an end to the tour. They
entered a street even narrower and filthier than any Leah
had seen before, and the carriage stopped beneath a sign
that bore, in flaking paint, the emblem of the Glove and
Falcon.

Kelley helped Leah to alight and escorted her to the alehouse as the carriage, a tenuous link with the respectable

world, clopped on down the street and was lost behind a row of houses.

The place was nearly deserted, with only a few men sitting crouched over trestle tables, nursing their drinks. In contrast to the sleek, well-dressed merchants and gentlefolk Leah had seen earlier, these men had a gaunt, hungry look, and their garments were much worn and patched. They looked up, eyes glittering, when Leah entered, but quickly minded their own business again when they saw Kelley. It was strange, she thought; in the Dees' dining hall he was an overbearing oaf, yet on the streets of London and in this dingy tavern he took on a whole new personality, knowledgeable and subtly tinged with menace. She didn't like this personality, either, however.

"Call your master," he said to the tavernkeeper, a cadaverous man with pockmarked cheeks, hardly the sort to promote happy camaraderie.

The tavernkeeper disappeared, and after a few moments another man appeared, small, swarthy and narrow-faced, yet tricked out in the garments of a gentleman of fashion. Lace dripped from his cuffs, and he wore a black narrow-brimmed hat with a pleated crown and a hip-length cloak of yellow leather. The oddest thing about him was that he sucked on an artifact of clay, and smoke poured from his nose and mouth. Leah saw that the bowl of the device was full of tiny live coals.

"This is my great friend Lord Foistwell," said Kelley.

"You must have brought me one fresh from the countryside," said Foist. "The way she stares, I don't think she's ever seen anyone indulging in tobacco before. One of the more useful discoveries of the New World. Hello, my dear. Edward tells me you're interested in learning 'the trade' from an expert."

Leah was overwhelmed for a moment by the smell of the

tobacco lingering on Lord Foist's breath, mingling with the strong musk scent of his perfume.

"Don't let her fool you," said Kelley. "She's a sharp one. She and her partner are running a fine game on Dr. Dee."

"I don't suppose that's so hard to do, is it?" asked Foist. "You've been doing the same thing for years." The two men laughed.

"You'll have to follow my rules here, girl," said Foist. "You'll work in my tavern on your off hours to help pay for your keep, and work till you drop in practice. I claim everything you bring back while you're under my roof, but when you go, you'll take away a skill that'll keep you in clover for the rest of your days. Not such a bad bargain, eh?"

"I do want to learn," said Leah, finding her voice. "And I don't mind working."

"That's my girl," said Kelley. "I've business of my own to tend to, so I'll be going, but I'll be back to check up on you after a few days. Think you can wait till then?" He chucked her under the chin familiarly.

"I think I can," said Leah. "Barely." She forced herself to smile up at him, and he went away, whistling to himself.

Leah was given a plate of bread crusts soaked in broth and shown to a dark, dank attic room, where one of the straw pallets was hers. She got as comfortable as possible, weary from all her travels. In the street below her, London's voices began to die away, and the rumble of rolling wheels grew faint. Somewhere in the street below she heard the voice of a watchman. "Ten o' the clock, look well to your lock, your fire and light, and so good night."

When she slept, she dreamed she was a little girl again in Avignon. It was the eve before the Passover Seder and she and her father were searching the house by candlelight for any trace of leaven, so that it could be burned before the festival began. Of course, they always found some, since Grandmère Zarah hid it, just for this purpose. A meticulous housekeeper, Zarah had always removed all traces of leaven from the house well before Passover, but Leah enjoyed this small ritual. The following day, at the Seder, the tale of how Moses led his people out of slavery in Egypt would be told, in dramatic form, with much festivity, and *matzoh*, unleavened bread, would be eaten, to remind them of the hardships of the long passage. But in her dream, as they searched, Scorpio took the place of her father, and she knew they were looking for the orb, but though they searched carefully in all of Grandmère Zarah's usual hiding places, nothing was found. The dream ended with the sight of Zarah's hands, age-spotted and arthritic, patting out the flat cakes of *matzoh*. Her voice was cold and toneless as she spoke. "The bread of freedom is a hard bread."

Chapter 7

*T*he next morning Leah was awakened by a loud knocking on the door. For a moment she didn't remember where she was, or more important, *when* she was. She expected Grandmère Zarah to come into her room to wake her up. What had she been saying? Then she heard muffled curses very near and saw the low-slanted bare beams of her garret bedroom, dust motes dancing in the beams of light through a many-paned window hazed with grime. The three others who shared her room were wriggling and stretching beneath the coverlets of their floor pallets like insects trying to break free of cocoons. Then one by one they all emerged, looking weary and dazed, lank, uncombed hair hanging about their shoulders.

Leah rubbed her eyes, realizing that being at home in Avignon again was only a dream, but that what Zarah had said about the bread of freedom seemed quite true at this moment. She had never been more free, or felt more lonely. Her roommates were girls her age or younger, apprentices in the thieves' school and part-time tavern wenches. Hard lives showed in faces weathered close to the bone and in sharp, darting eyes. They ignored Leah, the stranger among them, as they chaffed each other in rough language.

After a breakfast scarcely better than the supper she'd had the night before, Leah and the other girls were directed to the large storeroom behind the tavern. Several boys

waited there, and they made rude comments as the girls
entered, some of which were answered in kind.

"None of that now," said Lord Foistwell as he entered
the room. The young people immediately grew quiet, sen-
sing an underlying menace in the man. He said everything
in a monotone and rarely raised his voice, yet they were
deferential to him, always calling him "Lord" Foistwell,
at least to his face, though obviously he was not lord of
anything, unless it be lord of pickpockets.

"You're here to learn, and you'll do well to keep your
eyes open and your mouths shut. It's a good rule on the
streets as well. You'll live longer that way. Here are your
teachers, Roger and Darby." Leah almost laughed as two
ragged and dirty little boys with unkempt manes of tow-
colored hair came in to stand beside him. Soot streaked their
cheeks and forehead so thickly that she wished for a cloth
to wash their faces clean. The tallest of them scarcely
reached to Lord Foistwell's waist, and the other kept wiping
a runny nose with his sleeve. Teachers indeed, thought
Leah. The elder can be no more than eight.

Some of her fellow students hooted aloud their derision
at considering as their teachers boys so much younger than
they were. "They're too little to even wash their own
faces," cried Joan, a tall, rawboned girl with coppery red
hair.

Lord Foist turned his cold eyes on her until she looked
uncomfortable and fell silent, and then said, "The look of
innocence is a great advantage to a thief, and who is more
innocent than a little child? Also, a few smears of soot
might sometimes keep a mark from identifying you afterward. It's a disguise that's always available. Now shut up
and watch this demonstration. When it's at an end, we'll
see if you can do as well."

As Leah watched, a man she recognized as the tavernkeeper sauntered across the room. A moment later she saw

Darby, approaching from the opposite direction and moving very quickly. The little boy slammed into the tavernkeeper as if by accident. Hardly had they collided when Roger came at him from behind and, with a movement so deft Leah didn't catch it, used a small knife or razor to cut through the strings holding the man's purse to his belt. This done, he veered away and was gone before the man could discover what was missing. Darby had also taken to his heels, so there was no culprit left to catch.

"There, think you can master that? I'll divide you off into threes and you can practice. Roger and Darby here will watch and give you some pointers."

Leah took the role of feinter on their first try, but it wasn't as easy as it looked to hit a walking target. Her first try missed, and she fell among empty wine casks with a bone-jarring thump. "Come now, try that again," said Roger with the insufferable tone of the expert, as she struggled to rise. Angry, she tried again and hit her target this time, though success only gave her new bruises to add to old. "Well done," proclaimed Roger, and she was even angrier at herself for being pleased by his praise.

"You must have begun your training at a young age to be such a proficient cutpurse," she said.

"I'm a quick study; that's what my mum says. I see a purse and 'snick-snack.'" He held up his knife and made a snipping motion.

"What's that on your thumb? Can I see it?" Leah examined the stiff thimblelike device as he held up his hand. The sharp blade of the knife and this thumb guard made quick work of any purse-fastening.

"They call me a knight of the horn thumb," said Roger.

After a time Lord Foist called the practice to a halt and introduced them to another of their teachers, a large woman with disheveled blond hair and red-rimmed watery blue eyes. She wore a loose, flowing gown of coarse weave, and nothing much beneath, from the way the fabric clung to generous breasts and thighs. Her name was Eleanor Waterby, or Ellie, as she was called. "My mum," said both Roger and Darby.

Leah discovered later that she was a prostitute as well as a free-lance fence and feinter. Ample flesh was here the mark of the harlot, since it was said that the greater the success she had, the more double chins she displayed.

"That's enough of purse-cutting for now," said Lord Foist. "It's obvious you've all got a great deal to learn. Let's do the lightfingers for a while." Roger and Darby grinned. The lightfingers consisted of attempting to lift a stickpin from the clothing of a partner who held a cane. Whenever a touch was felt, the cane was brought down smartly on the student's hand. Leah cradled her aching hand, thinking that if all the drills were so painful, she'd be glad to consider a life of honesty.

After that first day Leah fell into the routine. Practice sessions alternated with serving ale in the tavern.

Not all practice was conducted in the musty tavern storeroom. One day Lord Foist sent Leah out with Ellie and the boys to "spy out" a neighborhood.

"What does he mean, 'spy out'?" asked Leah.

"Lord Foist maintains that a thief's greatest advantage is to know the terrain," Ellie answered. "If you know every possible hiding place, no matter how unlikely, you can disappear when the law gets on your trail. It's also a good idea to know any places where they might try to trap you, like dead-end streets or blind alleys." She stopped to separate Roger and Darby, who were having a noisy argument that was just coming to blows.

"I suppose that makes sense," said Leah.

"And, of course, it's useful to know just what might be

available in the area, and not too well guarded, as well as what sort of people might pass through and what sort of pickings you can expect from them. Oh, there's a great deal to be learned by exploring every nook and cranny of an area.''

Leah took the importance of this activity on faith, though it didn't sound terribly interesting. Not the sort of glamour in this I thought, she told herself.

The neighborhood they chose was one of dilapidated houses and nearly deserted streets. It seemed as though the city's vitality had moved off in other directions, leaving this one corner forgotten. The filth of the streets was even worse here, as if the scavenger carts gave it a wide berth.

When Ellie suggested she explore a dank, stinking alley, she went forward cautiously, hearing noises inside. When she was partway in, she was confronted by a huge, grizzled rat the size of a small cat. The rat held its ground and stared at her as she stood there, trembling. Finally, she was the one to turn and run.

Roger was laughing at her. ''An old King Rat,'' he chuckled. ''Gets 'em every time.''

Leah was distracted by the people of this place. They were scrawny and pale, and only looked at her sidelong as she passed. She saw a half-clad child in a doorway, eyes enormous in a skull-like face, every rib distinct beneath bluish skin. She saw an old woman scavenging for a morsel of food among the debris of the street. When she rushed over to her and put a coin in her hand, the woman only looked at her dumbly, as if she couldn't conceive of anything so bizarre as an act of kindness.

''What did you go and do that for?'' asked Ellie. ''It'll only encourage more begging. Whenever there's a bad year in the countryside, armies of beggars flood into the city.''

''Then there are other neighborhoods like this, other poor people?''

"Common as dirt in London. I suppose where you come from everyone was rich."

Leah was silent. She knew there were poor in Avignon. But she had the feeling the poverty here was worse, possibly because she knew of the great bounty that existed elsewhere. "I thought, perhaps with the growth of business and trade, that there wouldn't be so many places like this."

"The poor are with us always," said Ellie, which seemed as far as she could go toward explaining the problem. Taking a pewter flask from where it nestled in her ample bosom, she took a healthy swig. She offered Leah a swallow, but it was declined.

"I don't know why you brought me here. There can't be anything left to steal."

"There's always something to steal," said Roger matter-of-factly. "Mark of a good thief."

"Even if we don't find anything," said Ellie, "we usually take beginners to places the law doesn't much care about. It's safer that way. You're not ready to take on the Keepers of the Queen's Peace just yet."

Leah sat on a wine keg in the practice room watching Joan attempt to reach into a pocket strung upon a cord. Little bells were fastened to the pocket's top. Inside were some coins, and the thief that could take out a coin without any noise was declared a "public foister." Alongside it was a purse, strung from the same cord. Anyone who could take a piece of silver out of it without ringing the bells was called a "judicial nipper." Joan moved her hand carefully, but the jingle of bells spoiled her attempt and she turned away, smothering a curse. Leah got down from the keg and went to the pocket. Hours of practice and a steady hand allowed her to reach carefully into the pocket. No bells rang. Smiling, she opened her hand and showed the coin.

"Don't gloat, my girl," said Joan. "Practice in a back

room ain't nothing like trying your luck on the streets.''

Leah sighed. ''I begin to think we'll never get a chance to put any of this to use. Perhaps Lord Foist just uses this thieves' school as a blind. All he really wants is unpaid labor in his tavern.'' She was beginning to feel that the cleverness of London thieves was vastly overrated. She had learned to do these things so quickly; there was nothing to it.

Impatient to try her hand in the real world, she asked Ellie when she'd be allowed to do her first job. She would have asked Lord Foist, but his personality was so chillingly forbidding that few students asked him anything.

''Are you sure you're ready?'' asked Ellie. ''You've been here only a fortnight. Hardly long enough to become a seasoned thief.''

''The exercises are so boring, the same thing over and over.''

''True, but considering the penalties if one is caught, it's best to be well practiced.''

Leah remembered that Kelley's ears had been forfeit for his crime of forgery. She had also heard of thieves who'd had their hands lopped off. This was done because everyone knew such a punishment would keep the culprit from stealing again. However, Leah had heard about the punishment from a successful one-handed thief she'd talked to at the Glove and Falcon. Still, Ellie had a point. If failure led to such dire punishment, it would be best to be fully prepared. But she knew she was ready now, so she persevered in asking. After all, she couldn't help Scorpio if she was buried in an alehouse forever.

Several days later Ellie came by as Leah was just getting off duty at the tavern.

''I know you're a stranger to London, dear. Maybe you'd

like to get away a bit, see some sights and have some fun for a change."

"I'd like that," said Leah, who had the feeling that Ellie was tired of her appeals to be given a chance to show what she had learned and was only finding another way to put her off. "But wouldn't Lord Foistwell object?"

"Oh, no, it's something his lordship would approve of. I can show you how easy the pickin's are where people congregate."

The four of them, Ellie, Leah, Roger and Darby, set out in a festive mood for the Bear Garden. That was what they called it. Leah knew what bears were, and what gardens were, but put them together, and she had no idea what she might see.

Roger and Darby gamboled on ahead of them, children again, their voices raised in some ongoing sibling argument, and Ellie walked quite briskly for her weight. It was a fine day, and Leah was glad to be away from the dirty tavern and the threatening presence of Lord Foistwell.

Whatever the Bear Garden was, it was located on the south bank of the river in an area more or less remote from the city proper. They left the close-clustering behind and walked past open fields where the sweetness of dried grass came as a surprise after the city's stench. In one sense they hadn't escaped the city because as they walked along, others began to join them, until it was obvious they were part of a crowd all moving in one direction. "I told you this is one way a good thief can line his pockets with gold," said Ellie, indicating how Roger and Darby moved like quicksilver among the ambling masses.

Ahead Leah saw a circular structure with a thatched roof upheld by widely spaced pillars. Beside this was a pond between two long sheds, with a smaller shed to one side. As she came nearer, she heard frantic yapping and barking from the long sheds and caught the musky scent of confined animals as the wind turned in her direction.

Leah couldn't help catching something of the holiday mood of this crowd. Brightly colored pennants were strung on the structures, and she could hear music, a shrill piping. "Give way, give way," shouted the people around her, and the crowd opened to admit a parade of sorts. Minstrels in colorful costumes played horns and flutes. Behind them came two men leading an immense, lumbering bear between them on stout chains.

"What bear is it, boys?" asked Ellie, trying to peer between members of the jostling crowd.

"It's Don Jon, Mum," said Roger.

"I see him," said Ellie. "I know him by his torn ear. He's a rare fighter. There'll be a good match today."

Leah began to have misgivings as they approached the arena. They paid their penny and were admitted inside. Seats for the spectators were provided all around the circle. This was roofed over, but the arena itself was open to the sky, probably to provide more light. Before the entertainment began, Leah noticed that many of the spectators were gathered in groups. Money was changing hands, and by the odd snatches of conversation she heard, she understood that odds were being taken on the outcome of whatever contest this was to be. She noticed that the people who gathered ran the spectrum of the social classes, from richly dressed lords and ladies to raggedly clothed apprentices and laborers. The only thing they had in common was the glitter of anticipation in their eyes.

After a time the bearkeepers led their charge into the center of the arena. The chains were fastened to a framework that gave the animal some freedom of movement, or as far as the chains would allow.

"Here come the mastiffs," shouted Darby, jumping up and down on his seat. Leah heard a chorus of yelps, barks, and whines with a counterpoint of harsh, deep-voiced growls as several large dogs were brought in, straining at their leashes.

"But what are we to see?" asked Leah, just as the keepers slipped the leashes and the dogs were set on the great bear.

When the bear stood up, it seemed eight feet tall, but none of the dogs hesitated. Two circled, barking loudly, while three more launched themselves directly at the bear's throat. Sweeps of immense shaggy paws sent dogs flying to left and right. One dog was hit squarely. He cried out in agony and was sent rolling. When he stopped, he tried to rise but fell back. His rib cage on one side looked crushed and a drool of blood descended from his open mouth. Occasionally, a dog would get through the bear's defenses and set his teeth in the hairy hide. Then the bear would shake himself violently to release the dog's hold, and the jaws would shear through hide and flesh, causing a jet of blood.

All the animals seemed half crazed by the blood scent that hung heavy in the air. All the animals, including the watchers, Leah thought, becoming nauseated at the sight. The people were drunk on the spectacle; they seemed to have no notion of the cruelty behind it.

She put a hand on Ellie's shoulder. She had to shake the woman to get her attention. "I've had enough of this," she said. "I'm going. You can stay if you want to."

Blindly, she fought free of the crowd and tried to close her ears to the noises behind her. She felt only a little better when she was outside, since she knew the brutal spectacle continued. After a moment she heard hurried footsteps and turned to see Ellie.

"What's the matter? Did the crowd frighten you?" asked Ellie. "Sometimes the spirit of the bear-baiting gets to them and fights break out among the men. They lay about with swords and daggers, cutting off fingers, ears—"

"Is that what you people do for sport here?" asked Leah.

"Well . . . some do, anyway," said Ellie, puzzled, as if she couldn't understand why anyone would object to such action and fun. "The sport we chiefly have in mind is the good old nip and foist. The noise and excitement are great cover. Roger and Darby are trying their luck now."

"Shall we wait for them?"

"No. They may have to flee quickly, and we'd only be an encumbrance."

Ellie conferred with Lord Foist, and it was decided that Leah should have the opportunity to put her learning to the test. "You'll be our 'stale,' " said Ellie, "our decoy. Try this." To Leah's shock and amazement, Ellie lifted her skirt until her whole calf and a part of her doughy thigh showed. Then she appeared to be refastening her garter. "Believe me, this stops the gentlemen in their tracks. It becomes an easy matter for Roger to creep up behind him. We certainly know where the gentleman's attention is going to be."

"B-but you showed practically your . . . whole leg!" said Leah dumbfoundedly. She was as shocked as if Ellie had calmly discussed disrobing on a street corner.

"It's just a leg, dear. Little enough to ask, that is, if you're really serious about doing a job."

"All right." Leah bit her lip and hoisted her skirt, but she knew she'd feel guilty about it for days afterward.

"It's not really a frivolous thing, after all," said Ellie. "Roger's life depends upon it, you know."

Leah felt a chill, considering this. Ellie was right. When you became an active participant in anything, it seemed the stakes went up.

Roger and Leah strolled along a busy street, appraising the passersby. When Roger spotted a well-dressed gentleman, he poked Leah and pointed him out. They walked nonchalantly past him and then darted down an alley to cut him off at the next street.

Feeling sweaty and disheveled, the very antithesis of what she must appear, Leah positioned herself where the gentleman couldn't miss seeing her as he came by. Men jostled each other on the street. She wouldn't just be displaying herself for their quarry. Everyone would see. She felt mortified. Better just break and run now, before Roger's life was jeopardized by her foolishness. But if I don't do this, I'll be giving up in defeat. I'll never learn what I need to know to get the talisman.

As he approached, Leah saw that the gentleman they'd chosen had a coarse, debauched-looking face. Maybe that was only her imagination. She took a deep breath and, pretending her garter had broken, lifted up her skirt.

She saw the gentleman slow down, pause, stop to stare, a grin smearing itself across his gross features. She froze as he began to approach her. Ellie told her she should smile, try to hold his attention as long as possible, but she felt paralyzed, riveted to the spot.

By this time Roger had come up silently behind the man and had done his part. She saw him wave jauntily in signal that it was time for her to flee as well.

"Hello, missy," began the man, coming very near.

Leah was in a panic. The real situation was so different than practice. She hadn't thought she'd be so scared that she would not be able to move.

As he carelessly put his hand to his hip, he discovered that his purse was gone, and reaching out, he grabbed Leah by the sleeve and began to cry out loudly. "Thieves, robbers! I've got one of 'em. Call the constable!"

Roger came up from one direction, Darby from another, shouting something about "Sister, sister, come home. Our mother's sick!" Roger pulled hard on the lacings that attached Leah's sleeve to the gown and they tore away. Feeling herself freed, Leah began to run. She heard pounding feet behind her, but now panic seemed to be helping her because she ran as she had never run before. Slipping through a gap in the heavy street traffic, she lost any pursuers for good, but even after she holed up in a hiding place discovered on one of her earlier explorations, she couldn't seem to stop shaking. All right, she told herself. This isn't so easy. And all didn't go as planned, but I made it. I'm still here, and all in one piece.

After a time she returned to the Glove and Falcon, sure that she would be in deep disgrace and that it would be a long time before anyone wanted to work with her again. When she arrived, she was in time to overhear Roger telling the other apprentices a riotous version of what had occurred. Her face reddened as the others looked up at her and laughed, but that was the only chastisement she received for her failure. She supposed that the real punishment for a thief's failure could be so severe it was the only threat needed. I'll do better next time, she vowed.

Ellie came into the practice room, walking a little unsteadily. Her breath was heavy with the smell of ale as she spoke to Leah. "I promised to show you a good time in London, and our last outing didn't work out so well. Come along with me and I swear you'll have a good time."

"I can't. I have to go on duty in a few more hours," said Leah, though after the debacle of the bear-baiting, she was glad to have this excuse.

"I guarantee you'll like this. No blood—well, nobody really gets hurt, in any case. And the crowd is almost as good as at the bear-baiting," said Ellie. "Come along. You can't go home from London and tell them you haven't seen a play."

Finally giving in to Ellie's promises, Leah agreed to go. She had overheard people talking excitedly about this new form of entertainment, and she had wanted to see it for herself. It would give her something to tell Scorpio when she got back. She knew she could never explain the bear-baiting to him.

"We'll have a bit of a walk," said Ellie. "Bluenose Puritans believe this sort of entertainment's rude and common. Stodgy old Lord Mayor would ban plays altogether, says the crowds gathering causes disease, and fires could be caused by stage directions like 'chambers shot off within.' So they built the theatre in Shoreditch where the city's writ isn't in force. The Queen thinks it's all right, though, and is always holding masques and plays at court. Good old Queen Bess." Ellie raised her flask in a toast and drank deeply.

After a long trudge, they reached the edge of the city where close-set buildings gave way to open fields. Leah saw a round structure set off to itself. As at the bear-baiting, a crowd had gathered and was streaming in through the entrances, evidently called by the blaring of trumpets and the raising of colorful flags that rippled in the wind. She couldn't help feeling excited. Ellie handed over a few coins to a man at the entrance, and he dropped the money into a box.

Leah found the building curious. There was no roof over the central part, though roofs and awnings covered the tiers of seats and private boxes along the sides where the wealthy folk sat. A square wooden platform extended out into the center. Crowds of the poor folk ebbed and flowed through this section; people ate, visited, joked.

At last another trumpet call sounded, and a group of flamboyantly dressed people trooped onto the platform. "What are they going to do?" asked Leah.

"Just watch."

Leah watched, mesmerized as action and pageantry unfolded before her. The speeches and actions seemed outlandish, yet there was a magic in it. More seasoned playgoers around her shouted their approval or tried to bandy words with the actors. A little later on, Leah screamed as one man seemed to stab another and blood splattered on the stage, sending a few drops out among the groundlings.

"It's real!" she said, turning on Ellie. "The bear-baiting was bad enough, but to watch two men rend each other—"

"It's only a bladder full of blood from the butcher's," said Ellie. "Makes it more realistic. Look, do you think a dead man could twitch like that." A moment later the dead man shouted a curse at a heckler in the audience, so Leah knew he was all right.

Then a little later she whispered to Ellie, "Am I wrong or is that lady . . . a boy?"

"Certainly she's a boy. You don't expect real womenfolk to get up there and disport themselves so shamefully, do you? He does make a pretty wench, though, don't he?"

Leah thought it odd that Ellie, considering her occupation, would talk about a shameful profession, but she was silent, caught up again in action that was obviously false, yet in another way quite real.

Then just when things were getting exciting, Leah felt a hand on her arm and turned to see Joan, from the thieves' school. "Lord Foist sent me to get you. Said you'd take the evening shift in place of your afternoon one or he'd raise hell."

Knowing how effective Lord Foist was at that endeavor, Leah turned reluctantly away. "Will you watch till the end and let me know how it turns out?" she asked Ellie.

Ellie nodded.

Some moments after Leah had gone, there was a sudden, brilliant flash of light on the stage, making Ellie and the other groundlings shield their eyes. Ellie knew about the trapdoor in the middle of the stage by which ghosts and the like were made to appear, but in conjunction with the flashing lights, it looked quite realistic.

Out of the afterimages stepped two figures. They were obviously masked actors in flowing black gowns, but the effect was startling. Their skin was a fearsome red. Each had a bone running lengthwise across his face, creating a beaklike appearance, and spiraling ram's horns to either side of his head. One of them, the taller, slenderer one, carried a small, glowing golden ball.

Ellie struggled to fit this apparition into the plot of the play. It must be some grave portent appearing to the King, she thought, but the King was backpedaling quickly, his crown falling from his head, and the "lady" whom Leah had remarked on was making a speedy exit, skirts flying around long, boyish legs.

Lethor awoke from what he thought was a strange dream, to find himself standing on a crude platform in a primitive building only half roofed, the center open to the sky. He saw that he and his companion, Ardon, were surrounded by a crowd of the species that inhabited this world, as if the Hunters were somehow on display for this ragged, ill-smelling herd. "I wonder what manner of place this is," he said aloud, though he expected no answer from his more burly companion, who was, after all, a Beta, not bred for thinking, though he followed orders well. The orb that he and Ardon held between them reminded him that they had followed Scorpio and the female indigene here because there was a small commitment as yet unfulfilled—Scorpio's death. The hunt had not gone well, Lethor admitted. What should have been simple had been complicated by the orb which Scorpio had stolen. And these native creatures had been involved in the chase, as well. Undisciplined, he thought, this will not do at all. Anxiety made his near-vision cut in, and he was treated to a closer sight of the faces of the groundlings, some pockmarked, some gap-toothed. With an effort, he suppressed this visual reflex.

A Hunter was supposed to feel no emotion toward his prey, but Lethor was finding it increasingly difficult not to feel something approaching anger toward the elusive Aquay.

He had hoped, when they emerged from orb space, to find some clue as to where his quarry had gone. After all, an alien could hardly go unnoticed here.

The crowd, which had been somewhat stunned by the first appearance of the orb-travelers, soon began to stamp their feet and shout for the play to continue. The actors had gathered at the edge of the stage and gesticulated as they talked things over. They appeared to be incensed that they had been driven from the stage. The King brandished his sword and began to approach aggressively, as if his training in the mock combat of the theater gave him confidence. "Ho there, we know you're from a rival company, sent here to spoil the performance."

Lethor experienced the same instant understanding of the creature's language as Leah had earlier, though there were enough alien concepts in the sentence to render it incomprehensible. He saw that Ardon, who often acted on reflex, had drawn his laser.

Lethor raised his hand to caution him against any unnecessary use of force. Like all Hunters, he found his sensibilities upset by purposeless violence. Meaningful violence was something else again.

The actor raised his sword as if to strike, and Ardon could wait no longer. His finger was quick on the firing stud, and a bolt of searing red light shot out. Only the haste of his shot saved the man; the stream of light passed close to one side, leaving a glowing hole in the lower edge of his cloak and charring a long, smoking groove into the planks of the stage.

"Fire," shouted one of the players as he saw the glowing light and the smoke.

"Fire!" echoed the patrons, and they began to bolt, fren-

zied, for the exits. Seeing the possibility of being caught in
the crush, Lethor quickly held the orb out to his companion.
With both their hands on the orb, their outlines began to
blur, though no one in the fleeing crowd noticed.

Ellie wasn't sure how she had made it outside without
getting trampled on. She felt her hip and shoulder where
bruises were surely forming.

"Some jape perpetrated by a rival company," said a man
standing beside her. "You know what these players are
like."

That seemed as good an explanation for it as any, and
since Ellie was not imaginative, that was how she would
present it to Leah. She would also chaff her about missing
all the fun.

Chapter
8

*T*hat evening Scorpio crept from the house unobserved. After what Leah had told him about Kelley's designs on the orb, it seemed best not to hide it in his chamber, where it might be easily found. Looking about the grounds, he saw the moon's reflection caught on the dead surface of the lake for which the house was named. Mortlake. Less a lake than a stagnant pool, its edges were ragged with reeds, and algae had turned the water dark and murky. Unseen frogs splashed a warning as he slid down the bank to the water's edge.

Dark and forbidding as it was, the water seemed to call him. He slipped from the hampering rough cloth of his monk's robes, palmed the orb and dived. He hit the water so cleanly there was scarcely a splash. His thick Aquay skin was impervious to the water's chill, and being back in his element again felt good. He spiraled to the bottom and hovered there feeling free as he never felt on dry land. As he held the orb, a warm sensation tingled his palm, and the orb's glow was cool and diffuse through the cloudy water. "Yes, we must separate again," he told it, not feeling foolish because there was so much about it that seemed alive. For all he knew, it could hear his words; if only there could be full communication. He knew the orb would be safe here, and easily recovered, at least for an Aquay. He placed the orb carefully in a slight depression in the lake bed where it half sank into the silt.

He pulled himself up the bank and donned the thick robes, feeling somewhat bereft, especially with Leah gone. She didn't understand this time any better than he did, but at least she was among her own kind. Humans were so different from him, he always felt at a loss. He did know he trusted Dr. Dee to help him if that were possible.

He nearly collided with Kelley as he returned to the house. "Where have you been?" Kelley demanded. "The doctor sent me out to look for you. Said he had important instructions regarding the séance, though I'm not sure why. He also said he was arranging a private audience for you with the Queen, and I'm not sure why he's doing that, either. Let Gloriana get a look at that face and—you're wet!"

Scorpio felt uneasy, his mind setting up an undercurrent of warning, "Run . . . Get away . . . Flee!" as it always did in Kelley's presence. The man was as rude and arrogant as Scorpio was diffident and retiring. "I-I fell into the lake when I was walking on the grounds."

"Fell into the lake, eh," said Kelley, laughing rudely.

Since Kelley seemed so angry about something, Scorpio only followed him back to the house without saying anything else. It was better just to go along with everything for now, until he understood more of what was happening. He wondered what was meant by a "queen." Possibly a ruler of some sort, like the Pope. That made his mind flutter with warnings again, as he remembered how he'd been betrayed in Avignon. He hoped that Kelley hadn't been standing there watching all the time he was hiding the orb. Even so, he didn't think a human would dare brave those cold, murky waters. That was one of the benefits of having an eel's skin, he supposed smugly.

Dr. Dee was waiting in his study. "Scorpio, I've decided that you will aid us in our séance with de Simier tomorrow.

I think your presence will make the ritual even more impressive."

"But I've gathered all the information you asked," said Kelley rather agitatedly. "All is in readiness. Having a novice present might spoil my concentration."

"Nonsense, Edward. You're an old hand at this by now, and I trust you to dazzle de Simier with your usual skill. Scorpio, with his unique appearance, will be just another dramatic device."

Kelley listened grudgingly as Dee outlined his plan, daring to make no protest. He began to wonder what place this interloper might eventually earn in Dee's favor. One would think the dotard thought of Scorpio as a son, the way they put their heads together over those old books at all hours. Heretofore Kelley had enjoyed a particular place in the doctor's good graces, purely by dint of his psychic talents. It was obvious to him that with his shady background, he wouldn't have gone far as a medium without Dee's patronage. He had grown used to sharing the doctor's fame and the occasional financial gifts from the court. Occasionally, Dee got out of sorts with him because of his drinking and his temper, but he always took him back again.

Someday, he knew, he could go out on his own as a medium and be a great success, but for now, he meant to keep this situation. He'd have to come up with some clever means to discredit Scorpio. He seemed innocent enough, but who knew what was going on in that ill-shaped head. He could be plotting their deaths at this moment and no one could read it on his face.

Dim candlelight caught and flickered in the crystal as Jean de Simier and his host entered the inner chamber. Kelley was already seated at the table, dressed in a robe of fine white linen on which had been embroidered a glittering webwork of arcane symbols. Dee set about the final prep-

arations, causing a suffumigation of bay leaves and pep-
perwort to perfume the air, and carefully drawing a ''magic
circle'' on the floor in yellow chalk, explaining that only
within the circle would one be safe from evil spirits, should
any be summoned by accident. He supposed this occult
chicanery should irk him, since what he sought was the real
Source, the Wellspring of all creation, but he had always
been enough of a showman to enjoy this part of his work
for Queen and country. The small room was close and
airless, the scent of herbs attaining an almost suffocating
quality, the only light a few slim candles burning in a wall
sconce.

De Simier, a handsome, black-bearded fellow in a doublet
of fawn brocade frothed with lace and embellished with
elegant silver buttons, watched all this with a sort of patient
amusement, taking out a silver snuffbox at intervals and
inhaling a pinch of snuff off his wrist with a practiced,
graceful gesture. He seemed to be saying he'd seen all this
before and wasn't impressed.

Good, thought Dee. The Frenchman would present a stim-
ulating challenge to his arts.

Dee closed the circle once they were inside it and began
to intone in a sonorous voice, ''Zapkiel, Agiel, Sabathiel.
Hamiel, Hagiel, Noguel. I conjure thee by the great living
God, the Sovereign Creator of all things, to appear, without
noise and without terror, to answer truly unto all questions
that I shall ask thee. Hereunto I conjure thee by the virtue
of these Holy and Sacred Names.''

As these words died into silence, Kelley began to thrash
about and to moan loudly. Out of the corner of his eye, Dee
watched his guest and thought he could distinguish the be-
ginnings of a feeling of uneasiness. Throwing back his head,
Kelley gave one last full-throated shriek for good measure
and lay back laxly, his eyes glazed.

Dee raised his arms in a theatrical gesture and then

brought his hands down suddenly to douse the flames of the candles. In the scent-laden darkness, a black drape was drawn off from before a hidden alcove by a spring device. Inside the alcove stood Scorpio, his alien features brought into startling prominence. It was helpful, Dee thought, to have a working knowledge of optics, although no amount of trickery could duplicate Scorpio's face. He had been given robes similar to Kelley's, and it looked as though he'd painted his face and hands as chalky white as the linen. It made him look like a shrouded corpse with huge, staring eyes. Of course, that made it all the better. If you couldn't have real magic, Dee supposed, artificial magic by means of clever devices was the next best thing.

Kelley nearly fell off his chair from surprise, so startling was the effect. He had to hand it to the stargazer, he really knew how to put on a show.

He didn't even have to look over to see how this was affecting de Simier. He heard the man's sudden indrawn breath, his whispered *Mon Dieu* and shuffling of feet as if only fear kept him from fleeing the protection of the magic circle.

"Speak, spirit. With the lips and tongue of this poor mortal. Impart your wisdom to us."

Kelley began his usual babble, but soon lapsed into more coherent speech. They went through the questions and answers that they'd rehearsed, mostly information about de Simier's home and family, to convince him that they had knowledge by supernatural means.

He hated to admit it, but Dee had been right about the boggart. One look at that face and the froggie was ready to jump. But it worked too well. How long would it be before Dee decided he could do this show without the medium?

He knew that de Simier would blame the "spirit" and not the medium for whatever message was sent. All he had to do was to come up with the message that would cause the most trouble. Of course! De Simier's houseman had assured him that d'Alençon was still pursuing his suit for the Queen's hand from the Netherlands, and that Elizabeth had paid for his military campaign there.

"The spirit is not confined by time or space," he intoned. "I see the Duc d'Alençon in the Netherlands drinking with his officers. He brags that he has won the heart of your Queen and that it is all in jest. He cares more for her Royal Treasury than her person.

"Ohhh, I grow dizzy. The spirit leaps across the Great Water as if it were a rivulet. I see d'Alençon's mother, Catherine de Médicis, resplendent in rich garments. She is gloating over her plan to trick her enemy Elizabeth into paying for d'Alençon's campaign. How she will enjoy telling everyone of it!"

"*Mais non*, that's not true," sputtered de Simier in an incoherent mix of English and French, but the spring device had been activated again and the room was plunged into darkness.

There were muffled curses, and when finally the candles were lit, de Simier had fled, outrage causing him to break the imaginary barrier of the circle.

From his alcove Scorpio pushed back the drape and blinked out confusedly, like an owl in daylight, uncertain about what had happened and his own part in it. He looked down embarrassedly at the whiteness of his hand. Aquay skin changed color to blend in with the surroundings; thus, he'd taken on the color of the robe. It was an Aquay principle always to blend in and not to stand out. Well, it was for all but him, he supposed.

"You fool," shouted Dee. "The Frenchman's gone off in a rage, probably to tell d'Alençon about this insult."

Kelley made rude grunting noises and attempted to focus his eyes. "Wha—uh? What happened? You know how easy

I slip into a trance state when I look at the crystal. I didn't mean to, but—''

"You were entranced? Then where did that message come from?" Dee looked suspiciously at Scorpio. "I must follow de Simier and try to undo the damage somehow."

"I thought everything went well. Was there some problem?" asked Scorpio when Dee had left.

"You know these Frenchmen," said Kelley. "They get emotional over nothing. You did a fine job." Kelley was about to put a friendly arm about Scorpio's shoulders, but the Aquay's alien appearance made him think better of it.

"Now the next thing Dr. Dee wants is for you to give the Queen herself the same message as the spirit imparted to us here. I hear you'll be having an audience with her soon. Let me repeat it so you'll be sure and get it right."

Scorpio was a quick study, thought Kelley later that night. Those few insulting words to the Queen and it would be "off to the Tower." No more worries about losing his fine situation with Dr. Dee. Of course, Dee might find himself in trouble as well, but that would leave Kelley in line as Royal Astrologer, and Leah could be his assistant. He went to sleep dreaming of that pleasant arrangement.

Chapter
9

"*F*orget purse-cutting practice today," said Ellie as Leah came down from her room sleepy-eyed. "We've got some real game to stalk. Remember that fine gown you showed me? Go put it on. You've got to seem like a lady today."

Leah returned to her room and put on the yellow gown Mistress Dee had given her, feeling uneasy because she didn't know what Ellie had in mind for her to do.

"You look real fine, darlin'. You're sure to turn the young gentlemen's heads in that getup."

"I thought I was to learn to turn out their purses, not turn their heads," said Leah suspiciously, knowing how Ellie earned most of her livelihood.

"In this case it's to be a bit of both," said Ellie. They joined the foot traffic in the street, jostling their way along. Ellie's two ragged boys followed them, arguing intently all the while. "You see," said Ellie, "Sir Walter Raleigh, a fine knight and gentleman, was walking with the Queen, and when they come to a puddle of water, he whipped off his elegant cloak and put it over the puddle."

"But it would get all soiled."

"Sure it did, muddy as hell, especially since he let Elizabeth walk over it. Y'see, that allowed her to keep her feet clean."

"That seems a stupid way to treat a perfectly good cloak.

I know I wouldn't have walked over somebody's clothes."

"But the point is that a cloak is usually a gentleman's most expensive garment; it shows how he values a lady. All of London was buzzing about it. Now everyone's competing to make grand gestures of gallantry, like Sir Walter. Whenever there's a puddle particularly, the cloaks fly."

"I don't know why you're telling me all this. I don't have a cloak."

"Ah, yes, that is the point, dear. You need a fine cloak to go with that lovely dress of yours, don't you think?"

They had reached St. Paul's Cathedral and had to slow their pace to thread their way through the crowd. This seemed to be a busy day here. Peddlers were taking full advantage, crying their wares in raucous voices. Customers dawdling in front of hucksters' booths, porters carrying bundles, and litters conveying ladies or gentlemen jostled for space.

"All right, look sharp now. Pick your mark, some fine gentleman of wealth, and make sure he's wearing a cloak. When you're sure he sees you, give a little girlish shiver and faint."

"In this crowd? Someone's sure to walk over *me* like the Queen did over Sir Walter's cloak."

"Let's get a little farther off from the crowd, then."

Leah strolled along, pretending to stop and look at a peddler's display of ribbons, though she was feeling nervous, remembering her other attempt. She saw a tall, handsome young man with neatly trimmed brown beard and short hair in the fashion of the times, and judged his wealth by his elegant costume: doublet of burgundy velvet with long, embroidered, jewel-encrusted sleeves slit to hang behind him, a small, flat hat with an ostrich plume and a blue cloak lined in sable. Feeling awkward, since she had never done such a thing, she caught his eye and smiled, she hoped, mysteriously. He smiled back, looking somewhat amused, and made a slight bow.

Leah was suddenly flustered, feeling heat rise into her cheeks. She knew what she was planning called for coolness and calculation, but she couldn't help noticing his mischievous green eyes and wondering what he was like. You know him already, she realized. He's a gentleman of fashion, a courtier; obviously, he's as shallow and self-centered as all his kind, no matter in what century one encounters them.

As the gentleman approached, Leah had the sudden desire to turn and run, but she forced herself to stand there, a stiff smile on her face. What can I say? her mind asked desperately, and then she realized that there need be no conversation at all. They would never exchange a word; there would never be an opportunity to know him. Pretending a sudden weakness, she wilted like a flower at his feet.

She felt strong arms around her, and she let her eyelids flutter open to be sure it was the man she'd chosen. This wasn't going well, and for all she knew she'd been scooped off the filthy street by a vagabond. She let her eyes close as she recognized him. If she looked into his face, she'd surely begin to wonder about him again, and he was only a victim, a "rabbit," as Lord Foist would say.

True to Ellie's word, he was wrapping his rich cloak around her. He lifted her to her feet.

"Thank you, sir, you're a true knight and gentleman." Ellie had appeared, somehow, out of the crowd, walking and talking briskly. "Come along, child, we've got to get you home now, so you can recover. You've never been strong."

"Make haste," Ellie whispered angrily into Leah's ear as the two of them set off down the street, hoping to become lost in the crowd. The crowd obliged them, closing in around tightly until they had made their escape.

• • •

Leah ran her hand over the luxurious fur. "We did it. It was so easy!"

"I told you it'd work. Show 'em a pretty young face and you can get away with anything." Leah caught a wistful look on Ellie's weathered countenance as she said this, as if remembering better times, but then she brightened. "Let's have a bit of fun. We can slip back now and watch what happens next."

"No, we can't go back. What if he sees us? What if he calls the guard?"

But Ellie was already leading her along, and before long she saw the gentleman she had robbed, searching fruitlessly through the cathedral. "Hide here, behind this column," said Ellie, "and watch the fun."

At first, Leah was petrified that she'd been seen and probably would be arrested. Then she began almost to like the feeling of flirting with danger, and felt pride at her skill in stealing the cloak without being caught. It hadn't been as hard as she'd thought. She could almost learn to enjoy this. And she had an advantage that other thieves did not: if things got too dangerous, she could always find Scorpio and the orb, and they could jump again.

As she watched, she saw Roger and Darby creeping up on the young man from either side. As Roger burst from the crowd to shout a foul oath, dodging away as the man reached for him, Darby came up from behind and almost casually used his thin-bladed knife to separate the thongs that held the gentleman's purse on his belt. By the time he felt the tug and reached to see what had happened to his purse, Darby had fled, laughing, into the crowd.

They left the gentleman there looking foolish and angry.

"I taught the boys well," said Ellie proudly.

Leah looked at Ellie's smiling face as she beamed with pride over her sons, as much as if they'd done some noble deed she could brag about, and felt a curious detachment.

It was as if Ellie and the boys, even the gentleman, weren't real to her. As if they were players on a stage, and when the play was done, they'd go off laughing, becoming altogether different people. Then the moment passed, and she knew they were real. She was the "player," not them. Their lives were real because this was all they had, and all they would ever have.

"They were wonderful," she said a little belatedly, to answer Ellie's comment about her boys, and it seemed to please the woman.

"Let's go back and you can show Lord Foistwell your trophy; a good day's work, I'd say."

Lord Foistwell narrowed his eyes to peer at the cloak and blew on the fur to judge the luxury of the pelt. "Must admit I had my doubts about training you," he said. "Kelley hasn't ever brought me a smart one yet, but this is a good job of work, and I hope to see much more." He reached out for it greedily.

"Can't I wear it?" asked Leah. "Just for this afternoon?"

"Let her. After all, she's earned it," said Ellie. "Don't you see how handsomely it complements her gown?"

"All right, but I'll check to see if it's soiled, and if it is—"

Leah wasn't sure why she wanted to hold onto the cloak; it didn't have anything to do with the vanity of wanting to wear it, as she'd told Lord Foist. It didn't have anything to do with the triumph she'd felt earlier about separating the gentleman from his finery. It was all right to take from the rich, she reasoned; after all, they'd taken enough from her. Aimeric would have taken her virtue, without a second thought. Pope Clement had stolen her father's life and her trust, all to advance his own position. Selfishness and wealth seemed to go hand in hand, and it was only fair that she took back something. She supposed she'd complete her training as a thief, and if need be, she would steal the old Kabbalist's secret, if that was what it took to help Scorpio. But somehow she knew she couldn't keep this cloak.

It was really very strange. She supposed her early training played a part, the way her father taught the Torah and agonized over the Talmud. She had been brought up among people who trusted each other because they had no one else to trust except their own kind. When she finally boiled it down to its essence, it was simply the way having stolen the cloak made her feel. It was as if she had wallowed in filth that could not be washed away, scrub as she might. It didn't help to realize that the gentleman had only been coming to her aid. She wondered what would happen to the next person who fainted or fell ill on the street as the young man passed.

It surprised her to realize that the code that forbade theft existed not only to protect property. A human being naturally wanted to feel good about herself, and injustice hurt. The freedom she had felt earlier when she imagined skipping from one time to another whenever things got too rough dissolved like a mirage.

Returning to St. Paul's, Leah began to retrace the gentleman's path. His clothing and handsome appearance were distinctive enough so that when she described him, she discovered that he was Lord Bothwell. She remembered Dee mentioning Bothwell as a young lord who had connections at court and a rich and powerful family. If I'm going to steal, she thought wryly, it might as well be from the richest. Following the leads of several passersby, she was able to locate him at last. She walked behind him among the pillars, trying to decide what to do. She could give a street urchin a coin to return the cloak for her, thus redeeming herself without embarrassment. But considering the children she had been exposed to so far, there was no guarantee that the urchin wouldn't end up with both the coin and the cloak. That meant she would have to put it into Bothwell's hands personally, even though she wasn't sure what he'd do when he saw her again. After a few minutes she gathered up enough courage to confront him.

Lord Bothwell strode along the pavement, not looking up to see who was coming, but depending upon his bulk and his frowning expression to keep people out of his way. It had begun as a fine day, with business to finalize and a few hours of leisure to mingle with the folk at St. Paul's. Things had really become promising when the yellow-gowned wench had caught his eye. She didn't seem at all like the women who came here to show off their finery or to entice the unwary. There had been something so innocent in her expression as she smiled at him that he couldn't be sure what her intentions were. That had intrigued him; after all, he'd come here for a bit of excitement. And then after she attracted his attention, she had fainted dead away before him. Damn, he'd been totally taken in by the vixen, holding her as if she were some sort of breakable doll and hoping she'd open those huge, dark eyes and look at him again. He had felt disappointed when the harridan took her away.

It had taken him a moment to realize that he'd been relieved of his cloak as well.

Then he'd been doubly gulled when those dirty-faced brats had surrounded him kicking and cursing like sailors, and suddenly he was missing his purse. What a day!

It wasn't that he couldn't afford to lose both cloak and purse, but who wanted to be made a fool of so publicly? He'd looked around for a constable, but of course, couldn't find one. If I'd seen her and her accomplice, I would have hauled the both of them off to gaol, one in each hand, he thought miserably.

Someone was making throat-clearing noises, very near.

He reached out a hand as if to brush intruders away. But then he felt someone impertinent enough to tug at his clothing and he looked down to see . . . her. It was the girl who had run off with his cloak, and she had the effrontery to be carrying it over her arm. He had an impulse to grab her, as if he were afraid she would fade back into the crowd like an apparition. But he hesitated. She didn't seem to be going anywhere. Best hear her out.

"You left abruptly," he said in an ironic tone. "I wanted to find you, to see if you'd recovered, though I suppose the speed at which you departed should have told me something of the state of your health."

"My chaperone is a dear soul, and very solicitous of my health. She wanted to bring me home as soon as possible lest the vile humors of the streets caused me to become ill again."

"You've been ill—well, of course, I can see how sickly, how delicate you look. Roses are as pale."

"She hurried me off so quickly I hadn't time to tell her that you'd wrapped your cloak around me. She assumed it was mine." She held out the cloak to him shyly.

Lord Bothwell stood a moment, saying nothing and making no movement toward the cloak. She stole it, and now she's returning it, just like that? he asked himself. Oh, no, my girl, maybe you've got something more in mind.

"Well, perhaps it was just a foolish mix-up," he said, taking the cloak back casually, as if he had given little thought to it. "It's unfortunate that your chaperone didn't come along to properly introduce us. I'm Andrew Haver, Lord Bothwell."

"I know," she said, not bothering to confide her own name. He realized that his stare was making her quite uncomfortable. "I really can't stay," she said hastily. "My chaperone is expecting me back."

"Of course not. This is no place for a fine lady."

"You know I'm not a fine lady," said Leah, and her sudden honesty, putting a stop to the badinage, startled him.

"I'm afraid I don't know what you are," he said. This was the time to seize her, to shout for the constable. She might well be planning something even worse. It was hard for him to see her as a danger; she had the look of a startled deer. "But I might enjoy finding out, I think."

Before he finished his sentence, she had wheeled and run. For a few paces he tried to follow, but the milling mobs of the street seemed to have swallowed her up. He stopped, smoothing the fur of his cloak, remembering her dark eyes and the direct way she looked at him. London is a large city, he thought, but not so large that I can't find you again.

Chapter
10

Scorpio, Dr. Dee and Kelley
waited nervously outside the audience chamber. Scorpio
looked down at himself. Mistress Dee had stitched up one
of her son's costumes to fit his odd physique and had padded
it out until it was difficult to see his differences without
looking closely. The stockings made his legs look even
skinnier, but as she'd told him, "Many a man has lanky
legs and is not thought the worse for it."

"Remember that the Queen loves to be flattered," said
Dee. "Did you commit to memory those compliments I
gave you?"

"Yes, I tried to," said Scorpio dutifully. "But what
exactly is flattery?"

"Pretty lies," said Dee.

"The Queen enjoys being lied to? She must be a curious
person, indeed."

"I think this is going to be a big mistake," said Kelley
in an undertone, as if to himself.

"The Queen will be charmed," said Dee, sounding as if
he wanted to convince himself. He was beginning to have
second thoughts about Scorpio's day in court. Scorpio
wasn't even human and knew nothing of the correct pro-
tocol. Who knew what he'd do to disgrace himself and his
sponsor. "Here, put this on before you go in."

"What is this?" asked Scorpio, turning the mask over in

his hands and wondering what part of the body it was supposed to fit over. It was a grotesque mask, a demon face with protruding snout covered over in blue spangles that looked like scales. Two tufts of feathers at either temple resembled wildly flowing hair.

"It's to cover your scarebabe face," said Kelley. "So the Queen won't bolt when she sees you."

"This is surely uglier than I am," said Scorpio, holding the mask beside his face.

Kelley laughed. "I'd say you were twins."

"Be quiet, Edward, if you can't be encouraging," said Dee, fastening the mask behind Scorpio's head with a thong. "We mustn't upset the delicate sensibilities of the Queen. Besides, the courtiers themselves often desport themselves in masks at balls and galas. You'll be right in fashion."

After a time a servant in elegant livery opened the door and beckoned Scorpio inside.

Dee watched his protégé enter the Audience Hall with a nagging feeling of anxiety. He knew that Elizabeth could be kind, but she could also be downright capricious and cruel at times, too. She made a bad enemy. He knew he'd kept Scorpio here overlong already by promising to help him learn to control his orb device. He didn't really have knowledge of its workings, but if Scorpio made a good impression on the Queen, Dee was sure to get the funds he needed to continue his scientific studies. Who knew what he could learn if he had funds and leisure to study the orb? The Queen's meeting with his celestial visitor was a necessity, but he wished he didn't feel as if he'd just sent a lamb to the slaughter.

"The honorable Scorpio of Aquay, Keeper of the Golden Orb," the servant bellowed as Scorpio began to walk down what seemed like a mile of red carpet leading to a three-tiered dais at the far end of the room. He wondered why he hadn't simply been announced by his name. There were no titles on Terrapin, since all were Aquay. Or at least that was the case before the Hunters came.

All the way down the aisle he kept getting messages from his subconscious: *Run. Hide. Danger!* But Dee had said it was important, for some reason, to please the Queen. Scorpio gathered it had something to do with the medium of exchange on this world—something Dee called money. Dee coveted it greatly. When the Queen was pleased, she was generous with this money. Dee had told Scorpio that he needed it to continue his researches.

Scorpio was a little puzzled. This had been called a private audience with the Queen, yet a half dozen of Elizabeth's gentlemen-pensioners surrounded the dais, stoic looks on their faces and gilt axes held upright beside them. He supposed they were there to protect the Queen—from him! It made him smile, but of course they couldn't know that the Aquay were nonaggressive by nature.

Upon the second level two men stood: the ministers Lord Burghley and Walsingham, according to what Dee had told him, though he couldn't tell one from the other. They both looked like slightly weary human males of middle years, and one of them wore an implacably worried look. Upon the upper tier sat a very fancy chair. The arms and legs of it were covered in shiny, golden metal and encrusted with gems—prized as much as money here, he had observed, though an Aquay would have little use for such sparkling rocks. On the chair was a woman, also, as he judged, of middle years, legs and feet hidden by a voluminous skirt. The gown she wore was sewn with what must have been thousands of the gems here called pearls. His world had these gems, too; they were the result of a piece of grit falling into a common mollusk, not his idea of something to be treasured. And if the padded and jeweled gown of amber brocade wasn't heavy enough, several necklaces and brooches of gold and jewels helped to weigh her down even more. He got the impression of a slender, wiry, strangely dynamic woman under all the padding and had a sinking feeling that his own disguise couldn't protect him from her perceptive gaze.

Elizabeth had hair of a brighter red than he'd previously seen on a human, so he suspected it might be artificial, though artificial hair seemed a bizarre concept. (Hair seemed a bizarre idea to him, for that matter; it reminded him strongly of the tentacles of a sort of jellyfish native to Terrapin.) And her skin was preternaturally white, almost phosphorescent. He had heard Dee's wife say that the Queen soaked her skin in some sort of potion made of egg whites, alum, borax and white poppyseed. Sounded disgusting, but he found this part of her the most attractive feature, since to him most humans looked unpleasantly pink, as if they'd been boiled. As to her beauty, which was legendary here, he couldn't presume to judge, but at the moment, to him at least, she seemed quite frightening.

Trembling inside, Scorpio paused on the lowest level of the tier and knelt, in the posture he'd been shown, waiting for some sign that he could speak.

He heard a soft laugh. "So you're Dr. Dee's latest toy. You certainly seem a novel one, and I hope you're more durable than his usual offerings. He's continually trying to create mechanical toys for me, a little man that walks, a bluebird that flaps its wings, but they always break. It's so disappointing. You have leave to speak."

"I wish Your Majesty good day," said Scorpio.

A silence ensued at the rippling, high-pitched sound of Scorpio's voice. The two men looked toward Elizabeth, as if judging what her reaction would be, so they would know what to do next.

"A voice like a songbird. So lilting and musical. Say aught else so we may listen." Though there were three of them present, Scorpio had the odd feeling that the Queen somehow considered herself plural.

"Your Majesty's face is as serene and pale as the moon and assuredly as cratered," said Scorpio. That *seemed* right; he knew that Dr. Dee had written something about the moon, and he had noted that this particular satellite had definite shadows indicating crater formations. Dee had made him memorize several such speeches, each more flowery and ridiculous than the one before it, since this sort of thing didn't come to him naturally. However, under stress, he tended to forget things. In fact, he had forgotten to tell Dr. Dee about this forgetfulness.

"Our thanks, sir," she said with a certain coldness. "We were told you come from domains remote from our England. So remote as to be another world. Is this true?"

"Yes. But of all the worlds I've visited, I've seen no woman more beauteous than Gloriana, nor one with such shining . . . tentacles." No, he thought desperately, that wasn't it.

The Queen pursed her lips as if sucking a lemon. "Someday we may send our ships thither," she said.

"It hardly seems likely," said Scorpio, forgetting the next flowery speech, but he supposed it was just as well, since the flattery ploy didn't seem to be working too well.

"Don't be so sure, otherworldling. Our domain is fated to be far-flung."

Sensitive to dangerous situations, Scorpio felt the tenor of the visit change, grow more strained.

"Dr. Dee has made claims. He calls you an angel, says that you're omniscient, that you know the secrets of the universe. Can you prophesy for us?"

"I would be delighted," said Scorpio, feeling a bit trapped. What if he said the wrong thing? This world was a barbaric one, after all, and maybe there would be consequences for displeasing as well as for pleasing a queen.

Despite the foolish ceremony, he had begun to feel the gravity of this meeting. He wasn't sure that he liked this Queen, but he did realize that Elizabeth was somehow a person of substance and wit, a swift intelligence coupled with a vast power.

"I have had a surfeit of pomp and glory," said Elizabeth, relaxing a bit and falling into the singular. "As any woman, my thoughts sometimes turn to love. Shall I find a constant lover? What are my chances?"

Scorpio tried to recall more of Dee's coaching, but everything was a formless jumble. He could remember nothing. A moment of agonizing silence passed. He dared tell nothing but the truth to this commanding presence.

Mistress Dee had often told him tales of Elizabeth stopping to listen attentively to one of her subjects, even though it might be the lowliest peasant. She was sometimes rude to her servants, her courtiers, but always had time for her people. "I think that your only faithful and lasting love will be your people," he stammered, "and it's love returned. I've heard they cheer you everywhere you go and grieve over your illnesses, as if one of their children were suffering."

"My ministers have always fretted about the lack of a successor," said Elizabeth, shooting a wicked glance at Burghley and Walsingham. "Tell me, will I produce an heir?"

He remembered Dr. Dee making some remark about the Queen being past the usual childbearing age. "Your Majesty, your heirs will be a thousandfold. Heirs of your indomitable spirit, not of your flesh."

"Well spoken, strangeling. I would have been well advised if I had Scorpio of the Aquay as one of my ministers. I have yearned for the things other women have—home, husband, children—but what other woman has a kingdom and such loyal subjects? My lover will be England; my

successor, my memory in the hearts of the people. So be
it! The time grows short. Do you have aught else to tell
me?''

In the roiling tumult of Scorpio's brain, the message
Kelley had told him to deliver came floating to the surface.
He didn't trust Kelley, but Dee considered him a true
psychic. Maybe this message was important to the Queen.
''The spirits also speak to me of your latest suitor, le Duc
d'Alençon.''

''This sounds interesting. Say on,'' urged the Queen.

''He no longer wishes to marry you. In fact, he was
merely interested in your treasury so that he might finance
his campaign.''

There was another strained silence in which Burghley and
Walsingham looked dumbstruck at the insult.

Elizabeth burst out into laughter. ''I never had any plans
to wed or bed my little froggie, so I'm glad his heart will
not be broken. There is no longer any benefit to be gained
from marrying the Frenchman. The price of a skirmish in
the Netherlands is a small one for the pleasure of outsmarting
both Henry III of France and his harridan of a mother and
my dear foolish Philip II of Spain.''

''There was more, I—'' stammered Scorpio, but he
couldn't remember the part about Catherine de Médicis. He
hoped it wasn't important.

''You are a charming innocent,'' said Elizabeth. ''And
you make me laugh. I hope to entertain you at court often.
And perhaps you'll not be so coy next time and allow me
to see your face. I think it may be a handsome one.''

Scorpio was about to deny this, but then realized that it
was the Queen's turn to bandy flattering words. Burghley
and Walsingham were nodding their agreement, though
Scorpio felt it would go hard with anyone who didn't agree.
Perhaps now things would work out. Dee would get his

money, his researches would allow him to help Scorpio master the orb and all would end happily.

"The audience is at an end," said Elizabeth. "Tell your sponsor, Dr. Dee, and his assistant that I would be pleased to entertain all of you at dinner. You otherworldlings do eat, don't you?"

"Yes, but we don't enjoy it," said Scorpio, still in a muddle.

Elizabeth burst into peals of laughter.

Scorpio went out to join the waiting Dr. Dee and Kelley. The latter seemed distinctly peeved to see Scorpio returning, as if he hadn't expected him to come back.

"Well, did you remember all the speeches I taught you?" asked Dee.

"Your Majesty's form is as agile and lithe as a . . . mighty oak," he parroted.

"No, her *steadfastness* is as the oak," moaned Dee. "What did you say in there? What did you do? My reputation is ruined, ruined!"

"I told you not to trust the slimy eel," said Kelley. "They're probably coming for all of us right now. It's the Tower for sure. But I'm only your assistant, remember? I'm not responsible for any of this and I don't want any part in it."

"I'm not sure," said Scorpio, "but I don't believe it went so badly. The Queen invited us to dine with her; is that good?"

Dee hugged Scorpio as he wriggled to be free, his overloaded brain sending muddled messages of fear.

"It's good. It's wonderful," said Dee, dancing him around. "I knew it, you're about to become a court favorite."

"We'll have riches beyond our dreams," said Kelley.

"You're only the assistant, remember?" said Dee. "But

we'll allow you to partake of the feast, as long as you're civil to Scorpio.''

As Dee went off to perfect his toilette for the coming honor, Kelley leaned threateningly close to Scorpio. "You got my message all jumbled up, too, didn't you? Or else you didn't deliver it like I told you to."

"No, I did deliver it, exactly as you said. Well, almost exactly. Her Majesty was quite amused, so I owe you my thanks for suggesting it."

Kelley's face seemed to grow quite red then, astounding Scorpio, who thought he was the only one on this world whose skin changed color.

*K*elley was hard at work in Dr. Dee's workshop at Mortlake. It was a large room, complete with a forge, and cluttered with tools and the bits and pieces of the mechanical toys Dee was so fond of making. Earlier that day Kelley had stormed through both Scorpio's and Leah's chambers in a fit of rage, throwing the bedding to the floor, ransacking the clothespress and trunks, all to no avail. The orb wasn't there.

Scorpio has hidden it someplace, he thought. If I had him to myself, I could get the secret from him, but now that he's a favorite of the Queen's, I can't touch him.

After pausing to calm himself, he began to wonder if the shining orb had been nothing but a cheap conjuror's trick. Just because the old man was gullible and believed the two were from outer realms didn't mean Kelley had to. If he could build something that resembled the orb, he could use it for his own séances. It would create a sensation, and he'd have no more reason to put up with Dr. Dee's crochets.

With this thought in mind, he had gone to the workshop to see if the effect of the orb might be duplicated. He had obtained some bladders from the butcher's leavings which now lay in a slimy mess on the tabletop. Into one of these, by dint of much effort, he had inserted a lighted candle, and he was trying, with great pains, to inflate the thing without extinguishing the candle. After a lengthy struggle, he managed it, and his eyes took in with satisfaction the glowing light inside the membrane, somewhat as he remembered the orb. Still, it seemed that the orb had had a certain quality he couldn't reproduce. As he leaned close to the experiment, suddenly the bladder burst and caught fire, filling his eyes with moisture and stinging smoke.

"Fire!" he shrieked, blundering about the room with his hands to his eyes. "Fire!"

After a moment, when no one seemed to be answering his summons, he stopped, uncovered his eyes and blinked. With arms folded, Mistress Dee stood in the doorway watching him. The remains of the bladder smoldered on the table, giving off a foul stench.

"What in the name of Tophet are you doing in here, Edward Kelley?" demanded Jane Dee. "The doctor will be most displeased. His whole workshop smells like flaming liverwurst."

"I was only, er, only conducting an experiment," Kelley said, trying to marshal his confidence against her intimidating stare.

"Well, I'll get you a bucket of water. I want this mess cleared away before the doctor gets home. Do you hear me, *Mister* Kelley?"

Later, as Kelley scrubbed energetically at the mess on the tabletop, he watched Mistress Dee out of the corner of his eye. I know she fancies me, he thought. And we're all alone here. What if I should pass by closely and steal a little kiss?

Scorpio sat idly in the study, thinking of the banquet with the Queen and her courtiers. It had been a festive occasion, and Elizabeth had given him the silver ring he now wore, bearing her royal seal. Dr. Dee told him that meant he had met with the Queen's favor and would receive many benefits. He was glad for Dee's sake, since it seemed to cheer him considerably, but powerful though she might be in her own realm, Elizabeth could do nothing to solve his own problem. He wished Leah were here now, so they could talk. There was no one else he could confide in. He wondered where she was. She had seemed to have some notion of how she could win the secret of the symbol from Jacob Auerman, but she hadn't told him what she had in mind.

We were so hopeful when we came here, he thought, but this world has as many dangers as the one we left. I hope she knows that, and I hope she's being careful, wherever she is, because if she doesn't come back . . .

He was surprised to find that his concern for Leah's safety was for her own sake and not just for the sake of his mission. He had told himself that everything he did on this world was only important in terms of how it would help his people, but he now realized that he was beginning to care about those he met.

He rose and wandered about the room, stopping to study a globe and then moving on to a shelf of books. On a table to one side rested a sphere of polished crystal smaller than the dark stone in Dee's séance room. He stared gloomily into it, but only saw the skewed reflection of his own face. If she doesn't come back, I must go on alone, he told himself, as long as there's still a chance I can help my people. But I feel so distant from them here. Unless I keep reminding myself of home, it's almost as if Terrapin had never existed.

I must concentrate, try to send my mind commands into this crystal. Perhaps it can tell me something of Leah. He sat in the chair beside the table and, placing a hand on either side of the crystal, fixed his eyes on it. He concentrated on Leah, hoping to form a picture of her within the glass or even to see her as she was at this moment. His eyes blurred from the strain, and he thought for a moment a cloudy picture was forming, but it quickly faded. He let his head droop to one side until it was resting on the tabletop.

He heard a rude laugh. "What're you trying to do there? I'd almost think you were trying to contact the angels if I didn't know you were one of 'em yourself. Or at least that's what the old stargazer believes."

Scorpio lifted his head, though he already knew it was Kelley. He had never seen him in a scullery maid's apron before, though, with his sleeves rolled back. There was also a fresh patch of bright red across his cheek, as if someone had struck him.

Scorpio couldn't suppress a warble of laughter. He supposed he should thank the man; it was the first time his spirits had been lifted all day.

Kelley tore the apron off himself, balled it up and tossed it away. "I forgot I still had that on," he growled. I'll teach the impudent eel to laugh at his betters, he thought, and then remembered what he'd said about not being able to touch him. Yet. "I was, um, just helping Mistress Dee with some cleaning. She likes to have me about. Claims I'm handy around the house."

Scorpio said nothing, but only peered into the crystal again in a melancholy way.

Maybe he's sick, thought Kelley hopefully, then aloud he said, "It's no use just staring into the crystal like that. You're not going to see anything. There's a trick to it. I could show you."

"I thought the crystal gazing was only what Dr. Dee called flummery. You know, the show we put on for the Frenchman."

"Well, that was done for a purpose, but that doesn't mean I don't have real psychic powers. Many times at Dee's urging I've looked into a scrying glass and gone into a trance. He always calls the spirits we contact angels, but who really knows what's out there?"

Scorpio saw the look of raw fear on the man's face when

he talked about contacting spirit beings, and realized that despite all of Dee's tricks, Kelley believed there was something to this scrying business. More than that, the man was terrified at what he might be in touch with. He simply covered the fear with bravado.

"Is it true, as you said during the séance, that the spirit of the showstone is able to move easily through all of time and space?"

"What I say during a trance state is always true. Do you think the spirits lie?"

"Is it possible to contact a world other than this one, to talk to the beings there?"

"Of course. There are no barriers in the astral realms."

"That seems rather hard to believe," said Scorpio haltingly.

"Get out of the way, there," said Kelley, taking a seat behind the crystal as Scorpio moved aside. "I'll show you, but don't become fainthearted when you hear voices from the other side."

Scorpio watched the man stare intently into the crystal until his eyes began to glaze over. Self-hypnosis, thought Scorpio. Is that all there is to it? A grown man scared to death of the things inside his own head? He thought about that a moment and decided that there were probably all kinds of things inside Kelley's head he preferred not to face. Scorpio preferred not to face them, either. He decided maybe this had gone too far and was about to reach out and shake Kelley's arm and awaken him.

"I see clumps of waving waterweed, schools of striped fish," said a voice so unlike Kelley's that it startled Scorpio. "Something like a castle made of pink coral. I see the people swimming in and out of openings in it, carrying bunches of seagrass and brightly colored flowers."

Scorpio stood uneasily by as the voice went on, describing what surely was the Festival of Harvest at Tridontia. He felt a chill; Kelley couldn't know about that. The strange voice coming from Kelley's mouth fell silent for a moment, then spoke again. "Scorpio. Scorpio. Don't forget me!" Kelley slumped over the table. Scorpio was trembling. Was he wrong, or did that sound like his friend Leandro's voice?

After a time Kelley looked up, his eyes clear. "You see, it's not a fake, after all. What did I say?"

"I-I didn't understand it," said Scorpio. "You must have been speaking in a strange celestial tongue."

"That's odd. Dr. Dee is always able to make out my messages. Now that you know my gifts are genuine, I'd be glad to teach you to do it for a very small consideration."

"I have nothing to pay you with."

"There's always the golden orb. You have it somewhere, anyway, even if you aren't telling where. Let's make a bargain. I teach you the skills of scrying, and you show me how to use the orb."

"That I can't teach," said Scorpio, "since I don't have the secret to controlling it myself. If I did, do you think I'd still be here?"

"If there is a secret to it at all," said Kelley, still half believing that the orb was only trickery. But I won't know, he thought, until I have a chance to hold it in my hands. There's something he isn't telling me about my trance, too. Even though I can't read that strange face of his, he was obviously nervous, as if I'd said something that frightened him. Still, I suppose hearing messages from the void would give anyone a fright. I'll have to get the wench back; she's the only one who can reason with him. I'll get my hands on the orb, whether it's truly magic or not, and then I'll dispatch this Scorpio just for the sheer pleasure of it.

Later, after some thought, Scorpio decided that it must have been his own desire for home that influenced the unconscious Kelley. It did have the effect of bringing thoughts of Terrapin to the surface of his mind. He wondered how he could have forgotten his home and resolved that nothing would stop him in his quest. Even if it hadn't been Leandro's voice, he would remember.

Chapter
12

The Glove and Falcon was full of roisterers, and Leah was weary from answering the cries of "More ale!," "Drink here, girl." She darted about the room, saying, "Anon! Anon, sir!" She had grown skillful at avoiding groping hands while she filled the tankards without spilling a drop. Or usually without spilling any. The drinks were mostly beer and ale with colorful names—huffcap, maddog, and angel's food were some of the more polite ones. It was a rude and lewd crew that filled the tables. Ellie called the regulars maltworms; they were loafers, vagabonds, men of low reputation. Working in Lord Foistwell's establishment did make a sort of sense, Leah thought, as it gave one a good reason to move quickly, although the others had told her he used their services out of penury alone.

Slipping out when the tavernkeeper wasn't looking, she sneaked into the storeroom and hid behind a pile of full casks. She sank to the floor, exhausted. She had to have a moment to get her wits together, because she was sure Lord Foist had been waiting for her to return the cloak.

Yesterday she had been so moral, so brave, but she had been acting on impulse rather than planning things out as she should have. It was probably too much to hope that Foist's attention had been distracted by something else and that he had forgotten all about the cloak.

She was just about to return to work when Lord Foist came through the door.

"Where's my cloak, girl? You only had it on loan because of my good nature. I hope you won't come up with some weak story about losing it."

That had been the story she was going to tell. She thought fast. "I returned it."

"You what?" Foist's pale eyes narrowed, and she felt a gaze that seemed to see clear through her.

Leah backed away a step. "I returned it, but be patient a moment. It was in a good cause. It belonged to Lord Bothwell. He has great influence at court. I'm sure you've heard of him."

"Of course. Who hasn't?"

"He was pleased to have the cloak back and was impressed when I told him I worked here for you, and you had advised me to do the honest thing."

"I know that he's influential. One could do worse than have a friend at court. Did you really tell him that about me?" asked Lord Foist.

"I swear it."

With an easy movement, Foist reached out and grabbed Leah's wrist. She felt suddenly vulnerable. Kelley was the only one who knew she'd come here, so nothing would point to Lord Foistwell if she would happen to disappear or if the body of a wayward girl bobbed to the surface of the Thames. He was quiet a moment, holding her easily, as if he knew she was sweating and he was savoring the knowledge. "That's a stupid lie," he said, "and you know it. I expected much better of you. Did you know you weren't the first girl Kelley has brought me to be trained? There have been several others, each more stupid than the one before. I don't know where he finds them.

"But you—you're not stupid. You have a delicate touch and a good mind. It's too soon to tell if you've got the thing that spoils many a promising thief, a conscience. You've got a real future here, if you don't throw it away. I know you're smart enough to be thinking that I can do whatever I want with you, and that's what I want you to think. It's true.''

Among the voices from the next room crying boisterously for ale, Leah suddenly recognized Kelley's. "Yes, it's our friend Edward,'' said Foist, letting go her wrist. "I'll give you another chance, for his sake, but *never* cross me in anything again, or—''

Leah's hands trembled so much as she poured Kelley's ale that the drink slopped onto the table. She had the feeling that Foist's anger was only stayed by his underlying fear of Kelley. Obviously, she had just been rescued.

"Less haste, my girl,'' said Kelley. "I wanted a drink, not a bath. Come join me a minute, the others will spare you.''

"How is Scorpio?'' she asked, seating herself opposite him.

"Can't you think of a better greeting for me than that?'' asked Kelley. "After all, I'm the one who set you up here.''

Leah pushed a strand of hair off her wet forehead. "Yes, thanks for this,'' she said with a wry smile.

"Don't blame me, you're the one who wanted to enter Lord Foistwell's school.''

"I'm sorry. It was kind of you to introduce me. I'm doing well; my training goes well. Want to see the 'clip and run'?''

"No, no thanks. You don't have to sweat here in this dirty tavern, you know. You could go anywhere you desired, if you only had the orb.''

Leah remembered that she had told Scorpio to hide the orb. This made it rather obvious that he had done so, and successfully. "I don't know where it is,'' she confessed. "And, besides, it belongs to Scorpio.''

Kelley covered Leah's hand on the tabletop with his and

leaned close to speak to her. Leah had to force herself not to pull away, remembering that in this place Kelley was actually her protector.

"But he trusts you. He would tell you where it is in a minute, if you only asked him. You're too pretty to be traveling companion to the likes of him. Get me the orb and I'll take care of him for good. With the golden crystal and my powers as a medium, our fortune would be made. Think of it—living like royalty with all of London at our feet."

Leah lowered her gaze, feigning shyness. That way she didn't have to say either yes or no.

Kelley smiled fatuously, as if he had her exactly where he wanted her. "Of course, a dainty thing like you can't make a quick decision. I can be patient. But in the meantime, Dee took our goggle-eyed friend to see the Queen, and for some reason she liked him and invited him to dine. I think he may have cast a spell upon her."

"He's been to see the Queen?" asked Leah. "But I wanted to—" Kelley looked at her. Of course. She wanted to see if Elizabeth was as beautiful as everyone said, and if she wore a gown dripping with gemstones.

I wanted to ask her, Leah thought, what it's like to be a ruler and a woman, and how she can bring herself to sign someone's death warrant. I would have told her how much it frightened me to think I might be responsible for a patient's life.

"You would have loved the banquet," said Kelley. "The yeomen of the guard, bareheaded and with scarlet livery with a golden rose on their backs, came in bringing a course of twenty-four dishes served in gold plate. There was a dish with a peacock roasted and then cunningly presented in his feathers so that he appeared alive again. Such a surfeit of dainties, I don't know what all. Each yeoman was given a morsel from the dish he had brought, since Her Majesty is always in danger of being poisoned.''

"It all sounds charming," said Leah, imagining what it would be like not to freely eat one's food. Yet rulers, women or not, had to live with the realities of power.

"I wish you could have gone with me; you would have been a great success."

She looked down at the shapeless gray gown the tavern wenches were given to wear, the splotches of ale drying on it. Scorpio was at court yesterday dining with the Queen, she thought, while I was scrubbing this alehouse floor.

"Like I said, missy," murmured Kelley persuasively, "you can be rid of Scorpio anytime you say." He cracked the knuckles of his big hands, as if he were breaking someone's bones—and enjoying it.

Kelley's crude gesture brought Leah's thoughts back to the present. If Scorpio went to see the Queen, it was with good reason, not just to be entertained. He's doing his part as I must do mine, she thought. But if I can, I must return to Mortlake and warn Scorpio of how dangerous Kelley really is.

"I think you know I'm a patient man," said Kelley, cupping Leah's chin roughly in his hand and making her look at him. "But I can't wait forever for your answer. Think it over. I'll be back soon for your decision."

He rose hastily and left. Leah scrubbed at her face with the cloth she used to wipe off the tables, trying to get rid of the feel of Kelley's fingers. Cries from the "maltworms" finally made her jump up to do her duty. She poured ale distractedly, wondering what she would do when he came back.

The following day Leah was stalking an obese gentleman under the stern eyes of Roger and Darby. She had been following him down the street, and now she moved faster to gain on him. She watched a temptingly full pouch bob at his hip and palmed her thin-bladed knife. I'm really going to do this, she told herself in amazement, and then a coach rumbled by so close it nearly hit her. She threw herself out of the way just in time, but sat down abruptly in a puddle of mud and offal at the street's edge. Where was that Sir Walter Raleigh when a girl really needed him, she thought wryly, and saw that the coach was a fine one, drawn by six matched black horses, the royal seal outlined in gold on the coach's side. The Queen, she thought. If I'm not to meet her, at least maybe I can see what she looks like.

Roger yelled something as she got to her feet and sprinted off down the street, holding her dripping skirt away from her legs. She darted into an alleyway so she could cut the coach off at the next corner and possibly get a peek in the windows.

She was both disappointed and excited when she saw that the occupants of the coach were Dr. Dee, Scorpio and Kelley. They were evidently on their way to Whitehall. I've got to warn Scorpio she thought; but how? I can hardly go to Whitehall like this. She looked at her torn and soiled gown.

As the coach was about to disappear from view, she saw it slow down. The door opened and a burly figure leapt to the street. Kelley. He must be on his way back to the tavern for her answer.

Only she wouldn't be there to give it.

I've wasted enough time, she thought. And I'll never be a better thief than I am now. Too bad there's not time to say goodbye to Ellie and the boys.

Determinedly, she set out for the Jewish quarter.

Chapter
13

Scorpio and Dr. Dee were in Dee's study, hemmed in by stacks of books and papers. Scorpio thought that Dee was in a sort of ecstasy amid the smell of moldering old paper and the sight of crabbed writing in faded brown ink. There was a certain comfort in the room, especially since he knew the wind blew keenly outside. A friendly fire crackled on the hearth, and the only sound for some time was the brittle turning of a page or Dr. Dee's muttering as he puzzled over a Kabbalistic symbol.

Scorpio had trouble concentrating on them. He could have sworn he'd seen Leah yesterday from the coach; it had looked so like her, but this woman had been wearing a ragged and filthy gown, and there were smears of soot on each cheek. Would Leah be wandering the streets disguised as an urchin, he wondered, and if so, then why? She had asked that he trust her, but she hadn't bothered to explain whatever plan she had in mind. He had gathered that London had more than its share of thieves, tricksters and the like. Thinking of Leah among them gave him an uneasy feeling.

"Don't you understand what he's saying here?" asked Dr. Dee, shoving a book toward Scorpio.

"No," said Scorpio.

"Oh, that's right, it's Leah who reads Hebrew."

"Is that important to understanding how to use the orb?"

"Well, I don't know as yet. It's a very important bit of

information, which I'll copy into my notebook for further study.'' Dr. Dee set to his copying work with zest as Scorpio watched. Dee was in love with knowledge for its own sake, and he would gladly wade through all the ancient texts whether or not any reference to the orb ever appeared. Though Dee had a mind that questioned, as opposed to the Pope's closed one, Scorpio felt that the doctor was still far distant from any real understanding of the orb. It had felt good, for a while, to work side by side with Dr. Dee, and no doubt Dee meant well, but there was no point in deluding himself. If he wasn't careful, he could end his days as a sorcerer's apprentice, and that would do his people no good.

Scorpio knew that his presence at court also added luster to Dr. Dee's reputation as a mage. It could become addictive to be the latest wonder in the glamorous court of the Virgin Queen, but Elizabeth was notoriously fickle, and the wonder would surely fade.

If anything had been learned in his studies with Dee, it was that the mind was a powerful tool. He knew that the orb had properties that made it seem a living thing, and since it could not speak or hear, the only way to enter into a communion with it was through concentration.

He found himself often walking by the lakeside, looking down into the moving water's surface dappled with sun and shadow and directing his thoughts toward the orb, where it lay on the bottom of the lake. One day he crouched on the bank for almost two hours, sending out questing tendrils of thought. It seemed an idle exercise, since nothing had ever come of it, but this time he was determined, and he kept at it until his brain was fogged with fatigue.

It was as if his thoughts were a searching hand, groping through the murk and mud of the bottom. A chill began at the base of his spine as he felt the imaginary fingers of his mind close on something—something round and solid, not cold as it should have been from its immersion in the frigid waters, but with an organic warmth, as if he held something frail and living within his hand.

Exhaustion numbed his mind, and he couldn't hold the thought; it was as if the fingers stiffened, threatened to drop the precious burden. He concentrated until thought became actively painful. He knew he couldn't hold the connection much longer, if it really was a connection.

How do I know? he asked himself in anguish, and as he asked, he saw a gleam of light ride the ripples in toward the shore. At first he thought he had imagined it, but no, it was there—cool, steady light radiating from deep within the lake, distorted and moved by the sluggish surge of water toward the bank. He let the thought go then and collapsed on the soft mud of the shore, knowing that for the first time he had actually communicated with it, if only for a fleeting second.

I must tell Leah, he thought. But how can I? I don't even know where she is. If there was only some way to contact her. He tried to send his thoughts spiraling out to wherever she was, but he was exhausted and couldn't hold the concentration. His head throbbed from the effort.

He picked himself up from the bank, brushing away mud and twigs. The Dees were going to begin wondering about all the time he spent out by this lake. I'll get some rest, he decided, and try again later.

Kelley had been watching Scorpio as he sat by the lakeside. He had often seen him come here and stare into the water as if he considered it some sort of huge crystal. He knew that some mediums did scry by means of a vessel of water, though he'd never heard of using an entire lake. The day was chill and Kelley wrapped his cloak about himself as he thought of the coldness of the murky depths. So the fool likes to stand by this dead lake and stare, he thought. That doesn't mean I must waste my time watching him. I could be by the fireside now, with a cup of mulled cider. Still, he kept his place, just out of sight behind a leafless hedge.

He remembered the first time he'd found Scorpio near the lake. He had surprised him coming back to the house dripping wet, having fallen into the water. It would have saved me a great deal of trouble if he had drowned that day, Kelley mused. At first it was only an idle thought, and then he began to wonder if Scorpio could swim. He suddenly realized he didn't have to give him that chance. If he fell in once, he could do so again. Kelley laughed under his breath as the thought occurred to him. No, he dared not. It was too bold, and of course, he didn't have the orb. Still, the girl might know where it was by now. She'd disappeared so mysteriously. Once Scorpio was out of the way, he could have the secret from her easily enough, and he didn't think he'd have such a good opportunity again.

His brain was sluggish, but his body was already moving him toward execution of his hastily made plan. He had begun to worm his way down the hillside, keeping to cover when possible, though his quarry wasn't really looking in his direction, anyway. He had come very close when he stepped on a stick that snapped, and Scorpio looked up and saw him.

Kelley thought he read surprise in those bulging eyes. All of the indignities he'd suffered over the past weeks suddenly boiled to the surface of his mind, and he blamed Scorpio for all of them. As always, when his temper flared, he did things he wouldn't be sure about later, but he did remember leaping forward to grab the creature by his skinny arms. Kelley discovered that there was surprising strength in that whiplike body. For a moment he thought he might have made a mistake, as Scorpio almost broke free of his grasp, but he hung on and proved the stronger. He felt all resistance give way as he began to push Scorpio toward the bank. They both went in with a splash, but by his superior strength, Kelley was able to hold his enemy under the water, even though Scorpio's arms and legs thrashed about fiercely. Kelley held him down for a long time, until he began to feel the chill of the water through the blood heat of his fading temper.

As always after one of these bouts, he came back to himself and looked around at the damage that had been done as if someone else had done it. Even drowned, the Aquay's body was too warm to his liking. He pushed the limp thing in his arms as far away as he could into the water's depths. It floated there a moment, looking rubbery and lifeless, and slowly sank. Only now beginning to feel fear, Kelley sloshed to the bank and fled. Like many things that had been done in the heat of his anger, Kelley half regretted the murder. Not that he wasn't happy to be rid of the imposter, but Dr. Dee was very clever about these things. If he found out, their long association and Kelley's psychic talents might not be enough to keep Dee from telling the authorities. Reflexively, Kelley reached for the side of his head. Murder was murder, he supposed, even of a semihuman entity. He sat up late, worrying, and in his dreams, black waters closed over his face, and he thrashed against their icy coils for what seemed like most of the night.

Chapter
14

$\mathcal{N}$ot bothering to return to Lord Foistwell's for fear of meeting Kelley, Leah continued on to the Jewish quarter. Her dress was muddy and torn, but that would go along with her plan. Rather than approaching Auerman's house from the front, she made her way around the newly built structures beside it and came up to the back door.

When she knocked, the same tiny, wrinkled woman appeared. She had a face like a little withered apple and, Leah suspected, a no-nonsense attitude. Leah had wrapped a kerchief around her hair and kept her head bowed, in hopes she wouldn't be remembered from the earlier visit. She also kept her voice to a timid whisper.

"What is it, girl? My old ears can't understand what you're muttering there," said the woman.

"I said I'm hungry and I'd be willing to work to earn a few pence to buy myself a meal."

"Begging, is it? I've never seen you around here before. Where do you come from?"

"I'm Leah de Bernay," she said, glad to be able to fall back into her own identity. "I've newly come from Avignon, escaping the persecution there. I'm very strong and I'd work hard."

"You don't look so very strong to me," said the woman as she grudgingly opened the door. "But I suppose I can find a little work for one of our own. I'm Esther Green.''

Leah followed her inside and found a kitchen little changed from the one in which she'd worked side by side with Grandmère Zarah. Burnished copper kettles, along with other equipment—pot hooks, frying pans, spits, graters, gridirons and the like—hung along one wall within easy reach. In a large stone fireplace something bubbled in a pot hung just above the flames. Antique cupboards occupied another wall, and bunches of leeks and dried herbs were suspended from the high ceiling beams. Leah had been turning into a pretty fair cook, according to Grandmère, until her studies with her father began to take up so much of her time. She was sure it would all come back to her.

"I suppose you could handle the dusting and polishing," said Esther Green, handing her a cloth and leading the way to the next room. Leah worked quickly and efficiently, rubbing the carven wood to a glow. She paused before Jacob Auerman's ornate study door. "Oh, my, no," said Esther. "The master would have a fit if anything were disturbed in there. And you don't want to go in, anyway, girl. My master's a magician, and you wouldn't want to know what goes on in his study."

Leah tried to look properly awed. "Black magic?" she asked.

"Good heavens, no! The master is a devout man, very learned. But see you stay out of his way; he would have no patience with a chit of a girl like you."

Leah nodded obediently, and Esther seemed pleased. She took Leah back into the kitchen and ladled out a bowl of stew from the pot over the fire. "Here, you said you were hungry."

Leah was hungry by now and found the stew delicious. "I suppose you have no place to stay," said Esther.

"No, I—"

"You can stay here for a few days and do some work I

have planned," said Esther. "This is a lonely sort of house, with just myself and the master. I hope you won't mind."

"No, no, I won't mind. And thank you."

Esther insisted on replacing Leah's coarse tavern wench's gown with one of her own stiff black dresses. For several days Leah worked about the house, keeping her eyes averted shyly when Jacob Auerman happened to come into the room, hoping that he wouldn't remember her from her previous visit.

But the oddest thing was that after a while Leah didn't feel she was playing a role, really. Her whole upbringing, except for the fluke of her father teaching her medicine, had prepared her to fit into a proper household. She had to admit she was more at ease here than in the Dees' fine mansion. It felt comforting to lapse back into this familiar way of life.

Each week the Sabbath began with light and wine. Auerman put aside his studies and consultations, Esther her assiduous housekeeping, and the three of them gathered for prayer and worship. As a child, Leah had always been certain that on the Sabbath she would get attention from her mother and father that she sometimes didn't get during the week. At the time, that was all it meant to her, yet there was a strong lesson in seeing everything of the workaday world unfailingly put aside for a day of rest and thanksgiving for blessings received. During the rest of the week, the family might be pulled in several different directions, there might be arguments, tempers lost, but the Sabbath drew them together again and made them know how lucky they were to have each other.

She supposed that remembering these things, now that her family was dead, should have been intensely painful, but she began to find a sense of peace in the slow pace and silence of the Sabbath. Six days for energy and achievement, the seventh for contemplation; it seemed a healthy idea.

As she enjoyed her time in Auerman's house, somewhere in the back of her mind was the knowledge that she had come to despoil the place, to rob Jacob Auerman of his precious secret. She pushed it further back as the days passed. She didn't have to do anything about it until Auerman gave her an opportunity, and so far he had not done so.

Lord Bothwell strolled through St. Paul's, feeling uneasy after what had happened to him there previously. He had sent some men out in search of the raven-haired young woman, but they'd returned saying they'd learned nothing of a girl who might have been a thief or in league with thieves. He wasn't a puling schoolboy, but he still thought of her occasionally and indulged his fantasies.

It was a fine day, and he met several congenial people he knew, so the events of last time had been pushed to the back of his mind, when he saw a prim figure approaching. Dark, severe dress, head covered, basket on arm, the very picture of the proper Jewish housewife . . . except he knew her. It was the girl who had stolen his cloak. Wasn't it? For a moment he hesitated to approach her, and then she seemed to see him, and there was no need to, because she was walking straight toward him.

"Good day, madam," he said stiffly.

Leah couldn't understand his discomfiture at first, then she realized that her whole image had changed from the time she last met him. She wondered what he thought of her now. "You wanted to know who or what I was," she said. "Well, I'm Leah de Bernay. Now you know who and what!"

Her words sounded like a challenge, but she wouldn't take them back.

"I did want to know," he said. "After you ran off with

my cloak and your friends took my purse, it was hard to forget you. Can I be sure you're who you appear to be now?''

Leah smiled in spite of herself. ''Perhaps not, your lordship.''

''Andrew,'' he said.

As they strolled along, they passed the wooden podium that was often used to make announcements. A man stood behind it now. He was wisp-thin and his skin was so pale as to be almost translucent, colorless hair flying wildly around his face as he gesticulated. With his body so emaciated, it seemed as if he were powered only by the mad light in his eyes. In a quavering voice he was exhorting the passersby, and several had stopped to listen, with more joining them all the time.

''Witches can be anybody. Your next-door neighbor, the tavernkeeper, a porter in the street. But in private when no one sees, they call on Satan himself.'' Leah saw that his words were beginning to inflame the listeners, who looked about one another with frantic eyes, as if trying to see a witch mark on the man or woman beside them.

''Satan is an abomination, worse than the Black Death, and the witch is a Plague-carrier that must be wiped out, ere our souls become sick unto death!'' The speaker continued in this way until he had the crowd shouting encouragement and milling about angrily.

''I don't like the look of this,'' said Bothwell. ''There have been several riots in the last month where mobs ran about, destroying the property of those they considered witches, and this fellow seems to be inciting to violence at this moment. I think I'd better get you out of here.''

Keeping himself between her and the growing mob, Bothwell hurried her along until they'd outdistanced the danger. When it was clear they were safe again, she remembered that Bothwell had connections at court. Maybe this would be the way to contact Scorpio. "I wonder if you'd do me a great favor. You're familiar with Queen Elizabeth's astrologer, Dr. John Dee?"

"Astrologer and sometime spy," he said, studying Leah with narrowed eyes. "Do you know him?"

"Yes, and it's important that I send him a message. Could you take it to him?"

"This begins to sound like some sort of plot," he said teasingly.

"It's harmless, really. I have a friend staying with Dr. Dee, Scorpio by name. I would like for him to meet me here, at St. Paul's in three days' time."

"Yes, the mysterious Scorpio, man from another world. The court is buzzing with it."

"You believe he's from another world?"

"I believe the Queen is entertained by the idea, and anything that makes the Queen happy is the truth for the hour. But what connection do you have with him, I wonder?"

"We are friends. You must have friends."

"One or two, when I'm not at my disagreeable worst."

"Then you'll tell him?"

"For a favor in return."

"What sort of favor?"

"Just the pleasure of your company."

"I thought that's what you were getting now."

He laughed. "I have a carriage. What'll it be? The Bear Garden? A play?"

Leah remembered her first tour of London. "Why not a voyage down the Thames?"

"A perfect choice."

When she saw the gaily decorated wherries bobbing at the quayside, Leah felt excitement. She chose one with a red-striped awning and fringes of silver. As the oarsman pulled the boat out onto the rapidly flowing water and the bank receded behind them, she began to worry that this might not be such a good idea. Bothwell pulled her playfully back onto the cushioned seats with him, and she wondered why she chose to be here with him now, when she had been terrified of being alone and far from shore with Kelley. She knew Kelley a great deal better than she knew this man. All she knew of Bothwell for sure was that he had made the gesture of wrapping his cloak around a stranger who had fainted in the street. Would Aimeric have done any less? Just another scapegrace with more gallantry than substance, she thought, remembering Aimeric. But I discovered that flattering words and grand gestures don't always make a man.

"You seem as if you're a thousand miles away," said Bothwell.

"And a few hundred years while we're at it," she said, smiling and undoing the kerchief about her hair. The breeze was good, and the smell from the water wasn't so bad when the wind was blowing stiffly. She saw a flotilla of swans making its graceful way along the distant bank.

Andrew drew closer, and at the moment he leaned over to kiss her, she realized she knew something like this would happen. Their lips met softly for some moments, and then he drew back. She had wanted this to happen, she realized. Living out of place and time, running the streets of London with thieves, had brought out her reckless streak. But still, she'd been taught that physical love was barren without its proper setting—commitment, home, children—and as Bothwell became more ardent, she drew away. Amazingly, the title of "gentleman" he bore was more than just a word. He released her gently.

"There's plenty of time for us," he said.

Leah was silent as they drifted past the notorious Tower of London, a forbidding monolith of weathered gray stone.

From the water, everything was quiet, no rumble of traffic, no cries of street vendors. London was a dream city, slowly passing down the time-stream. She knew somehow that what he had just said was wrong. She didn't belong here and didn't think she'd be here forever. So they really had very little time to get to know each other. A tear slipped from beneath her eyelid and made its way down her cheek. She wiped it away quickly so that Bothwell wouldn't see.

The rest of the ride was spent in conversation, and Leah was in better spirits by the time they arrived back at the quay. Bothwell brought her hand to his lips and wished her farewell, but only, as he said, "until our next meeting."

Leah considered that idea, her cheeks burning, all the way back to Jacob Auerman's, but then she turned her thoughts to more practical matters. I've spent a whole afternoon daydreaming and lollygagging, she thought, and Scorpio's still in danger. Maybe Andrew will deliver my message at court, and maybe he won't. I wish there were some way to contact Scorpio. We should have arranged something before I left. Dr. Dee set great store by telepathic messages. I wonder—

I don't know where my common sense has gone, considering such a course, she thought, but it can't really hurt anything to try.

The next day Leah was scrubbing the walls in Auerman's parlor and thinking how foolish she must have looked sitting in her cubbyhole of a room and concentrating on getting a message through to Scorpio. She hadn't gotten anything but a headache from it. As she approached the door to Auerman's study, she heard a regular, rasping sound. She looked around to see if Esther was nearby, then placed her ear to the heavy door. The sounds continued. They sounded like the deep, resonant breaths of one peacefully asleep and snoring.

She pushed on the door and found it open. This was risky. If she was wrong—

But she saw Auerman lying forward on his desk fast asleep, his nose pressed against some text he'd been deciphering. This was the only chance she'd been given to get her hands on the amulet. At his throat she could see the thin cord from which it descended.

Esther had given her a small scissors to use in her needlework, and that now hung from her belt in an enameled case. With the training she'd had, it should be a simple matter to clip the cord and make away with the amulet.

It would have been simple when she first came here, worming her way into Esther's good graces. But when she was accepted, she'd fallen back into the old traditions. Perhaps these came too easily to her. She had hardly believed she would miss a way of life that promised to keep her tied to a kitchen for the rest of her days, but she had to admit that there were things about life here that were quite satisfying.

She had now been here long enough to know how much Auerman prized the secret symbol in his amulet. Every evening she brought him prayer shawl and phylacteries, and he would take out the slip of parchment, fragile and yellowed. She would see his wrinkled old face intent in the glow of flickering candles—the *merkabah* rider, ascending to spiritual heights by means of meditation.

Leah knew she had to act quickly. There wouldn't be that many chances, and everything was going according to plan, yet still she hesitated.

To take his amulet from him would be like stealing away a bit of his soul, and she couldn't do it.

First the cloak and now this. I'm a total failure as a thief, she thought.

It was a moment before she realized that Auerman's eyes were open. He straightened in his chair and stretched. Although he acted startled to see her, she had the distinct impression that he'd been watching her for a while.

"I'm sorry I disturbed you," she said, backing toward the door.

"You did not disturb me," he said. "I was deep in study, that's all."

"I'll return to my work."

"There's time for that later. Stay awhile."

"Your study frightens me," said Leah, playing the part.

"No, I don't think it does," he said. "I think it fascinates you, or at least you seemed interested that first day when you came here accompanied by those charlatans."

"I didn't think you remembered."

"Well, I'll admit, I wasn't sure you could be the same girl I remembered. When I first met you, you seemed quite unnatural. You knew how to read, and worse, you used your knowledge to contradict your elder. Then I saw you in a whole new light: doing your proper work and making the house more cheerful with your presence. I wondered at first what brought you here, but I see now that you were only out of place and needed to fit yourself back into the natural order of things. Esther has been very pleased with your work, and you've made her less lonely for a time. But I think you won't be with us much longer."

"I've been happy here," said Leah, this time not playing a part. "Your natural order of things won't ever be quite right for me again, but it's good to remember that for every path one takes, another, equally worthy path goes untraveled. That doesn't keep one from choosing a way, but it does tend to teach humility." As she spoke, she seemed to see the eyes of the women in the baths at Avignon, and she would no longer be haunted by them. They'd conveyed their message.

"I hope you'll stay long enough to help me with some of my translations."

"You'd let me?"

"I don't see why not. Since by some mischance you've been taught to read, it would be wasteful not to use the talent. I know that you read Hebrew. Tell me, what of your Latin?"

"I'm fair at Latin and Greek and even better at Provençal."

"You speak Provençal? You're not just a prodigy, but a wonder!" Jacob seemed very excited about this discovery, but she thought that she had been about as bold as she dared for the moment. "Perhaps I'd better see if Esther needs help preparing dinner," she said.

"Yes, yes, perhaps you should," he said, but he still wore a satisfied smile.

Leah was happy now that she didn't have to hide her desire to learn. She and Auerman labored over translations the next morning, and in the afternoon she helped Esther with the housework. But she began to have a restless feeling as she worked, and she didn't know why. Thoughts of Scorpio began to resonate in her mind until she couldn't think of anything else. Scorpio in danger from Kelley, deep in conversation with Dr. Dee, or just looking wistfully down at the glowing orb. Finally, she began to realize that maybe the idea of telepathy wasn't just foolery, after all. Maybe two minds that tried to seek each other out could relay a message. She resolved to find a quiet time that evening so she could be "open" to such a message if it came.

In one of the poorer districts of London, Een Bright was going fishing. It was near midnight, he judged, as he ambled down the narrow lanes between cottages ranked in silence and shadow, carrying across his shoulder a long pole with a small hook at its tip. A fog had crept in, as it was wont to do of nights, and lay in the low places like cotton wool, but that didn't bother Ben. By the lord mayor's edict, lanterns were to be hung on the houses to lighten the gloomy streets, but especially in the poorer quarters this was not done. The streets were left to whoever dared walk them—usually folk like Ben Bright.

He crept up to the window of a cottage and waited there a moment to be sure there was no sound within. Surely, all the folk were abed by now. The window had been carelessly left open, and Ben thrust the long pole within. He had spent the last few days walking along these lanes, peering into this or that window to see what valuables might be lying about, especially those made of cloth. He also noted which householders were careless enough to leave their windows open occasionally.

Aha, thought Ben, as he withdrew the pole, landing a linen tablecloth. A fence will give me a good price for this.

Times being poor in the countryside, Ben had come to London to seek his fortune. He was one of a number of sturdy beggars and rogues who earned their living any way they could, as long as it didn't entail work of any sort.

He knew men who would put rat's bane on their flesh to create sores. Wrapping their limbs in bloody rags, they would go about begging. Himself, he was an Abraham man, someone who pretended to be mad. The clothes he wore were filthy and so tattered they left his arms and legs bare. His hair was as matted as a bird's nest. Country housewives often gave him food as a bribe to get him out of their sight, but he got his best effect by sucking on a piece of soap so that he could throw a frothing fit in front of some poor wretch of good conscience and full purse.

His attention full upon maneuvering his pole to see whether he might hook a plump velvet cushion he had seen earlier, he felt himself gripped firmly by two large hands. Such hands he supposed a constable might have, though how anyone could have slipped up on him he didn't know, since he prided himself on his keen senses.

He was just about to attempt some excuse for his actions when he felt himself, of a sudden, lifted clear of the ground as no constable would be capable of, Ben being a substantial sort. Speechless, he found himself carried like a babe in arms down the sleeping streets. He thought he heard his captor cursing or muttering under his breath in some foreign tongue as he strode along.

Ben was carried in through the courtyard of an old inn, long since fallen into disrepair and abandonment, and was deposited on the littered floor. He landed with a thud. Ben looked around furtively. There was a light in the room, though its glow was of low intensity and far steadier than any lamp should have been. There were two figures, indistinct in the dim light. The larger, the one who had brought him here, was moaning as if in pain. Quickly, he went to the strange lamp and began to rub it over his skin, sighing in relief as he did so.

"Damnable climate," said the smaller one. "The dampness of these fogs set our skin afire."

Now that he had had a moment to collect his thoughts, Ben sat up. "This ain't no pageant," he said raspingly, in a voice that had terrified many a country housewife. "So why have the two of you tricked yourselves out like the Lord of Misrule or some other devilish creature?" They were dressed identically, like mummers at a celebration, in black robes and masks of red lacquer.

"At least he speaks," said the smaller figure. "Some you brought me could only babble, and the rest knew nothing at all. I hope we do better this time, but you certainly chose a poor specimen."

"No one else was abroad."

"No matter, as long as we can question him." The figure came nearer, light playing off the shiny surface of his face—

of his mask, Ben assured himself. He knew that what he was seeing had to be some kind of disguise, but it made the hair stand up on the back of his neck all the same.

"We have come in search of Scorpio the Aquay. He may be accompanied by a female of your species. Do you know if he is in London?"

"I know nothing of this Scorpio," said Ben, hedging to gain time. It seemed he had heard that name recently in idle tavern gossip.

The mummer reached down and grabbed Ben by his ragged garment and began to shake him until Ben felt like a rat in the jaws of a terrier.

"Scorpio . . . He's the famous . . . celestial . . . traveler . . . at court . . . The man . . . from another world," said Ben between bounces, repeating the rumors he had heard about the Queen's latest prodigy.

"So where might we find this otherworldling?" The shaking stopped, but it only brought that nightmare face into greater focus, making Ben turn away rather than look at it.

"Everyone knows that he's with Dr. Dee." A hand grasped his ragged clothes again. "At his home at Mortlake in Surrey," Ben added hastily.

"At last we can finish our quest and get out of this hellish climate."

As the figure turned, the robe flared and Ben got a look at the thing's feet. It was no wonder he had heard no footfalls. The foot, split into two nailless toes in front, was soled in a spongy layer of what looked like thick callus.

No longer able to assure himself that the beings were only men in strange disguise, Ben shrieked and rolled into a ball. He was still lying there, mumbling to himself, when the two left a few moments later, though he heard no door open or close. The worst thing was, he told himself, that when Ben Bright the madman tried to tell the authorities what he had seen, no one would believe him.

Chapter
15

*T*he next morning Kelley came whistling to the breakfast table. He knew there were clouds in the sky, with rain threatening, but to him it was a beautiful day. No more eel threatening my position with Dr. Dee, he thought. Everything is going to be—As he sat down, he looked across the table and saw . . . Scorpio. Kelley sat there staring dumbly until Mistress Dee reminded him it was impolite to stare. And not only did Scorpio not look dead, he looked positively cheerful, as he set upon an immense breakfast. "What's the matter with you, Edward?" asked Dee.

"Yes, is there a problem?" asked Scorpio, fixing Kelley with his protuberant green eyes. Except for the murderous intent of the man, Scorpio had felt the whole thing was somewhat of a joke. It was hard to kill Aquays by drowning, since they could stay underwater for much longer than a human being. As soon as he had realized what Kelley intended, he played along, pretending to be the weaker, though there was a great deal of wiry strength in his slim body. He had thrashed about and then went limp, and by the look of the man's face, he had been completely fooled.

This isn't happening, Kelley told himself. He's dead. He has to be dead. I drowned him. I remember it. He looked at his hands and remembered the struggles.

147

"Care for some conger in sauce?" asked Scorpio, passing a dish.

How could someone clearly dead now be alive? Kelley studied Scorpio with narrowed eyes. Could he be a master conjuror and not just a fake? But what sort of powers must a man have to return from the dead? Kelley racked his brain trying to remember the incident, but since it had happened in a fit of anger, he had problems bringing it back in clear detail. Is it possible, he wondered, that being angry at Scorpio, I dreamed it all? Sometimes when the anger takes me, I have almost no memory of what occurred. It may have been only a particularly vivid dream. In fact, since Scorpio still does everything that the living do, that must be what happened. But it was so real!

Later that day Scorpio sat beside the lake, letting his mind fall into a state of utter relaxation. He replayed the breakfast scene in his mind, much to his own amusement, though he supposed that someone hating him enough to try and commit murder wasn't really a laughing matter. Still, there had been someone trying to kill him for some time now, and he was almost getting used to the feeling.

Leah had been in his thoughts a lot this morning, too. He saw her preening in the yellow gown Mistress Dee had given her; running through the streets in ragged garb; mourning the death of her family. This was the first time today that he'd had the opportunity to be alone and really try to send out his thoughts. He had learned a little more about the technique of it after that first time when he'd exhausted himself. It was better to let the mind float, as one floats on water. He watched a dead leaf rock on the lake's surface and let the thoughts of Leah flow through his mind unimpeded. He wasn't sure whether they were his own thoughts or not.

After a time, behind the images of Leah, he thought he

saw a familiar background appearing. It was fragmentary
at first. Stately pillars, impressive windows, an architecture
of arches and soaring towers, like a cathedral. St. Paul's.
He realized he was seeing St. Paul's Cathedral in London.
And in all the images the sun was at its zenith, so the time
must be around noon. He'd also been told St. Paul's was
a meeting place, so what better location for Leah and himself
to meet. He had seen it, but only from a distance as the
carriage passed, so he sent his own fleeting impression of
the place as if in reassurance that the message had been
received. He still had half an idea that he was deluding
himself. There was only one way to find out. He must
arrange with the Dees for a carriage to take him to London
immediately. There was just time to arrive before noon.

Kelley sat at Dr. Dee's writing desk, also deep in concentration, as he struggled to compose a letter to Burghley
and Walsingham. He had been practically illiterate when he
first came here, but Dee had been insistent about him learning his letters. He still had problems with spelling. The
letter read, more or less legibly:

> I have discoverd some information that may be very
> important as regards Her Majesty's safety and welfaire,
> but must conferr with you in pryvate. I will be coming
> to London tomorrow and hope that you will meet with
> me. Relying upon your wise judgement in this matter,
> I remain . . .

Remembering the vividness of the dream in which he'd
dispatched Scorpio, he began to tremble, and his shaking
hand made a blot on the page. Damn. My life's been a
shambles ever since those two showed up. And there's more
to that Scorpio than meets the eye, even though what does
meet the eye is ugly enough. Him with that stupid mask,

and the Queen always teasing at him to remove it in her presence. If I can ever get him to do so, she'll probably fall over in a dead faint.

With the crowds of London at a fever pitch about witches in their midst, the Queen would dare not protect him once he was shown to be a sorcerer.

Dr. Dee appeared in the doorway. "Where have you been? I've been looking all over for you. I'm busy with my astrological calculations, and farmer Rolfe has arrived to consult about his lost cow. I told him you'd be right with him."

Kelley cursed under his breath. Since finances were so straitened, Dee had been taking in money any way he could, even to locating lost articles for the common folk—a cloak, a sack of grain and now even a lost cow. Dr. Dee usually managed to be conveniently busy on these occasions, and Kelley had to use the glass alone.

Grumbling, he went to the séance room. Farmer Rolfe was a great, oafish lout of a man with sun-reddened face who looked and smelled as if he'd come directly from the barnyard.

"The last time I seen her was in the south pasture. We're in sore need without a cow to give milk, so I hope you can help us," said Rolfe as Kelley gritted his teeth and took his place behind the glass.

On such occasions he set aside all the usual flummery that was reserved for richer clients. Simply keeping the room dark was enough to properly awe the countryfolk, who were superstitious to begin with, anyway.

Kelley's eyes inadvertently went to the glass, and he thought he saw shifting patterns of light within it. He averted his eyes slightly and began to work up a proper trance state. The whole thing could be done in a few minutes if he worked it right. He began to spout gibberish in a sonorous voice, noting with satisfaction that Rolfe looked terrified. When I go out on my own, thought Kelley, I'll have an assistant to handle these commonplace matters.

The gibberish suddenly stuck in his throat as he saw curved reflections dancing on the wall before him. Light shimmered like a giant golden bubble, and two figures were taking shape inside it. It's happening, thought Kelley in a panic, what I always feared. Without knowing it, I've called something. He sat paralyzed in the chair as the apparitions came clearer, two man shapes, one broad and muscular, the other thinner with a regal bearing. Both had hideous, bird-like faces, and black robes flapped about their bodies where there should have been no wind blowing. Their red skin and coiling black horns made them look suspiciously like devils. The slender one carried a glowing, golden orb.

Rolfe had been growing more fidgety all the time, and now he couldn't seem to keep himself from throwing a glance over his shoulder where Kelley was staring so fixedly. He looked from the shapes back at Kelley with a new awe.

The figures ballooned large for an instant, then came into reality with an almost audible snap.

"Are they going to help look for my cow?" asked Rolfe innocently as Kelley cowered back from the visitants.

"You fool, they're not part of the show. I don't know where they came from."

This was too much for farmer Rolfe; with a half-suppressed scream he bolted for the door and was gone.

Kelley would have liked to run, too, but the apparitions were between himself and the door. "Avaunt, begone, spirits, I command thee!" he shouted with more conviction than he felt. The two only continued to look at him curiously. He had a sinking feeling that he should have bothered about a magic circle this time.

Ignoring Kelley, the two visitors walked around the sé-ance room, inspecting everything carefully. They were most interested in the crystal, looking into it and seeing their weird faces appear even more distorted, and making noises that sounded to him like evil laughter.

"I conjure thee in the name of—" Kelley began again.

"Silence, worm," said the thinner one. "We seek Scorpio. What can you tell us of him? Lie and I'll move you around a dimensional corner and turn you inside out. You'll be able to look down and see the beating of your own heart."

He prostrated himself, babbling almost incoherently. "Scorpio. He was here, but he went to London for some purpose. I don't know why. St. Paul's, he said. That is all I know, your lordships, your Graces, Your Worships. Please do not harm me!" Being turned inside out didn't sound like an impossible threat coming from these two.

Seeming to laugh again at Kelley's fear, the spirits grasped the orb between them and it emitted a burst of light. Concentric rings of radiance blinded Kelley for the moment, and when he looked again, they were gone.

Dr. Dee was working busily in his study when Kelley came bursting in, wild-eyed. "I quit," he said. "I quit your employ as of now."

"Calm down, man, what's the matter?"

"You kept pushing me into contacting the spirits. Angels, you said. Don't tell me the things I just saw were angels. They were red and had horns; tails, too, I think. Yes, definitely tails. They were carrying a golden orb, and—"

It just now occurred to him where he had seen a glowing sphere like that before, and he also now reflected that there was something similar between the faces of the apparitions and that of Scorpio.

"Scorpio," he said. "I never thought to see another face as misshapen as his. They were looking for him, and they had an orb, too. He's real, not a fake. A real sorcerer! I killed him, you know. Yes, I held him underwater until he stopped breathing. All the time he was only laughing at me, playing with me.''

"Calm yourself, man, you look ready for a fit of apoplexy.''

A real sorcerer, thought Kelley. And all the time, I accused him of being a charlatan. I wonder what awful plans he has for the Queen and the realm. Now it's more important than ever that I unmask him and turn him over to the authorities. Those speaking out against witches are right; there *are* unnatural things about. Once I tell the constable what I know, Scorpio's certain to be imprisoned, maybe even burned as a witch, and then my troubles with him will be over.

Chapter 16

*T*he sun stood just at noon, wreathed in a veil of cloud, as Leah made her way to the cathedral. For all she knew, this was just a fool's errand. It seemed impossible to send messages through the air. But maybe Bothwell had delivered the message for her; there was still a chance that Scorpio had received it that way. It didn't really matter, as long as the result was the same.

She lingered in the nave for a few minutes, and then when no one appeared, she began to walk around the grounds. St. Paul's was a large place. He could be here and she could miss him. No, it would be better to stay in one spot. She stopped by an ornamental fountain.

A moment later she saw Scorpio running toward her.

Leah ran to meet him, and then they both stopped, looking at each other somewhat embarrassedly. Then on impulse Leah reached out and enfolded Scorpio in a hug, oblivious of those who stared at his odd appearance.

"I didn't think it would work. It couldn't work, and yet . . . " stammered Scorpio, looking embarrassed again as Leah released him, as if he were uncertain how to react to her gesture.

"We read each other's thoughts," said Leah. "I seem to remember something about that." She strove to recall what had happened in that dream womb so long ago, but it was no use.

"Perhaps this means that we can control the orb with the power of our minds, as Dr. Dee told me," said Scorpio. "Do you know what that would mean?"

"It would mean we'd have our pick of all time and space. We could go anywhere, anywhen."

"We could go back to before your father first became involved with de Signac's intrigues," said Scorpio. "Or better yet, even before you met me."

"I don't know if I'd want that."

"You could have your life back."

"It wouldn't really be my life anymore. Not after all this. I'd surely spend my days waiting for the appearance of a troublesome demon that never arrived."

"Well, you wouldn't have to go back. How about forward? Live in the time that pleases you best."

"It sounds tempting. Then you could go back to your own world."

She supposed she didn't understand what it must be like to be in the midst of folk who were so alien. Terrapin was the only place for him, but still Leah felt almost bereft when she thought of going on to an unknown future without him. Foolish, she thought, to think he could have the same feelings as a human being.

"Anyway, the reason I asked you to meet me here was to warn you about Edward Kelley," she said. "He doesn't just want to steal the orb; he wants you out of the way."

"Thanks for the warning," said Scorpio, "but I'm afraid he's already done his worst."

"Has he actually made an attempt on your life?"

"Better than that, he killed me," said Scorpio with a burble of laughter. He shared the story with Leah, who didn't seem to find it all that humorous.

"I shouldn't have left you there. What if he'd tried something that didn't involve water?"

"I never thought of that," said Scorpio. "But now he won't get the chance."

"I'll have some stories to tell you when there's more time. Anyway, I think I've got Jacob Auerman almost convinced to show us his mysterious talisman. It might still be of help."

"Yes, while I was playing at sorcerer with Dr. Dee, you've been working hard."

"I'll take you to him now."

As they walked by the podium, Leah noticed that the pale, thin speaker was there again, loudly exhorting a knot of interested passersby about the imminent dangers of witchcraft. "Let's hurry; there was almost a riot here earlier," she said.

As the man stood there, gesticulating wildly, behind him a vision began to form, within expanding rings of golden light. His audience, some of whom had been heckling him, suddenly became riveted, and the speaker waxed even more eloquent.

Leah and Scorpio stood frozen in fear as the apparitions grew more solid and recognizable. "Hunters! Here!" said Leah. "I thought we had lost them centuries ago."

"Run, hide!" shouted Scorpio, for once letting his instincts have full sway. They both turned to run, but the crowd began to scream and panic as they became aware of the alien visitors, jostling and pushing Scorpio and Leah and giving them no room to run.

Ardon, the larger of the two Hunters, put out a hand and grabbed the skinny speaker around the neck, lifting him straight up off the ground and cutting his discourse short. Then he tossed the man aside as easily as if he were a bag of meal and pointed toward Scorpio. "Lethor, there he is! Let's get him!"

A voice cut through the noise. "There, that deformed man is the sorcerer." Leah saw Kelley alight from a carriage and run toward them. "He's the demon-conjuror. And the woman is his apprentice. Seize them or all is lost!"

The crowd rallied, their attention still divided. A pot-bellied merchant looked as if he were about to lay hands on Scorpio, who tossed back the cowl of his robe. Seeing this alien visage, the merchant and those standing nearby recoiled, leaving an avenue of escape.

Leah and Scorpio wasted no time taking advantage of this; they began to run.

"Don't be afraid. He can't resist all of you," shouted Kelley. The mob took his words to heart and gave chase.

The two Hunters also tried to follow, but they were effectively cut off from their prey by a ravening mob. Ardon drew his laser and looked as if he were about to cut his way through the crowd, but Lethor gestured for him to put it away. "There are too many of them for that to be effective," he said. Hunter ethics prevented gratuitous slaughter. Killing was always done with a purpose in mind.

"This way," panted Leah, pushing Scorpio toward the cathedral and sparing a look over her shoulder to see how close the front runners of the mob had come. She judged that they were still far enough ahead for what she had in mind.

"We can never outrun them," gasped Scorpio.

"We don't have to. I learned a little something while I was gone."

She remembered Lord Foistwell holding forth about knowing every nook and cranny of a place before planning a crime there. She didn't really know every detail about St. Paul's, since it was such a large place, but she thought she remembered something that would be helpful. There had been ongoing attempts at repair of the crumbling old building, and she had earlier noticed where a loose wooden panel in the wall had been put back carelessly. There was only a very small space behind it. She hoped that both she and

Scorpio would fit. There was little time to try it for size; they crammed themselves into the musty crevice, and Leah let the panel fall back over them.

They heard the thunder of the crowd's feet as they dashed by, shouting, "Death to the witches. This way, I can hear their footsteps!"

"We must wait until we're sure they have gone," whispered Leah. The cramped space gave her a claustrophobic feeling, and if the sharp eyes of the Hunters should notice that this section of the paneling didn't quite fit together— She shivered, remembering previous experiences with the alien beings.

Time passed and the dark, cramped quarters began to remind her of the dream womb inside the orb where both their minds had been linked. The telepathy that had brought them to St. Paul's was a poor thing compared to it, but she realized that that was where the link had originated. More orb travel would no doubt accentuate it. She wondered whether it was a good idea for beings so different to share such a close communion. They had already decided they were bound for separate futures, once their problems with the orb and the Hunters were resolved.

When they peered out after a wait of several more minutes, the mob had passed, and there was no sign of the Hunters. No doubt they'd followed the others.

"Lord Foist was right," said Leah. "Now we must make our way to the Jewish quarter."

Chapter
17

*L*eah and Scorpio hurried toward the Jewish quarter, keeping a close eye for any sign of possible pursuers.

"I don't understand," said Scorpio. "You say you enrolled in a thieves' school in order to get the amulet away from Auerman."

"I learned all the lessons quite well," said Leah, "but I failed the final test, which was to actually steal something. I must have been the school's biggest failure."

"But you think you're going to have access to the secret because you *didn't* steal it."

"It seems so."

"This is a confusing world, isn't it?"

"That's a conclusion I have often come to."

Esther Green gave Scorpio a sharp look, but she escorted them to Auerman's study. "You said earlier that if Jacob Auerman had a chance to listen to your story, he might help," said Leah. "I think you were right. I could have tried to explain, but you're the logical one to plead your case."

Auerman greeted them in the study, and this time listened patiently to all that Scorpio had to tell. When he finished his tale, Auerman's expression was rapt. It was as if he had discovered that his ideas about the possibilities of En Sof,

161

the infinite, were even greater than he had imagined.

"About this other world," he said. "I believe you. And to return to save the lives of your people is something I understand. Do you truly think the secret of the symbol will help you master your orb-craft?"

"We have to try," said Leah.

"Yes, I can see that you do." The old Kabbalist bent his head and took the amulet from around his neck. Deliberately, he handed it to Scorpio, as if he feared to let it get out of his possession after all these years.

Leah took it and carefully unrolled the tiny scroll, using the dexterity Lord Foist had taught her.

"I can't read it," said Auerman. "But perhaps you can. It's written in Provençal by an early Kabbalist scholar."

Haltingly, she read the words written in fading sepia ink: "On the Chariot Throne sat a being with two aspects. On the right, the male, on the left, female. Neither could see the other and each was kept from moving by the opposing force of the other. The Matrona, the female, spread out from her place and adhered to the male side until he moved away from his side and she came to unite with him face-to-face. And when they united, they appeared as veritably one body. When they were one, the moon waxed full—" Here Leah paused.

"Or maybe the sphere became complete," she said uncertainly, and then continued. "And the fiery chariot ascended to the realm of dreams."

There was more, on the same order. When Leah had finished reading, she looked at Auerman expectantly. "Do you know what this signifies?"

"There is an ancient Kabbalistic tradition that the Deity has a feminine counterpart, not, as one might think, representing softness and kindness, but rather, stern judgment and demonic power. Her symbol is the moon. It may mean only that a man should keep in touch with the feminine aspect of reality by taking a good wife, but it may mean much more. It is too soon to judge. We must study this further to see what it might mean. Can you come tomorrow?''

"I'm sorry," said Scorpio, "but our time here grows short.''

Thanking Auerman, they left and paused outside, deciding what to do next. "Do you think anything we learned will prove useful?" asked Leah. "It talked of a cooperation between the male and the female. We are male and female.''

"Yes, but that should mean that we can master the orb, but that the Hunters cannot. That's the exact opposite of how it is.''

"There was mention of a glowing orb.''

"Or only the moon," said Scorpio. "I'm afraid it was too arcane to give us any help with our present problem.''

"Your experiments with mind control of the orb are promising, but there's so much we don't know," said Leah. "We may have to consider any possible clue, even the most obscure. We simply have to keep trying until we master it.''

"The mobs here make me nervous," said Scorpio. "Maybe we'd best return to Mortlake. The Dees' carriage is still waiting at Whitehall.''

"That's a good idea, but perhaps we should travel separately. Someone might spot us and remember that we were together at the cathedral. It will also give the Hunters two different trails to follow. It could confuse them.''

"All right," said Scorpio, "I'll meet you back at Mortlake, but be careful.''

Chapter
18

Ardon picked his way down a street littered with disgusting substances, wondering what sort of people could live in these hovels. Above, clouds were gathering and beginning to rumble with thunder. Ardon muttered to himself about the uncomfortable tightness of his skin in this high humidity. If it began to rain, they would have to duck under a roof quickly before the moisture made their hides blister and crack. Both Hunters bore the scars of being drenched while chasing Scorpio in Avignon. Hopefully, the rain would hold off until they'd done this little job.

Ardon lifted his hand in signal to Lethor to show that he had checked out this side of the street and had seen nothing of the Aquay or the girl. That was like an Aquay, he thought, dragging a native into what should have been kept private. But since the female had chosen to play a role in this, she would have to take what came. She could certainly expect no mercy from him; that was the rule the Hunters always played by, and they were scrupulous about their own rules.

Having their orb to bear them to different locations didn't help because this city was a maze of dirty streets, and the only way to find their prey now was to search every one in the general vicinity.

They moved on down the street, store owners slamming closed their shutters at sight of them, passersby tending to

165

pass by on the opposite side of the thoroughfare. They would have captured them at the cathedral if that earless rogue had not interfered. Ardon's hatred was slow and methodical, like all of his emotions. As he lumbered along, he considered the ways and means of Kelley's death for a long time. That was pleasant. But he saw that Lethor was signaling to him to enter the next street. Lethor liked to do things fast, and it was sometimes hard to figure out what he wanted.

Ahead of him in the narrow, winding street, he saw a familiar figure; he homed his near-vision in on her to make sure. It was she, the girl Leah. He raised his hand and waved it in the prearranged gesture that meant the prey had been identified. Of course, it would have been much easier for the two of them to slink up behind her and drill a hole in her back with laserfire, but tradition said a Hunter had to let his victim see him first. The hunt became more exciting that way. Ardon began to feel excited, despite his phlegmatic disposition.

He saw Lethor dart back behind the buildings, evidently trying to get ahead of her. Sure enough, he saw his lean companion leap from the shadow of one of the shops, and it was obvious the prey had seen him, because she began to run in earnest. It didn't matter, thought Ardon, because the Hunters would always run faster.

Leah felt clumsy and foolish as the Hunter appeared so nonchalantly before her, as if he'd been tracking her all this time without her knowing it. This was the warning Scorpio had talked about, Hunter etiquette. She stood in front of a barbershop. The white pole with its red striping, indicative that the barber also bled people as a cure for illness, seemed a ghastly symbol under the circumstances. She knew that there were two of them, but she didn't see the other. Perhaps, like she and Scorpio, they had decided to split their forces to cover more ground. She could only hope so. The

Hunter was larger and stronger than she was and could outrun and outjump her. The only advantage she might possibly have was that she'd worked this neighborhood as a thief, and she knew the terrain. Perhaps the alien did not. She scanned the sky. Perhaps it was too much to hope that a downpour would make the aliens seek shelter.

She ran with all her might, ducking into alleys, crawling under broken foundations, dodging past oncoming traffic, her terror making her reckless. Daring a look over her shoulder, she could not see a pursuer. Possibly, her strategies had worked. Her spirits fell when she caught a glimpse of another silhouette at a corner. He moved back, to hide behind a pile of crates, but he didn't move fast enough to escape detection. Seeing him forced her to move off in an unplanned direction. She had the panicked feeling that the two of them were herding her to a place she didn't wish to go.

She was sure of this later when she reached the mouth of an alleyway and darted inside, the stink of corruption rising around her. In the semidarkness she heard scuttling noises and saw a rat's naked tail slip behind a pile of debris. She was so aware of the real threat behind her that nothing so familiar as a rat could frighten her now.

From the positions of the two pursuers behind her, the alley was the only place she had left to go. It appeared to be a blind alley from the street, but previous experience with this quarter told her that between a building and a mound of rubble was a small egress, wide enough for a small person to squeeze through. She didn't think she'd be able to do it with them so close on her trail, though. She needed time to make her escape, a distraction—anything.

She heard the inexorable *pad-pad-pad* of the Hunters' feet on the cobbles and realized they were closer than she had thought. As her hand brushed the pouch at her side, she felt something angular through the cloth. She'd forgotten about this. Maybe it would work. At this point she had to try.

Ardon was beginning to feel a little fatigue from the long chase. This female was stronger than she looked, and she had been good prey. Ardon hoped that Lethor would give her the honor of dying with a clean shot between the eyes, rather than drawing it out, as he sometimes did, for fun. Obviously, this stench-filled corridor between structures was closed at one end by a slide of rubble, so now that she was in, she was trapped. All that was left to do was for Lethor to go in and make the kill. It was dark inside, but the prey was surely not dangerous. Ardon wondered why his companion was hesitating.

"I hear something," said Lethor. "She can't escape, perhaps she's coming this way."

"Do you hear her footsteps?"

"I hear something, some odd noise. But she is the only one who went in there and the only one who could be stirring."

"Except possibly vermin."

"Other vermin," said Lethor, and they shared a laugh. Who ever said Hunters didn't have a good sense of humor? Ardon wondered. Now he could hear the sound, too. Something was coming this way, but it was an odd, buzzing, clicking sort of sound.

It was coming closer. Both of them tensed, fingers on the studs of their weapons.

A mannikin made of metal whirred and clicked as it walked shakily down the alleyway's cobblestone surface. Lethor's curse was loud in the confined space. He turned his laser on the toy and incinerated it and then dashed into the alley. Ardon heard him curse again and ran in, to see Lethor staring at a very small escape hatch through the pile of rubble.

"She looked too tired to get far," said Lethor hopefully.

Then both of them looked up as they heard raindrops begin to patter in the streets outside. "Take cover," screamed Ardon as an errant raindrop touched his skin with a sizzling sound.

Chapter 19

*S*corpio made his way back to where he'd left Dr. Dee's carriage and hastened toward it. A slight shower had washed the streets, leaving them glistening, but now the clouds were clearing away. He hoped Leah was safe. He should have insisted she come back with him and ride to Mortlake in the carriage, but at the moment it had seemed like a good idea to split up to confuse the Hunters.

He was about to greet the driver when he saw that the carriage was occupied. Edward Kelley sat with a stout, muscular man in some sort of official-looking uniform with an emblem on it. Two others, armed guardsmen, sat opposite them. Scorpio didn't think he liked the look of things. It appeared to be a trap.

In the confusion of the moment, he retreated, but found himself approaching the palace. He still carried the mask he had worn, in a fold of his robe, so he stopped and donned it. He approached the guards at the front gate, holding out his hand to show the signet ring the Queen had given him as a token. "You know this seal," he said. "Her Majesty has summoned me on a matter of great import."

The guards, seeing Elizabeth's seal on the ring, let him pass.

Hide! Flee! his instincts were telling him, but he knew the palace was large, and there would surely be a spot he could hide in until Kelley gave up his search.

"Scorpio," said a voice. He looked up to see a woman dressed like a fairy princess, with a sparkling mask and frail wings of gauze attached at either shoulder. He thought he recognized her as one of the ladies of the Privy Chamber, though he didn't know them all by name.

"The Queen was not expecting you."

"I was not expecting myself," he said, which made the lady laugh.

"We're preparing for a masked ball this evening. Why not attend? You're already dressed for it."

"Well, I don't—I'm not—" he began, but the lady soon had him in tow, chattering at him animatedly. He was always at a loss on human social occasions, but perhaps his luck was not entirely bad. Surely, Kelley's search could not include the Queen's hall in the midst of a gala celebration.

He heard lively music playing from behind huge double doors, and as he entered, he felt in the midst of chaos. It was as if this were a convocation of worlds, and each one had sent as a representative its most bizarre and colorful species. Velvets, spangles, and cloth of gold had been used in lavish display. Outlandish masks covered the faces of the guests, and for the first time since he'd been here, he felt inconspicuous.

Tables, running the length of the hall, offered a vast selection of wines and dainties, so he lingered here, nibbling this or that morsel, hoping to lie low until Kelley gave up.

A man dressed in Roman toga with a silver mask of comedy held before his face jostled Scorpio at the banquet table. Though these were courtiers, Scorpio noticed that their behavior was uninhibited. They drank and danced unrestrainedly and were likely to play coarse practical jokes or indulge in rude jests.

"Did you hear the latest? Musicians are healthy because they live by good airs," said the man, slapping Scorpio on

the back and laughing loudly. "D'you get it, music ...
airs?"

Though he tried to squirm away, the man continued. "Did
you know a cannibal is the lovingest man to his enemy, for
willingly no man eats what he loves not."

After a few more of these *bons mots*, Scorpio was able
to excuse himself and escape from the jokester.

Kelley was arguing loudly with the guardsmen at the gate
just as Walsingham's carriage arrived. "What's this all
about?" Walsingham asked, recognizing Kelley as Dee's
assistant.

"This lout allowed a dangerous sorcerer to pass the gates,
and for all I know he's gone to work his evil magics on the
Queen herself."

"A threat against the Queen—" began Walsingham, his
protective instincts aroused. "Who is the scoundrel?"

"You know him as Scorpio of the Aquay, and I believe
he's managed to worm his way into Her Majesty's good
graces, but I've come into possession of some interesting
information concerning the invoking of demons."

"I never cared for that mask and that shrilling voice,"
said Walsingham. "I should have known there was something amiss about him. You say he's gone to harm the
Queen?"

"Yes, and I've brought the law with me to deal with the
beggar," said Kelley, gesturing toward the constable and
three guardsmen who had accompanied him. "But these
fools have let him enter."

"He had the Queen's seal," said the gateman. "How
was I to know?"

"Let us in and we'll apprehend the felon," said the constable self-importantly.

"Do you realize the court is holding a masked ball this
evening?" demanded Walsingham. "I don't approve of

such mummery, of course, but the Queen loves her entertainments. But, see here, I can't let you go barging in among the guests. It would cause a scandal.''

''We must uphold the law,'' said the constable.

''Then you must do it in costume,'' said Walsingham, ''and you must cause no disturbance. If you search and find that Scorpio isn't there, you must go away quietly.''

''All right,'' said Kelley, ''but I'm sure he'll be there.''

Once inside, Walsingham sent a servant to fetch costumes for Kelley and his men. Grumblingly, they put them on. Kelley was given a jester's motley, and bells jingled at every step as he approached the hall. Now I'll have my revenge on the boggart, he thought. Walking closely together, they strolled among the guests. ''Remember that this is the Queen's hall,'' he whispered to the others. ''We can have no disturbance here or it may be our heads.''

''Are you enjoying yourself, Scorpio?'' asked the lady who had conducted him here.

''Yes, very much,'' he said.

''I think the costumes are so very exciting,'' she said. ''Some are quite grotesque. You should have seen the pair in black robes and skullcaps. I don't know how they did it, but they'd varnished their skin a brilliant red. And those ram's horns on their heads—''

''Where? Where did you see them?'' asked Scorpio, suddenly feeling panic. A crowd of bizarrely dressed folk that could hide *him* could hide others as well. ''If you see them again, don't go near them,'' he said. ''I'm afraid I must go now.''

''But you haven't yet danced.''

''I'm ignorant of such a human custom, my lady.''

The orchestra struck up a pavane.

''It's easy to learn. I could teach you.''

Scorpio was about to take flight when he realized that the

man in the jester costume was approaching him rapidly, and he didn't look friendly. In fact, a closer look at him revealed Kelley's general build and swaggering walk. The lady was pulling him toward the line of dancers, so he let himself be towed there and tried to mimic her motions.

It was no use. He, who was as graceful as a shark in water, was totally at a loss on a dance floor. Some of the other dancers got out of his way; others stopped to laugh at him. His face was hot with shame until he realized the room had gone silent and someone was standing before him.

Her head was hidden in a casque set with black brilliants, from which rose tall, feathery antennae. A black domino obscured her eyes. Behind her head was an enormous lace collar in the fanciful shape of a butterfly, sprinkled with sparkling, varicolored gems. Her immense, flaring skirt was yellow with black butterfly markings.

Those around her were bowing, but he would have known her anyway by the long-fingered white hand she held out to him. She signaled the orchestra to play on, and in the midst of the costumed court, Elizabeth asked him to dance.

"I couldn't, Your Majesty," he said. "With my clumsiness I'll make a spectacle of us both."

"That's the beauty of being a queen," she said. "I can make a spectacle of myself whenever I wish, and no one *dares* laugh."

"I thank you, Your Majesty," said Scorpio when the dance ended. "I feel very honored, but I really must go. It would be better for everyone concerned."

Before he had a chance to leave, Kelley jingled up to him, flanked by the men of the law. "Pardon us, your ladyship," said Kelley, who had evidently not recognized the Queen, "but you don't know who you were dancing with. He is an evil sorcerer, master of the black arts. I personally have seen the devils he conjured forth."

"You think I'm a charlatan like yourself," said Scorpio,

"because you trick the gullible out of a few coins with your so-called talent of scrying."

"So-called," sputtered Kelley. "I'll have you know that I've been very successful in calling up the spirits by means of a crystal. My contacts, Madimi and Medicina, have imparted to me many arcane secrets, which Dr. Dee writes in his book."

The constable began to eye Kelley as he bragged of his prowess with the showstone. "I think the authorities would also be interested in one who calls up the spirits," he said. "Surely, this, too, is unnatural."

"No, no, you misunderstand. It is angels I speak with . . . angels."

"You call them angels. Well, we can sort all that out at Newgate Prison," said the constable. "Scorpio of Aquay, I arrest you in the name of—"

"The name of the Queen?" said Elizabeth, lowering her domino so they could see to whom they spoke.

"Begging your pardon, Your . . . Your Majesty," said Kelley, doffing his belled cap.

Though the others were riveted by fear, a long-standing grudge made Kelley sidle toward Scorpio. When he was close enough, he reached up and plucked the mask from the being's face.

Several ladies standing nearby screamed when Scorpio was unmasked. And the Queen looked shocked at first.

"There, you see, unmasked as a conjuror," said Kelley. "Can you not see it by his face?"

"It is as I had once guessed," said Elizabeth softly. "A handsome countenance. Though, I'll admit, very different than how I had imagined it. I think you told the truth when you said you came from a world far from here."

She spoke more sternly. "Would anyone dare to interrupt *my* festivities, to threaten *my* honored guests?" And the guardsmen retreated, leaving Kelley alone with Elizabeth's wrath.

The answer to the Queen's question seemed to be yes, because at that moment Scorpio saw two tall, black-draped figures cross the room and focus their weapons on him.

He whirled around and began to run, hoping to draw them away from the Queen and her courtiers. A flash of laserfire sizzled along a tabletop beside him, turning every dish to flambé as he took to his heels. A glance over his shoulder showed him that two of the Queen's gentlemen-pensioners had advanced to protect her, drawing their swords.

He saw a laser burst hit a sword blade, and the poor guardsman watched as his steel bowed, melted and puddled on the floor. Then Scorpio saw no more as he darted from the room.

Chapter
20

*L*eah, having hitched a ride with a farmer on his dray, arrived at Mortlake, expecting to find Scorpio there. When she didn't see him, she couldn't hide her concern from Dr. Dee.

"Something's wrong, isn't it?" he said. "I should have known it when Edward came in here like a man demented, offering to quit my service and babbling that the angels we summoned were really devils."

"That means the Hunters have been here," said Leah.

"Can you explain any of this to me?"

"Only that the Hunters are aliens like Scorpio, and they want to kill us." She explained to him how his clockwork mannikin had diverted the Hunters' attention long enough for her to escape, and Dr. Dee laughed at the idea of the savage aliens waiting at the mouth of the alley for one of his toys to walk out. "I thought it was clever to come here by different routes, but maybe we should have stayed together. It's getting late. Maybe they've already found him."

"You're going to go, aren't you?" said Dee.

"We have to, if it isn't already too late." Leah paced the room, waiting, as night fell.

At last a dispirited-looking Scorpio entered, having come most of the way on foot.

"I thought they'd caught you," said Leah. This time she held back from embracing him. It wouldn't do to embarrass him with her human concern for his welfare. She couldn't help feeling it, though, however much it was wasted.

"They·did, but they lost me again," he said in an exhausted voice. "I hope we'll be safe here, at least for a little while."

"We won't be safe," said Leah. "They've already been here, looking for us. Kelley saw them. When they can't find us in London, they'll surely think of Mortlake. We have to get the orb and jump again."

Scorpio covered his face with his hands. "They have an orb, too. No matter where we go in time and space, they'll seek us out. I don't know why I thought I could make a difference all by myself; none of my people would have thought of such a thing, except maybe Leandro," he amended softly.

"You're not by yourself," said Leah. "You have me."

"And me," added Dr. Dee.

"That's the problem, don't you understand? I've turned your lives upside down, moving in times and places I have no business in. I have no right to bring my problems into your lives or to cause you to care about them."

"Don't say that," said Dr. Dee. "Mankind must continue to discover, and explore, whether it be in time and space or in the realm of ideas."

"And so must womankind," said Leah.

Scorpio looked up. "The scroll," he said. "The way your society is set up, the natural assumption is that men think with logic and women by intuition, but what if it wasn't talking about male and female at all? What if that was only a metaphor for the two aspects of the mind: the side that plods along, putting one fact together with another, and the side that makes wild intuitive leaps of the imagination? Could my problem with controlling the orb be that I'm trying too hard for control?"

"At the primordial point, all opposites must be understood as potentially present," said Dee thoughtfully. "You might be able to balance your mind between logic and dream. A worthy theory, but theories need proving."

"We don't have any time for proving theories," said Leah.

The sudden rattling of the door latch startled them.

"The Hunters!" said Leah. "Who else could it be? A locked door won't keep them out for long."

Dee opened one of the windows. "Make your exit this way. I'll try to delay them a few moments."

"Don't put yourself in danger," said Scorpio. "They're deadly assassins."

"Don't you see, I want to find out what they're like, even though they might be dangerous."

"Thank you, Dr. Dee," said Scorpio as Leah frantically pushed him toward the window. They tumbled into the wet grass below and began to run toward the stagnant lake. Scorpio sent out a tendril of thought and plunged it deep into the water. A ray of light, like a beacon, shot skyward from the orb hidden on the murky bottom, guiding them.

Scorpio tried to ignore the two looming silhouettes that paced them from behind, but they became impossible to ignore as a laser burst arced into the grass beside him with a hissing sound. Another shot sped past so close to Leah that it caught her skirt on fire. He heard her scream, saw her slap at the flames.

"That's all right," he told her. "We're close enough. Grab me and hold on tight."

Scorpio felt her fingers dig into his rib cage, and he leapt. He heard the fire go out with a sizzle. Water closed around him, feeling heavy and smothering at first, then giving way to the buoyancy and freedom he always felt in the water.

He swam strongly. The Hunters wouldn't dive because of the damage it would do to their skins.

Following his tendril of thought, Scorpio went unerringly

to where the orb lay half buried in mud and slime. Leah let go her hold with one hand, and the water made her swirl around him as if they danced. A moment later they held the orb between them, and Scorpio could feel the mind connection, like a three-way link, solid, reassuring. Neither of them could stay down here indefinitely without surfacing, though he could stay longer. But it didn't matter; the Hunters waited above, and there was only one way out.

Jump, said Leah's mind.

Jump, came the echo from his own.

And the future waited.

COMING MAY 2005

SCORPIO, Vol. 2
DRAGON'S BLOOD
by Alex McDonough
ISBN: 1-4165-0430-3

**2 BOOKS IN 1! A JOURNEY THROUGH TIME
AND SPACE, PERFECT FOR WORLDWIDE
FANS OF *DOCTOR WHO*!**

Savage Hunters are tracking the alien known as
Scorpio. The chase has crossed two planets and
thousands of years, and the Hunters are finally
catching up. In a last, desperate gamble, Scorpio flees
blindly through time with his only ally: a human girl
named Leah de Bernay, a fugitive in time from the
14th century.

From a Russia on the eve of revolution to the age
of the dinosaurs, and back to the killing fields of 20th
century Cambodia, the time travelers race to stay one
step ahead of their pursuers while Scorpio searches
for a way to save his people from extinction!

GHOSTBUSTERS™

THE RETURN
by Sholly Fisch
ISBN: 0-7434-7948-3

**THE FIRST-EVER ORIGINAL
GHOSTBUSTERS NOVEL, BASED ON THE
SMASH HIT FILM FRANCHISE!**

Two years after the events of *Ghostbusters II*, the group finds themselves once again neck-deep in ghosts and ghouls as some of the most unsettling urban legends—like the hook-handed killer in Lovers' Lane and The Vanishing Hitchhiker—all come to deadly life!

But the worst is yet to come for Ray Stantz, Egon Spengler, and Winston Zeddemore—and quite possibly the people of New York: the Ghostbusters' leader, Peter Venkman, has been chosen by an independent political party to be their candidate… for Mayor!

With the city reeling under a supernatural reign of terror, can the Ghostbusters stop the arrival of an ancient fear-demon in time to save Election Day—or should Venkman start looking for another job already?

DEFENDER™
HYPERSWARM
by Tim Waggoner
ISBN: 0-7434-9310-9

THE FIRST ORIGINAL NOVEL BASED ON THE POPULAR GAME FRANCHISE!

The aliens known as the Manti have been destroyed by Defender pilot Mei Kyoto when she helped the AI called Memory crash the moon into Manti-occupied Earth. The remnants of humanity that live on the Solar Colonies have been saved, but at the cost of their homeworld. Several years have passed, and Kyoto has become a controversial figure. While some view her as a hero, others demonize her as the destroyer of Earth.

Detroit Adams—now a general and head of the Galactic Stargate Authority—has convinced Kyoto to use her celebrity status as a goodwill ambassador to the Colonies, in the hope of keeping them unified... or at least prevent open hostilities from breaking out....

PHASES OF THE MOON
STORIES OF SIX DECADES
by Robert Silverberg
ISBN: 0-7434-9801-1

**A COMPREHENSIVE COLLECTION OF
THE BEST ROBERT SILVERBERG STORIES,
SELECTED BY THE AUTHOR HIMSELF!**

"So now, looking back over my long career, bringing
together a representative sampling of stories from
each of the six decades—so far—in which my work
has found publication, I shake my head in wonder at
the way it all turned out, and give silent thanks to
all…"—Robert Silverberg, from his Introduction

In addition to early efforts ("The Road to Nightfall,"
"The Macauley Circuit") and classics ("Good News
from the Vatican," and "Sailing to Byzantium," to
name but two), this amazing collection includes a
small volume's worth of the Science Fiction Writers
of America Grand Master's introductions and mem-
oirs.

"These short works represent all that science
fiction can and should be."
                        —*Publishers Weekly* **(starred review)**